TO TONI

The Big Payback

by

T. J. Denton

DORRANCE
PUBLISHING CO
EST. 1920
PITTSBURGH, PENNSYLVANIA 15238

The contents of this work, including, but not limited to, the accuracy of events, people, and places depicted; opinions expressed; permission to use, previously published materials included; and any advice given or actions advocated are solely the responsibility of the author, who assumes all liability for said work and indemnifies the publisher against any claims stemming from publication of the work.

All Rights Reserved
Copyright © 2015 by T. J. Denton

No part of this book may be reproduced or transmitted, downloaded, distributed, reverse engineered, or stored in or introduced into any information storage and retrieval system, in any form or by any means, including photocopying and recording, whether electronic or mechanical, now known or hereinafter invented without permission in writing from the publisher.

Dorrance Publishing Co
585 Alpha Drive
Suite 103
Pittsburgh, PA 15238
Visit our website at *www.dorrancebookstore.com*

ISBN: 978-1-4809-1083-6
eISBN 978-1-4809-1406-6

The Big Payback

Early one December morning, Thomas got up from bed and began to start his daily routine. He went into the bathroom and began brushing his teeth and then jumped into the shower. This, however, was a different day from the norm, a special day you could say. Thomas had no idea at the time that something different was about to happen to him; something that would change the rest of his life.

Beverly, Thomas's wife, got up shortly after Tom and went toward the kitchen to start preparing breakfast. Beverly took out some pots and pans from the pantry and sat them on the counter. She then went back up the stairs to wake up the kids, so that they could start preparing for school. The kids had taken their showers last night, so they needed only to choose their clothes, get dressed, and prepare for breakfast. Thomas was dressed before everyone else, so he went downstairs and let Samson out. Samson was the family dog, a very large Siberian husky. Tom said to Samson, "Good boy, way to watch the house last night, but your watch is over, you're relieved." Samson jumped up on Thomas and Thomas rubbed him on his head and petted him, and then opened up the door into the backyard and let him go out for the day.

Thomas then went over to the kitchen area and began to cook breakfast for the family. Thomas began with a pot of grits, and then some scrambled eggs, and threw some turkey bacon into the oven. At 0645 the rest of the family came downstairs and into the kitchen, with what seemed to be a very healthy appetite by the way they filed to the breakfast table.

Melvin, Thomas's twelve-year-old son said, "Dad, did you fix some potatoes this morning for breakfast?"

And Thomas replied, "No, man, I hooked up with something better; I hooked up some grits."

Melvin replied, "Hey, Dad, I need lots of carbs, you know? I need carbs to grow."

Thomas replied, "Man, let me tell you, grits have 40 grams of carbs, per every 5-ounce serving and no fat."

Melvin replied back, "My dad, the nutritionist."

Then Thomas said almost before Melvin could finish his sentence, and also anticipating what Melvin was actually going to say, "Son, I guess you forgot I used to be a personal trainer."

Tina, Thomas's thirteen-year-old daughter came on to add, "Hey, Melvin, Dad is the one who informed you what to eat in order to grow in the first place, so when did your source of information become more advanced that Dad's all of a sudden?"

Melvin replied, "This conversation is none of your business, in the first place, and in the second place, I told you about talking over my head. I know that whatever the heck you said, you were just trying to put me down."

Thomas jumped in and said, "Okay, you two, that's enough," and they both went silent immediately.

Elijah, Thomas's oldest son at fourteen, and Elizabeth his oldest daughter who was fifteen years old, both came down to the breakfast table. Elizabeth said, "Good morning, Mom; good morning, Dad."

Thomas and Bev both replied, "Good morning, Elizabeth."

Elijah said, "Good morning, Dad; good morning, Mom."

Thomas and Bev replied, "Good morning, Elijah; good morning, son."

Beverly asked Thomas, "Hey, honey, did you make the coffee, yet?"

Tom answered, "Oh no, I forgot."

Bev said, "Don't worry; I'll fix it real quick."

After breakfast was over, Thomas shouted, "Okay, listen up! At 0730 I'm taking off; the train leaves on time! All passengers that are taking the train this morning please be advised that we are boarding on time as scheduled, and if you are not onboard by takeoff time, the train will proceed without you! That is all!"

The rest of the family laughed and Elizabeth looked at the clock on the wall in the kitchen and saw it was already 0720 and shouted, "You guys better hustle up!" and the kids broke out running up the stairs to gather their gear together for school.

Beverly said to Tom, "Hey, sweetheart, I can pick up the kids this evening because I'm leaving the office early; I only have eight clients today and they're all scheduled between 0900 and 1400 hours. I should be out of there no later than 1500 hours."

Thomas said, "That's cool, then I'll just stop off somewhere on the way home and pick up dinner for us for tonight."

Beverly said, "That's fine. Oh baby, I almost forgot about Elijah; he has football practice today from 0500 to 0700."

Thomas replied, "That's not a problem, I'll just stop off and pick up dinner before I pick him up from practice. Man, I'm kinda glad that we only have one more week of the regular season of football. I mean, I'm glad his team made the playoffs, but this has been an awfully long season."

Beverly said, "Yes, it sure has; but remember, if they take state, then it goes to nationals and then we're looking at December 20 for the nationals title game."

"Yes, well I guess that's a good thing," he answered.

Tom kissed Bev on the lips and said, "Baby, I love you and I'll talk to you a little later; have a good day."

"Thank you, honey," said Beverly, "I love you, as well; be safe." Bev got into her BMW 745Li and took off for the office. Beverly ran a real estate office located on Florence and Normandy.

Thomas jumped into his SUV, a GMC XL, and all four kids piled in, threw their gear in the rear, and off they all went. Thomas owned and managed a fitness gym. The gym had state-of-the art equipment and also had a clothing line by designer Phil Parsons, who Tom spent time with in the United States Marine Corps. Thomas and Phil saw action at the end of the Vietnam conflict, as well as Special Ops in the Contras and Granada.

Thomas dropped off the kids at their respective schools and then headed for the gym. The Gym/Fitness Center opened up at 0500 hours. The center specialized in personal, one-on-one training, and was very successful; however, with the constant growth of the clientele, the center was in desperate need of expansion. Thomas arrived at the center and parked his vehicle in his personalized slot. He walked through the front doors and was greeted by his staff at the Customer Service Desk.

"Good morning, Mr. Dugmal."

Looking at every one of his staff, Thomas replied, "Good morning back at ya." Tom walked past the front desk and headed down the hallway toward his office. He opened up the door, walked in, and then turned on his computer and sat down in his chair at his desk. He looked on his desk and noticed three messages, which he received yesterday.

As he began to review the messages, Phil popped his head into the office and said, "What's up, man? How are you doing?"

Tom replied, "Man, everything, just everything. Hey, bro', I need to talk to you about some things."

"Sure man," Phil said, "you know we spilled some blood together. I carried you out of the bush, so you can cover my flank; you know, bro', the world is ours."

Toms laughed and said, "Man, it's nothing like that; man, come on in and have a seat."

Phil sat down and said, "What's up?"

Thomas went on to ask, "Hey, man, do you remember we were discussing the idea of expanding the business and making the place larger and better; adding a restaurant with health food items on the menu?"

"Hell, yes," replied Phil, "I remember; man; I'm past ready to go through with this."

Tom said, "Well, it's just a matter of when we will get funded for the project."

Phil, in a display of excitement shouted out, "Man, who do we need to knock out or roll over to make this thing work?"

"Hold your horses. I wanted to tell you this…I went down to Western Stage Coach Bank and presented a proposal, along with a cost and profit analysis and they're going to let me know today if we're approved for the loan or not."

Phil asked, "Today?" in amazement.

Tom replied, "That's what I've been trying to tell you, man; they're coming in today."

Phil asked, "Man, what can I do to help you?"

"Nothing, bro'; just be here with me when they arrive," said Thomas.

"I am so excited," answered Phil, "I'm going out front to tell the crew to make sure that the place is 'A J squared away' when the representatives arrive. I'll catch you later, bro'."

Tom shouted out, "Hey, man, they are scheduled to arrive at 1330 hours!"

As the day progressed, the crew got the place in tip-top 100 percent 'A J squared away' condition. At 1320 hours, the Western Stage Coach Bank representatives arrived and were met at the front desk. "Good afternoon, I'm Taria; welcome to the T & B Fitness Center. Do you have an appointment?"

One of the four people stepped out in front and extended her hand out in effort to shake Taria's hand and introduce herself. "Sarah, from Western Stage Coach Bank; these are my consultants and, yes, we do have an appointment for 1:30 P.M. with Mr. Dugmal."

Taria replied, "Pleased to meet you; if you'll just hold on for a moment, I'll call Mr. Dugmal and inform him that you have arrived."

Sarah responded, "Thank you very much."

Taria picked up the phone and called Tom's office; as Thomas answered, Taria said, "Mr. D, your guest has arrived."

"Thanks, Taria; please show them to my office." Thomas hung up the phone and called Phil's office, two rooms down from his and said, "Man, our guests have arrived."

Phil responded, "Roger that; I'll be right over."

Phil got to Tom's office just seconds before Taria arrived with the foursome from Western Stage Coach Bank. As the guests arrived in the entranceway, Taria smiled with her beautiful smile and said, "Sir, your guests."

"Thank you, Taria; that will be all," said Thomas.

Phil extended his hand to Sarah and said, "Hi, I'm Phillip Upchurch, operations manager, and I'd like to introduce you to Thomas Dugmal, CEO and owner of T & B Fitness Center."

Sarah replied, "Pleased to meet you, Phillip."

Phil interrupted Sarah and said, "Please, call me Phil."

Sarah responded, "Okay, Phil," and smiled, then looked at Thomas and said, "It's a pleasure to finally meet you face-to-face rather than talking to you on the phone. I'm Sarah Daniels, Loan Approvals Manager."

Sarah is a very attractive lady, thirty-three years of age, and very aggressive; a lady that's very sure of herself and who is not afraid of speaking exactly what she's thinking and going after exactly what she wants. Sarah is 5' 4" tall, and unmarried because she has not found the guy that can be comfortable with her and allow her to be who she wants to be. Sarah does, however, want someone in her life to share her success, yet, understand her position in life. What Sarah is lacking, however, is the willingness to compromise and meet the other person halfway. Sarah has long brunette hair to the middle of her back, and has had work done to enhance her breasts. She has very nice legs, well-built calves, thick ankles, a small waist, and God has blessed her in the south of the border area. Sarah has a B.S. degree in business from MIT of NYC. Sarah enjoys exploiting weak mean and admires the strong type, not just physically, but emotionally and mentally, as well.

Sarah shook Tom's hand and said, "I would like you to meet Peter Ware, our finance manager," and the two shook hands, "and Linda Whitehead, our loan specialist." They shook hands. "And this is Randy Boil; he runs the monitors business department." They also shook hands.

Thomas said, "It's a pleasure to meet each and every one of you; please come in and have a seat." Thomas's office is set up with a conference table and eight chairs. Thomas took a seat at the head of the table. He looked at Sarah and asked, "Can I get you anything—coffee or some fruit and water."

Sarah replied, "Yes, that would be great."

Phil had gotten a portable food tray and was wheeling it in as Thomas was asking. Phil pushed the cart to the far corner of the room, took off the fruit tray, carried it, and placed it in the middle of the conference table. Phil then grabbed a stack of paper plates and napkins, along with some plastic forks and knives, and placed them on the table, as well. Then Phil placed glasses on the table in front of everyone.

Thomas looked to his left where Sarah was sitting and asked, "Can I pour you some water?"

Sarah responded in an almost school girl type tone, "Oh, why yes, please," and Tom picked up the pitcher of water and poured some water into her waiting glass.

After everyone had a plate of food in front of them, Thomas looked around the table and said, "People, please enjoy the fruit; all of it was organically grown in my reserve private garden. That will be where all of the fruits and vegetables will come from to supply the health club restaurant when we open it up as part of the new center." Thomas looked over at Phil and asked, "Phil, please pass out the outline proposals and plans packages."

Phil said, "Sure," and handed the copies to all four of the representatives.

Thomas looked over at Sarah and said, "If everyone opens the package up to page one, you will see that the blueprints for the floor plans and specs are all in order. If you'll turn to page four, you'll see the projection for the cost and profit analysis for the next five years. Now based on the current trends with the market, compared to last year and the prior three years of business with T & B Fitness Center, the profits made and lost in restaurants in the local and sounding areas, in conjunction with the fact that people are driving toward a healthier living and dining style, we project the net gains and continuation in net gains for the next seven years. Ladies and gentlemen, we're looking at supply and demand at the most opportune time, and this is exactly what people are looking for, but don't have anywhere to find it. We call our plan Healthier Living (Eureka)."

Sarah looked over at Thomas and said, "I really like this plan. I believe that if you use the correct marketing and strategies, you will become a total success."

Randy Boil added, "I believe with affordable cost for the meal and affordable membership fees, you'll have the support of the entire minorities market, and you should blow all other companies out of the water."

Linda Whitehead looked across the table at Phil and said, "We will have to go over the final projection and figures; however, I don't see why this project should not fly."

Peter Ware said to Thomas, "Looking at your last three years in profit growth, your assets netted $756,000 less than what you had to pay out in labor and maintenance cost, so you still cleared $322, 000. Now, please understand that you do not qualify under the small business loan area; you are looking more realistically at a mid-size business loan, but we can qualify you under the Minority Business Rights Act. I see no reason for not approving this loan."

Thomas smiled and looked over at Phil, who was looking over at Tom at the same time. Phil stood and asked, "Can we break out the champagne now?"

Sarah replied, "No, let's wait until the signing of the final paperwork has been completed and the check is in hand." She continued, "I believe that's all we need from you at the moment. I'll draw up the final paperwork and contracts and have them ready for the signing by tomorrow afternoon, 3:00 P.M. at the latest."

Thomas asked Sarah, "Should we come down to the bank, or will you come by here?"

Sarah answered, "I'll bring everything back here; that way the final process will be in a more relaxed and comfortable environment for you."

"Well," said Thomas, "I am certainly obliged to you all for coming down, and for all of the trouble, as well as efforts in assisting us to secure this business venture."

Sarah replied, "It has been an absolute pleasure."

Phil stood up and said, "I'll walk you good people to the door." The group walked out of Tom's office and headed toward the front door.

"You guys go on ahead," said Sarah, "I want to leave Mr. Dugmal one of my business cards, and have a last word with him."

So, the rest of the group continued to the front door with Phil leading the charge. Sarah turned around and headed back toward Thomas's office. Thomas was facing the back of his office when Sarah came to the entrance of the doorway and knocked. Thomas looked around and saw that Sarah had returned, and asked, "Don't tell me you changed your mind about approving the loan?"

Sarah laughed and responded, "No, quite to the contrary. Can I have a word with you in private, Tom?"

"Sure, of course; how can I help you?" he answered.

Sarah walked into his office and Tom went over and shut the office door. Thomas then said," Sarah, have a seat please."

Sarah said, "This will only take a minute."

"Sure, I'm all ears," Tom replied.

Sarah paused for a minute, looked over at Thomas, and said, "I'm going to be straight forward with you, if I may."

Thomas answered, "Please do, by all means."

Sarah went on to say, "I just wanted to let you know that I'm very impressed by you. You really surprised me with your presentation and intelligence."

Thomas responded, "Well, thank you very much, Sarah."

"I have some paperwork for you to review and sign that's already drawn up, but I left them back at the office." Sarah continued, "I would like to get this paperwork taken care of and out of the way, so we can fund you as quickly as possible."

Thomas said, "Well, I'll have some extra time on my hands this evening before I have to pick up my son from football practice."

Sarah said with a smile on her face, "Are you suggesting we meet somewhere for a while?"

"No," replied Thomas, "I was just saying that we could get the paperwork knocked out this evening."

"Oh well, I was hoping that you were asking me out this evening. I must admit, Thomas, you have made me feel something that…it's hard to explain; to be quite truthful, I have not felt this way about a man in a very long time. I guess what I'm trying to tell you, Thomas, is you turn me on like a light switch in a candle factory."

Thomas paused for a moment, then said, "Sarah, I find you very attractive and intelligent, as well; however, I am married with children."

Sarah responded, "You know, the strangest thing is, I know all of that but it makes me want you that much more. I'm not asking you to leave your wife or family. I just believe it would be worth both our whiles to explore new horizons."

"Sarah, I just believe that the connection is present, but the timing is off."

"Thomas, I believe things are going to change."

"Sarah, is there anything else I can help you with?"

Sarah said, "Yes, why don't you give me your cell phone number so I can reach you later on this evening, so we can set things up for the paperwork signing."

Thomas said, "Okay then," as he reached into his desk drawer, pulled out one of his business cards, and handed it to Sarah, "my cell phone number is on my card; see it says cell phone number' right here," Tom pointed out the number on the card for Sarah.

"Well, Thomas, I'm going to join the rest of my group before they leave me."

Thomas looked at Sarah and said, "Well, I'll see you later on this evening and thank you for everything you've done; you have been most helpful."

Sarah turned and left Tom's office and headed toward the front door to catch up with the rest of her group in the parking lot. They all got into their vehicle and took off.

Phil ran into Thomas's office and, with a big smile on his face, said, "Hey, man, did she ask you out? Man, I'm telling you, she was sprung for days, and she looked good as hell, too."

"Man, you know it," Thomas said. "Yes, she looked pretty good and all that, but everything stayed on a professional level; you know it's not that kind of party with me."

Phil looked at Thomas and busted into a laugh and said, "Yeah right, man."

"Well, anyway, thank God this thing is finally coming through."

Phil said, "Yes, Lord. Do you want me to make an announcement to the rest of the crew?"

"No, no let's wait till tomorrow when we have the check in our hands," said Thomas.

Phil said, "Okay, but man I just can't wait. Well, I'm going to do some work in my office; if you need me, you know where I'll be."

Five o'clock rolled around and the shift changed up front with the crew; Taria walked into Thomas's office and said, "Mr. D, how did the meeting go with the Western Stage Coach Bank people?"

Tom answered with a smile on his face that displayed relief and delight at the same time. "It went well, Taria; thanks for asking."

"Well, will you make an announcement anytime soon?"

Thomas said, "Taria, please keep this under your hat for a while, at least until we confirm everything tomorrow."

"Sure, no problem. Oh, by the way, Mr. D, don't forget to pick up your son from football practice and get dinner for your family."

"Oh yeah; thanks, Taria." Tom continued, "You know, when the place is finished and we've completed the new floor plan, I would like to sit down with you and discuss, perhaps, a management position in the restaurant. That is, if you're interested?"

Taria's eyes opened as large as life itself as she shouted, "Of course, I'd like nothing more! Thank you very much, Mr. D; you are the best boss I have ever worked for, I mean it! You are a good person, a good dad, a good husband, and a blessed man!"

Thomas said, "Thanks, Taria, but please, stop while you're ahead," and then smiled.

Taria laughed as she said, "Okay, Mr. D, have a great evening and good night."

"Good night, Taria."

Thomas looked down at his watch and noticed it was 1725, so he gathered his belongings and started out the door. The evening crew said, "Good night, Mr. Dugmal."

Thomas got twelve feet in front of his truck and his cell phone rang. "Hello," he answered.

"Hello, Mr. Dugmal, this is Sarah Daniels from Western Stage Coach Bank; did I catch you at a bad time?"

Thomas answered, "No, not at all, how can I help you?"

Sarah replied, "Well, I have some documents you should go over to ensure everything is correct."

"Are there any foreseeable problems with the figures or anything with the projections?"

Sarah answered, "Well, that's what we need to go over."

"Well," said Thomas, "I can come by first thing in the morning."

"Well, to be honest with you, this needs to be finalized before I turn in anything in the morning before processing."

Thomas looked around and said, "I was sure everything was intact." He thought *I'd better check this out.* Tom asked Sarah, "What's the latest we can meet because I have prior obligations, and I won't be free until around eight o'clock; is that too much of an inconvenience for you?"

"No," Sarah replied, "I don't have anything else pending tonight; besides this is very important, so I don't really mind."

Thomas asked, "Would you like to come over to my house? You can eat dinner with the family and we can take care of business at the same time."

Sarah quickly replied, "No, we are not encouraged to meet at a client's place of residence to conduct business, but can I offer to meet you at Clam's House of Ribs? The dinner will be on Western Stage Coach Bank and it's a public place. It should not take too long of a process to review the paperwork and have a bite to eat, as well."

Thomas said, "Well, I guess that would be okay. Can I meet you there, say around eight o'clock?"

"Yes, 8:00 P.M. it is."

Thomas drove over to Los Pollos Market and picked up dinner for his family and then proceeded to the football field to pick up his son Melvin. As he arrived at the field, Melvin came running toward the truck. Thomas parked the truck and got out and opened the passenger doors in the front and back. As Elijah approached, Thomas said, "Hey, man, put your gear in the rear."

Elijah shouted, "I know, Dad!" as he executed the move. Then he jumped into the front seat.

Thomas asked him, "So, son; how was practice today?"

"It was great, Dad. I ran the scrimmage at the halfback position and I took it to the house, man; I actually scored a touchdown. And, on defense, I had two quarterback sacks from the middle linebacker blitz. Dad, I'm a bad man."

Thomas smiled, looked at Elijah, and said, "Be as bad as you want to be, but stay humble."

Elijah looked at his dad and said, "Dad, I'm working on it," as they pulled up to their driveway.

Thomas looked at the garage door to the house, and noticed the garage door was open. Beverly had just pulled into the garage. Thomas pulled up and parked. He jumped out of the truck and said, "Hey, baby, how was your day?" and walked over to greet her.

As the two meet face-to-face, Beverly reached over and kissed Tom on his lips. Beverly replied, "Boy, I was busy from the time I got into the office until it was time for me to leave. The Bradley family wanted to stay in the home they were looking at for an hour and a half. They just could not make up their minds if that was the house they really wanted. And I couldn't say, 'Well, what are you guys going to do?' although that's what I really wanted to say," with a small snicker of a laugh. "Anyway, sweetheart, how was your day?"

Thomas looked at Beverly and said, "Well, my day was quite interesting; the Western Stage Coach Bank's Loan Department came by and they liked what we presented. I do believe they are going to fund us; one of the representatives wants to meet with me tonight at 2000 hours to review the final contract and they should have everything ready to sign and have it processed by the morning, and closed by 1500 tomorrow."

Beverly said with an exuberant look on her face, "Congratulations. I know this baby is your dream come true. And it finally has, and you really deserve it. Hey, it is 7:45 now; you better get going. I trust you know what you're doing, Tom, so I'll just let you handle this. Please be careful and make sure you read over and understand the entire contract."

Thomas replied, "I will do so, you know that." Thomas kissed Beverly on the lips and said, "I'll try not to get back late, baby."

And Beverly said, "Nine-thirty P.M. So I'll talk to you in the morning."

"Okay, baby," Thomas responded, "I'll try not to wake you up."

So, Thomas took off, headed toward the restaurant. He arrived at the restaurant at 7:59 P.M. and walked inside.

As he entered, a waiter asked, "Are you Mr. Dugmal?" and Thomas answered, "Yes, I am." The waiter asked, "Please follow me, your table is ready and your guest is already seated."

"I'm impressed," said Thomas to the waiter, as he walked Tom to the table that's located in a private section of the restaurant. The area was in the rear and divided off in sections with signs that read RESERVED. As Thomas gracefully followed, the waiter came to the area where Sarah was seated. Thomas looked at her and said, "Hello, Sarah, long time, no see."

Sarah laughed and said, "Thomas, please sit down."

Thomas looked around the room and noticed the size of the room. It appeared to be 75' x 125' all the way around and there were only three couples in the whole room. Thomas said to Sarah, "How did you manage to swing this?"

Sarah replied, "Well, I did tell you that this would be on Western Stage Coach Bank."

"Yes, you sure did tell me that, but I still had no idea."

Sarah said, "This is the section that we have a lot of our meetings in."

Thomas looks over across the table and noticed a pail of ice and a bottle being chilled.

Sarah asked Thomas, "Would you like to look at the menu?"

He replied, "Well, this is the house of prime rib. No thanks, I don't need a menu; I'll have the 12-oz. prime rib, please, cooked medium."

Sarah called the waiter over. The waiter for that particular section stayed there and took care of the reserved area only. The waiter came over and said, "Yes, madam, are you ready to order?"

Sarah replied, "Yes, we are."

Thomas looked at Sarah and said, "You order first, please," and Sarah said, "Thank you very much, that was very considerate of you."

Sarah ordered a 12-oz. prime rib, medium well, and a baked potato with mixed vegetables.

Then Thomas placed his order, "I'll have the 12-oz. prime rib, as well, cooked medium with mashed potatoes and broccoli."

The waiter told both of them, "Thank you and we'll place your orders at once."

Sarah picked up a large envelope and placed it on the table.

Thomas asked, "Is that the paperwork for review?"

"Yes, you just need to sign it."

Thomas asked, "What about the changes?"

Sarah smiled, "The documents were fine the way they were, Thomas."

Thomas looked Sarah in the eyes and said, "I don't understand what the deal is then."

Sarah answered, "The deal is this; I am terribly attracted to you, and I know that you are married with children, but I had to express my feelings to you without embarrassing myself. I know that I may not be as attractive as your wife, but I know I look good and I can do a lot for you, with no strings attached whatsoever. Please, before you reply, Tom, let's just enjoy this moment, and drink some of this free champagne, compliments of Western Stage Coach Bank."

Thomas thought for a moment and said, "Okay, what the heck; I could use a drink right about now." Thomas reached into the bucket and pulled out the bottle of champagne and poured some into Sarah's glass and then poured some into his glass.

Sarah said, "I would like to propose a toast. This is to your loan approval and the start of your business success and to a whole new friendship."

Thomas lifted his glass and tapped Sarah's glass and said, "Hear, hear."

They both drank their champagne. Thomas picked up the champagne bottle and asked Sarah, "Want more?"

Sarah answered, "Yes, please."

Thomas filled her glass up once again, and then filled his glass. Thomas lifted up his glass and said, "Here's to people helping people."

Sarah said, "Hear, hear."

They both drank down the second glass. Thomas picked up the bottle once again and poured more champagne into Sarah's glass and then his own. This time, there was only enough to half fill both glasses. Sarah said, "Well, I can order another bottle."

Thomas asked, "Is it free?"

"Yes, it's on Western Stage Coach."

"Well, order more," replied Thomas.

When the waiter returned to the table, he placed their food on the table in front of them and asked, "Is there anything else I can do for you?"

"Yes," responded Sarah, "another bottle of champagne, if you please."

The waiter replied, "It would be my pleasure."

Thomas looked over at Sarah without saying a word. Sarah looked back at him and asked, "What is it?"

Thomas said, "I've been thinking about the question you asked me earlier."

Sarah asked, "Well, what do you think?"

Thomas looked down, then back into her eyes, and said, "Sarah, I find you very attractive, and you seem like you would be a fun person to be around; however, I'm married with a ton of obligations. You don't want to get tangled up in a web of a mess like that."

"You know, I'm a big girl now, and I've handled extremely large accounts dealing with movie stars and sports professionals. I can handle a hell of a lot more than you think."

He said, "These things never work out. In the end, someone or several people wind up getting hurt in the process."

Sarah responded, "Well, I have known of some cases, where situations start out like this and end up in no mess at all. I'm willing to go out on a limb and take this chance, because this chance may never come around again, and then you will miss the love you never had."

"Sarah, a lot of people could get hurt if this does not work out and gets into the open."

She responded, "It can work out; I know it. I feel it in my heart. I can be so good to you and for you, as well. No one can give you what I can give you, Tom. I know that you're attracted to me, as well. I see the way you look in my eyes and you can't deny that."

Thomas looked at Sarah and then looked down and then back up at her. "Sarah, I am a very attentive person. I'm sorry if you got the wrong impression. To be honest with you, I was drawn to you just as nearly every man has and will be. However, you can't just act on impulse, or succumb to lavish or carnal thoughts."

"Well," Sarah replied, "with that, Thomas, let's finish up here with dinner. You've signed everything you need to sign, and we have a long day ahead of us tomorrow. Everything should be processed in the morning and you should be funded by 3:00 P.M."

"Thank you very much for everything, Sarah," he said as they both stood up.

Sarah reached out her right hand to shake Thomas's hand. As Thomas made contact with Sarah's hand, she pulled herself closer to Thomas, until they were standing face-to-face with each other, and could feel each other's breath on their skins. Sarah said, "Please, forgive me, Thomas," and leaned forward and kissed him on the lips, ever so softly and gently, and after several seconds opened her mouth and inserted her tongue into Thomas's mouth.

At that point, Thomas was not only taken by surprise, but after a few glasses of champagne, the feel of a soft warm body pressing up against his, and the subtle pleasure of soft lips with the throbbing passionate penetration of Sarah's tongue, Thomas found himself in a trance and offered no resistance. After forty-seven seconds had gone by, the two ceased their display of passion, as Thomas commented, "Wow, that was deep."

Sarah said, "Are you sure that you want to go home now, Thomas?"

"Sarah, we have to be strong, and I know what I have to do."

Sarah asked, "Well, can you at least walk me to my car? I just have to sign for the meal," and Thomas responded, "Yes, I can walk you to your car."

Sarah signed for the meal and they both walked toward the front door without any words being exchanged between them. As they approached the front door, Thomas walked ahead and opened the door for Sarah to exit first.

Sarah turned to Thomas and said, "Nothing turns me on more than a man that's a gentleman, as well."

Thomas said, "Well, I can't go back on what I was taught by my dad in my early years growing up."

As they walked to Sarah's car, she turned to Thomas and said, "You know, I've had too much to drink and really don't want to drive in my condition, can you please take me home?"

Thomas answered, "Well, I don't know if I really should, can't we just call you a cab?"

Sarah asked, "What if in my present state of mind the cab driver takes advantage of me? You'll have to live with that on your conscience."

Thomas said, "I'm only going to take you home, Sarah, and that's it."

Sarah replied, "Of course, what else would it be?"

"Can you get someone from your work to bring you back here in the morning so you can pick your car up?"

She answered, "Sure, of course."

They both walked over to Thomas's truck. Thomas opened the passenger door and let Sarah get in, and closed it. Thomas got in and started the engine; they took off and Thomas turned to Sarah and said, "You'll have to stay awake and give me directions, Sarah."

She replied, "I'll do my best. Thomas, why did you allow me to drink so much?"

Thomas smiled, "I was busy trying to keep up with you."

Sarah stayed awake long enough to give Thomas directions to her front door. She said, "There...we're here; home sweet home."

"Wait, I'll get the door for you," cautioned Thomas.

Sarah said, "Thomas, wait...something's wrong. I can't get this seat belt to release."

"Wait a moment," he said, "and I'll come around and try to assist you." When Thomas walked around, he opened up the passenger door, reached over Sarah's lap, and said, "Excuse me, please; I should be able to set you free pretty quickly."

He struggled with the belt release, and commented this had never happened before, and Sarah said laughing, "I've heard that one before."

Thomas stepped up on the truck's running board in an effort to gain a little leverage. As his body crossed over, Sarah could not resist taking advantage of an opportunity to put her hands on Thomas's thighs.

"Sarah, what are to doing?"

Sarah didn't answer, but moved her hands to his crotch and began rubbing him in an up and down motion. Thomas's body had become totally immobile at this point, and as Thomas, in his mind, wanted to back off and out of the vehicle, his body wanted to do something completely different. Sarah continued stroking with one hand, and with the other she grabbed around his neck and pulled him close enough to kiss him once again. She began panting and breathing heavily and rapidly. She discontinued kissing and said, "Tom, I need you very badly; I can feel you in my body already. I promise you no strings attached; please, just make this a night to remember for me and this time we spend together will last a lifetime for me in my mind and soul."

"Sarah, I just don't know if this is right…to give my love to you tonight."

Sarah said, "Thomas, people do things for other people all of the time. I do good things for people all of the time; just this one time would you do something nice for me, something that I need, something that I desire. I feel I deserve it every once in a while."

Thomas looked at Sarah, gazing into her glossy eyes, took a few seconds to gather some thoughts, and said, "Sarah, I'm not a bad person and I try to do good all of the time. I really love my wife, my kids, and my life. One night with you is not worth losing all of that."

"Thomas, you don't have to lose anything. After tonight, you can resume your life as usual, as I will, and you'll have your business booming with wealth and popularity, and we both will have done something to help each other in a time of need."

"Okay, Sarah, but this night never happened in the real world."

Sarah said, "Thomas, what night? Let's go into my house."

They went into Sarah's house; she walked over to the stereo and put on a Temptations CD entitled *Songs for Lovers*. Sarah said, "Let's go up to the bedroom."

Thomas looked around and said, "Wow! This is one of the largest master bedrooms that I've ever seen, and you have surround-sound speakers up here, as well."

"Thomas, make yourself comfortable."

"Sarah, can we take a shower first?"

Sarah replied, "Yes, we can."

They both removed their clothing and headed toward the bathroom with Sarah leading the way. Thomas took the opportunity to view Sarah's goods from the rear view and the sight was very pleasing, as Sarah had an extremely enticing figure. They both entered into a large shower area.

Sarah asked, "Thomas, can you soap my back?"

"I thought you'd never ask."

Thomas began soaping Sarah. He lathered her from behind, starting at the neck and moving down to her shoulders and on down the buttocks, between the 'cheeks,' and then moving forward to the vaginal area.

By this time, Sarah was panting and breathing hard. She bent over slightly and put her hands on the wall in front of her. Thomas caressed her vaginal area, paying particular attention to the clitoris. Sarah, at this point, had come half a heartbeat away from an orgasm. Thomas continued down her thighs to her calves and down to her toes. He turned Sarah around and began soaping the front of her body, starting with her neck and then slowly stroking the front of her shoulders. He moved ever so slowly and gently to the middle of her chest and then started massaging her breasts. He began rubbing her nipples until they were as erect as the Statue of Liberty. Sarah held her head back and started to pant and moan out loud.

She cried out, "Thomas, I need you so bad. Please, take me now."

Thomas calmly said, "Wait, I want you to enjoy yourself a little while longer."

"I can't stand it any longer," Sarah cried, "I feel like I'm going to explode. I need you inside me right now."

Thomas smiled and said, "In due time. Smile, Sarah; you asked for this, now you're getting it."

Sarah continued to moan and groan and pant heavily. Thomas worked his way down Sarah's body until he reached the vaginal area. He then began stroking gently on her clitoris, stroking her left nipple with his tongue at the same time. This sent Sarah to a different time zone. He grabbed her hair with both hands and started pulling it back in pleasure that was so tantalizing that she began to shake uncontrollably. Thomas moved up to Sarah's face and she swiftly grabbed his head with both hands and began kissing him as passionately as one can, losing her tongue in his mouth and discovering his in hers. This went on for another twenty minutes and Thomas said, "Okay, Sarah, it's time now."

As they left the shower and dried off, Sarah looked at Thomas and said, "I have never in my life had an orgasm without penetration and with just foreplay."

Thomas looked back at Sarah, "Well, then you're in for a really nice treat."

As they made their way to the bed, Sarah grabbed Thomas by the waist and began kissing him once again. She led him backwards until they reached the bed. She then forced him to lie down on his back on the bed. She started kissing and licking him...his neck, and working her way to his chest. Sarah commented, "You have a very nice shaped chest."

Thomas smiled and said, "Thank you, Sarah; I have put a lot of work into maintaining my body."

Sarah replied, "Well, it shows," as she worked her way past his stomach to his navel and stopping a minute, she ran her tongue in and around his belly button, and then continued on a downward quest. As she reached his groin area, she smiled and said, "Thomas, you are blessed, aren't you?"

"I guess, I am."

Sarah said, "Yes, you are," and began to stroke his penis with her mouth. She began very slowly and meticulously, and then began to pick up the tempo. Sarah began panting again, as if the art she was performing was giving her as much pleasure as it was giving him. Sarah continued until she had about brought him to the point of no return. She said, "No, honey, it's not that time, yet; the best is yet to come." Sarah climbed on top of Thomas, startling him and said, "Now it's time to come home; I want you inside of me."

Thomas positioned himself in alignment with Sarah and began to penetrate. Sarah gasped and said, "Please, honey, enter me slowly; I have to adjust to your size."

Sarah was dripping wet on the inside of her inner walls. Love juice began to run out of her and flow down on Thomas's firm shaft. As Sarah relaxed, she was able to consume the whole of Thomas's unit. She began to sway back and forth with controlled motion. Her speed increased until her whole body began to tremble and quake. Sarah released a groan and then began to move up and down on Thomas. After a few minutes, Sarah released yet another orgasm, and then laid her limp body down on Thomas.

Thomas said softly to Sarah, "Roll over."

As she rolled over onto her back, Thomas slowly moved on top of Sarah. He positioned his body in between her legs as Sarah spread them open and wrapped them around his backside. Thomas entered into Sarah's open and waiting cavity slowly and methodically. He began a slow rhythm from left to right and then right to left, contentedly changing to up and down, then back and forth.

By this time, Sarah was enjoying herself like she never thought was possible. She took hold of Thomas's back like GI Joe with a kung fu grip.

Thomas continued his art for twenty-five more minutes and then exploded like the Fourth of July. Sarah continued her hold onto Thomas as Thomas did not release her. After seven or eight minutes, Thomas rolled off Sarah. He stared at the ceiling, not saying anything.

Sarah had a look on her face that said it all. She was pleased in the most splendid way. Sarah looked over at Thomas and asked, "What's wrong? Because I feel better than I've ever felt before."

Thomas answered, "You know this is the first and last time I'll ever do anything like this."

Again Sarah said, "You know, you haven't done anything wrong; no one got hurt and no one is going to get hurt."

"Well," said Thomas, "I hope no one will; but nevertheless, this cannot happen again. I just don't feel good about it."

She said, "Relax, Thomas, your secret is safe with me."

Thomas replied, "I'll just shower off real quick; I have to get going."

Sarah replied, "Sure, I understand. Please, Thomas, don't feel guilty about what we did; we did something that made both of us feel good—good about another human being, good about ourselves. That's nothing to be ashamed about."

Thomas looked at Sarah for a moment, and then turned and headed for the shower. Thomas washed off quickly and got dressed.

As he was leaving, Sarah said, "Thomas, you made me feel better than any man has made me feel and, for that, I thank you. Remember, the docs will go in for processing in the morning, and your check for funding should be ready no later than three o'clock."

"Thanks, Sarah; I look forward to hearing from you later." Thomas took off and headed home. When he got home, everyone was asleep. He disrobed and crawled into bed. Beverly, who had gone through a very exhausting day, did not budge when Thomas adjusted himself. He looked at Beverly for a couple of minutes and thought to himself *how could I have ever cheated on you, baby?* His eyes filled with water as he turned and laid his head down and went to sleep.

Friday morning, Thomas got up bright and early and then jumped out of bed. Beverly woke up, looked at Thomas, and said, "Honey, what is wrong with you? You normally wait for ten minutes before you get up."

"Baby, this is the day things change. The loan will come through today, baby; this is a good day for us. I think I'll schedule the start of construction to begin on Monday. Man, I have so much to do."

Beverly asked, "Are you going to shut the gym down for the construction period?"

"No, we can't do that. What's going to happen is we'll close the rear and keep the front open with limited access, and full use of all the equipment, but not the locker rooms and showers; hopefully, for no more than forty-five days. There can be no delays because I don't want to lose any of the good client base, so time is of the essence."

Bev replied, "I know what you mean. Do you have your marketing strategy completed, yet?"

Thomas answered, "Yes, as a matter of fact, I do; the television ad starts running next week. We worked in the studio last month at FOX and had a mock version of the complete club and restaurant. It was so cool."

Beverly looked at Thomas with a pleasing glow of approval in her eyes and said, "Thomas, I am so proud of you, honey. You took this dream of yours and turned it into a reality."

"Thank you, baby, for all of your support and actually believing in me." He continued, "Hey, baby, I'm too excited to eat any breakfast, so I'll go down to the gym and exercise and get pumped up; I'll grab some breakfast afterwards."

She said, "Okay, just give me a call when everything comes through."

"Sure thing." Thomas hurried and showered up, and then put on his gym clothes, grabbed his suit, and started out of the door.

The kids ran out after him shouting, "Hey, Dad; you're not going to wait for us?"

Thomas said, "I'm sorry; I was in such a hurry… Your mom is taking you to school today; I have to get to the gym to take care of some things this morning, so we can close the deal on the loan."

Beverly said, "That's right, your dad is sending us into the big times with the new center."

Melvin said, "Good luck, Dad; let us know about the news this evening."

"Sure thing, son," Thomas said as he headed out of the front door. On his way out he shouted, "Please feed Samson this morning and everyone have a good day!" Thomas jumped into his truck and took off. After arriving at the gym, he warmed up on the treadmill and then went into his routine; after an hour and fifteen minutes had passed by, Thomas completed his routine and hit the showers. He then put his suit on, went into his office, turned his computer on, and began to check on his past email messages.

At 0945 Thomas started going over the marketing plans and Phil popped his head into Thomas's office and said, "Good morning D, what's up?"

Thomas smiled and said, "Nothing much, good morning to you."

Phil asked, "You had chow, yet?"

Thomas replied, "No, matter of fact, I have not; and I am so hungry, I can see biscuits walking around on crutches."

Phil laughed out loud and said, "Hey, let's move; breakfast is on me."

"You made an offer I cannot refuse."

Thomas and Phil headed out the door and Thomas turned to Taria saying, "Good morning, young lady, we're going to breakfast; we'll be back in a couple of hours."

"Good morning Mr. D," responded Taria. "Okay, I'll take messages for you."

Thomas and Phil jumped into Phil's H2 Hummer. As they pulled out of the parking lot, Thomas asked, "Where are we going?"

"Roscoe's Chicken and Waffles on La Cienaga," replied Phil.

"That's cool with me."

They pulled into the parking lot and discovered quite a few people had the same idea about having breakfast at Roscoe's. Phil found a parking space and they rushed into the restaurant. Inside they found people sitting down waiting to be seated and another group waiting to have their names added to the wait list. Thomas and Phil stood in line and discussed strategies concerning the gym—when it closes, maintaining the front portion of the gym, etc. After agreeing and coming up with a game plan for shifts and personnel, the two finally reached the hostess, who asked "How many in your party?"

Phil answered, "Three, including you."

The hostess smiled and said, "I sure wish I could have breakfast with you fine gentlemen; however, we aren't supposed to fraternize with the guests."

Phil said, "Well, well, that's just too bad. What if we were more than guests, and you didn't work here?"

The hostess replied, "Then I could have breakfast with you under those circumstances."

Phil smiled at the hostess and said, "Who do I need to talk to in order to make that happen?"

The hostess said, "Who's asking?"

"Phillip Upchurch and Thomas Dugmal from T & B Fitness for Life."

The hostess exploded with a Kool-Aid ear-to-ear smile and said, "No, you're not the ones from the gym on 45th and State Street?"

Thomas answered, "Yes, I'm the owner and Phil is my partner in crime."
The hostess said, "Everyone is talking about your gym. I'm even thinking about joining. Hey, I'm sure there is no waiting for you gentlemen; let me just confirm it with my manager. I'm sure we can seat you pretty quick; there is a forty-five minute wait, but I'll be right back."

Thomas and Phil thanked the young lady. She returned two minutes later with her manager and excitedly introduced him to Thomas and Phil.

Thomas said, "Hi, I'm Thomas Dugmal and my partner Phillip Upchurch."

The manager responded, "Hi, I'm Bertil Karton; it's a pleasure to have you in my restaurant. I can seat you right away, if you will just follow me, please." As he was walking Thomas and Phil to their table, Bertil said, "I know you are the owners of the gym, and I used to work out when I was younger back at home in the islands and want to get back into it. Do you have anything special going on right now?"

Phil answered, "Come down to the gym and we'll talk shop there, about what you really want to do with your body, your mind, and what you consume, as well."

Bertil asked, "All of that?"

"Weight training is a way of life," said Thomas, "that means you have to have the right mindset, as well. You can look at it this way…you have the ability to add ten to fifteen quality years to your life expectancy; now is it worth it or not? It's a question only an individual can answer for themselves."

Bertil replied, "Well, if you put it that way, I'm ready to join."

"Bertil, why don't you make plans for March to start the program," Phil said. "That's when the gym will be completed with the new additions and we'll get you started the right way."

"That would be great, and I will be ready to do it right." Bertil then said, "You gentleman please enjoy your meals, and this one is on me, so order up."

Thomas said, "Bertil, you don't have to go out of your way like that."

Bertil replied, "It's not going out of my way and, if you don't accept the offer, I would be highly offended."

Phil said, "No, no, no, we would not offend you in any way, so we gladly accept your offer and are very thankful."

"Thank you very much," said Bertil, "and I'll leave you alone to order and, if there is anything I can do, please don't hesitate to ask."

Thomas and Phil said, "Thank you very much."

The waitress said, "I can take you order now."

"Now that's what I call service," said Phil. "I'll have the chicken wing breakfast special with an extra stack of waffles and extra chicken, and could you bring me a pitcher of H2O, please?"

Thomas said, "That sounds good, but I don't need any extra waffles and chicken, but I'll have the same special."

The waitress said, "Thank you, I will have your order brought to you as soon as I can."

Both Thomas and Phil said, "Thanks a lot."

Thomas pulled out the marketing plans and pointed out the demographic areas that he plans to target that have not been tapped into, yet. As Phil looked at the target areas, he said, "That's good, my only question is what strategy can we use to attract...let's say...the Latin community, Middle Eastern, and Asian communities?"

"I already consulted with a national marketing specialist," stated Thomas. "The plan that we've come up with is not veering off too far from the beaten path targeted in the African-American community. We will broadcast and advertise the high levels of high blood pressure, stress, and poor dieting habits which lead to lower life expectancy. Our goal will be to educate people in these areas with our service, along with having on-site doctors taking blood pressure readings and measures to relieve tension and stress. We'll have to spend a little money in advertisement, but the return in revenue will balance that out. My only concern at this point will be to make sure that our staff is taken well care of, so we don't experience the 'through the revolving door' process. We'll offer good medical and dental plans and offer a 401k, as well. I looked into this already and reviewed all of the packages. We have a meeting with a representative from the Labor Board and Commission out of Sacramento next, so that aspect will be taken care of beforehand and will be out of the way."

Phil said, "Hot dang, Devil Dog (an LA term used to describe marines) you are a bad MOFO. I believe that we are going to blow up."

"Man, this is my dream," replied Thomas. "I've put a hell of a lot of thought, combined with careful planning, and tons of prayer into this and because of a few good men, this is going to happen."

Phil then asked, "Man, but I still want to know more about that fine-looking young lady from Western Stage Coach Bank that came by the other day."

"Well, what would you like to know, brother?"

Phil said, "You know what the hell I mean—is she single, is she married, does she have any kids, does she like men?"

Thomas laughed, and said, "Man, you are as crazy as a Texas road lizard. I mean you're the kind of brother that would fart in a bathtub and turn around to see if you could bite the bubbles before they pop." They both broke out into joyful laughter.

"When it's all said and done, I still would like to hit that," declared Phil.

Thomas said, "Well, be my guest. I believe she likes men and I just happen to know that she is not married as of yet, but if the right man comes around and can accept her success and not attempt to distract her from her goals, and is willing to allow her to be herself, then she's down for that."

"I just want to tap it," stated Phil.

At this time, the food came out and Thomas and Phil secured their conversation and began to chow down on the waffles and chicken. After the fine meal, the two departed the restaurant. Before leaving, Thomas handed the cashier at the front one of his business cards and said, "Please give this to Bertil for me. Thank you very much." The cashier gladly accepted the card and assured Thomas that it would be delivered to Bertil.

As Thomas and Phil jumped into Phil's H2, Phil looked over at Thomas and said, "Man, I'm full as hell."

Thomas replied, "I'm full as a Texas tick myself." They both laughed out loud as Phil drove off.

When Thomas and Phil made it back to the gym, as they were walking in the door, Taria walked up to Thomas and said, "Mr. D, you had a call from Ms. Daniels and she asked if you could please return her call."

"Thanks, Taria." Thomas told Phil, "Hey bro', I'm going to my office to use the phone; hopefully, this is the call saying everything is approved and the check has been cut."

Phil said, "Man, let me be the first to know."

"You bet." Thomas went into his office and closed the door behind him. He sat and pulled out Sarah's business card.

He dialed the number and Sarah Daniels answered saying, "Thank you for calling Western Stage Coach Bank, Sarah Daniels speaking, how may I help you today?"

Thomas said, "Good morning Sarah, how are you?"

Sarah replied "Hi, I'm fine; wait a moment, let me close my office door." Sarah closed the door.

Thomas said, "That's fine, I hope you have some good news for me."

Sarah replied, "I have great news for you, Thomas. Everything is approved and signed and the check will be processed and cut by one o'clock this afternoon."

"Oh man," said Thomas, "I hope I don't go into cardiac arrest before this afternoon."

Sarah said, "I hope that you don't go into cardiac arrest at all."

Thomas said, "That was just a figure of speech. Sarah, I want to thank you for everything you've done to help this project go through smoothly and quickly."

"You know, Thomas, on a personal note, you thanked me enough last night. I wanted to tell you that no man has ever made me feel the way you made me feel last night. I can't really explain it, but I can tell you this, I can't stop thinking about you, no matter how hard I try. I've tried to put you in the back of my mind and you keep popping up to the front. I can't understand this right now, and it's really starting to frustrate me, because I normally have more control over myself than this. I, I would really like to know your thoughts on this, Thomas."

Thomas paused for a moment, then responded, "Sarah, please don't think I'm ignoring you or anything like that, but let me think for a minute. That was pretty heavy what you just laid on me and I'll have to allow what you said to digest for a brief moment."

"You know I don't want to feel this way," said Sarah, "just as I know you don't want me to, but the fact of the matter is that I do feel like this, so the question remains, what in the hell are we going to do?"

"Sarah, we did discuss this matter before we actually got involved. I was under the impression we would be strong enough to move on and accept what happened between us that night as a one-time thing that would stay in the past."

Sarah said, "You know, on the night in question, if you put it on paper, it all sounds good and looks good in writing, but we're talking real life... reality... in your face feelings and it's not something that you can put an eraser on and make it go away; it just doesn't work like that, Thomas."

"Okay, Sarah; first let's calm down. We have to keep in mind what's at stake here. You were on company time and became personally involved with a client. I allowed myself to engage in extra- marital activities. We have both jeopardized our careers at this point and now we are being forced to deal with some harsh realities that could probably have some major repercussions. I suggest that since the experience is so fresh, that we step back and allow emotions to lower themselves a couple notches and look at the big picture; take some time to conduct some serious soul searching and revisit this subject at a later date. I'm not saying forget anything ever happened, but take some time to compile our thoughts and revisit this when we're more rational and not emotionally overwhelmed. How does that sound, Sarah?"

"Well, that does sound fair, but I do need a time frame as to when a revisit, as you say, will happen."

Thomas said, "Well, I'm not an expert in this field or anything like that, but we can say a fair amount of time would be about three weeks to a month. What do you say about that?"

"I'm going to trust you on this one and go with what you say."

Thomas said, "Well, I believe this is the best way for all involved."

"That's fine," agreed Sarah. "Okay, let's get back to business. I'll have the check by three o'clock. We usually give you an option of picking up the check from the bank or us dropping it off personally."

Thomas thought for a second and said, "Why don't you bring the check to the gym and I can make the announcement to my entire staff at the same time; I'll call it a celebration."

"Consider it done; I will see you at three-thirty."

"Very well; thank you very much and see you then," Thomas said as he hung up the phone and thought to himself *boy oh boy what have you gotten yourself into now? I guess what's more important is what am I going to do to fix this?*

Phil knocked on Thomas's door, and then opened it and said, "So, what's up?"

Thomas looked up and said, "Well, I'll tell you like this…we're good to go."

Phil jumped up and down, ran into Thomas's office, and stepped in front of him, cheering, "Oorah, Devil Dog; high-five," as Thomas stood up and they both high-fived each other.

Thomas responded, "Oorah."

Phil asked, "Man, is there a 'but' coming sometime soon?"

"No man, no buts. Close the door and have a seat."

Phil did as Thomas instructed him to, and looked at Thomas and asked, "What's up, man?"

Thomas replied, "Bro', I did something that I should not have done— had sex with Sarah Daniels the other night."

"No you didn't, I know that she was just too fine to pass up…"

Thomas said, "No man, it wasn't anything like that. She called me a couple of times after the meeting and she made several comments to me about how she was attracted to me. I was a fool for pleasure; I was taken in for pleasure. Man, we met for dinner to go over some paperwork, we had a few drinks and next thing I know, I was in her bed. She happened to catch me on a good night, I guess; I was pumped because I knew the loan was about to be approved and her persistence, coupled with her beauty, I fell into a tangled web of adultery."

"Man," said Phil, "people have done worse and then asked for forgiveness and moved on. No one was killed or wounded in action; hell, everyone goes home. What's the problem?"

Thomas looked down in despair, then looked back up at Phil and said, "Man, damage was done. This woman has fallen in love from our only encounter."

Phil said, "Damn, most guys would die to have that happen to them and you're upset."

Thomas looked at Phil with a thousand-yard stare (oh, a look only another marine that has been involved in combat would know) and Phil said, "Alright, man, I thought I would throw a little humor in there. What's the worst case scenario?"

Thomas said, "Well, I have not had the opportunity to give this thing a heck of a lot of thought, yet, but I would say, if I didn't continue seeing her, she would threaten me with going to my wife with this."

Phil asked, "Do you think she would really go that far?"

"Well, I'll tell you like this, the professional side of her went out of the window for a brief period and the emotional woman aspect side took over, and it really got scary for a moment. I was able to convince her to take a hard look at this situation and see and understand that there could be some serious repercussions and consequences behind these actions, and she agreed to step back for a while and revisit this at a later date."

Phil said, "Damn, Thomas, you defused this thing for the time being, but what are you going to do as a permanent fix?"

Thomas replied, "Man, I just don't know. I'll tell you this…I made my bed like my dad use to tell me…and now I'll have to lay in it. I briefly thought if I beat her to it and tell Beverly about it, then the worst will be over."

Phil said, "Man," then let out a laugh, "you think the worst will be over if you tell Beverly that you not only slept with another woman, but a white woman at that, it will be the least of you worries?"

Thomas paused and then replied, "Why does it have to be a white woman, why not just a woman?"

"Bro', when you tell her about what you did, the first question will be, why did you do it? And the second question will be, who was she?"

"And, again, I say my reply stays the same, it was just another woman."

Phil said, "Well, my brother, I simply suggest that you not only give this some more careful thought, but think long and hard, because I think your thought s are clouded right now."

"You know, you're right about that, and I do intend to think this thing out more carefully and also how not to let this kind of thing happen again."

"Amen to that," Phil said as he looked at Thomas and continued. "Man, I got your back, no matter what goes down. We shed blood together in Cambodia, you carried me when I was wounded; in Ghana I carried you. We have bled, cried, sweated, and damn near died together; so to this, let's get through this together." The two grasped hands in the power shake and then embraced, as Phil said, "Man, this is now time for celebration; tell me what you want to do baby baba."

Thomas said, "We're going to party like its 1999. Phil, do me a favor. Go out there on the floor and tell everyone that we will announce some good news at 1530 hours this afternoon. Have Taria go through the employee phone list and call all of our employees and have them come in at 1500. If any of them need babysitters, have them bring the kids with them; I don't care what they're doing, have them come in."

Phil said, "Now that's the Thomas Dugmal I know; welcome back, bro'."

Thomas smiled and said, "Get outta here."

Thomas picked up the phone and called Beverly.

She picked up the receiver and answered, "Good afternoon, the People's Choice Real Estate, may I help you?"

Thomas said, "Hey, baby, you want to fool around?"

Beverly replied, "Well, let me check with my husband on that."

"Well, he can't be as good looking as me and smart and as strong as me, so what do you say sexy thing?"

Beverly smiled (knowing it's Thomas, but playing along anyway), "It's okay with me, you seem like you would qualify as competition, but do your qualifications include decorated marine, good father, good husband, and, perhaps, one day US Senator?"

Thomas paused, "That's not fair; you used the rear flank assault on me."

"You should be ready for anything, at least that's what you taught me," she replied.

Thomas said (smiling), "Okay, you win. I called to share the good news with you."

With excitement in her voice, Beverly said, "You mean it came through?"

"Yes, baby, in a big way."

Beverly yelled through her office. Three of her co-workers ran over and asked what happened, what's all the excitement about? Beverly said, "My husband has been approved for expansion for the business."

Gloria, another real estate agent asked Beverly, "So, what exactly does that mean, where it would cause all this excitement?"

Beverly said, "Well, it only means we will be owner of the largest health and fitness club and restaurant in both Southern and Northern California."

Gloria started jumping up and down as the rest of the office joined in the celebration.

Thomas asked, "Beverly, are you still there, baby?"

Beverly answered, "Yes, but I can barely hear you."

"Well, tell those guys over there they can continue their celebration without you."

Beverly said, "What did you say? I can barely hear you?"

Thomas shouted out, "Be here at the gym by 1500!"

Beverly shouted into the receiver, "Did you say three o'clock come down?"

"Yes, 1500, be here; can you hear me now?"

Beverly laughs and said, "I'll be there." She hung up the phone and said, "I have to leave to go to the gym at about two forty-five."

Gloria looked at Beverly and asked, "With the expansion and growth of the business, do I detect that you'll be telling us you're leaving us?"

Beverly grabbed Gloria's hands, held them, and answered, "Yes, Gloria, I will have to leave you at this office, but that does not change the status of our friendship whatsoever, and that goes for everyone here." The whole office responded by coming over to Beverly and embracing her and, some of her co-workers even began shedding some tears. Beverly broke out and yelled, "You guys stop this, you're making it seem as though I'm going away to die or something. I will come by here and visit, as well as do some consulting for the company. And besides, I won't leave until the construction is about complete. Anyway, so we're looking at around a month to two before I go anywhere."

Gloria smiled in between tears and said, "Well, that's sure good to know." Beverly and her office crew continued to reminisce about when they first started out in the real estate business and how hard it was adapting to the business.

Thomas made a phone call to Justin from the construction company and informed him that his crew could begin the construction project next Monday. Justin confirmed and assured Thomas he'd have his crew ready to rock and roll.

Phil came back into Thomas's office and said, "Man, your girl came through for you, and every one of the employees is coming in for the announcement between 1500 and 1515."

"That's great."

"Is everything set up on your end?" asked Phil.

"Yes, I called the construction company, and set the startup date for Monday, January 4."

"Outstanding."

Thomas said, "I also called Beverly and gave her the good news."

"Oh yeah, how did she respond?"

Thomas said, "She'll be down here at 1500."

Phil paused, looked at Thomas, and asked, "So, Bev is coming down here at 1500, and Sarah Daniels is coming down at 1530 to drop off the check, right?"

Thomas replied, "Right."

"Well, I got your back on this one," said Phil. "I know you had no choice; if you had not called Bev for the signing...no there is no such thing as not calling Bev for that; hey, brother, we have to work with this. I'll keep Sarah occupied and let's just keep our wits about us."

Thomas looked at Phil and said, "Well, we're in the heat of the jungle again."

Phil replied, "Yes, we are, and we're going to get past this just as we have in the past."

"Amen to that."

By this time, it was two o'clock and Phil went to the front of the gym and instructed Taria to turn down the music in the gym. Taria asked, "Down how much?"

Phil answered, "All the way down. It's just for a couple of minutes."

"Okay."

Phil said, "We have an important announcement to make."

Taria said, "Okay."

After Taria turned the music down, Phil grabbed the microphone, cleared his throat, and said, "May I have your attention, please; all the staff personnel, we have a special announcement to make, so we will need all staff personnel to muster at the front desk at 1530 hours. To all you civilian personnel, that means 3:30 P.M." Three o'clock rolled around and off-duty staff started to come in, and as they greeted each other, talk started to generate. Word was something big was going down, the only question was will it be something negative or positive?

Taria said, "I don't know exactly what it's going to be, but I can almost assure you that it's positive."

Allen, one of the staff trainers asked, "How do you know? What if the gym is going under and we'll be out of work?"

Jan, another staff trainer answered, "Come on, man; if that was the case, we would have been brought into Mr. Dugmal's office individually and been informed."

Shortly after three-o-five, Beverly walked in. All of the staff personnel in the front portion of the gym knew and loved Beverly. Beverly was a warm person, who when she asked how are you doing…she really wanted to know, how you were doing and it made people feel really comfortable around her. Everyone came over to greet her, since she did not frequently come to the gym. Beverly was returning the greetings back to each individual, and Allen came up to Beverly and said, "Hi, Mrs. Dugmal, how have you been?"

Beverly replied, "Fine, thank you and how about yourself?"

Allen said, "I hope I'm fine, as well; I'm just wondering why this meeting has been called and kind of worried that we are going to receive bad news."

Beverly smiled and said, "Allen, I assure you that we are going to share good news with you all, so stop worrying."

With a sign of relief, Allen said, "Thank you very much."

Beverly spoke to a couple more of the staff and then made her way to the back where the offices were. Phil met her before she got to Thomas's office. "Hey girl," he said to Beverly.

"Hey, Phil; how ya doing?"

"Great," Phil replied as they embraced one another. "I was just heading for Thomas's office," and Beverly said, "So was I."

They both walked up to Thomas's door, which was closed. Phil knocked and entered. "Guess who I found?"

Thomas had his head turned in the direction of his computer, which had his back toward the door. "Who did you find, bro'?"

Phil said, "Only the finest sister this side of the Rio Grande."

Thomas turned around and said, "Baby, you made it."

Beverly walked over (as Thomas stood up), embraced him, and they kissed on the lips. Beverly (while still holding Thomas) said, "Honey, I am so proud of you and I want you to know that I will stand by you 100 percent."

Thomas said, "Baby, thank you for believing in me the way you do."

Phil shouted out, "Hey, I did something too ya know; I should be able to get some love!"

"Man, you're right," said Thomas, "but, unfortunately, you'll have to get love from some other source." They laughed.

Taria walked to the doorway, knocked, and said, "I really hate to break up this Kodak moment you all, but Ms. Daniels is here; she says she has a three-thirty appointment with you, Mr. Dugmal."

"That's fine, Taria; we'll be right out."

Phil looked at Thomas, "I'll go out first."

As the three approached the front, Beverly said, "Hey, honey, I have my camera, and I want to take a picture when the check is handed to you."

Thomas said, "Okay, baby, but you know I don't like being photographed."

"Oh, stop being such a baby," Beverly said with a smile.

The three walked up to Sarah Daniels and Phil shook her hand and said, "Nice to see you again."

Sarah smiled and said, "The pleasure is all mine."

Thomas shook Sarah's hand and said, "Thanks for coming over."

"I wouldn't allow anyone else to come."

Thomas said, "Sarah, I would like you to meet my wife, Beverly."

The two shook hands and Sarah said, "You are very lovely, Mrs. Dugmal."

Beverly said, "Thank you very much, and please call me Beverly."

Sarah said, "Thank you, I feel like I know you already."

Thomas said, "Well three-thirty and time to make the announcement."

"I have the check right here, how do you want to do this?" asked Sarah.

"Please," said Phil, "wait just a minute while I gather everyone together."

Phil told Taria to turn the music down once again. He picked up the microphone and said, "May I have your attention please; we need everyone to gather around the front here where we are; we have the pleasure of making a very special announcement. I now present to you Mr. Thomas Dugmal."

Everyone clapped as Thomas walked up and said, "I'm not going to use the microphone. What I do want to say is…for those of you that have been with me for the five years that we've been open here at the gym, and those of you that have hung in there through the good times as well as bad times—there were some difficult times a few years ago when paychecks were two and three weeks late. You guys talked about me, oh yes, I knew what you guys were saying about me, but you hung in there with me, with pride and commitment you would see the payoff in the long run, you just had to see the big picture. Well, now is payoff time; if you look over to your left you'll see a layout of the new T & B Fitness for the gym and restaurant."

Phil unveiled the scale model that was sitting on a table. Everyone looked at it and some of the staff shed a tear.

Thomas then said, "Construction starts on Monday."

Everyone started clapping and after thirty seconds Thomas said, "Ladies and gentleman. Please join me in celebrating the signing of the check for the project, being presented by Sarah Daniels of the Western Stage Coach Bank. Ms. Daniels…,"

Thomas reached out his hand and Sarah joined him as she made her way to the front where he was. Sarah held up the check. Beverly made her way to the front with her camera out and started taking pictures.

Sarah said, "It is with great pleasure I present this check to you on the behalf of Western Stage Coach Bank; good luck and congratulations."

As everyone began clapping once again, Sarah looked at Thomas and said, "I need to talk to you in private," (more or less in Thomas's ear).

Thomas said, "Anything else?"

Phil walked over to Sarah, grabbed her hand, and said, "Sarah, could I show you the layout for the plans?"

Sarah looked at Thomas and answered Phil, "Sure, that would be great." Then the two walked off.

Beverly walked over to Thomas and said, "You probably need to go and secure that check or take it to the bank."

Thomas replied, "You're right. I'll put it in the safe in my office."

"Good," said Beverly, "I'll walk with you back to your office."

As they headed back to Thomas's office, several of the staff come over to Thomas and said, "Congratulations."

Thomas replied, "Thank you, thank you very much."

When they got to Thomas's office, they both walked in and Thomas walked over to the safe in the back of the room, and then turned around, and asked, "Baby, can you close the door, please?"

"Sure," said Beverly, and closed the door.

Thomas began turning the cylinder on the safe and Beverly commented, "Sarah Daniels is beautiful, isn't she?"

Thomas answered, "Yes, she is nice looking."

Beverly asked, "Is she married?"

"I really don't know," said Thomas, "why, do you have someone in mind for her to date if she's not married?"

Beverly said, "No, not really. Have you noticed how she looks at you?"

Now having trouble remembering the combination to the safe, Thomas replied, "I have not noticed anything different than the normal, if that answers your question."

Beverly says, "Well, I just noticed something about her, and the look in her eyes when she looks at you."

Thomas turned around and looked at Beverly and said, "You don't suspect she is on dope or anything, do you?"

Beverly said, "No, that's not what I'm saying. I guess you would have to be a woman to understand what I'm saying."

Thomas said, "No thanks, I like the way God arranged things for me the first time."

Beverly laughed and said, "Get that safe open so you can put that check away."

Thomas, with a feeling of relief opened the safe and put the check in, and then closed the door and spun the cylinder. He walked over to Beverly, grabbed and hugged her and said, "Baby, I love you very much and just hope that you never lose that twinkle in your eyes for me, the same as I have for you."

Beverly said, "I would go through the fire and through the storm and hell and back for you."

"Yeah, that's my girl. Now let's go and celebrate with the rest of the crew."

Beverly said, "Let's do it."

The two walked back out to the front and several of the staff went over to Thomas and Beverly and expressed their gratitude and congratulations, and just general conversations.

Phil was talking to Sarah in another corner of the gym when she spotted Thomas and started glaring in his direction. Phil noticed and looked to see what or who had her attention and saw that it was Thomas. Phil asked Sarah if she would like to go and have a couple of drinks. Sarah did not respond. Phil walked in front of her and asked again, "Would you like to go and have a couple of drinks with me? And I won't accept no for an answer the second time."

Sarah looked at Phil and said, "What do you mean a second time?"

"Well, I asked you the first time and I got no response."

Sarah smiled and said, "I'm sorry Phil; I have so much on my mind. I don't know if I should go out tonight."

Phil said, "Well, you said that you have a lot on your mind, I don't know any way better than having a couple of tall ones to take whatever it is off your mind. And I promise, we will not be out late and I am the perfect gentleman."

Sarah said, "You know, I do need to speak with Thomas on an issue that needs to be resolved."

"Not a problem," said Phil, "you do have his cell phone number, don't you?"

Sarah said, "Yes, I do."

"Well, why don't you just give him a call a little later; I promise I'll remind you."

Sarah looked at Phil and said, "Maybe you're right." Sarah was looking at Thomas across the room once again and Thomas continued his conversations with some of his staff, and he was so engrossed with them, he didn't even notice Sarah attempting to get his attention with eye contact.

However, Beverly was scanning the room and noticed Sarah across the room. Beverly looked at her for a moment and saw that her eyes were fixated on someone in particular. Beverly looked at what she believed was the object of her fixation and the two made eye contact. Sarah had a surprised look in her eyes, much like that of a deer at night that walked in the middle of the wood and saw headlights.

Beverly then walked over to Thomas and rejoined him.

Sarah said to Phil, "Now about that drink; you promise I won't be out that late and the place we go will be a safe watering hole?"

Phil said, "Cross my heart and hope to die, if I should fib or I should lie."

Sarah responded, "Okay, it's a deal," so Phil and Sarah grabbed their belongings and left the gym. It was now four-fifteen and the staff that came in for the meeting was beginning to disburse.

All the time, Beverly was watching Sarah leaving with Phil. Beverly said to Thomas, "Well, it's time to go and pick up the kids."

Thomas said, "Well, I have a suggestion; you go and get half of the family and I'll grab the other half, and let's meet at the restaurant for dinner and make the announcement together to the kids."

Beverly said, "That sounds like a plan, where do you want to go?"

"How about the Dallas Ranch Steak House?"

Beverly said, "Excellent choice; let's all meet there, say around six o'-clock."

Thomas said so long as he looked around to make sure that he didn't still see Sarah in the gym. After carefully scanning the place, Thomas was assured that Sarah had departed the gym, which caused him to release a sigh of relief. Thomas walked around and found Taria, and said to her, "Taria, I need to talk to you in my office."

Taria said, "Sure thing, Mr. D."

Thomas walked back into his office and sat down in front of his computer and began to stroke out some words in the WordPerfect program.

Taria walked in and said, "You wanted to see me, Mr. D?"

Thomas answered, "Yes, Taria, please come in; come in and have a seat." Thomas finished up his sentence and turned around in his chair. Thomas said, "Taria, first I wanted to inform you that I'm in process of generating a memo informing all of the staff that we will begin construction on the new gym project on Monday. This means that we will have to alter some of the schedules, as well as gym hours."

Taria asked, "What will the hours change to?"

Thomas answered, "Well, I was strongly leaning toward 4 A.M. to 8 P.M. until construction is completed. I have a deal worked out with the construction company that the heaviest construction will be conducted after 6 P.M. and go until 10 P.M. without creating any overtime. This will save money for the gym toward the construction. What I propose to offer…the staff that normally works the off hours will be allowed the option to start work earlier, or take vacation for two weeks and I'll pay for one week, by which time the construction in the back of the gym should be near completion give or take a week or two. The second shift can overlap with the first and third shift and can temporarily move to day or second shift overlap."

Taria said, "That sounds more than fair, Mr. D; after you've written it out I'll review it and get copies made up, and I'll get with all of the crew and get back with you by Sunday evening."

"Thank you, Taria; you are definitely my right hand as well as foot."

Taria smiled and said, "Thank you Mr. D, will there be anything else?"

Thomas said, "Taria, what I really wanted to talk to you about is running the restaurant side. Now please, keep in mind that this project will be extremely stressful and is going to require 100 percent of your efforts to oversee it, so I just need to know from you, are you really up for the challenge?"

Taria said, "Mr. D, I do believe in myself and if you believed in me, as well, I know that I can do this."

Thomas said, "Taria, you will have all the support you'll need, and I have an online program for you to go through before the restaurant opens. I know that you're young, by the way, are you 21 or 22 years old?"

Taria answered, "Mr. D, I'm 23 years old now."

Thomas asked, "And when will you obtain your degree?"

"This May I will earn my Bachelor of Arts."

Thomas said, "Very well, it looks like the stage is set, so I'll get everything in motion."

Taria stood up and said, "Mr. D, you are a good man, and I really mean that. It's not very often when a black man hits success and pulls along everyone involved up the ladder, as well. I love you like a father and a good friend, as well. You really deserve the best that life has to offer you."

Thomas said, "Thank you very much, Taria, however I'm not an angel by any stretch of the imagination and I've done my fair share of dirt and wrong. But through it all, I believe that we learn from our mistakes and when given the chance for a fresh start and to make amends and the right wrongs done, you grow and gain wisdom and move onward and upward. This means helping as many along the way as possible whenever feasible. Well, I've said enough now, so run along with the rest of the crew and I'll finish up this memo and get it to you for review and distribution."

Taria smiled and said, "Yes, sir, Mr. D," and then walked out and returned to the rest of the crew as they continued to celebrate the occasion.

Thomas finished up the memo and printed out a copy, looked at his watch, and saw that it's 1645 hours and time to pick up the boys from school. He shut down his computer and grabbed his bag and jacket, heading down the hallway toward the front of the gym, as the entire crew waved to Thomas and a few of them yelled out, "Are you leaving already?"

Thomas yelled, "You guys enjoy the evening and I'll see you later."

Everyone yelled, "Goodnight, Mr. Dugmal."

Thomas jumped into his truck and started to take off, but before he could get out of the parking lot, his cell phone rang.

Sarah and Phil were at the club called the Blue Room. Sarah said, "Excuse me please, Phil, I'll have to visit the ladies room."

Phil said, "Sure, not a problem."

Sarah excused herself and went into the ladies restroom; she pulled out her cell phone and went into one of the stalls. She dialed Thomas's cell number.

Thomas stopped the truck just before leaving the parking lot of the gym. He said, "Hello, Thomas speaking, may I help you?"

Sarah paused for a moment.

Thomas said, "Hello, is there anyone there?"

Sarah answered, "Yes, yes there is; hi, Thomas."

Thomas paused for a moment. "Sarah, is that you?"

"Yes, it is me."

Thomas asked, "Are you okay? Is there anything wrong?"

Sarah responded, "Thomas, I need to see you."

Thomas said, "Sarah, please; let's not go through this right now. We both agreed that we would not revisit this issue until a couple of weeks from now."

"Well, I thought that I could wait until then, but I can't and I want to… I mean I need to see you, Thomas."

"Sarah, I'm on my way to meet up with my family as we speak. There's nothing that I can do to help you, even if I wanted to."

Sarah said, "Then after you've met, what were you going to do? I'll settle for afterwards."

"Okay, Sarah, since you don't get it, I'll explain it to you as if I was your drama teacher; we cannot meet tonight at all, under any circumstances. Now I'm sorry, but that's how it goes."

"Thomas, I don't know why you're being so unreasonable, but I'm going to back off and allow you to win this round, but please understand that I am used to having things just like Burger King…my way."

Thomas said, "Sarah, I will get back with you first chance I get, tomorrow morning sometime."

"Very well, then," said Sarah and hung up.

Thomas hung up, paused, and thought to himself *boy I hope this does not get out of hand.* He then proceeded to the school to pick up the kids. Thomas picked up Elizabeth and Elijah. Thomas parked in front of the school and Elizabeth jumped in the front seat first and said, "Hi, Dad, how are you?"

Thomas answered, "Fine, thanks for asking."

Elizabeth looked at Thomas and asked, "Dad, what in the heck is happening? Why are you talking like that?"

Thomas responded, "Well, I guess I'll just have to tell you what exactly is happening a little later."

Then Elijah jumped into the back and said, "Hi Dad, hi Sis."

Thomas said, "Hi, Son."

"Elijah," said Elizabeth, "something is wrong with Dad."

Elijah said, "Something, like what?"

"Well, he won't say right now," replied his sister, "but he will tell us a little later on tonight."

Thomas proceeded to drive home, and to meet up with Beverly at the house. On the way home, Thomas turned on the radio to KGFS 'oldies but goodies.' A song came on and Thomas said, "Man ain't this about a blip?"

Elijah said, "What are you tripping on, Dad?"

Thomas said, "Oh man, you could not understand, even if you wanted to. I was just thinking back to the days when this song came out…what I was doing at that time." After the introduction had finished, the words began. "If loving you is wrong, I don't want to be right. If being right means being without you, I'd rather be wrong than right."

Elizabeth shouted, "Isn't this song about infidelity?"

Elijah answered, "No, it's about two people getting caught up. He should have just hit it and quit it and forget it."

Elizabeth says, "You are a true form of man's best friend."

"You guys stop it," said Thomas. "This song is about someone being honest and letting others know that he, as well as millions of other people in the world, has gotten into situations with another for whatever reason, and confusion gets in the way of doubt and discovers love has multiple definitions for multiple situations."

Elijah said, "Man, Dad, that was deep; you ought to write a book on relationships."

Elizabeth said, "No, Dad, you sound like the voice of experience."

Thomas looked over at Elizabeth and said, "Baby girl, listen to this…just live a little longer and love a little stronger and then and only then will you understand."

Elizabeth replied, "You know, if love has that much drama then I just might stay away from it."

They all laughed together as the truck pulled into the driveway and Thomas touched the button on the ceiling, and the garage door opened. When they got into the garage, Elijah said, "Dad, for now, whatever happens in Vegas, stays in Vegas," and they all laughed as they exited the truck and headed for the door to enter the house.

When they got into the house Bev, Tina, and Melvin were already inside as everyone greeted one another. Bev went over to Thomas and kissed him on the lips and asked, "How's everything going these days?"

Thomas replied, "Fairly well; what about things at the office, how are they going?"

Bev said, "Really busy, I've just about everyone trained to take over when I leave."

"Well," said Thomas, "I hope that this will be a smooth transition."

Bev said, "Oh, by the way, I have a message for you; Sarah called and said sorry she missed you, but would like to catch up with you in the morning, maybe over breakfast."

Thomas looked over at Bev and his eyes were open wide with sweat beads on his forehead. He asked, "Did she mention if anything was wrong or not? Or, if we needed to go over more paperwork?"

"No, she did state that it was not business related, but was of personal nature."

Thomas paused and looked at Bev and asked, "Did she mention if it was important or not?"

"No, she did not mention, but she did say that she would like to see you alone and she would talk to me at a later date, concerning some issues at hand."

Thomas looked at Bev then dropped his head in an effort not to make eye contact with her.

Their silence lasted 45 seconds, and Bev said, "Tom, is there anything you want to tell me?"

"As a matter of fact, baby, there is; can we go upstairs and talk in private?"

Bev answered, "No, we can talk right here in front of the kids."

"Bev, now let's be reasonable."

Bev said, "Is that what you call it now, reason?"

"Bev, you've trusted me in the past, now I need for you to trust me on this one. Now can we go upstairs and discuss this?"

"Well, I can't wait to hear this," Bev said as she started upstairs.

Bev and Thomas went up the stairs and walked into the bedroom. Bev entered first and Thomas followed, closing the bedroom door behind him. Thomas thought to himself for a moment, trying to formulate in his mind how he was going to break his confession to Bev. Thomas thought *I was stupid; I was weak when I should have been strong and let someone take advantage of me.*

Bev looked over at Thomas while she stood by the window. Thomas looked over at Bev and made eye contact, almost detecting that Bev was anticipating facing a blow that would deliver pain from words that were about to be spoken.

Thomas said, "Bev, I'm going to sit down in my chair over here; would you please sit down, as well, on the bed?"

Beverly looked down, took a deep breath, and said, "Okay, Tom, I'll sit on the bed; please let's get everything out in the open and be completely honest with each other."

Thomas paused and answered, "That's just what I plan to do," without changing his tone. Bev sat down and Thomas looked directly into her eyes and said, "Baby, I messed up this time."

Beverly responded, "I know you're not going to stop now, you're starting out pretty good."

"I won't go into explicit detail, but I've been unfaithful to you and it was no fault of yours," declared Thomas. "It's on me 100 percent. I had sex with Sarah, the young lady that works for Western Stage Coach Loan Approvals."

Beverly stopped Tom and said, "I remember that bitch. I could tell she had her eye on you from the very beginning, and I know as sure as I sighted her, she made the first move."

"I let myself be taken in when I should have been strong. I truly do not love this woman by any stretch of the imagination. The evening we signed the closing papers, we celebrated with drinks and I allowed my irrational mind to go against all of my moral standards and violate the vows I made before God and to you my wife and the integrity of my kids, as well. For that I ask you to find it in your heart to forgive me. However, I do not ask you to forget this incident, but put it behind us and allow us to move forward, if you're willing to do that."

Beverly looked at Thomas; she noticed tears coming from his eyes, running down his cheeks. Beverly had tears, as well, running down her face. Beverly said, "I have to respect you for coming clean and I commend you for not making any excuses. Thomas, this hurts like no knife wound or gunshot can compare to. I have given you my all and all without conditions, reservations, or restrictions. I have known only you only for eighteen years, and to know for one night's pleasure you would take a risk in losing all that we have built... it's unbelievable. I know it takes two to tango, but love should not allow you to succumb to the Devil. You know, Thomas, I'm hurt, but feel sorry for you right now."

Thomas said, "For the hurt that I have caused you, I'm sorry, but my question to you is why do you feel sorry for me?"

"I've already talked to Sarah Daniels. She told me everything in a nutshell, and I know you are being honest with me, and for that you do get brownie points. But, Tom, you have bigger problems right now. That bitch says, that she is in love with you, and if I don't give you up she will destroy your whole life as you know it. We had a few words with each other and I informed her that I will not just give you up. It doesn't quite work like that; you are my husband and I would stick by your side no matter what may come. No, I did not want to let on to her that, though I love you, right now I can't live with you, either. I'm not saying that it's over between us, but right now I do need some distance. You do understand?"

"Yes, I do understand," said Thomas, "and I must respect your decision, as well. Baby, I do love you and wish this thing had never happened, but it did and now we must get past it; conquer the evil that's attempting to destroy our lives."

Beverly said, "Okay now, Tom, this is not like the Vietnam War in Ghana. What we'll do is go about business as normal; the construction project will be finished next month, so I'll move in with my sister along with the kids and you'll spend the majority of the time at the gym overseeing the project and, as far as anyone else is concerned, the reason I'm spending time with my family is because of the time your spending at the gym. Now, by the time the project is completed, hopefully, this will be behind us and I feel enough for you to get back together as a family. But you have to make a promise to me, and I don't care what's going on, you will never violate our vows again."

"Baby, I do promise that and more. I admit I've been a fool and any treatment you give or hand down to me now, I deserve it and will accept sentence."

"Thomas, you know, if you did get involved with anyone it would have to be a psycho bitch," and they both laughed.

Thomas said, "Baby, I'm going to call Sarah tomorrow and explain to her that we've laid everything out on the table and we're working on reconciling, so there's nothing for her to attempt to 'white mail' me with and if she does not get out of my life, I will make her disappear; just as sure as a monkey takes a crap in the jungle, I will erase her."

Bev said, "Please be careful, Thomas; remember a women scorned is like a wounded lion, it's going to be more dangerous."

Thomas replied, "I'll keep that in mind; I'll try using diplomacy first."

Thomas and Beverly prepared for bed and Thomas got on his knees and thanked God for being so merciful and allowing Beverly to see the forest through the trees.

The next morning, everyone got up and began their daily routines and Bev went to the kids and told them there would be a change in routine. "Please pack an overnight bag with a change in clothes for at least three days. We're going to go over to your grandmother's and grandfather's house for a few days this week."

Elijah asked, "Nothing is wrong is there, perhaps, that we should know about?"

Thomas answered, "No, son, they are finishing up the gym, I will be spending the majority of my time there at the gym, and your mom just would feel better there in my absence."

"Hey," said Melvin, "it's not a problem, Dad; we can stay here and I'll look after the family, being I'm the next in command. I'm the next marine, anyway."

Beverly smiled and said, "That's all well and good, Melvin, but just the same, we're going over to Grandmom's and Dad's house, so let's get it together." So, all of the kids went their respective ways to prepare their bags.

Once the kids left the room and Thomas and Beverly were alone, Thomas walked over to Beverly and stood in front of her, looking into her eyes and said, "Baby, I just want to thank you once again for your understanding and sticking by me in the midst of my shortcomings and brain farts."

Beverly responded, "Hey, man, I'm you wife, not your high school sweetheart; I love you, man, and I'll stick by your side come thick and thin, but if you pull anything like this again, I'll beat you like an Alabama runaway field slave."

They embraced and kissed each other on the lips. Thomas said, "Well, baby, what's the plan?"

"Thomas, I have a feeling that this deranged psycho bitch may get stupid, so we need to come up with a plan to counter her."

"You're right; I've thought about this and I believe if she is led to believe that she has caused our separation, then she will leave you and the kids out of the equation."

"Yes," replied Beverly, "but she'll still need a pawn to leave her with the advantage over you, so I'll make sure that I'm available and accessible to talk to and make her believe she has my ear. In the meantime, you just act as though everything is the same."

Thomas asked, "So, baby, just so I have this straight, I'm going to play this thing out and see how far this woman wants to take this and we will deal with it as it raises its ugly head?"

"Yes, that's right, but that doesn't mean you will get stupid with it. I mean you will not have sex or hit or anything like that, but don't let her know that everything is cool with us; as long as she feels we are on the outs then she will believe that she has the upper hand, but it will be just a smoke screen."

"Roger that, let's make it work." The phone rang and Thomas said, "I'll get it." Thomas picked up the phone on the third ring and said, "Dugmal residence."

Phil was on the other end and said, "Thomas, kill the proper talk: man, let's get busy. I got a call from the ad agency and they want to gather today at 1000 hours to go over the grand opening next week. Man, we have news and camera coverage for our grand opening day; I can't believe this shit."

Thomas said, "Man, slow your roll, brother man; let's not count our chickens before they hatch. Let's just take this one step at a time. Now, I'll meet you at Roscoe's at 0830."

Phil responded, "That's a bet, bro', I'll see you then."

Thomas asked, "Hey, baby, are you dropping off the kids at school?"

"Yes, I am," replied Beverly, "what do you have going on?"

He responded, "Well, Phil and I are meeting for breakfast to go over the marketing strategy that we will roll out to the press that will be hooking up with us at 1000 hours this morning. It would be nice if you could join us for breakfast and meet with the media, as well."

"That would be nice. Let me get the kids off to school and I'll join you at Roscoe's."

"Okay, baby, that's cool; so, I'll order ahead for you?"

Beverly answered, "Yes, I'll have the three wings and a waffle and a cup of coffee please, and I'll be there not too long after 0825."

Thomas said, "Okay, so shall it be." Thomas grabbed his suit coat and told the kids, "I'll see you guys in three days; make sure you're minding your manners and do what your mom and your grandmother and father say to do."

All of the kids acknowledged, "Yes, sir."

Thomas went downstairs and yelled, "Baby, I'll see you a little later."

Beverly responded, "Okay, sweetheart."

Thomas left the house and jumped into the Yukon XL and drove off. He arrived at the restaurant at 0820 and found that Phil had already beaten him there.

Phil came over and greeted Thomas at his truck and said, "Hey, man, what's up?"

Thomas replied, "*Nada, compadre.* Hey, bro'; you beat me here, which means you have to buy breakfast this morning."

Phil said, "No biggie, bro', let's do this."

"Bet on that," said Thomas.

As they were entering the waffle house, Thomas opened up the restaurant door and motioned for Phil to enter first. Phil said, "Thanks, man," as he walked past Thomas.

After Phil walked in, Thomas followed and said, "Hey, Phil; by the way, Beverly will be joining us this morning," and smiled.

Phil looked at Thomas and said, "Okay, Devil Dog, you got me on that one," and smiled back.

After they were seated, the waitress came over and said, "Good morning, gentlemen; I don't understand why you are here without any female company."

Phil responded intentionally before Thomas could and said, "You know, I was just asking myself that same question and an idea came to mind. What time do you get off?"

The waitress responded, "Two o'clock, why?"

"Well," said Phil, "this is the middle of the week and I was just wondering if maybe you would like to go out for dinner this evening and, perhaps, for drinks afterward. I promise I won't keep you out late."

The waitress replied, "You won't; whatever or wherever you had in mind, I drive myself and you'll drive yourself."

Phil laughed and said, "I guess I can't argue with that."

The waitress looked over at Thomas and said, "Well, you're being awfully quiet; are you married or something else, because I do have lots of friends who are single and available."

Thomas laughed and then responded, "You are a very lovely young lady and I trust that you do have nice-looking friends, but you'll see why I can't go out with you guys in (Thomas looked at his watch) about seven minutes."

Phil looked at the waitress and said, "Well, that does not apply to me, so let's exchange phone numbers and we'll discuss where and when we are going to meet."

The waitress said, "Okay, then."

So, Phil and the waitress exchanged information and Thomas placed the food order for himself and Beverly. Phil then placed his order and the waitress headed off to the kitchen. The clock reaches 0845 and in walked Beverly. Thomas and Phil both stood up and Beverly walked over to Thomas, he grabbed her up to him, and kissed her on the lips.

Phil said, "Oh hell, no; I know you're not going to just give Thomas some love."

Beverly laughed and said, "Phil, you crazy marine; I'll give you a hug, that's about it."

"Well, that's good enough," replied Phil, and they embraced. After everyone had properly greeted one another, they all sat down in their seats.

They began a conversation concerning who would be the spokesperson for the media coverage; Phil spoke up and said, "Well, I believe that I should be the spokesperson because I'm the only one who is not married and I believe that would draw the customers to believe that I'm the honest and sincere person."

"Man, do you know how you sound?" said Thomas.

Beverly interrupted and said, "Wait a minute, Phil, before you answer that question, let me tell both of you this. Remember, we are attempting to bring in customers, which means an intelligent marketing strategy."

Phil looked at Thomas and they both nodded their heads in agreement. Thomas looked back in Beverly's direction and said, "Baby, please elaborate, if you feel so inclined."

Beverly responded, "If I may... Well, as we all know or should know, if we want to target the male market for just about anything, who do you get to capture their attention?"

Thomas replied quite naturally, "A female."

"Now, if we want to capture the female market, who do we look to?"

Phil said, "Beverly, I think we get it now. So, what you're saying is we need both of us to address the media."

Beverly said, "That's exactly what I'm saying. And we have to be extremely careful what we say and how we say it, you know?"

Phil shouted out, "Roger that!"

Thomas said, "Okay, I've written down what we will say on the letter for our marketing campaign." Thomas pulled out his folder from his briefcase and took two sheets of paper out and handed one to Beverly and one to Phil. Thomas said, "I had my speech writer prepare this material. Phil, I know that you're dying to have your fifteen minutes of fame, so here's your chance. And Bev, as good as you look and as articulate as you are, you'll definitely make Phil look good, and you can pick Phil up if he stumbles, as well."

Phil laughed and said, "Hey, and if she falls, I'll pick her up." They all laughed.

Beverly said, "Well, this looks pretty good, Thomas, I'm impressed. I think I'll just have to go over this a couple of times and I can have it memorized."

Phil looked at his copy of the script, and then said, "Well, what I can't memorize, I'll adlib."

Thomas said, "Man, that's not good enough; I need you to follow the plan and stick to the script."

Beverly jumped in and said, "Boys, what Phil can't remember, I'll prompt him; I'll have this whole thing memorized anyway...mine and his."

"Now, I can live with that," said Phil.

Thomas agreed, "Well, that's good for me, as well."

They all finished eating, drinking coffee, and reviewing the script materials for the media. Thomas looked at his watch and realized that it was 0940. He shouted out, "Woo, we have exactly twenty minutes to get to the gym!"

Beverly suggested, "Thomas, why don't you drive us over there; there's no need in taking three vehicles, plus it will buy us a little more time to study."

Thomas said, "Let's do it!"

Phil said, "I was going to suggest that, but you beat me to it."

"Yeah, right man," teased Thomas.

They all got up from the table and exited the restaurant. Beverly caught the attention of the restaurant manager and beckoned him outside where she was standing. The manager looked out at her and then looked to his left and then to his right, in order to be sure that she was really motioning to him. When he realized that she really was motioning to him, he looked over at the hostess and told her, "I'll be right back."

By this time, Thomas and Phil had already piled into the truck and were waiting for Beverly to join them. When the manager came out, he began to adjust his tie, and straighten his pants and shirt. He had a very bold and joyful look on his face, thinking that Beverly was interested or, hopefully, he had a chance to get with her. When he got directly in front of her, with a big smile on his face, he asked, "How may I help you, pretty lady?"

Beverly smiled and said, "You really think I'm pretty?"

The manager answered, "Actually, I think you're fine; however, I'm trying my damnedest to maintain my professionalism."

Beverly smiled with the look of a school girl, very shyly, and replied, "I wish my husband would think the same way that you do."

The manager said, "Well, if he doesn't, then he can't tell gold from silver."

"You are too kind," said Beverly. "I was just going to compliment you and your restaurant and staff on what a good job you're doing, and I still want to extend that; however, if I might add, since you have been such a gentleman, I was just wondering if I could leave my car here. I'll return a little later in the afternoon to retrieve it and, hopefully, you'll still be here and if it so happens you are, maybe we can have lunch."

The manager stuck out his chest as if he was as proud as a peacock and replied, "You betcha, you can leave it here as long as you like. When you return, just come into the restaurant, and, if I'm not standing around front, just ask one of the waitresses to go and get me."

Beverly said, "That's wonderful, you are such a kind, considerate person; I'm impressed already."

The manager couldn't control his smiles at this point, and found no words would come out of his mouth.

Beverly looked him in the eyes and said, "Okay then, here's the plan. Those two people in that SUV over there are my business associates and I'll be riding with them. One of them will leave his vehicle here, as well, if that's okay with you?"

The manager replied, "No problem at all."

"So, then I'll have them drop me back off here after we've completed our business and when I return I'll come in and ask for you."

The manager (still with a Kool-Aid smile) replied, "I can't wait."

Beverly smiled at the manager with very sultry eyes, which almost melted the man, and said, "Okay then, I'll see you a little later." She turned and walked away; knowing that he was still watching her as she walked off, she put a little extra into her already masterful strut, and smiled, acknowledging that she had his attention hook, line, and sinker.

The manager turned around and thought to himself, *Man, I must be one of the luckiest brothers in the world; I'm going to hit that real good.*

As Beverly reached the door, she thought to herself, *Boy, that must be the most gullible person I have ever come across; he couldn't really think it would be that easy to get with a sister like me, I know.*

As she opened the door and got in, Thomas asked, "What was that conversation all about?"

Beverly replied, "We get to park our cars here until we finish with our business meetings and all I had to do is smile a little; I swear, you men are weak as lambs when it comes to thinking you're going to get a piece or a little something, something from a lady or that there's even a chance you could."

Thomas replied, "Yeah, you women definitely have us at a disadvantage there."

Phil shouted out, "It's not a joke; you women have brought down the nation, started wars, and destroyed countries!"

Beverly turned to both Phil and Thomas and said, "You guys just remember that when you think that you can pull one over on us."

Thomas looked at his watch and said, "We're cutting it close, we better step on it," then sped up and caused the attention to shift from conversation to the road.

Beverly took out her speech and started reviewing it, and Phil thought it was a good idea if he did the same. It did not take Thomas long to reach his destination. As Thomas pulled into the parking lot of the gym, he had hardly put his truck into park and looked up, when he saw the news van pulling into the lot.

Phil looked around and said, "Hey, they're here already; we had better double-time it out of here."

Thomas hopped out and ran around to open the door for Beverly. The three of them got out and walked to the front door and waited to greet the news crew.

The person conducting the interview was Nathaniel Archibald. When Nat gathered the crew together, he walked over to the trio and introduced himself, "Hi, I'm Nathaniel Archibald and I'll be conducting the interview today. This is my camera crew (pointing to a man carrying a long pole with a microphone at the end of it), and then my lighting crew (pointing to a young lady holding a pole with lighting equipment attached to it)."

Phil said, "Damn, man, I thought that this would be a simple exercise; this looks like coverage when we fought in Beirut." They had to laugh at what Phil said.

Nathaniel asked, "Who is Mr. Dugmal?"

Thomas shook his head and said, "I'm sorry, I got caught up in all the drama. I'm Thomas Dugmal and this is my wife, Beverly, and over here is the one and only Philip (USMC) Upchurch."

Phil added, "But you can call me Phil or Devil Dog."

They all shook hands and Phil said, "Well, let's step inside and you can set up where you need to."

Nathaniel agreed, as he motioned for the crew with a wave of his hands to follow him inside of the gym. When they got inside, Nathaniel looked around and was amazed at what he saw. He looked over at Thomas and said, "Man, I'm really impressed; this gym is not only huge, but nice, as well."

Thomas said, "Thank you. I put a hell of a lot of time and effort in planning this particular design and it's really a dream become reality for me. I'm truly blessed to be able to make this dream a reality and to have the support from my truly lovely wife, Beverly, and best friend and business partner Philip Upchurch, and my entire family, as well."

"Please," said Nathaniel, "save that speech for the camera and the interview."

Thomas laughed and said, "Well, Beverly (pointing over at her) and Phil have been selected for the speaking part; you can get me for the tour and the basic information."

"Okay, can we take a quick tour so I can decipher where we will set up?" asked Nat.

Thomas replied, "Sure, let's get started."

Amy, one of the lighting assistants said, "Hey, boss (referring to Nathaniel), I caught Mr. Dugmal on tape expressing the success of his dreams; would you like for me to rap that up in the editing later?"

Nathaniel said, "Yes, please; good job, Amy. Thomas, shall we begin the tour?" Nathaniel gladly followed Thomas.

Thomas said, "This first floor is where we have our clothing line and store; the majority of the clothing design came from Philip. And, of course, we sell several different lines from different manufacturers. We also have supplements from different suppliers, as well as my own personal line of products."

Nathaniel asked, "You actually do the lab work yourself?"

"No, what I've done through research and study groups, was sat down and studied the different groups through a period of time, like six months, used the leading brand of supplements, and came up with points to compare against for the different ethnic groups, being each group was different genetically, and came up with a different line of products for each group to accommodate the differences; I found the research to be successful 79.6 percent of the time in my case studies."

Nathaniel said, "Man, you're blowing me away."

"No, really, everyone is different, so it was about time to make a few changes for the good and not sit around and waste time waiting for someone else to do it, when they got around to it," added Thomas.

Nathaniel said, "Amen to that."

They walked out of the store and Thomas walked Nathaniel over to the restaurant. Nathaniel asked Thomas, "Now, what inspired you to open a full service restaurant inside of a gym?"

Thomas replied, "I'm glad you asked. I started out by saying, the hardest thing to understand about getting into shape, weight training, bodybuilding, or whatever phase of sport you're in football, basketball, baseball, or what have you—you can find my gym to go to. But the workout is just one piece of a very complicated puzzle that has to have all of the pieces to be complete. That's where the nutrition aspect comes in. Most common everyday layman, and even athletes, do not know what to eat and even when to eat. You basically have a two-hour window to put nutrition into your body, be it carbohydrates, proteins, supplements, or vitamins; it's vitally important to the success of your training. To not have this oh so vital information, would mean little or no chance for progress, which means no success, and we can't have that."

"No, we can't," agreed Nathaniel.

"All of the staff in the prep department are board certified nutritionists, who will work directly with the trainer for each client in order to formulate a nutrition plan that best suits the need of the individual client."

Nathaniel asked, "Will this plan work for everyone including, let's say, me—an average everyday Joe that just wants to get into shape and learn to eat right?"

"Yes, of course; please understand, by us having the restaurant here on the facility, you are encouraged to eat here because you know what you're getting and, instead of going out to eat in these fast-paced times when no one has the chance to prepare home cooked meals at home, this is the best way to go. We have, as you see, calorie counters, carb counters, protein, fat, sodium, and everything you need to know. We will serve pasta dishes, fish prepared grilled; I don't mean on the cooking grill. I mean a real canister barrel grill. No by-products or pork in the kitchen, only natural products grown here in this area from local farmers."

Nathaniel asked, "Will I be able to sample any of the restaurant food?"

"Yes, I'll arrange to reserve a table for you during our grand opening. I would like to open the restaurant to the general public, but I can't; I'll have to restrict it to members only and paying customers. My wife conducted a survey and discovered that it will be in a very large demand for customers that want to come in just to dine and get quality foods that are healthy and planned out for their specific needs. What I will have is, if your health plan covers and approves it, we'll accommodate you, by appointment only. The restaurant maximum occupancy is 175 people; however, I did have them put in a restricting wall that will retract 20 yards and give room for an additional 175 people for a total of 350 people."

Nathaniel said (with a look of amazement on his face), "That's incredible."

"No man," said Thomas, "that's for real; our target will be minorities, because for some reason, the minorities just don't get the education on proper nutrition or the importance of exercising and staying fit. So, this will be an excellent means of getting that."

Nathaniel asked, "What makes you so sure that you can reach all of these people out there and actually draw them in?"

Thomas answered, "Well, I'm glad you asked that; when we closed down for the short time for remodeling, we sent out membership applications. There was a requirement based on income level, and membership fees were due when the applications were turned in. It seems we have got an overwhelming response from members joining the gym and actually paying the fees from six months in advance to three years in advance. As of this day and date, we have 7,500 members—old and new."

"Wow, can you accommodate all of these people?"

With a smile on his face, Thomas replied, "Yes, of course. Remember, these clients will not be in every day and we'll be open seven days a week, plus our hours of operation will be 4 A.M. to 12 A.M., so we will only close for four hours. That closing will be to restock the kitchen and clean machines, restaurant, restrooms, and things like that, so we are here to serve and connect to success."

Nathaniel said, "Well, you have certainly impressed me."

"Well," said Thomas, "let's take a look at the workout areas, the locker rooms, and the children's center."

"You have a children's center?"

"Yes, of course, we have a place where the kids go while the parents are exercising."

Nathaniel said, "That is a brilliant plan; everyone, no matter what their income level is, will be able to learn how to live longer and take better care of themselves, especially minorities."

"Yes, that's my plan and, hopefully, this concept will spread," said Thomas. "I mean I know there will be several copy cats that will open and try to compete, and I have no problem with that as long as they keep it real and focus on the people and not get in it for the money alone, you know?"

And Nathaniel said, "Yes, sir, I completely understand."

Thomas took Nathaniel around and showed him the rest of the center. They went into the area where the swimming pool was and the basketball courts were, then upstairs on the second level where the fitness center was, where aerobics, cycling, step class, cardio boxing, and dance stepping class took place. The shower area was located on the second level, then they moved up the stairs to the third level. This is where the hard core training was done. You had a section for nothing but free weights, benches, and equipment, and on the other side of the upper level gym were machine weights where the personal training was conducted.

Nathaniel ran his fingers over his head and through his hair because he was just in awe. He turned to Thomas and said, "Man, this has to be one of the most well thought out plans for a gym that I have ever seen. I have a confession to make; I'm jealous, however, that I did not come up with this plan, but then again you are smarter than me, so what the heck."

Thomas smiled and said, "To be honest with you, Nathaniel, all this that you see before you, I had nothing to do with. It is all by the grace of God and his mercy on me. I am a working vessel and he is working through me for the people."

"Well, Thomas, I can say this, whatever you're doing you must be doing it right, so keep doing it."

"Thanks, man, I will, even more than ever because I am already invested in this." They both laughed out loud. Thomas said, "Well, I've given you a complete tour of the place, so let's go back down and you can set up and get started shooting."

"Cool, let's go," said Nat.

Thomas asked, "Do you want to walk down the stairs or take the elevator down?"

"You didn't tell me you have an elevator in the place."

"Well, you never asked. Plus, I was saving the best for last."

They walked over to the elevator and Nathaniel said, "Hey, I saw this on the second floor; I thought it was just a glass door leading to another room."

"No, not at all; I just wanted glass so you can see out every side and enter from any side. I brought in some elevator engineers from Japan for this one and this was their first creation of this type."

"Right," said Nathaniel, "I'm going to make sure that I get shots and print this, as well."

Thomas just smiled as they entered into the glass elevator and rode down to the ground floor level. When they reached the ground level, they exited and Nathaniel went over to his crew and started giving instructions on where to start setting up. Beverly and Phil were standing over in front of Phil's office going over the speeches.

Thomas walked over to Beverly and said, "Hey, baby, I'm just going to sit down in the back here in the cut and observe from a distance and stay out of the way."

Phil said, "Man, don't you want a part of this action?"

"Brother, trust me, I've had about as much action as I need in one year. Trust me, you two help yourselves and take advantage of your fifteen minutes of fame; it only comes once in a lifetime."

Beverly said, "Baby, this fame will be for the both of us." Beverly walked over to Thomas and kissed him on the lips and said, "Honey, I love you very much and, despite all your screw ups, I'm still proud to be your wife."

Thomas said, "Thank you, baby, that means a lot to me. A man has no limitations as to how far he can go when he has a woman by his side."

Phil looked at the both of them and said, "Hey, don't I get some love, too?" They both looked at Phil and laughed.

"Man, you get some love always," said Thomas. "Man, you guys go on up front so you can get started with the interviews."

They headed to the front and met up with Nathaniel and began the interview, beginning with Beverly; she explained how she and Thomas first met and when the idea about the gym first materialized. Beverly explained that Thomas had a smaller gym that was originally a gym that specialized in personal training. They basically grew out of that gym due to the high number of members that the gym was acquiring. It had been expanded twice already and the number of clients continued to grow steadily.

Nathaniel asked had there been any obstacles heading toward the success of the business, because there is always a period of hard times and tragedy. Beverly explained, "We did have pitfalls, trials, and tribulations. We have four kids…" and laughed. Nathaniel laughed and nodded in agreement. Beverly explained that the family foundation had to be solid, not just to find success, but based on values and not giving up on your dreams, no matter how far away they may seem; and the most important factor of all, was sticking to it no matter how hard times get and get through it together.

Nathaniel asked Beverly a few more questions and then they told her they were going to turn to Philip now. Nat looked at Phil and waited until he got the cue from the camera crew. After Nathaniel received the cue, he asked, "So, Phillip, where do you fit into this puzzle? Please, start out with your full name."

Phil cleared his throat and said, "My name is Philip Upchurch, but my friends call me Phil. Thomas and I go way back; we met in 1973 across a few thousand miles of water separating us from the rest of the world. We saved each other's lives on one or more occasions. We served proudly in the United Sates Marine Corps. After two tours, we separated and met up again on vacation on a little remote island called Granada. After that, you could not separate us, even by death; we would have partnered up then. We both got out of our beloved corps after twelve wonderful years of service and decided to make sure wherever we decided to live, it would be the same place. We worked for a local law enforcement agency for a few years. We opened up a small gym first and it began to take off. The gym was Thomas's idea and he even put up the money for it. I remember when he opened up the first gym. He came home and told Beverly that he had just bought a gym and opened it up. Beverly asked him had he lost his ever-loving mind. After one and a half years, we were able to retire from our law enforcement positions and go full charge with the business. Beverly never doubted Thomas, but going into your own business can be very frightening. Look at us, here we are now. I work as a personal trainer and in charge of operations. I love what we do and especially enjoy working with people and helping people obtain goals and reach expectations. In recent years, it truly has been a joy, seeing people obtain their goals, and seeing people that you've helped in situations where they were on medication to moderate blood pressure or something like that and, because of proper exercise and nutrition, were able to get off of their medications and actually live longer. Or, even watching young people develop into adults, playing sports and actually making it to the pros. It's been great."

Nathaniel said, "So, I guess I can say you really enjoy your job."

Phil replied, "Enjoy...I love what I do."

Nathaniel asked a few more questions of Beverly, and then Phil; then called for a wrap up. The camera crew started breaking down the equipment and Nathaniel walked toward the back offices, looking for Thomas. Thomas was just finishing up a phone conversation and hanging up. Thomas saw Nathaniel approaching him and started walking toward him.

"You're finished already?" asked Thomas.

Nathaniel answered, "Yes, I just wanted to touch bases with you on a couple of things."

"Well, let's go into my office." Nathaniel followed Thomas into his office as Thomas said, "Please have a seat."

Nathaniel said, "Thank you, but this won't take too long," and sat in the very comfortable black leather chair.

Thomas looked at Nathaniel, smiled, and asked "So what's on your mind?"

Nathaniel answered, "Well, I just want to thank you for this opportunity to cover your gym story and opening. I also want to inform you that I plan to include our discussion about your grand opening date. Okay, we will cover your grand opening live. We will only have a thirteen minute slot, so we'll have to be brief."

"Not a problem," said Thomas.

"The show will air at 7:00 P.M. that same day and will cover approximately 13 minutes. Now don't rush everything because 13 minutes is a lot longer than you think it is."

Thomas asked, "It is?"

Nathaniel answered, "Yes, actual recording time will be 33 minutes, but after editing commercials, it will average out to 13 minutes."

Thomas looked amazed, and said, "That's wild, but if that's the way it works, so be it."

Nathaniel extended his hand to shake with Thomas and Thomas returned the gesture. Nathaniel said, "I'll see you next week and good luck, once again, in your business and congratulations." By the time Nathaniel got to the front door, the camera crew was taking out the last of the equipment.

Thomas looked around for Phil and spotted him standing in the front area by the clothing store talking to a vendor that he'll be doing business with. Thomas shouted out to Devil Dog; Phil immediately turned and Thomas said, "Man, when you get a chance, come and see me in my office!"

Phil nodded his head in agreement and gave the thumbs up.

Thomas looked around and saw Beverly talking to a young lady at the receptionist desk. He walked over to where they were, and was able to hear their conversation. Beverly was asking the young lady, "Are you 100 percent sure that LAN will deliver these flowers by 5:00 A.M. next Monday?"

The lady was saying, "Yes, I'm sure it won't be a problem."

Beverly said, "Yes, there will be a problem if the flowers are late, or you don't come at all. Now we are going to have the media here on Monday around 5:30 in the morning setting up; the grand opening is set for 6:00 A.M. and it's going to be aired live. I can't afford any type of margin for error."

The young lady said, "Ma'am, I will oversee this project myself. I will personally put the arrangements together myself and a couple of staff will be here no later than 5:00 on Monday morning."

Thomas stepped in and said, "That sounds fair as you can get, doesn't it, baby?"

Beverly paused for a moment then said, "Yes, I believe I'm okay with that." Beverly looked at the florist and said, "Please, if you have any problems or anything, please call me ASAP."

The florist replied, "Yes, ma'am, any problems." The young lady turned and walked out the door.

Thomas grabbed Beverly by the hand and said, "Come with me, baby." They headed off down the hall in the direction of the offices; he led Beverly into his office and asked, "What do you say we have a party tonight?"

Beverly said, "Okay, but where?"

Thomas said, "Here… If we wait until Monday, we will be too busy with the opening to enjoy it."

Beverly said, "You're right; I'll call the restaurant staff and have them come in and start on the grill."

"Very good," said Thomas. "I'm going to have…"

(In popped Phil) "What's up?"

"Phil," Thomas continued, "Call all of the staff and have them come in for a party tonight at 2000 hours. Phil, you got that?"

"Roger that. I'll get started right away calling everyone. Damn it, I forgot I have date with that young lady from the waffle house…"

Beverly said, "Man, you can bring her here. That would be considered a date."

Phil responded, "You know, I guess your right; that would be a date. Well, let me get started on the phone tree." Phil started making his calls from the phone that was located in his office.

Beverly picked up the phone in Thomas's office and began calling the restaurant crew. She explained that they needed to celebrate the grand opening by having the party in advance in order that everyone got an opportunity to attend and to fully enjoy themselves.

Phil called up Taria, and informed her that the celebration would be tonight. Taria was extremely excited to hear this news.

Taria said, "That sounds good, I'll be there; can I call Alicia and the rest of the staff?"

Phil said, "Yes, that would be cool, then I don't have to call them. Just let me know if you need a number or someone needs a ride or something."

Taria said, "Okay and I'll see you 8:00 P.M., unless I have something else come up."

"Ooh, righty then," said Phil and hung up the phone, went into Thomas's office and said, "Hey guys, everything is set up; we're on for tonight."

Beverly said, "Well, I have the restaurant staff coming in, so that's all set."

Thomas added, "I contacted the DJ and that's set up. We're going to have a seventies theme going on."

"How did I know it was going to be a seventies theme party?" Phil laughed.

"Because the seventies was the bomb," Thomas looked at Phil, "and you know this, man."

Beverly looked at her watch and said, "Wow, it's after three o'clock; I have to get out of here and pick up the kids."

"Right," said Phil, "and I have a couple of errands to run myself. Hey, Bev I'll give you a ride."

Thomas said, "Both of you are tripping, because both of your cars are still at the chicken and waffle house."

Beverly laughed with embarrassment; Phil just threw up his hands in the air and said, "That's why you're in charge of things."

Thomas smiled and said, "Man, out of here with that."

Beverly enjoyed the laughter and said, "Well, we had better get going." They all headed toward the door and departed the gym. When they got out and walked over to Thomas's window, which was down, Bev kissed him on the lips and said, "Honey, I'll grab the kids and drop them off at Mom's house and then clean up at the house, and I will return before 8:00."

Thomas said, "Look, baby, I brought some threads with me; I'm going to go by the warehouse and grab my old school music, so we can groove to the sound of real music."

Beverly said, "Okay, I'll see you in a couple of hours."

Phil was in his car by this time and yelled out, "I'll see you in a few, bro'."

Thomas shouted back and said, "Right on, bro'!" Thomas went by the warehouse where he kept additional equipment and such for the gym and private items, and picked out all of his old school albums and CDs. He looked over them carefully and thought to himself, *Man, 1972...I still remember back on the block...all of the parties in the basement and garage...the blue lights... what memories. Well, I had better get back and make sure everything is set up.*

Thomas got back to the gym, looked at the clock, and thought *Boy, I still have time to hit it real quick.* So, he changed into his workout clothes and began his workout. After fifty-five minutes, Thomas completed his workout, and said, *Ooh, boy, that was intense.* He walked back to his office, grabbed his gym bag and dress clothes, and started heading for the door; but before he could get out of his office, the phone rang. Thomas looked at the clock and wondered, *Should I let it go, I'm pressed for time,* but followed his first thought and put down his things in the chair, went over to his desk, and picked up his phone on the fifth ring. He answered, "Good afternoon, Thomas speaking; how may I help you?" No one said anything for about twelve seconds and Thomas was thinking to himself, *This is a call to my direct line, so it has to be someone that knows me.* Thomas asked, "Is anyone on the line? Can you hear me now?"

There was another pause for ten seconds and then a voice—soft and low— responded, "Hi, honey, I really miss you a lot."

Thomas sat down in the chair and asked, realizing who it might be, "Who's speaking, please?"

The voice said, "Thomas, please tell me that you have not forgotten me already, as much as we shared together."

Thomas said, "There's nothing to remember and enjoy, that's reason to forget; now I'll only ask you one more time, please identify yourself."

"Please, Thomas," the voice answered, "this is Sarah. I really don't understand why you're treating me like this."

Thomas responded, "Sarah, first off, there is no way to treat you. It was understood in the beginning that whatever happened between us, was just what it was—in the past. And secondly, if you want to threaten me by going directly to my wife about what happened between us, please be advised I've already come clean to her, so there's nothing you can say to her that she doesn't already know."

"So you've told her everything, huh?"

"Yes, everything," replied Thomas.

Sarah said, "Okay, sweetheart, so you don't mind if I call her and speak directly to her, and ask her just for the sake of my satisfaction?"

"Sarah, I know that you already have my home phone number because you've called several times already, so please feel free to call now."

"Well, nothing personal, Tom, I still love you and trust you; I just want to come clean. I just want her to know that there is a child involved now and that kind of turns the tides in the cesspool."

Thomas took a couple of deep breaths and said, "A child? You never mentioned anything at all about a child."

"Sweetheart; you never gave me a chance. You see, I knew the first time that we made love, you hit the jackpot; everything was so perfect and right."

"You know, Sarah, if this is true what you say about the child, then I'll deal with it. I've made my bed and I can lay in it, as well."

"Thomas, it would probably be in your best interest to leave your wife; hell, I'm younger, I'm smarter, and I have a more promising future than her. Shit, she'll start manipulating you soon, and you don't want to deal with that, no man does. We'll already have one kid, we can have one more, and our lives will be perfect. She can have the business, I'm sure that's all she will want anyway; we can start another business together, something bigger and better. How does that sound to you?"

Thomas answered, "You sound like a mad woman; I'm not going to turn my back on my family or my wife, or the business that I bled, sweated, and fought to build. I should not have ever succumbed to you; however, I did and now I'm willing to deal with it, and that's going to be that."

"I'm sorry that you feel that way, Thomas," Sarah replied, "I'm going to teach you one of the most expensive lessons that you will ever learn in life."

"Sarah, I'm going to take that as a threat and, believe me, I'm already prepared for a war."

"Okay, Tom; remember you did have a choice."

Thomas hung up the phone. He sat in the chair for two minutes and then said to himself, *It's started*, got up and went to the shower room to get cleaned up.

At 1920, Thomas was dressed, helping the DJ set up the music and speakers and such. Phil walked in with the young lady that he met in the restaurant that morning, and said, "Hey, baby boy, look at what the dog has drug in this time."

Thomas walked over and said, "Nice to see you again, young lady."

She responded as she put her hand out to shake his, "Well, it's a pleasure to see you again, Mr. Dugmal; my name is Lisa Turner."

Thomas walked closer to Lisa and said, "My name is Thomas, please call me by my first name, and it's customary to embrace upon meeting and greeting someone special." Lisa smiled and opened her arms to receive a warm embrace from Thomas. Thomas said, "Please enjoy yourself tonight; there is going to be good food, good music, good company, and good fun."

"I'm looking forward to it," replied Lisa.

Thomas said, "Well, I'm going to have to excuse myself real quick now," as he saw Beverly coming in the door. Beverly had a look of concern on her face. The first thing Thomas thought was Sarah had contacted her already and she was upset. Thomas prepared himself as he approached Beverly.

Before Thomas could say anything, Beverly hurried over to him and almost frantically asked, "Thomas, please tell me that the restaurant crew is here and have started?"

Thomas sighed and smiled and answered, "Yes, baby. Calm down, everything is going like clockwork—the DJ is here, the chefs are here, the employees are filtering in, and everything is going to be fine."

Beverly smiles and said, "Thank you, Thomas, but you know how I get about events and having to rely on other people."

"I know, baby, and that's why I love you so much, because you always want the best."

"Thanks again," said Beverly.

Thomas continued, "I'm going to finish up the set up with the DJ. I'm almost finished here, we'll do a sound check, and then I'll come and check up on you in the kitchen and make sure everything is in order."

Beverly said okay and headed for the restaurant.

Thomas continued the set up for the music and then conducted the sound check. Everything checked out fine and Thomas gave final instructions for the music line up. Thomas told the DJ, "Now, we'll start out with *Celebration* followed up with *Fantastic Voyage*, *It's All the Way Live* and then *Let's Have Some Fun*. After that, just mix it up in 1999."

PJ the DJ responded, "Mr. Dugmal, trust me, sir; I got this shit down to the bone."

Thomas said, "Whatever, man, just make it happen. I'll let you know when to announce the Soul Train line."

"Okay," replied PJ the DJ, "I'll wait for your cue."

All of the employees knew how much of a stickler for time Thomas was, so by 8:00 P.M. the gym was packed with all of his employees and friends and family that were attending. Thomas got on the microphone at the DJ's table and said, "May I have your attention, please; first, I would like to thank each and every one of you for coming out to celebrate a dream come true. And, to all of my employees, thank you all for your dedication and the hard work. I know that the pay was not the greatest for you when we first opened and started out of the gates, but you trusted me when I told you that if you stuck with me, it would be well worth the time and effort that you put into it. And to Phil, for sticking by me throughout the years and being able to take my tantrums and yelling at him at times and for saving my ass under fire more times than I can remember..."

Phil yelled out, "You know that's right; I'm charging up double for my salary, too." Everyone started laughing.

Thomas continued, "To my lovely wife, Beverly, the one who never stopped believing in my dream and in me. I know that I don't even deserve to have a woman as good as her, but I do thank God for her every waking day."

Beverly blinked her eyes and nodded her head in acknowledgement, as her eyes began to well up with tears.

"I love all of you," said Thomas, "and together we will succeed." Everyone started clapping and started to high-five each other. Thomas said, "Okay, now the food is ready, go eat and get your grub on."

It did not take long for them to clear out of the lobby area and make their way to the restaurant.

Thomas said, "Well, PJ, lay down some nice jazz; just put on these CDs." Thomas handed PJ *Grover Washington Jr.'s Greatest Hits* and Najee's *Day by Day* CD. Thomas started heading for the restaurant. PJ shouted, "Mr. D, can I come and get some grub, too?"

Thomas smiled and said, "Come on, man." PJ set the CDs to play and took off for the restaurant.

Everyone was eating and enjoying the food. Beverly was sitting with Thomas, and looked at him and asked, "Hey, honey, do you think I should have made more of a selection to order from?"

Thomas said, "No, baby, we have steak, baked chicken, and smoked salmon; veggies, salad, potato salad, yams, green beans, black, navy, and white rice…that's enough already."

Beverly smiled and said, "Well, I guess you're right; I should stop worrying so much."

Thomas said, "Right, baby, just take it easy and enjoy this time, that's why we're doing this."

"Well, I guess you're right; I'll stop worrying and enjoy myself."

The dinner party went well and everyone was enjoying themselves when Phil walked over to Thomas and said, "Hey, man, I just wanted to know if it would be cool to show Lisa around the place?"

"Of course, my brother, but make sure you mind your manners."

Lisa smiled and remarked, "Don't worry about that, Mr. Dugmal…I mean, Thomas; he'll have no other options."

Phil looked at her, smiled, and said, "Hey, I like a woman with a Marine Corp demeanor." They all shared a laugh as Phil grabbed Lisa's hand and led her away.

After dinner, Thomas informed everyone in the restaurant that drinks and dancing awaited them in the main front of the gym area. PJ the DJ shoved the rest of his steak down and began to put a 'to-go' plate together to take with him to the DJ booth. As people began to get up from the tables, the bus people began picking up plates and silverware from the tables and taking them to the back of the kitchen to be washed and stacked.

Bruce, the chef, said to the crew, "Huddle up and get this place cleaned up, and then after it's been cleaned and inspected, you all can go and join the party and dancing in the gym." This brought smiles to the crew that lit up the whole room. The crew looked at each other and without any exchange of words, read each other, and immediately started double-timing it, in an effort to get everything cleaned up as soon as possible.

Meanwhile, PJ the DJ started the party by putting on *Celebration* courtesy of Kool and the Gang. As the music began to play, almost the whole crowd present started heading for the dance floor. Thomas looked around for

Beverly, when he discovered her standing near the clothing store area, just looking around as if she could not believe that a dream had come true at last and how they would handle the success. Thomas walked over to her and asked, "Hey, baby a penny for your thoughts, a nickel for a kiss, and a dime if you tell me that you love me."

Beverly laughed and said, "Honey, you know I love you, and I will give you one million kisses before I die, I promise you that. Honey, I am the most fortunate girl in the world. I mean, I know that I am not perfect, nor are you for that matter. I even know that our marriage is not perfect, but to have a dream actually come true in spite of all of the obstacles in our path…. We have each other and believe in one another, and I believe in my heart that after some time, I will be able to put behind what happened with you a couple of months ago."

Thomas grabbed Beverly and pulled her close to him, embracing her. "Baby, I love you with all my heart and all my soul. I know that I hurt you and, in essence, I hurt myself as well because we are one, and you can't hurt without me feeling hurt, as well. But, I'll tell you this, I will only be foolish like that one time in my life, and I've already used up my one time."

Beverly looked into Thomas's eyes and said, "Enough said."

Thomas said, "Baby, I do need to talk to you about that situation; however, I would like to wait until the celebration is over. I don't want the devil to steal our joy."

Beverly smiled and said, "Okay, honey, but if it's about Sarah being pregnant, I already know." Thomas had a look of surprise on his face, and Beverly said, "Man, don't look like you're the only person that's privy to information; it's my job to stay up on things." Bev smiled and said, "Honey, let's go dance before the song goes off."

Thomas agreed, "Right, let's do it." So, they headed off to the dance floor.

After an hour and a half of straight get down, old school funk, PJ the DJ made an announcement. "May I have your attention, please?" It took a second time; PJ had to make another announcement to get everyone to stop and pay attention to him. After everyone was quiet, he said, "Well, it looks like everyone is enjoying themselves."

The place erupted with clapping and whistling and shouts, "Hell yeah, the party's right here!"

PJ said, "Well, I have a special treat for you, then. I want all of my ladies to form a line and stand next to each other facing the center of the dance floor." The ladies, without hesitation, did what they were instructed to do. "Now, all of the men, the same thing goes for you, but you're going to face the ladies." The men carried out their instructions.

Someone yelled out, "Is this going to be a gang war?" Everyone laughed.

PJ said, "No, man; it's a Soul Train line." Everyone began clapping and PJ said, "I want the people that are facing each other to pair up; the ones that are closest to my DJ booth to start out."

The first couple paired off and started going down the line and doing their thing, while the rest of the group watched and waited for them to get to the end of the line. They clapped in rhythm and moved side-to-side with a smooth glide. The people partied so hard that when Thomas looked at his watch and discovered it was after 2400 hours, he said to himself, *Woo, I better end this thing; its later then I thought.* Thomas went over to PJ and motioned for him to bend down so he could talk to him for a minute. PJ bent down and said, "What up, money; I know I'm turning this mother out."

Thomas replied, "Yeah, man, you are turning it out, but it's also time to turn it off."

"Are you saying it's time to stop the party?" asked PJ.

Thomas answered, "Yes, it's after midnight."

PJ said, "Hey, boss, this is your world; I'm just a squirrel trying to get a nut."

Thomas smiled, shook his head, and walked away. Beverly walked up to Thomas and asked, "Sweetheart, how much longer? It's getting late."

"I told PJ the DJ to wrap it up."

Beverly said, "Well, I'm going to make sure the kitchen is in order and I'll be right back."

"Cool, I'll help PJ break everything down, so we can get out of here pretty fast."

PJ made his announcement to everyone on the dance floor. "That time has come again, ladies and gentlemen, that the party must end, or at least that's what the clock on the wall says, so this is your last call for alcohol and last chance to dance. After that I would like to say thanks for coming and sharing in this special celebration. I hope that everyone has enjoyed themselves as much as we have enjoyed you and, as always in parting, we offer you Love, Peace, and..." everyone yelled at the same time, "Soul." Everyone clapped and acknowledged that they had a good time.

After the place had been cleaned up and the DJ had packed up his things and loaded them into his van, Thomas looked at Beverly and Phil and said, "Hey, that was the bomb."

Phil said, "I really enjoyed myself."

Lisa said, "I think that you are really some wonderful people. It's people like you that make people feel like their lives are worth living."

Phil said, "Man, that's deep."

Thomas said, "Thank you very much, Lisa, but we are just being ourselves."

Beverly asked, "Lisa, are you okay getting home?"

"Yes," replied Lisa, "Phil is going to see me home."

Thomas said, "Lisa, I think that's what Beverly was asking; are you okay with Phil taking you home?" Beverly, Lisa, and Thomas laughed.

Phil whined, "Hey, man, that's not funny; I'm a perfect gentleman, haven't I been, Lisa?"

Lisa, slowing down her laughter, answered, "Yes, you have been, Phil; I feel I'll be just fine with you seeing me home."

Thomas set the alarm in the gym and locked the doors.

Beverly said to Lisa, "You two have a good night."

Lisa said, "Thank you; you, too."

Phil said, "I will."

Thomas said to Phil, "We need to be here tomorrow morning no later than 0930 to go over staffing and schedules."

Phil said, "Man, 0930; that's early."

Thomas said, "Hey, man, up in the morning to the rising of the sun..."

Phil finished the verse, "The work doesn't stop till the work is done. Bet I'll be there, sir."

Beverly looked at Lisa and said, "That's Marine talk."

"Thanks for clarifying that for me," said Lisa, "because I was lost."

They smiled and Phil and Lisa got into Phil's car and Thomas opened the door for Beverly to get in theirs, then they drove off. While on the way home, Beverly asked, "Has Sarah contacted you lately?"

Thomas answered, "Yes, last night. She informed me that she was 'with child' and it was mine."

Beverly said, "Well, I want to inform you that I hired a private investigator to keep track of her movements and intentions. He did report to me that she has seen an OB/GYN and confirmed that she was pregnant. What is her next move...the trump card?"

"Either leave you and the kids and come with her, or she would first call and inform you of the latest developments, and if I did not comply at that point, she would begin to make my life as I know it, a living hell here on earth."

Beverly responded, "Oh, yeah?"

Thomas said, "Ooh, yeah."

Beverly then said, "Well, I know there's got to be more because I know that you just let her say whatever the hell she wanted to say and you just sat there."

Thomas answered, "No, baby, I didn't just sit there. I should have thought before I responded, but in light of the situation that I was in, I responded by telling her that she just threatened the wrong Marine, and that if she attempted to disrupt my family's life in any way, shape, or form, then I promised I would make her disappear without a trace like she never existed here on earth."

Beverly paused for a second and said, "Tom, that's scary; even I would have backed off if you said that to me. Did you really mean that?"

Thomas answered, "Yes, I did, only if she really meant what she said about my family. You can't back me up against the wall and not expect the three supporting walls not to fall. If she wants to fight me, I know she is going to fight dirty and have quite a bit of help and people behind her; so, if that's the case, then she had better prepare for all hell to break loose on my side."

"Tom, please; I don't really like for you to talk like that, but I know that you know what you're doing. Please, just don't tell me the plan. I don't think I can handle it, anyway. But I will say this, honey, please be careful. I know that you've seen action plenty of times, but this is on American soil and the cards are already stacked against you."

Thomas said, "Baby, I'm aware of that, but I have no other recourse."

By this time, they were driving up into the driveway and the garage door recognized the sensor in Thomas's truck and automatically opened up. They both got out and entered the house through the garage door leading into the house. They both turned in for the night.

The next morning just before 6:00 A.M., Beverly was awakened by her cell phone ringing. She looked at the caller ID and did not recognize the number. She looked over at Thomas and saw he was still sleeping, so she picked up the phone and walked over to the bathroom, turned on the light, and went in. She asked, "Who is this?"

The voice on the other end answered, "This is Sarah Daniels; do you remember me?"

Beverly turned to see if Thomas was still asleep. He was, so Beverly said to Sarah, "Please, hold on a minute." She looked at the alarm clock and noticed that it's 5:59 A.M. and the alarm on the clock was set to go off at 6:00. She rushed over and turned the alarm off before it went off in an effort not to wake Thomas. Beverly then went back into the bathroom and closed the door behind her. She then went into the shower portion of the bath that has a door separating the two, and closed that one.

"Sarah, how may I help you?"

"Can you talk now?" asked Sarah.

Beverly began to get agitated now and answered with a much stronger tone. "What do you want to talk to me about?"

Sarah said, "Well, I just thought you needed to know about my current situation."

"Well, I'm waiting, please continue."

"Well, I'm pregnant and it's Thomas's baby."

Beverly then asked, "Have you gotten a DNA blood test as proof?"

Sarah laughed and said, "Thomas is the only man that I've been with for the past year and a half. So, if it's necessary to go down that path, it's not a problem, but I was hoping to avoid all that negative press."

Beverly said, "Well, I would have to have proof beyond a reasonable doubt before we can move forward. And what are you driving at anyway, because it seems like you're giving me some sort of an ultimatum."

Sarah replied, "An ultimatum sounds like too heavy of a word and it doesn't fit this situation. Let's just say I'm offering you a way out woman to woman, and we can both come out of this ahead."

Beverly said, "Now you're talking like someone who is completely mad."

Sarah said, "Just a minute, bitch, I'm trying to help out and you are too dumb to see the light."

Beverly took a breath and said, "Listen, you stupid little whore; you were the one that slept with a married man, knowing beforehand that he was married and went into it with both eyes open, so if anyone is a nasty skank ass bitch, it's you. Now you had better say what you want to say before I really get pissed off, Sarah."

"Well, I don't want to rub anything in your face, but I can say that I did fuck both you and your husband because I did suck his cock and I remember tasting some of you, so you have a lot at stake in this. So, listen carefully; you allow Thomas to walk away and meet his responsibility like a man is supposed to, and I'll allow him to offer you a nice pay off, something that will take care of you and the children for the rest of your miserable lives...let's say in the area of $500,000...and you can have the business, but not own the rights to the name, and full control of the one business. I believe that is more than reasonable, don't you?"

Beverly responded, "Man, you are really a piece of work. I'll tell you what; you just blew me away with quite a bit to ponder over. Give me at least a few days to sort this out and give you a definitive answer."

"That sounds reasonable to me," replied Sarah, "I'll give you three days."

Beverly said, "Well, let's make it four more days; we have our grand opening; at least wait until after the opening."

"Okay, I'll give you until Friday of next week after the grand opening, and I want you to contact me; I don't want to have to contact you."

Beverly said, "Bitch, you sure have a lot of nerve."

Sarah said, "You don't even know the half of it, yet," and hung up on Beverly.

Beverly slumped down to the floor and stared at the ceiling. She whispered, "Lord, I'm looking up to the hill from where my strength comes, and you know I need help with this one." She took another ten minutes to gather herself and then got up and jumped into the shower. When she finished, she put on her bathrobe, walked out into the bedroom, and walked over to Thomas, who was still sleeping. She stood over him and just looked down and thought, *Brother, you don't even know. If I didn't really love you and my family, and you, my darling, weren't worth fighting for, even if you were weak and stupid for a night and allowed this madness to take place....*

At that time, Thomas woke up and looked at Beverly. He said, "Hey, baby, you're up already? I didn't even hear the alarm go off. You smell really good and fresh. Have you showered already?"

Beverly answered, "Yes I've showered, and the alarm clock didn't go off. I was awakened by something alarming, however."

Thomas sat up in the bed and asked, "What's up, baby?"

Beverly sat down beside Thomas and said, "Honey, of all the people in the city, or state for that matter, you picked the craziest sickest woman you could find to have an affair with."

Thomas responded, "I really don't believe I could feel worse than I do about the situation. And I am willing to do whatever it takes to right this ship."

Beverly looked at Thomas and said, "You know, I really do believe you."

"Wait, has she contacted you this morning?"

Beverly answered, "Yes, we had a very interesting conversation this morning." Beverly went on to explain what she had discussed with Sarah.

After Thomas had heard Beverly out, he said, "Man, oh man alive. Well, I know what I must do now."

Beverly said, "Wait a minute, now; she gave me until next Friday to make a decision, so let's wait and see if we can call her bluff."

"But, baby," Thomas answered, "you never want to let the enemy get the upper hand and get a drop on you, or you'll get outflanked every time."

"Oh, Thomas; not every situation is war. You did things your way first and screwed everything up, now let's try my way and see how things are going to unfold and take it from there."

"Okay, but I'm telling you, if you let the enemy get the upper hand then you're playing catch up."

Beverly said, "Well, nevertheless, we're going to wait this one out."

"Okay, we do it your way, but if it does not end up in your favor, then we do agree that at that time, we do it my way because the shit will be hitting the fan."

Beverly said, "Let's get started," so they began the day.

Thomas got dressed and went down to the gym. As he walked in the doors, he was greeted by Taria, the receptionist. "Good morning, Mr. D; how are you this morning? I had such a good time last night; you really know how to throw a party."

"Good morning, little sunshine. Boy, you are bursting with energy this morning. We're going to have to bottle that energy up and sell it. I could make a fortune on it."

Taria said, "Fine, just make sure you cut me in with a fair share."

"Taria, do you remember when we had a discussion concerning moving you up into management?"

"Well, yes, but I didn't really think you meant it."

"Well, I did really mean it and I want to start off with some training. Mrs. Dugmal will be coming in and you'll be under her direction."

Taria said, "Mr. D, I love you; you're the greatest."

Thomas replied, "I don't know about the greatest, but you do deserve this opportunity. Your position will be Director of Operations and Training. I will get with you a little later on today to go over the details, but for now, I have some work to do in my office. Please hold all of my calls unless they have an appointment."

Taria said, "Yes, sir, you mean everyone?"

"You know what I mean, Taria."

"No problem, Mr. D."

Thomas started back to his office then he stopped and said, "Taria, is Phil in yet?"

"No, Mr. D. He probably won't be in until late. Did you see that young 'tenderonie' he was with last night? I know he's not getting up anytime soon," and began to laugh at what she had just said.

Thomas smiles and said, "Taria, Taria, Taria; I did see that young lady he was with and, yes, I do expect him in this morning no later than 0930."

Taria said, "Okay, Mr. D, whatever you say, but if he's not here by 0930, then you owe me a sandwich."

"You're on; that sounds fun," then continued back to his office.

The clock turned 0930 and no Phil in sight. Thomas looked up and shook his head, *Just lost to a kid. Now I have to buy her a sandwich. Oh well.* Thomas made a couple of phone calls and looked up and saw Phil sneaking in quietly. Thomas called out, "Phil."

Phil answered and said, "They were working on the streets and had a road block up. A train hit a person on the track, I had a flat tire, but I'm here at last. Thomas, ooh, look it's late we better start our meeting; I'll go in your office."

Thomas shook his head as if to say 'I just don't believe this guy' and headed toward his office, as well. Thomas turned around and looked at Taria and said, "Taria, what time is it?"

Taria says, "It's 0948, Mr. D, why?"

Thomas said, "Let's just say when you get my lunch for me, please make it a turkey on wheat, mustard, onions, and tomatoes, thank you."

Taria said, "That's cold."

Thomas turned around, laughed, and said, "No, that's just how it goes." Thomas went into his office and Phil was already sitting down, waiting for him. Thomas said, "Man, we have a lot to go over in preparation for the grand opening. Beverly has already drawn up a schedule for the crew, and she'll oversee the restaurant staff."

Phil asked, "Well, what do you want me to do?"

"I'm glad you asked. You will need to contact all of the staff who are not here and those who are not starting until Monday and give them their schedules. Now, it's very critical that you get in contact with everyone because we're going to have an extremely large number of new customers joining Monday and we need everyone on deck. We have eleven new positions to fill, which means we will interview and hire on Friday, Saturday, and Sunday, and they will have to be ready to start on Monday."

Phil asked, "I thought that we were only going to hire ten new employees?"

Thomas replied, "Well, I've decided to promote Taria to our management team and will rely on her to oversee the staff. She will report directly to you, and that will free you up to make sure that you have the time to ensure all of your responsibilities are met."

Phil said, "Thanks, bro'. It's about time I got some help. Well, is there anything else?"

"No, man, that's it for now."

"Okay," said Phil, "then I'm going to get with Taria and look over all the applicants, and start making calls and setting up some interviews for the next three days."

"Okay."

Phil asked, "Did we receive a good number of applications?"

Thomas laughed and answered, "Not that many; you have about three hundred and something."

Phil's eyes bugged out, he stood up, and repeated, "Three hundred and something; damn man, we'll be here all day."

"Well, I suggest you hurry and get started then."

Phil said, "You can bet on that, but you set me up on that one." They both laughed out loud.

Phil left Thomas's office and went up front with Taria to start work on the phone list.

Beverly dropped the kids off at school and then headed for the gym. When she got there, she walked in and the staff at the front door greeted her with a warm 'good morning.' Beverly responded in the same manner, then walked promptly toward Thomas's office. She walked in and saw Thomas reviewing some paperwork. She greeted him, "Hi, honey."

Thomas looked up and saw that it was Beverly, stood up and said, "Hi, baby, I didn't even hear you come in."

"What are you so wrapped up in?" she asked.

"Well, I was going over the projection numbers so we can check before opening."

Beverly said, "Good. I'll take some of that so we cover all of the loose ends."

Thomas said, "Thanks, baby," as he gave Beverly two spreadsheets.

She took off her sweater and put down her purse on the desk. As she began to review the first spreadsheet she looked over at Thomas and noticed he was spacing out, not really reading, and unfocused.

Beverly said, "Thomas," and Thomas did not respond. She called out once again, "Thomas," and he lifted his head up and looked over toward Beverly.

"Yes, baby, what can I help you with?" he asked.

Beverly said, "What's wrong? I know something else is on your mind."

Thomas answered, "Well, I was just thinking about Sarah Daniels; man, I have to take care of this situation."

Beverly said, "You will do no such thing. I told you wait until she contacts me on Friday and I'm sure things will work themselves out."

Thomas asked, "But, baby, what if things don't and this situation escalates?"

Beverly replied, "Well, we will deal with it accordingly at that time."

Thomas said, "Okay, but I'm telling you, I believe this woman can be extremely dangerous. She has a lot of contacts and the banking business is very political, which means things can get very messy."

Beverly said, "Thomas, I have never seen you afraid of anyone or anything."

"Baby, it's not that I'm afraid; but, I do not enjoy my enemy having an edge on me."

"We'll just have to respond without delay and try to reason with her," said Beverly.

"You can't reason with the devil."

"I think that you're over-reacting. Honey, please relax and let's get these projections knocked out and prepare to have one of the best grand openings ever."

Thomas smiled and said, "You're right and you're such a good person. I know that I let you down, as well at the kids and even myself, for that matter, and I know that I probably do not deserve a good woman like you, but I'm going to make things right once again for us as a family."

Beverly said, "Honey, I love you and we'll get through this together."

Thomas smiled and they both got back to work.

Phil and Taria organized all of the applicants' paperwork together and started calling them and scheduling appointments. They worked diligently on interviewing and conducting background investigations until Sunday afternoon.

The big day finally arrived and it was about 4:00 Monday morning, and Beverly was waiting patiently outside for the flowers to arrive. Finally at 4:30 the flowers arrived and Beverly looked relieved, as she couldn't wait for the woman to park her van. Beverly walked over to the van almost at a double time pace. She opened up the cargo door and started inspecting the arrangements inside.

The florist smiled and said, "Good morning, Mrs. Dugmal."

Beverly responded, "I'm so sorry; good morning to you. I just wanted to make sure that everything was going all right; you do understand, don't you?"

The florist answered, "Yes, ma'am, I do understand. And don't worry, everything will be just perfect, I assure you of that."

Beverly said, "When we get everything set up, I'll relax."

The florist then said, "Let's get this done."

They started taking the arrangements out and walking them into the building. It did not take them long to get the arrangements together and set up and Beverly started feeling relieved.

Thomas said, "Now, hopefully, all of the staff gets here ahead of time so we can kick this thing off right."

So, just like clockwork, all of the staff started entering at 0500 and Phil looked over to where he was.

Taria walked over to Phil and asked, "What's up, Phil?"

He said, "What I need for you to do is establish yourself as the director of staffing and floor operations. Now, what you must do is convince them that we are a team, and there is no 'I' in team; we all work together for one goal and one love. You can put it in your own words if you like, but the message should be clear concerning your expectations on a smooth running operation, and 100 percent customer satisfaction and results at T & B Fitness for Life. Are you cool with that?"

Taria replied, "Yes, I'm cool with that, and I will put my message in my own words because I want everyone to feel me coming from the heart. You feel me, Phil?"

Phil smiled and said, "Yeah, I do feel you."

Taria said, "You know, Phil, this is the first time that I will actually be over people. A lot of the people are going to be older than me; I just hope there will be no friction or any type of player hating or anything like that."

Phil said, "Well, Taria, you are a very talented young lady, as you know, you're very beautiful, and intelligent, as well; otherwise, Thomas would not have chosen you to run the floor. He knows that you can handle this. Now keep in mind you are going to go through growing pains because you're dealing with some angry personalities, but you'll learn quickly because of the fact that the test will come before the lesson on this subject; if you stumble, remember to get right back up. If you need my help, always ask; the worst thing that you can do is try and cover up a fault. Does that all make sense to you?"

Taria said, "Perfectly, and I'm ready to do this."

Phil said, "Okay, gather your troops together and let's get ready for war."

Taria gathered all of the staff together and gave them their goals and the importance of teamwork and family. This really went over very well with the new employees because it gave them a sense of fitting in and being welcomed in with open arms and a warm heart. It seemed that everyone was receptive of Taria and her new position.

At 0600 Thomas put the red ribbon across the front of the entrance. The news crews were rolling the tape, as the lines to gain entry started to grow. Some people gathered around with no intentions of coming in, but just to look at the cutting of the ribbon and for some to try and get in view of the cameras so they can say that they were on TV. Thomas was talking to Nathaniel Archibald from *Fox News*, who informed Thomas that they were going live in two minutes.

Thomas shouted, "Everyone, please get ready; we have one minute 'til show time!"

Lisa Turner drove up, parked her car, and ran over and looked for Phil. Beverly spotted Lisa and called her over. When Lisa moved over to Beverly's location, she frantically asked, "Hi Beverly, have you seen Phil?"

Beverly smiled and answered, "Oh dear, he's standing right in front of the entranceway. He'll be opening the front doors when we cut the ribbon; go on over there where he is."

Lisa said, "I can? Thanks a lot, Beverly," and ran over toward the front door.

Thomas called over to Beverly and said, "Hey, baby, come on over. It's time to cut the ribbon."

Nathaniel cued the cameras and then cued Thomas. He said with great pleasure, "We cut this ribbon," (as Beverly cut the ribbon with the large scissors), "and reopen with a new beginning to a new year and a new you. Our doors are now open."

Thomas and Beverly stepped to the side and Phil opened the front doors; the crowd that was waiting for entry began to walk in. As they would walk in, Taria would inform them, "If you already have membership, you're welcome to go and do your routine; if you want to sign up for membership, the line is over to your right." Thomas had hired a temp service that specialized in sign ups and start-ups.

All of the crew, as well as their stations, were busy as soon as the gym opened and were signing up people just like clockwork. Thomas had thought this one out very carefully; everything was flowing fluidly. As people signed up and received their membership card, they would go directly to the locker room, change, and start working out. By 0630 a full spinning class was going on, as well as a step aerobics class. By 0715 the second level began to fill up and by 0745 the gym floor on the third level was filled with the serious hard-core people that craved heavy iron. At 1000 hours, the camera crews had all gone and the line was slimmed down, but was still fairly long.

Beverly walked over to Thomas and hugged him, giving him a kiss on the lips, and said, "Baby, this was perfect; the opening, the crowd, I mean everything."

Thomas said, "Yes, baby, it was. All of our hard work and dedication has finally paid off," as he gave Beverly another kiss and smiled at her.

Beverly said, "I'm going to the restaurant and check in there to make sure everything is going well."

Thomas said, "That's fine, baby. I'm going to the store and see how things are going in there."

As Thomas walked into the clothing store, he saw that the lines were long with people buying gear to work out in. Thomas smiled and thought to himself, *This is beautiful; I just love it when a plan comes together.* He walked over to one of the cashiers who was busy ringing up a customer. Thomas said, "Good morning," and the cashier looked over at Thomas and said, "Good morning, Mr. Dugmal; man, it has been nonstop here for over an hour and a half."

Thomas asked, "No one has had a break, yet?"

The cashier said, "No, sir. We only have three cashiers on duty today."

Thomas said, "Okay, I'll get you some help."

The cashier replied, "Thank you very much, Mr. Dugmal."

Thomas left the store, went to the front counter, and asked the receptionist, "Where is Phil?"

The receptionist responded, "Hold on one minute." The receptionist made an announcement over the intercom system, "Mr. Upchurch to the reception area, please."

It did not take Phil very long to make his way to the reception area. Phil looked at Thomas and said, "What's up, man?"

"I need you to do me a favor and relieve the cashiers in the store for breaks; it's been nonstop for them and they're running with only a staff of three."

Phil replied, "It's done, bro'."

Thomas said, "Wait a minute; please take Taria with you so you guys can give a break to two at a time."

Phil replied, "Sure…oh…you think it would be cool if Lisa helped out?"

Thomas said, "Not a problem, bro'; as long as she is not on the clock."

Phil said, "Cool, but I do need to talk to you about some things later."

"Cool," replied Thomas as he went back to his office and sat down, leaned back and took a deep breath, thinking to himself, *man, this sure is great how things have worked out, but I still have a problem that needs to be solved. But you know as of right now, I'm going to break in my own pleasure zone.* So, he put the weekly schedules up on the bulletin board and went back out to the floor.

Thomas was amazed and overwhelmed at the turn out for the opening. He walked to the store and saw that the lines were still long. He walked over to the restaurant and discovered that it was filled to capacity. He then made his way to the second level and, again, it was full. Finally, he ended up on the third level and just like the rest of the gym, the entire floor was full to capacity. He walked toward the area where the flat benches and Smith machines were and noticed there was a crowd standing around. He naturally assumed someone was benching pretty heavy and impressing other people, so Thomas walked over to the area to see what all of the commotion was about. When he finally cleared the crowds and looked down at who was hoisting up 410 pounds for reps on the bench press, he shook his head in amazement because he could not believe what his eyes were seeing. There, lying under the weights was no one other than Ronnie Coleman—the eight times Mr. Olympia— and to add to the surprise, Kevin Levrone was spotting him.

Thomas's heart started racing like a little kid that just opened up his toys on Christmas morning. Thomas could hardly contain himself, but he knew that he had to. He waited 'til Ronnie Coleman had finished his sets and stood up. Thomas walked over to Ronnie Coleman and extended his hand for Ronnie to shake. Ronnie extended his in return and the two shook hands. Thomas said, "Welcome to my gym, Mr. Coleman, I'm an avid fan of yours and have followed you for a number of years."

Ronnie said, "Man, you have a hell of a gym here. I really like it."

Thomas replied, "Thank you very much; you are welcome here any time."

"Thanks a lot," said Ronnie, "whenever I'm in town, I will definitely come and work out here."

Thomas turned to Kevin Levrone and extended his hand, once again, for Kevin to shake. Kevin returned the gesture. Thomas said, "Kevin Levrone, I just don't know what to say about you. We call you Mr. Improvement, because of all the setbacks that you've endured and injuries, you still come back bigger and better than ever."

Kevin asked, "So you have been following me?"

Thomas answered, "Of course, the cream always rises to the top." They then shook hands and had a laugh together. "Man, if there is anything that you need, don't hesitate to ask; and please do visit our restaurant. I believe that you will be pleasantly pleased and this one is on me."

Kevin looked at Ronnie and said, "Well, I don't know about you, but I'm gonna check it out when I'm finished."

Ronnie said, "I'm right behind you, man."

Thomas smiled and began walking away, saying, "I don't want to take any more time from your workout, so please enjoy yourselves."

Ronnie said, "Thank you very much, man," and Kevin spoke out, "Yeah, thanks a lot, bro'."

Thomas headed back toward the stairs leading to the lower level. The place stayed busy all day and into the evening and, around 1900 hours, Thomas was sitting in his office reviewing some paperwork and Beverly walked in and said, "Hi, sweetheart, how are you?"

Thomas said, "Hi, baby, I'm fine; just a little tired, but feeling great. Come on in."

Beverly walked in and plopped down in a large leather chair.

Thomas looked at Beverly and asked, "We did arrange for someone to pick the kids up, didn't we?"

Beverly laughed and said, "Yes, my dad picked them up two hours ago."

Thomas laughed and said, "You know, it's just that I'm tired."

"I know," said Beverly, "I am, too."

Thomas said, "Well, I'm going to stick around for thirty more minutes and then I'm going to call it a day."

"Baby, I'm with you. The second shift is already in place and things are running like clockwork."

Thomas said, "Great, let's make sure everything stays tight and then let's head for the Ponderosa."

"Well, let's get this done," so they both said their goodbyes and headed for home. On the ride home, Beverly said to Thomas, "You know that the kids are staying at Dad's place tonight, so why don't you just drop me off over there and the kids and I will catch you in the morning."

Thomas said, "Okay, that's probably not a bad idea." Thomas dropped Beverly at her parents' home, saw her in, and headed for home.

Things went great all week at the gym—people were signing up, new membership was picking up, and the gym seemed to be one of the hottest things to open for the time being. It was now Thursday afternoon and Beverly was sampling a new soup that was prepared by one of the chefs in the restaurant. As she finished her sample and informed the chef that the soup was very good, and gave her stamp of approval to serve the soup to the clientele, a thought struck her...*Oh no, it's Thursday; that crazy woman is going to call me in the morning expecting to get an answer.* Beverly told the chef, "That soup is excellent, go ahead and make this dish the special of the day; I have to run."

Beverly left the restaurant. As she headed toward Thomas's office, all along the way, people were stopping her and speaking to her, asking how everything was going. Beverly tried to be as polite as possible and, at the same time, let people know that she was in a hurry and would get back with them a little later. By the time Beverly had gotten back to Thomas's office, she was winded.

She walked through the doorway and Thomas said, "Hey, baby, what's wrong?"

Beverly said, "I almost forgot that stupid woman will be calling me in the morning."

Thomas said, "Oh yeah, that's right; we have to prepare to stage war."

"No, that's not the way we are going to deal with this," replied Beverly, "we will get more flies with honey than we will with vinegar."

"Well, I hope that you have a well thought out strategy for that witch."

"I'm a woman; I will always think things out first and then have a backup plan."

Thomas said, "Well, baby, I'll tell you this, if you've exhausted all of your plans and desire to use mine, then please be sure to let me know because you may not approve of my methods, but they have been tried, tested, and proven to be most effective in extreme test situations."

"You know, I really don't want to know what you're talking about; but if we do have to resort to your measures, then Lord help us."

Thomas said, "Baby, if we have to resort to my measures, then Lord help everyone." Thomas kissed Beverly goodnight and made his way back to the truck. He drove home and after he had gotten into the house, he made himself a drink and sat on the couch in the den. He took a sip of his drink and then another sip. A thought popped into his head. Thomas toyed with the thought, *Hey, I know how these people play; this situation is going to unravel. I need to start planning now or I'll be a victim of reaction and I know that I need to be pro-active.*

Thomas reached over, picked up the telephone, and dialed a number. After the third ring, the person on the other end of the line said, "Hello, this better be important?"

Thomas said, "Hey bro', we need to have a sit down."

"Hey bro', are you okay?" asked Phil.

Thomas replied, "Hey man, it's time to cowboy up."

"Okay, now you've got my attention. When do you want to meet?"

"How is 30 minutes?"

"How about 45 minutes?" asked Phil.

Thomas said, "Cool, the door will be open."

"I'm there." Phil hung up and looked once at Lisa. Lisa looked at Phil with a very dissatisfied face and said, "Oh, hell no, I know that you're not just going to turn this stuff down for your friend?"

Phil said, "Hey, baby doll, check this out; you remember when we first met at the restaurant?"

"Yes, I do, and this had better be...."

Phil interrupted, "Recall when I said that when we were in the shit overseas, and Thomas saved my ass more than once?"

"Yes..." Lisa said with a more understanding tone this time.

Phil continued to say, "Well, I was not just figuratively speaking; I mean, back in Nam, we were in a minority—black, Puerto Rican, Mexican, Indian, and poor white trash. We had gotten down to seventeen men and had started out with sixty-five. Thomas was the sergeant, which means he was running shit. Thomas had his staff together enough that when some of the boys were panicking because they saw that we were outnumbered, outmanned, outgunned, and darn near out of ammo; no food left and we had not had any sleep in over three days, he pulled all of us together and we grouped up.

Thomas said, 'Hey, I'm going to give it to you guys straight up; we are surrounded on all flanks.' The guys looked at each other and fright was too shallow of a word to describe what the boys were feeling. Thomas said, 'Well, I don't know about you guys, but I know that Marines have a special place in heaven and not only that, Marines can't die without special permissions.' He had everyone's attention at this time, including mine. Thomas said, 'Charlie does not know this, and the way I see it, we have an advantage on him.' The men were starting to lose their fear and courage began to take over. Thomas said, 'There's seventeen of us left; it looks to be maybe one and a half platoons, at best, of Charlie coming; that's roughly one hundred and thirty or forty-five of them. Now the way I see it, every Marine is equal to at least seven of Charlie, so the advantage goes to us. I want every marine to make one shot, one kill...45-meter spreads, 7-yard intervals. I want one shot every three seconds and every shot a head shot. We'll go four on four on all four flanks and call your shots; men it's time to cowboy up. And if one of you sons of bitches has the fortunate pleasure to be called to duty at heaven's gates, then make sure to ask Saint Peter to save some room for us.'"

Phil continued, "I'm telling you, I have never seen a group of men ready to lay down their lives in a manner like that before. Even I didn't care if I died at that time. Well, Charlie came the distance and Thomas shouted out, 'Do not commence fire until I give the command!' and no one even questioned him. Charlie began to close in, running and yelling in their native tongue. Some of them were even speaking English saying, 'Yankees go home, screw Babe Ruth, and fuck Donald Duck.' Thomas shouted, 'Steady boys, steady!' until Charlie came so close, I swear on butter beans and ham hocks, we could smell the fish and rice and sweat coming from their pores; and then Thomas shouted, 'Commence firing!' We all started firing in repetition just as Thomas had instructed. Everyone was squeezing off rounds in 3-second intervals and Charlie started dropping like rocks in a pond. I continued firing as bullets whizzed past my helmet. It was a stone trip because I did not even care that the rounds were so close, that if one were to strike me, it could be fatal. Thomas shouted, 'If you get hit (talking to all of us), then continue firing until you cannot fire anymore! Remember, Marines do not surrender and we don't give up! There are no POWs in Marine ranks!' I continued firing and I saw Link fall down and shouted, 'Link, are you okay?' Link did not answer. I reached down and put my hand on his neck to see if I could find a pulse; but, it was to no avail. I called to Jessie and told him to cover the left flank for

Link. Jessie covered and we continued to fire. As we continued to drop Charlie, one by one and two by three, I saw that Charlie had slowed down on their advance. Thomas shouted, 'Hold steady, men; continue firing, but reduce to 5-second intervals!' All of us complied. After 27 minutes of intense fire, Charlie retreated back into the brush. Thomas shouted, 'Cease fire, cease fire!' We all complied. Thomas looked around, and said, 'Lord have mercy. I want all of you men to gather up our casualties and stack them right over there by that hollowed log. I want you do it as fast as you can and get back over here.' The men moved right away. After the bodies had been gathered and stacked, everyone was standing tall in front of Thomas. Thomas said, 'Well, we lost seven men; that leaves us with ten.' Jose asked, 'Hey, Sergeant, aren't those mother fuckers gone? I mean they aren't coming back, are they? We kicked their asses good.' Thomas smiled and said, 'At ease, men. Charlie got a very special surprise today, but they only retreated so they can regroup and come back and finish what they started.'"

Phil said, "I asked Thomas, 'How much time do we have?' Thomas said, 'Well, I'll tell you this; if they thought we surprised them earlier, then this one is going to kill them.' All of the men started laughing. Thomas looked out at Lightfoot and Andy Hernandez, and said, 'I want my two snipers up in those trees, one on the east side and the other on the west; nest in tight as a Texas tick. Make sure you use your flash suppresser so you don't jeopardize your cover.' Lightfoot and Andy Hernandez double-timed it to their positions. Thomas instructed the rest of us to position ourselves at 20-meter spreads; 'This will have the illusion of there being more of us than there really is. We will hold our positions and advance no more than 45 meters, so we can use the cover fire from our snipers from vantage points. No, I want everyone to gather any additional rounds from our fallen, and from any mother loving dead ass Charlies that you can find.'"

Phil continued, "We all did as Thomas said and, as sure as a donkey stinks, Charlie came back in full effect. Thomas gave the commence fire order and while everyone was in place, just as before, Charlie began to drop just like before. We started advancing and they continued to put up a fight. I was firing away, feeling like I was on top of the world. As I fixed my sights on one of the ugliest gooks that I had ever seen, I squeezed the trigger, just knowing that I would hit him with a round right between the eyes. As my trigger finger reached the back of the trigger guard, no round was dispensed. I squeezed again and nothing happened. I saw this ugly, rotten teeth, bad breath gook get so close, I saw the flash from his muzzle light up; but I was so focused, I reached down and grabbed my sidearm .45 pistol and after I had confirmed he was a non-threat to mankind, I began firing again at other targets. After a while, I began to feel light-headed, but I just thought that because of all the adrenalin flowing I was just tripping. Then I started feeling weak. I fell to one knee and the .45 pistol became extremely heavy. I remember attempting to point the muzzle at a figure that was advancing toward me, and I could not lift the pistol to sight in on him. I saw the figure rush toward me with his arm extended and a knife coming right at me. I remember thinking *what a way to go* and saying, 'Lord, I need an application for up there.' As I had prepared myself for my final blow, a body leaped in front of me and forced me to fall on my left side. I heard a grunt and then, 'It's time for you to be properly introduced to the reaper, you slant-eyed mother fucker.' I looked over my right shoulder and I saw Thomas with a machete raised in the air with both hands on the handle and, with one mighty swing down, chop the head completely off of the gook that wanted to send me to meet St. Peter. I looked at Thomas and said, 'Hey man, do not think because you saved my ass, we are going to hold hands or take warm showers together in the wee hours of morning.' Thomas smiled and said, 'You dumb ass, I'd have to meet your parents first anyway.' We both laughed. Thomas said, 'First, I'm going to stop my bleeding.' Charlie got Thomas in the side of the belly, but I knew Thomas wasn't going to die because he was just too damn angry. Then he said, 'I'm going to patch you up and get us both the hell up out of here.' I said, 'That sounds like a plan to me.'"

Phil said, "Thomas got us out of that situation and there were only seven of us left. All seven of us are still alive to this day and tight as Rockefeller's wealth. We all made a vow that if Thomas ever needed us, no matter what is or was entailed, we would be there and even put our lives down for him."

Lisa said, "It really seems like you guys love Thomas a lot."

"You girls say love. We men, as Marines, say respect goes farther than love. Love can be betrayed; respect can cause wars and end them, as well, and holds a great deal more power."

Phil continued, "There were a couple of more times Thomas saved me, as well, and I only had the opportunity to return the favor once. I would lay my life down for that man, and I don't think that you could ever understand that."

Lisa replied, "I don't completely understand, but I do to a certain degree, and would like to understand more if you would allow me to, because

I would very much like to be a part of your life forever and I trust you, as well. Please, go to Thomas and I'll wait for you for as long as it will take for you to return."

Phil looked at Lisa and said as he finished putting on his clothes, "Thanks, baby, now that's what I'm talking about. When I find out what's going on I will fill you in."

"Okay, baby, now go to him," Lisa said.

Phil rushed out and headed toward Thomas's house. Phil got there and let himself in as the door was unlocked just as Thomas said it would be. Phil called out to Thomas, "Hey, young blood."

Thomas shouted, "Here… in the den!"

Phil walked into the den and said, "Hey, man, what's up? I was just about to get real deep into some trim, so this had better be good."

"Okay, man," said Thomas, "make yourself a drink and grab a sit down."

Phil took Thomas's suggestion and when comfortable in his chair, said, "Okay, bro', give it to me."

Thomas began, "Okay, from the top. Do you remember that young lady from the bank that worked with us on the loan?"

"You mean the fine…er, what was her name? Oh yeah, sweet Sarah."

Thomas said, "Yeah, right. Well, Sarah was not so sweet after all."

"Man, I knew you hit that," said Phil. "Man, what's the deal?"

"Man, it was totally unplanned," said Thomas, "and some things went down one night and just got out of wack from there."

"Well, if you hit it just once, what's the problem?"

Thomas answered, "Well, she wanted more; I played her off and told her that the one time should not have happened, but she could not accept that what happened could not go any further."

"I know you, brother; you had to tell her in a way that I know she understood that if you said this was it, then that was it."

"Man, I just wish that it could have been that simple," said Thomas. "After some time had passed by, she started to get a lot more persistent, and aggressive; I figured things were getting a little messy, so I had a sit down with Beverly and laid it out."

"Oh shit, Thomas, you did what?"

"Calm down, man. I thought this thing out carefully and felt it was the best way to go."

"Okay, Thomas, I'm with you so far."

"Man," continued Thomas, "I guessed that if there's nothing to hide, then Beverly and I could move forward."

Phil said, "True. Now, what else could there be, unless that bitch played a fatal attraction on you?"

"Man, worse than that. Two months later, she comes back and informs me that she is carrying my child."

Shocked, Phil said, "Man, I can't say anything right now, go on."

"To make a long story short, she got a DNA test and is supposed to have the results by tomorrow morning and call Beverly, and have her meet up with her to show her the results and prove that the baby is mine."

Phil said, "Man, that is the wildest shit that I have ever heard."

"Man, there's more."

"Man, I think I would rather go back to the bushes in Uganda than to hear this crap," said Phil.

Thomas continued, "Man, this woman has given me an ultimatum—divorce Beverly and marry her, and she would give Beverly the business, but not let her own the company name, and pay Beverly off with $500,000, plus pay for the kids' college education, or she would expose me and ruin my reputation with the investors, as well as the banks, the media, and talk shows."

"Wow! It sounds like you got a 100 percent certifiable."

Thomas continued, "It actually is worse because she's smart; she has thought up a way to completely shut me down from operating, ruin my relationship with my family, and slander my name in the business world…cause me to cease to function."

"Well, Thomas, knowing the man that you are, I know that you are going to counter her attack."

"What's my name?" said Thomas

"That's what I'm talking about," Phil said. "What do I need to do?"

"Well, that's where you come in bro'. Phil, I want you to assemble all of the boys from Company C."

"You mean we're going to reassemble the 'Magnificent Seven'? Oh shit, that means that this is going down big."

Thomas explained, "Well, I'm hoping that it doesn't have to go down like this, but if it does, then I want to be ready. Like my daddy used to say, always hope for the best, but be prepared for the worst."

Phil said, "Man, you know that's right. So, what's the plan?"

Thomas answered, "I will run it down to you later; just get the boys together for a meeting for Friday night at 2000 hours and I will fill everyone in at that time."

Phil said, "Consider it done."

Friday morning Sarah went down to the medical lab and arrived at 0800 hours. She walked in and went up to the window to inform the receptionist that she was here to receive the test results from a DNA paternity test.

The young lady at the window said, "Good morning, ma'am, may I please have your name," and asked her to sign in, "and I will need to see one form of picture ID." Sarah complied with all of her requests. The young lady said to Sarah, "Please have a seat and the doctor will be with you momentarily."

Sarah sat down for eight minutes and the doctor opened a door, walked to the doorway, and said, "Sarah Daniels?"

Sarah stepped up and answered, "Yes, I'm Sarah."

The doctor said, "Please, come on in."

Sarah took a deep breath and headed in the direction the doctor was pointing for her to go. The doctor led her into an office room on the right-hand side of the hallway. To Sarah, it was one of the longest walks of her life. When she reached the room, she turned and walked in.

The doctor walked in right behind Sarah and said, "Please have a seat," pointing to a chair in the far corner of the room. After Sarah had taken her seat, the doctor opened a file folder and said the results of the test came back positive 99.99 percent, that the father of her child was, in fact, a match for a one, as the doctor read down several paragraphs, and said, "Oh yes, Mr. Thomas Dugmal. Now, I don't know if this is good news for you or bad, but the facts are the facts."

Sarah looked at the doctor and said, "Well now, I really don't believe that it's any of your business to be concerned with whether it's good or bad news for me. I just wanted the results from the test. That is what I'm paying you for."

The doctor looked at Sarah with a bewildered expression and said, "I'm sorry, you're right, here are the results," and handed her a 3-page report and said, "here is an envelope for the paperwork to go in. Ms. Daniels, have a good day."

Sarah carefully looked the papers over, smiled, and placed them in the envelope. Sarah said, "Thank you," and walked out of the office. Sarah could hardly wait to get out of the building before she grabbed her cell phone and dialed Beverly's phone number. As the phone was ringing, she glanced at her watch and noticed that the time was 0855 hours.

Beverly picked up her cell phone and said, "Hello."

Sarah said, "Good morning, Beverly, this is Sarah, can you talk?"

"Hold on a minute," Beverly said as got up and walked over to the den, making sure that the door was locked behind her. "Yes, I can talk."

Sarah said, "I have the results from the test, now are you prepared to take me up on my offer?"

Beverly replied, "You know that I still need to see proof of these results, so is there a place where we can meet?"

"Yes," Sarah said, "but it must be in a public place where there will be a lot of people."

Beverly agreed, "No problem with that, I can meet you wherever in one hour."

"Very well, then, how about the South Beverly Mall?"

"Sure, what location?"

Sarah said, "How about Zim's Restaurant? It's outside seating and there are always lots of people."

"Okay," said Beverly, "its 8:45 now; I'll meet you there at 9:45."

Sarah said, "See you there," and hung up.

Beverly clicked the cell phone off, stood there, and just stared into space thinking, *What am I going to say to this crazy woman? Well, I know that I need to maintain my cool. I think I'll just say a prayer before I meet with this lunatic.* Beverly started getting dressed. After she had gotten herself cleaned up and dressed, she ran downstairs and asked her dad if he could take the kids and drop them off at school. Of course, this would be no problem for her dad, as he's always eager to do something for his grandkids. Beverly rushed out of the house, almost forgetting to tell the kids goodbye. She ran back in and hugged each of them and instructed them to make sure that they stayed on their best behavior and she would pick them up this after-noon after school.

After all of the hugs and kisses were completed, she hurried off, once again, like a woman on a mission. Beverly was driving in her car and realized that she forgot to inform Thomas about what was going on. She pushed the phone access button on the dash, the phone activated through the speaker system, and then the voice, "Good morning, Mrs. Dugmal, what number, please?"

Beverly said, "Thomas's cell, please."

The voice said, "Thank you, dialing the number," and the next voice was Thomas saying, "Hello."

Beverly said, "Good morning, baby."

"Good morning, sweetheart," Thomas replied. "Is everything okay?"

"Funny, you should ask, Thomas."

"What's up, baby?"

Beverly said, "Well, I am on my way to see Sarah Daniels."

Thomas responded, "Sarah, this morning? Right now?"

"Yes, right now. Thomas, calm down, I have this under control."

"Well, where are you going to meet her? I'll be right there."

Beverly said, "No, honey, I have this one; I will call you as soon as we adjourn from our meeting and give you the results, but I have to handle this my way for right now."

"Baby, please be extremely careful, always watch your six o'clock and cover your flanks."

"I know, honey," said Beverly. "I remember everything that you taught me; trust me, I'll be fine."

"What time are you scheduled to meet her?"

Beverly said, "At 0945."

"Okay, I expect to hear from you at least by 1100 hours," said Thomas.

"Do not panic, if I don't call you by 1100 hours, please wait; it'll just mean that our meeting went over. I'll call you soon after, don't worry."

"Okay, I'll stand by to stand down."

"Fine," said Beverly, "then I'll talk to you later; baby, I love you."

"Baby, you know that I love you, as well," Thomas said as they both hung up their cell phones.

Beverly finally arrived at the South Beverly Mall. She found a nearby parking spot, parked, and rushed to the entrance in an effort to be in place and waiting for Sarah, before Sarah arrived. When Beverly reached her roundabout point, she carefully looked around and saw that she had gotten there before Sarah had arrived. Beverly looked around and then at her watch. She noticed that she had twenty-seven minutes to spare, so she went over to the café service counter and ordered a bagel and green tea. She received her order and walked to an outside table area and looked around to choose a spot where she would have a good vantage point. She found a perfect spot where she could see pretty much all angles of the café, the entrance, and outside perimeters. Beverly took her knife and began to spread her cream cheese on her bagel. She would occasionally glance around to survey the area as the café was starting to fill up with morning breakfast worshippers.

At 0940 Beverly looked to her three o'clock and saw Sarah slowly approaching with a white blouse and gold and white mid-heel pumps. Sarah, as she approached, was looking around as if expecting to see someone else she knew or was expecting to see. When Sarah finally arrived at the table where Beverly was sitting, she stopped in front of the table and said, "Well, are we alone?"

Beverly replied, "Yes, unless you brought someone with you."

"I came alone, just as I promised," said Sarah.

"Well then, have a seat and we can begin."

Sarah sat down and decided to take another 360-degree glance around the area. Beverly smiled and said, "You know, for someone who can talk as much trash as you on the phone and make all those threats and promises, you sure are acting very nervous."

Sarah smiled and responded, "Nervous, no; cautious, yes. I did not get to where I am in my career and in life, for that matter, being messy or careless."

Beverly said, "Well, that's just your personal opinion from your own observation of yourself, but enough about the personal crap. Let's get down to business."

"Let's. Now, the way I see it, I was pretty damn clear the first time we spoke; now, do you have an answer for me? I mean, what are you going to do?"

Beverly interrupted her and said, "Shit, you..." Beverly paused for a moment for a breath and looked Sarah in the eyes. "...you know, Sarah, my dad used to tell us when we were young..."

Now Sarah interrupted and said, "Oh, spare me the 'my dad used to say' shit, you..."

Again, Beverly interrupted her and said, "Listen, you little tramp, you called me making demands to me about my husband and conditions that are going to affect my life and my kids, as well, so you're going to listen to whatever I have to say and whatever the hell my dad had to say. Now...before I was so rudely interrupted, my dad used to say, 'Look into a person's eyes; you'll be able to tell a lot by their eyes, because the eyes cannot tell a lie.' And, do you know why, Sarah, the eyes cannot tell a lie?"

Sarah said. "No, I don't know why; suppose you enlighten me."

"My dad said that the eyes are the windows to your soul," answered Beverly. "And what I'm looking at and reading in your eyes, Sarah, is a heartless, selfish person with no constitution, and consideration for no one or nothing but yourself and your benefits."

Sarah paused for a moment and smiled, almost as if she was a demon possessed and then responded, "Well, that was the most accurate assessment of me that I have ever heard. I am truly moved and honored by the way you have flattered me. I swear I have to give it to you; you have inspired me to press onward. I want to know now, what in the hell are you going to do? I hope you'll come to your senses and take your brats and the money I offered you and run away like a good little dog."

Beverly looked at Sarah and with a tear in one eye responded to Sarah by saying, "You know, I have made every attempt possible to reason with you. Your goal is to break up a family to benefit yourself, for greed, and guess what? Greed is what's going to take you down. Remember, good always prevails over evil. And you are evil in the flesh. My answer is, 'hell NO' to all of your demands, and you're crazy in the head if you think that Thomas would have you after you have threatened his family and livelihood; you know you can go back to hell and tell your father Lucifer that you both will lose because you are going up against a Marine that will kill in hell forever with you two in it."

Sarah replied, "Is that supposed to scare me into changing my mind? No, I'd rather die than lose Thomas."

"You fool," mocked Beverly, "Thomas is not yours to lose, but then again, you're suffering from dementia schizo demoniac paranoid disorder, so I see why you feel so confused."

Sarah shot back, "Well, you can call it whatever you want to, but the bottom line is I'll walk away with Thomas and everything else I want, and there's nothing you can do to stop this from happening."

Beverly asked, "So is this your final decision; you're really going through with this madness?"

Sarah stood up and said, "I already had my mind made up long ago, but I thought that I would give you the common courtesy and decency to back down when you know that you've been bitten, but apparently you're not smart enough to tell the difference between fact and fiction, so I'm just going to have to teach you a very valuable lesson in life."

Beverly stood up and said, "Okay, where do we go from here?"

Sarah turned and started to walk away, stopped, turned back around, faced Beverly and said, "It begins now, and you'll see very soon my next move."

"Okay, I'll be ready," said Beverly, as Sarah turned and walked away.

Beverly stood there and watched her walk away and, when she was sure Sarah had gone from the café, she pulled out her cell phone, and speed dialed Thomas.

Thomas heard his phone ringing, looked at the caller ID, and saw that it was Beverly. He pushed the receiver button and said, "Hi, baby, how did it go?"

Beverly answered, "Well, I do think we're in for an all out assault by an insane woman."

"That's just what I thought. Now it's time to do what I do."

"Thomas, wait now; remember we have kids that this madness could possibly affect."

"Bev, baby, I can't just stand by and wait for this crazy women to hit me first."

"You have no choice; now we can sit down and discuss a counter plan, take notes, keep records, and monitor her actions, but that's about all that we can do at this point."

"Okay, baby, we'll wait to counter her first move; but as soon as she has shown her first hand, then I will deal a new deck of cards."

Beverly said, "Fair enough."

Thomas and Beverly went on about their business, as normal, and enjoyed watching their business flourish and grow. After eight months of steady growth with the gym, Thomas was now meeting with investors, concerning opening up a chain of health clubs. The planning began regarding locations and cost analysis and starts-up costs. Twelve months and the business had progressed into the black, so far that the profit margin went past $1.2 million. Thomas had been contacted by the investors, who informed him that he had the backing to open five more health clubs in the Southern California area, and four in Northern California, plans for twenty-seven other states with at least one in each of those states, and in some of the larger states two health clubs.

Thomas called Beverly and shared the good news with her. Beverly said, "Can we handle all of that?"

Thomas said, "Baby, we won't have to. The way it works in the business world is, we will own the name and then franchise the units out to independent owners."

"Okay, the way I understand it is we will share the profit margin of all the expansions that we have out there without having to do all of the work?"

"Well, by George, I think you've got it," teased Thomas.

"Thomas, come on now, don't patronize me; I have it now. We don't have anything to worry about anymore."

"That's just what I mean; that's what I'm talking about." So, they got off of the phone.

Thomas was sitting in his office and called the front desk, instructing the receptionist to get in contact with Phil. Two minutes later, Phil called Thomas and said, "Hey, man, I was just about to call you when my phone rang."

"What were you calling me for?"

Phil said, "Man, I have some news for your ass; it's going to blow your socks off of your feet."

"Well, I don't know if your news can top mine, but you go first since your seem so excited."

"No, man, I got your call first, so you go," said Phil.

"Okay, but you have to sit down first. I just received a call from our investors and they told me that it's a go for a chain of health clubs throughout the country; I'm talking about close to forty states."

"Man," said Phil, "I don't know what to say. I told you that you were the man with the master plan and I'm just lucky to be able to share a piece of your world."

"You know this, man, you will always have a part in this success, and that's for life."

"Man...I...I can't talk right now; please give me a minute."

Thomas said, "Man, take your time, bro'. Hey, Phil, what was it that you wanted to tell me?"

"Man, what you told me makes what I have to tell you seem dwarfed."

"Man, get out of here with that; tell me what you wanted to say," said Thomas.

"Okay, I just wanted to let you know that I asked Lisa to marry me and she accepted."

"Man, that's great news! When is the big day?"

"Well," replied Phil, "she wants to do the 'I do' as soon as possible, so we're looking at February 10."

"Cool, brother; that gives us one month, right?"

"I know that it's not much time, but we just figured that we could do it here at the gym and invite most of the members and our close friends and family."

"Man, consider it done," said Thomas. "I'll spring for the restaurant and photographer. That will be our gift to you two."

"Hey, bro'; you're the greatest friend a guy could have."

Thomas replied, "And you know it, man...," and they both shared a laugh.

"Oh yeah, one more thing, man…"

"I'm almost afraid to ask…what is it?"

Phil said, "Hey, brother, I would be honored if you would be my best man."

Thomas swallowed and paused for a moment, and replied, "Hey, bro', I would be honored to be your best man."

"Cool, I believe that Lisa is on the phone with Beverly as we speak, asking her to be her maid of honor and help her with the planning of the wedding."

Thomas said, "Well, I can tell you that she made the right choice in asking Beverly to help with the planning because Beverly will be detailed to the letter." They shared another laugh. "Phil, I'm proud of you and I just want you to know that you have my blessings on your choice of a wife; I do not believe that you could have picked a more compatible companion than Lisa."

Phil said, "Thanks, man, but I do have to agree with you; that girl is so good to me and good for me."

"Okay, we have to set up the bachelor party for you, and you know that we have to do it right."

"There's only one way to do it and that's right," said Phil. "I need to wrap up some things here, and then I'm on my way to the gym."

"Okay then, I'll see you in a few."

They both hung up their phones and Thomas sat back in his chair and said, "Man, if that don't beat all," and had to laugh out loud.

Later on that night, Thomas and Beverly got home from working at the gym all day and as they went upstairs and to the bedroom, Thomas looked at Beverly, smiled, and asked, "Baby, do you believe it? Phil is finally jumping the broom."

Beverly laughed and answered, "You know it had to happen sooner or later; it just so happened to be later." They both laughed. "I think we will keep it very simple given the short time frame that we have to work within."

Thomas said, "Well, I know, if anyone can do it, you can; just let me know what you need."

"I have this covered," said Beverly. "You concentrate on the chain of events."

Thomas replied, "Oh, you know I'm already on it."

They both smiled at each other, and then Beverly looked at Thomas and said, "You know that you messed up last year, don't you?"

Thomas hung his head down and answered, "Yes, I do know that I messed up; but know this…I love you and I will always love you. I realize that it makes no sense to hurt myself, you know self-infliction, and when I hurt you, I was just hurting myself, as well. I'm so sorry and I will do my very best to keep hurt out of our lives as long as you will have me."

Beverly replied, "Oh, you silly man; if I did not love you, I would have been gone long ago or I would have probably killed you or something. Now, I truly believe that love conquers all, but only true love."

"Baby, you're the greatest," said Thomas as Beverly kissed his lips and they both had tears drop from their eyes.

Their kisses became more and more passionate and Beverly began to breathe a little faster. Thomas pulled his body closer to Beverly so, at this point, you could not get a simple sheet of paper between them. Beverly allowed her gown to slip all the way down from her arms down to her waist.

Thomas began to kiss Beverly on the neck, very gently and very softly. The look on her face showed that she was enjoying this treatment to the fullest. He continued the soft caressing kisses with her ear lobes and all around her ears. She began panting at this point. Thomas gently caressed her breast, as he softly rubbed her hardened and erect nipples. He began to gently caress her nipples with the tip of his tongue.

Beverly whispered, "Baby, please don't stop."

Thomas smiled and his tongue explored the rim of her breast. He worked his way down to her belly button. He stuck his tongue in ever so softly, and Beverly began to quiver. She put her hands behind her head and grabbed her pillow, and began to squeeze it with both hands. Thomas ventured down a little lower and started gently kissing her outer thighs. He slowly worked his way to her vaginal area. He lifted the outer skin covering her clitoris and began stroking it with his tongue. As he continued, the clitoris became erect. She put her hands on the sides of his head.

Thomas smiled because he knew that she was feeling the passion. Thomas continued and began to notice that she was shaking and panting. Thomas picked up the pace. He would stroke with his tongue for a few seconds, and then he would gently put his lips up to her clit and suck it. She released some juices of joy and squeezed Thomas's head even tighter.

She softly whispered, "Ooh baby...please baby, baby don't stop; that feels so good I could just scream."

Thomas just smiled and continued to give her pleasure at her pleasure zone. After a few minutes, Beverly released her tight grip from around Thomas's head. She laid her head back on the pillow and released a sigh of contentment that completely convinced Thomas that his mission to please had been accomplished.

Thomas covered her body with his. She embraced him very tightly as every sense on his body began to rise and tighten up. She reached her hands down to find his semi-erect penis. She began to stroke up and down with her hands, as if she were performing artwork. As she stroked with her hands, Thomas's pride and joy responded.

She then slipped her body down and turned Thomas over on to his back at the same time. She slowly worked her way down and began to massage his shaft with her tongue. She began to cover the head of his shaft with her mouth and then rotate her tongue from side to side. Then she allowed her entire mouth to cover his shaft all the way to the halfway point, and then started going up and down with her mouth. Thomas was enjoying this treatment to the fullest.

She would go up slowly and then back down, trying to cover more and more ground on every attempt. After a few minutes of this mind-blowing pleasure, she looked up at him and softly asked, "Are you ready, baby?"

Thomas answered, "Yes, I'm ready."

She climbed on top of him and straddled his hips, as Thomas said, "Okay, baby, guide me home."

Beverly smiled and said, "I'm on my way," as she led his shaft into her vagina. She began a rocking motion—back and forth and then from side to side—with the most graceful rhythm, as though they were performing to music from a string quartet.

After several minutes of this performance, Thomas grabbed her by her thighs and lifted her body up, rotating her from the top position to the bottom. He then re-entered her and began a rhythmic motion, from side to side, rotating up and down and back and forth. They continued for the next forty-five minutes until they both exploded in glorious ecstasy.

Beverly's face was glistening with sweat beads as she grabbed and embraced Thomas as tight as she could. Thomas had broken into a full blown sweat on his face, as well as his upper body, down to his mid- and lower section. After that, they both fell fast asleep in each other's arms.

The next morning, Thomas and Beverly arose and greeted each other with a kiss as they both, as one would describe, had the glow of love on their faces. Beverly said, "I'm going to get down to the gym and wrap up the planning for the wedding."

"Well, we can ride in together," said Thomas. "I have to go and make some phone calls and set up meetings with the investors."

"What about the plans for Phil's part in the wedding?"

Thomas smiled and answered, "Hey, that's easy; I'm already setting up the spot for the bachelor party and the rest is history."

"Hey, wait a minute now; there is more to Phil's part than that. What about the minister and floral arrangements?"

"Baby, I have that covered. Taria is covering all of that and it's a done deal. Now, I'm in the shower first, so if you will go downstairs and let Elizabeth know that she has the honor of taking everyone to school and picking them up...."

Beverly replied, "Okay, but hurry up; you know that it takes me longer to get ready than you."

"I know, but I was never one to push perfection."

"Okay, man, flattery will get you everywhere with me."

They both got ready to head out to the gym and they said their goodbyes to the kids and headed off. Thomas said, "Let's take your car since Elizabeth has the whole crew, she'll need the space of the truck."

"You're right, we'll take the 745."

As the day progressed, Beverly had made all of the calls that she needed to make and everything for the planning of the wedding was set in motion.

Thomas picked out the perfect spot for the bachelor party and booked it up. He then made a phone call to his investors and set up an appointment. He also called his financial advisor and attorney, so they could be present to go over the paperwork and finalize the plans.

On Wednesday, Thomas met up with the investors; he presented the proposal, design, and finalized projections. The investors advised Thomas that they would carefully review everything and get back with him in 72 hours. By this time, Phil's wedding would be in five days.

The 72-hour time frame had expired and Thomas was getting worried because he had not received the phone call that he was expecting. Phil came into Thomas's office and said, "What's up, man; how are you doing?"

"I should've heard from those investors by now. They could at least call me and say we changed our minds, or screw you, or something."

"Man, calm down. This is going to happen, man, don't worry. I'll tell you what; let me buy you a drink."

"It's too early for that," replied Thomas. "It's only 1430."

"That's my point; it's time for a drink, now let's go and it will be my treat. We won't stay long and I'll have you back here in time so that you won't get into any trouble from Bev."

Thomas agreed, "Okay, bro', let's go."

"Cool, I'll drive."

So, they both took off, and as Thomas was passing the reception desk, he told the receptionist, "Take any message I get and I will be back from running errands in two hours."

They walked out of the front door and got into Phil's car. As they pulled out of the parking lot, Thomas's cell phone went off.

Phil said, "That's you, man; I'll bet that it's Beverly."

Thomas looked down at the caller ID and said, "Bet it's not Bev... Hello."

The voice on the other end said, "Hello, this is Mike Stone with Stone Investments."

"Hi, Mike, I've been expecting your call."

Mike said, "I'm sorry that it took so long for us to get back with you, but things went a little better than we thought."

"Better than you thought?" asked Thomas.

Mike replied, "Yes, better Mr. Dugmal; through word of mouth you were recommended to a few NFL team owners. They want to not only invest in the business, but want to use you as their new personal trainer, and they want you to set up a strength training program for their players and use you as a consultant for linemen to become lean, big, and fast. We have also had some discussions with some universities and they want to track your progress with the NFL for six months and, if it proves to be successful for the NFL, then they would be interested in taking you on for the same services at the university level."

Thomas said, "Man, I don't know if you're talking too fast and not allowing me to absorb all of this, or if I'm really asleep and just dreaming all of this."

"Well, Thomas," replied Mike Stone, "this is not just a dream. I can assure you of that because we have an advance check for you for $27 million, but I do have some other things that I need to discuss with you."

Thomas asked, "Is this going to require that I have an attorney present?"

Mike said, "No. We have already taken care of that, we have staff that will cover all of that. The only thing is, we will need to meet right away because this is very hot and someone else could come and move right in with the same idea and plan, so we need to seal the deal now."

"Very well," Thomas said, "I can go and grab my wife and Phil. Just tell me where you want to meet."

Mike answered, "Everything is already set up here in my office, so as soon as you get here we'll talk, and if everything is to your liking and you're in agreement with our terms, it's a go."

"Fine, I'll see you in one hour." They both hung up.

Thomas said, "Phil, stop the car right now; pull the heck over."

"Are you okay, man? I heard you mention $27 million. What was that all about?"

"Man, hold on just a minute." Thomas dialed Beverly's cell number on speed dial.

Beverly answered the phone, "Hello."

Thomas said, "Baby, do not move, stay right there; you are at the gym, right?"

Beverly answered, "Yes, I am at the gym; is everything okay, what's going on?"

Thomas replied, "Baby, I will explain it to you when I get there, just be ready to go; I'm about ten minutes away."

"Okay, Honey, I'll be ready to go." They both hung up.

Phil looked over at Thomas and asked, "Now can I drive?"

"Yeah, man, back to the gym as fast as you can without getting a ticket."

Phil said, "Come on, homey, when did that stop me?" Phil turned the car around and headed back toward the gym.

"Man, this thing has grown bigger than all of us."

"Hey, bro'," said Phil, "anytime you feel like filling me in on it; please feel free to do so."

"Well, I'll tell you this, not only is the deal going down with fitness centers in other states, now some NFL teams and college universities are interested."

"What, man?" said Phil. "We are set for life and so are our kids, and our families. Man this is the shit."

Thomas said, "There are some terms that we need to review, but we have to close on the deal today due to the fact that we have no patents pending or copyrights."

"Boy, we are not there, yet?"

"Man, you're wrong; as soon as we pick up Bev, we're there."

"Boy, I can't wait to share the news with Lisa; she is going to be thrilled."

Thomas said, "Hey, brother, why don't you wait for a few days before you share this with her? I do love her because you love her and she is going to be your wife, but would just prefer that you wait until the deal is sealed and she is your wife."

"I can respect that, bro', I trust that you know what's right."

By this time they were pulling up in front of the gym. Thomas said, "Man, don't even park. I'm going to run in, get Bev, and we're gone."

Phil said, "Bet on that, man."

Thomas ran to the doorway of the gym and Beverly was waiting for him. As she saw him running up, she opened the door and greeted him with a hug. Thomas kissed her on the lips and said, "Baby, I love you, let's go," and grabbed her by the hand and took off toward the awaiting car. Thomas opened the front passenger door for Beverly and she got in. Thomas jumped in the rear seat and said, "Hey, bro', we're not gone, yet?"

Phil took off without even saying anything to Thomas in response.

Beverly turned around to face Thomas in the backseat. She said, "Okay, are you going to tell me now?"

Thomas said 'yes' and proceeded to fill Beverly in on what's going on and where they were going. When Thomas had finished informing her, Bev just looked at Thomas for a few seconds, and then she looked at Phil. Phil looked back a Beverly and said, "Hey, don't look at me like that; I can't believe it either."

Beverly refocused on Thomas and said, "You know with all you have told me, we tend to make millions, on top of those millions, but you know what they are going to want us to do, don't you?"

Thomas replied, "I have a pretty good idea, but do you feel that's our only recourse?"

"Well," Beverly said, "you did say that one of their attorneys is going to be present, which means they most likely have the contracts drawn up."

Phil said, "Wait a minute; excuse the hell outta me, but I don't have a college degree like you two, I'm just regular Joe here. What are you two talking about; make it simple, I mean break it down to me like I was a five years old."

Thomas and Beverly looked at each other and laughed. Beverly said after smiling, "Well, because we would actually be going what they call in the business world 'global,' us being a small business, large investors being more credible and fluid would buy us outright. We would own rights to the gym or business name and we would receive proceeds and dividends, but they would run the company and hold a certain portion of stocks and shares."

Phil said, "Am I to understand, they would say how much they would pay us and when?"

"Not completely," Beverly explained. "We'll come to an agreement—that's why they want to meet us now—on exactly how much of a share is going to be split between us, for what period of time, and so forth."

Phil asked, "We're going to be able to negotiate this in one sitting?"

Thomas said, "They are going to present us with a contract proposal, and if we agree, then it's a go; if we don't agree, we'll discuss it's fairness until we come to an agreement and they'll draw up another contract to offer."

"You know what," said Phil, "that's a little past me; I can't keep up with that. I think I'll just sit in the car and wait for you two educated people to do your thing. I know you will do the right thing."

Thomas smiled and said, "Bro', sometimes it's not always about understanding everything. I'll need you this time for something else."

"Oh yeah, like what?"

Thomas said, "You're a big guy—5'11", 245 lbs. with 24" guns—if someone is not dealing right, you tend to have a way of convincing people that maybe, for their sakes, they'd better retract and come correct. I don't know what it is about you, but you do give out that sense of intimidation."

Phil smiled and said, "Man, you could probably talk me into buying a bridge in South Africa. I'll go up with you, but I'll just sit and listen."

"That's all I need you to do, and worse comes to worse, you'll learn something about business savvy and strategy."

Phil said, "You know that's right."

They pulled up in front of the building and parked; they went into the building and Beverly said, "Okay, Michael Stone and Associates, third floor." They got into the elevator and headed up to the third floor.

Thomas said, "Okay, Bev. I want you to review the contract because you have more experience in that area. If something is in question, please address it to me and I will, in turn, direct it to Mike for interpretation. I want you to sit down in between the two of us, Beverly. I take the far end seat, Bev you in to middle, and I want you sitting on the outer end seat, Phil, where you can see the door, the windows, and keep an eye on the other people in the room. But, you need to continually scan the room, you follow me?"

Phil replied, "I got you, bro'...10-4."

They got up to the third floor and arrived at Mike Stone's office; they knocked on the door and the door opened. Mike Stone was standing up behind his extremely large desk that had been carved from the best cherry wood available. To his right stood his accountant and to his left, his investment partner. To his far right stood a recorder, and to the right of him, his attorney.

Mike said, "Thomas, I'm so glad you came so quickly."

"Hey, I didn't come so quickly." Everyone laughed.

Mike stuck his hand out to greet Thomas and Thomas returned the greeting. Mike then shook Beverly's hand, and then Phil's. Mike said, "All of you, please be seated and we'll get started."

Thomas said, "If you don't mind, I would like to change the order of seating."

"Okay, if you don't like my arrangement, I'm open to new ideas."

"It's not that," said Thomas, "and don't take it personal, but I was taught that when you come into a man's backyard, he has the unfair advantage; so I would just like to even the playing field just a little, if you don't mind, then that way everyone will feel comfortable, and that's what we want now, isn't it?"

Mike answered, "Yes, of course; I did almost forget that you are a former marine."

Thomas said, "It's nice of you to have remembered. Mike, if you'll just excuse me for a moment, this will be very brief."

"By all means," said Mike, "go right ahead."

Thomas looked at Beverly and Phil and said, "Let's take our positions." Phil moved to the outside right and Beverly moved to the middle seat. Thomas walked over to the inside closest to the window and asked the recorder to move over. After every one was in position, Thomas looked at Mike and said, "We can start now."

Mike smiled and said, "Mr. Dugmal that was very impressive. You are definitely the right person conducting this business; hell I would feel right safe with you in command of national affairs. Well, now, let's get started."

Mike motioned to the attorney and the attorney went into his briefcase and pulled out a folder filled with a business contract. The attorney handed it over to Thomas; Thomas handed the folder to Beverly, who began reviewing the contents immediately.

Mike said, "You'll find that everything is pretty cut and dried. Now, we want to offer a $27 million signing bonus to start off with. Now, what you'll see is a proposal for projections that you submitted. We're looking at net profits from each health club to be in the vicinity of $1.3 to $4.4 million per location, depending on the state and city."

Beverly continued to review the contracts as the papers turned and she was reading as fast as possible. Phil continued to scan the whole room as he was paying attention to everyone's body language and facial expressions.

Thomas looked over at Beverly and said, "Hey, baby, take your time; it is no rush."

Beverly said, "Thanks, honey, but I'm just fine."

Mike looked at Thomas and said, "Thomas, I can't believe that you don't trust me."

"Hey, Dad always told me that the only person that you put all of your trust in is God."

Mike replied, "Well, he did have an unarguable point there."

Thomas said, "Yes, he spoke a lot of truth to us, and we believed in him."

"Thomas," said Beverly, "this portion says that all further proceeds and profits will be renegotiated."

"We will definitely need to reword that one. If we are to renegotiate, then let's do it now. That's about all, for now."

Mike said, "Very well now, any other changes, I trust it will not be anything significant."

"The rest looks okay," said Beverly.

Mike replied, "Good, then we will give you your copy and we have ours; we just need for you to sign and date it."

"Very good," said Thomas.

So they signed the contracts. Beverly said, "I want to review some of this a little closer at home."

Mike said, "No problem, but ten o'clock tomorrow morning, I'm sending everything in to New York, so please get with me before then for any changes."

"That sounds good," said Thomas.

They all got up and said their goodbyes, then took off. When they got to the car, Phil said, "Man, that was a hell of a lot to absorb at one time. I hope that you two were able to follow along with all of that better than I could."

Beverly responded, "Well, I was reading and browsing over a few things, but in actuality, in order for us to reduce our risk of loss in profit, it will definitely behoove us to allow them to buy us out under conditions; that way, our contract guarantees us our share outright and upfront, and if any of the fitness centers suffers heavy losses, then it would not affect us at all."

"That's right," agreed Thomas, "so we need to close this. I just did not want those guys to think that we were so overexcited that we were not able to see clearly. I'll just call him in the morning and drop off the signed contracts."

Phil said, "Now, I do understand that kind of talk."

The next morning, Thomas instructed Phil to take the contracts back to Mike's office at 0830. Phil carried out that task and then headed back to the gym. Phil walked into Thomas's office and said, "What's up, man? Mission accomplished."

"Good job, man. Now we should hear from them in 72 hours, which means we should receive some checks, as well."

Phil said, "You don't mean the $27 million type do you?"

Thomas smiled and said, "Well, it could mean that."

"Man, this is unbelievable."

"No," said Thomas, "what's unbelievable is you're getting married in two weeks and your bachelor party is next. Let's get ready for that."

Phil said, "Man, I'm already for that because I know that you are going to do it like it should be done; I mean, we are going to do this to death."

"That's right, how are we going to do this?" asked Thomas.

Phil answered "We're going to do this to death. Man, this is going to be funkier than nine cans of shaving cream."

Thomas laughed and said, "Man, we're going to take this back to the old school flavor of things."

"Man, I just can't wait."

The following week finally arrived and Thomas had everything set up at the club Purple Rose. The club was rented out to Thomas for the night for the private event. All of Phil's current friends were present, and Thomas also had the boys from Charlie Company there, along with some members of the gym and Thomas's friends. All together, there were approximately one hundred seven people at the kick off. Thomas had already requested the DJ to make sure that the music theme was of the old school seventies and late sixties era.

When the party started, champagne was served and a toast to the last ray of freedom as Phil would know it as a single man. Thomas surprised Phil by having several women come out of the storage room so that the boys would have someone other than themselves to dance with. This kicked everything off just right. The DJ started the party off with James Brown's *Gonna Have a Funky Good Time.* The music was right. The company was right and the atmosphere was perfect. The party was highlighted by a large balloon being rolled to the middle of the floor and out popped one of Phil's favorite actresses Lisa Raye. Phil almost had a heart attack, but managed to stay alive and dance with Lisa Ray to the beat of *Love on a Two-Way Street.* The party continued to bump strong until 2:30 A.M. and Thomas had arranged for taxi cab service for all of the participants that needed a ride back home.

After everything was over, Phil went up to Thomas and said, "Hey, bro', this party was the bomb. I truly had a blast that I know will last. I have much love for you, man."

Thomas said, "I know, man, this was your night because next weekend your life is over." They both started to laugh.

That following week, everyone was busy making final arrangements for Phil's wedding. They had almost forgotten that a mega deal was in the making.

Wednesday morning Thomas received a phone call from Mike Stone. Thomas picked up the phone and said, "Good morning, Mr. Stone. How are things?"

Mike replied, "Good morning, Mr. Dugmal; all is well, but I should be addressing you as sir. Your contract has been accepted."

Thomas dropped the phone and had to pick it up. He said, "Sorry about that, I dropped the phone."

Mike said, "No problem, I would have dropped the phone if I heard that kind of news."

Thomas asked, "So where does that leave us at this point?"

Mike said, "Well, what is going to happen is there will be a joint meeting with all the investors, they will review the contracts, and come to a mutual agreement on terms and conditions. They will hold another joint meeting to confirm plans on dates of completion of new structures and start-up costs. So, we are looking at about two months of meetings before all plans are put into action. The good thing is you will receive your bonus interest upfront and outright."

Thomas asked, "Are you telling me that I'm waiting for a check for $27 million to be signed over to me at any time now?"

Mike replied, "Not exactly in that order."

"Then what order are we talking about?"

"Thomas, I have the check already waiting for you here in my office as we speak."

"Man, unbelievable," said Thomas.

"Quite the contrary; it's believable and it's a fact."

"One other question I have for you…"

Mike said, "Shoot."

"Just to confirm, we will own the rights to the name and logo, but it will be owned by the partners or investors?"

"That is exactly correct."

Thomas said, "You know, I can live with that."

"Okay then, I can expect to see you here today?"

"Yes, you will see me there today," Thomas said. "I'll give you a call when I'm on my way."

Mike said, "Sure thing," so they hung up.

Thomas took a deep breath and sat there for a moment and allowed the thought of being a millionaire digest. Then he got up and walked out of his office and looked around. He walked past the restaurant and looked in and smiled at one of the chefs, the chef smiled back and waved at him. Thomas continued to walk around the gym. He walked to the clothing store and looked in. He saw Beverly in there, so he walked in. Beverly was talking to one of the clerks. They were discussing customer service and an issue that came up with him and a customer. Thomas stood by and waited for Beverly to finish up her conversation with the clerk.

Beverly turned around and saw Thomas standing there. She said, "Hi, Thomas, I didn't know you were there. How long have you been waiting?"

"Not that long. I was just waiting until you finished with your lecture."

Beverly said, "That was not a lecture; I was giving corrective criticism."

"Well, anyway, I need to talk to you for a moment."

"Sure," said Beverly, "let's walk out of the store." They walked out of the store and onto the floor of the gym.

Thomas said, "Baby, we probably need to go to my office and talk there."

"Thomas, this is not any bad news or anything like that, is it?"

"No, as a matter of fact, it's good news."

Beverly said, "That's good because I don't know if I would be able to handle any bad news after going through what we did the last go round."

"I hear you."

As they got to Thomas's office, Thomas allowed Beverly to go in first. She walked in and took a seat in the comfortable leather chair. Thomas walked over to his desk after closing the door behind him. He said, "Baby, we need to go and pick up the check from Mike Stone for $27 million at his office."

Beverly paused for a moment and then said, "Honey, are you sure it's ours free and clear?"

"Yes, don't you just want to feel that check in your hands? Just to say yes, I have it, it's mine."

"Okay," said Beverly, "so what happens next? I mean when we pick up the check?"

"What do we do with it?" Thomas said, "I knew that you were going to ask that. So, that's why I pulled you in here. We need to decide if we are going to open up a new account at the bank or what bank we can trust."

Beverly answered, "You now that we cannot put the check into our regular account. I suggest opening up an account at a savings and loan. Secure it in a mutual fund and label the account in the business name."

"I have no argument with that, let's do it." Thomas continued, "Oh yes, by the way, I'm not going to say anything to Phil or anyone else about this right now. We do have the wedding this weekend and all."

"I agree," Beverly said. "I won't say anything to anyone. Okay, let's go and take care of this and get back."

Thomas and Beverly ran down to Mike Stone's office and picked up the check. They went to open a new account at the People's Choice Savings and Loan. When they got back, Phil was walking back from the direction of Thomas's office.

"Hey, I was looking for you guys."

Beverly asked, "Why are you looking for us?"

"I have two more days of being a bachelor and I don't know if I'm ready for this or not."

Thomas and Beverly started laughing at him. Phil automatically took on a defensive attitude.

Thomas said, "Okay, bro', we need to talk."

Phil looked over at Beverly and said, "Okay, we all got jokes now, huh? Well, why do they have to be at my expense?"

Beverly said, "Phil, we're laughing with you. You have what we call 'cold feet'; trust me, everyone goes through it."

Thomas said, "Come on into my office."

"I'll just go and check on things around the gym," Beverly said.

So, Phil went into Thomas's office and Thomas ran down the process of having cold feet. After their little talk, Phil felt much better and, most of all, he felt like going through with the wedding ceremony. Thomas, Beverly, Phil, and Lisa worked extremely hard the next two days to make sure that everything was set up for the wedding on Saturday.

When Saturday rolled around, everyone was in place and the time had come. It was 10:00 A.M. and everything was in place. Beverly was with Lisa in the dressing room and asked her, "Are you ready to go through with this, Lisa?"

"Beverly, to be honest with you, I am scared to death about going through with this. Is this normal?"

Beverly smiled and answered, "Lisa, it's perfectly normal and you should be afraid. This is one of the biggest steps that you're going to take in life. This is going to affect not only you, but your family and friends, as well. Just keep in mind that the respect of your vows is the secret commodity that you have. Working on keeping your marriage together and healthy is a daily struggle. There are going to be times when you feel that it would be easier to throw your hand in and go out and start over somewhere else. But you can't because you promised that you would not give up. The best advice that I can give you is you're going to be forced to bend, but be careful not to break. Be supportive, as supportive as you possibly can. Nothing in life is stronger that when a husband and a wife stick together and fight for the right against an outside force. And, Lisa, always keep the channels of communication open; they are so important in your relationship. Help him to learn you, the real you, because that's the only way that he will get to know you. You continue to ask him how to learn him. Once he sees that you are interested in learning him through and through, he will feel the bond between the two of you. That's a good thing."

Lisa wiped a tear from her eye and said, "Beverly, you have me crying. I'm going to mess up my makeup."

Beverly smiled and said, "I believe that Phil is going to mess up your makeup tonight anyway." They shared a laugh and then continued to get ready for the ceremony.

Phil had his tuxedo on and was eager to go. Thomas says, "Hey, bro', are you ready to do this?"

Phil said, "Hell yes, and you know this, man." They both laughed.

The time was at hand and everything went off as planned. The wedding vows were exchanged in fine fashion and the two known as Mr. and Mrs. Phillip Michael Upchurch were one in union. The reception was being held at the Bonaventure West Hotel in the Grand Ballroom. Of course, more people showed up at the wedding and reception than expected. It's funny how you send out RSVPs and not everyone responds, but feel that they can just show up for the event anyway.

Phillip had changed from his tux to his tailor-made-to-fit suit. He knew that he was the cat's meow this night. Phil said to Thomas, "Man, how do I look, I mean really?"

Thomas had a glass of champagne in his hand and said, "Hold up a moment." Thomas stepped back about three paces, looked Phil up and then down. Thomas said "Hey, brother; you look like you're as clean as a Baptist preacher stepping into church on Easter Sunday morning. Man, if you were any cleaner, you would get a certificate of approval from the board of health."

Phil smiled and said, "Man, I knew that; I just wanted to hear it from you." They both laughed.

Thomas said, "But seriously, bro', I need to rap to you about a few things."

"Everything's cool, isn't it?" asked Phil.

"Yes, of course, I just need to share a few things with you since you are now a family man; some things are important for you to know."

Phil said, "Okay, let's go outside; I need some air anyway."

They both took a walk outside to the front of the hotel; on the way out, they saw several people from the wedding and people were offering congratulations. When they got outside, Thomas said, "Let's go over there at the side of the hotel so we can have some privacy."

When they got to the side, they both sat down on a large hood that came up from the basement. Phil looked at Thomas and said, "What's up, man?"

Thomas said, "First, I just wanted to tell you congratulations; I believe you made a wise decision marrying Lisa. I just wanted to let you know, even though I know you already know, I am here for you; whatever you need, I am here for you. I love you like a brother; hell, you are a brother. So know this. I will always have your back."

"Hey, bro', you got to give me some love," said Phil.

Thomas stood up and the two embraced and Phil said, "Man, it is truly a blessing to have you in my life. If we have any kids, you know I want you and Beverly to be the godparents."

Thomas said, "For sure."

"Good," said Phil. "Now let's get back in there to the reception before my wife misses me."

Thomas said, "One more thing I need to share with you, bro'."

"What?"

"Phil, you probably ought to sit down for this one."

"Man, you got me all pumped up, what is it?"

"Well," said Thomas, "we got the check last week."

"The check from Mike Stone Investors?"

"That's the one."

"So you're telling me we have, what was it, $27 million?"

"Yes, that's what I'm telling you," replied Thomas.

Phil jumped up and shouted, "Oorah!"

Thomas said, "Hey, bro', you have to keep this under your hat for the time being. We did put the check into a special account and Beverly and I are the only ones who can draw from it."

"That's not a problem," Phil said. "How do we go about getting funds for this and that and if I need cash for this and that?"

"Well, of course, we will incorporate a finance committee and when you or anyone needs to draw from it, you will present your request before the committee for approval."

Phil said, "Damn man, you're a genius, a real life genius."

Thomas replied, "Man, I'm no different from anyone else. I just try and think of what's right for all of us and look out for our best interests."

Phil said, "Man, I feel so good, let's get back inside; I feel the need to party, with my new wife, of course."

"Cool, let's do it."

The rest of the night went extremely well for the new bride and groom. The party was going strong and the hands on the clock said 12:47 A.M. Beverly walked over to Thomas and asked, "Baby, when was the last time that you saw Lisa and Phil?"

Thomas looked at his watch and laughed before he answered, "You know, they took off about 2315 and I have not heard from them since."

Beverly said, "And, you're not going to hear from them, at least not for the next few hours."

"That's true, especially if I know my boy, the way I think I know him."

"Okay," said Beverly, "that's more information than I need to know, but if I can convince someone special to take me home; I could probably make it worth his while."

"Well, I believe that I could make some arrangements for us to have the house to ourselves."

Beverly said, "Oh no, my brother, I'm way ahead of you. I've already arranged for the kids to stay with Mom and Dad and when they get up in the morning they are going to Baja, Mexico, for two days of fun and sun."

"Baby, you're the greatest."

As they embraced, Beverly said, "Okay, let's get the heck out of here." Thomas and Beverly said their goodbyes and goodnights and took off.

They pretty much stayed in the house and enjoyed each other for the next two days. Then, it was back to business. Phil and Lisa were still enjoying their honeymoon on the beaches of Hawaii. Thomas was sitting down in his office, going over some reports and Beverly was sitting down at her desk, on the phone with a local food distributor.

Thomas's phone rang, so he answered it. The voice on the other end said, "Good afternoon, Mr. Dugmal; this is Mike Stone."

Thomas's face lit up and he said, "Hi, Mike, how are things going?"

Mike replied, "Well, Thomas; I wish things were going better."

Thomas asked, "Are the construction plans delayed, or is there a problem with one of the contracts?"

"No, not exactly."

"Okay, so suppose you tell me the purpose of this phone call."

Mike said, "Okay, I will; I'll give it to you straight. I just received a call from Broadwick and Kelley."

Thomas questioned, "And what are they supposed to mean to me?"

"I'll tell you, they are very powerful attorneys. They're a firm, the largest on the West Coast."

"I'm still listening," said Thomas.

Mike went on to say, "Well, I was informed that you had a lawsuit pending that started two years ago and you evaded negotiations to settle out of court and would not cooperate with the firm, changing contact numbers and threatening the life of the plaintiff."

Thomas said, "That is the most ridiculous thing I have ever heard there is no validation to their allegations. The location of my home and business has not changed in the past ten years, why was I not served?"

Mike went on, "Well, you were, in fact, served two years ago; and there are witnesses with documentation to back it up."

"This will have to be proven to me and I have attorneys, as well; I'm sure all of this misunderstanding will be cleared up in no time."

Beverly heard Thomas's tone change on the phone, so she asked the distributor if it would be okay if she called him back later. The distributor said of course, and they hung up. Beverly then got up and went over, and closed and locked the office door. She then pulled the blinds shut. Beverly sat in the leather chair in front of Thomas's desk. Thomas looked at Beverly and shook his head from side to side. She could visibly see Thomas was getting angrier by the moment. He pushed the intercom so Beverly could hear the conversation, but Mike had no way of knowing on the other end.

Mike said, "Thomas, the committee met this morning and it was determined that we can't afford to wait this thing out while in litigation. We don't need the publicity, the press, or the exposure that this thing is capable of bearing."

Thomas asked, "What are you telling me? Come out with it already."

"I thought I made it clear already; we're pulling the contract from you."

Thomas said, "Mike, now I'm losing what little respect that I did have for you. First, you don't even have the common courtesy to ask me to come down to your office to discuss this face to face, let alone ask if any of the allegations are, in fact, correct. Now, you're telling me over the phone that you are pulling the plug on a multi-million dollar deal; have you lost your ever loving mind? Do you think that I'm just going to take this sitting down and not even put up a fight?"

"Thomas, you can do whatever it is you want to do, the fact still remains that you are just another black man in our world trying to get a piece of our pie anyway you can. Now you got caught with your hand in the cookie jar and you have to grow up and be a man for once, 'boy,' and face the consequences."

"You know, Mike, I'm glad I can see your true colors now."

Beverly got Thomas's attention, when she motioned for him with her hands to take it down a couple of levels. Thomas took her advice, took a deep breath, and said, "Mike, twenty-five years ago, I would have been in your office already and you would be explaining to your wife and kids how you as a grown man pissed in your pants. But, I've had enough experience with snakes of your breed. So, I say this to you, I'm down, but I'm not out," and Thomas hung up the phone.

Beverly ran over to the desk and started flipping through the Rolodex, as Thomas said, "Baby, what are you doing?"

Beverly came to the number she's looking for, picked up the phone, and began dialing. She looked at Thomas and said with trepidation, "I'm checking on the account."

"Good idea."

Beverly got the savings and loan and gives them the information needed. The bank told her that all assets had been frozen; Beverly's head dropped.

Thomas said, "Let's get in contact with the attorneys and see what course of action we need to take."

Beverly went through the Rolodex once again and found the attorney's number. As she was dialing, there was a knock on the office door. Thomas got up and went to the door and opened it.

Taria said, "Hi, Mr. D, a man came in with this envelope and said that he needed to give it to you. I told him that I was your daughter and that I could sign for it. So, here it is."

"Thank you, Taria." Thomas took the envelope and closed the door, re-locked it, and went back over to his desk.

By this time, Beverly had gotten in contact with the attorneys and was setting up an appointment to meet with them. Beverly said, "Two days, we don't have two days; we need to meet with you right away." She paused for a moment and said, "Well, how about tonight? I don't care how late it is; we need to meet with you ASAP." There's another pause and she said, "Good, I'll see you at our house at 10:30 P.M. Thank you."

Thomas was working on getting the envelope open, as Beverly asked, "Who is that from?"

Thomas looked at her and said, "It's from the IRS."

"What now?" asked Beverly.

Thomas finally got the envelope open and pulled out a 4-page letter. He began to read it. Beverly waited very patiently for Thomas to finish reading it. Thomas looked over at Beverly and said, "This letter says that the Western Stage Coach Bank has foreclosed on our loan due to false representation on the loan application and false collateral. Now everything we have inside of this facility is going to be confiscated and auctioned off. As of this date, the state has suspended our business license and we are not authorized to open a business."

"This is a setup, Thomas, and I bet I know who's behind it all."

Thomas asked, "Is it who I'm thinking it could be?"

"Honey, I think that we are on the same page."

"Okay," Thomas said, "we'll meet with the attorneys tonight and see what we can do from a legal standpoint."

"You're right, Thomas, we need to calm down and not let this thing consume us."

Thomas said, "Baby, that's why I love you so; you are truly the voice of reason. I'll tell you that weasel Mike Stone knows I could crush him with one hand and it's amazing that he could muster up and use his American Express card for a set of balls and say what he said to me over the phone."

"Thomas, please don't even go there with that fool. He'll get his and you won't have to even lift a finger."

"Yeah, and you know that's right."

Thomas and Beverly went home that evening and when 10:30 came around, the attorneys arrived, as scheduled. Thomas invited them in and he and Beverly laid out for them everything that had transpired. The attorneys looked over the letters from the IRS and after carefully reviewing them, told Thomas and Beverly that everything was covered as far as the legal aspects of the course of action taken by the IRS. Now, the grounds leading up to this was in question.

Beverly asked, "What can we do in the meantime to prevent the business from closing down?"

One of the attorneys stated, "Actually nothing, because when the IRS steps in for an investigation then everything is suspended pending the outcome of the investigation."

Thomas asked, "If we are found innocent of all allegations, will we be able to recoup our losses in our business?"

The attorney answered, "Yes, but not from the IRS; you would be suing the party that was responsible for bringing up the charges."

"You know what, that is messed up!" said Thomas. "For someone to have the ability to just come in and ruin another person's life and have the system on their side backing them up."

One of the attorneys asked, "Who is it that you pissed off so badly and why?"

Beverly answered, "There's no one that we pissed off so badly; this person is operating with a very twisted view on life and is about to get a serious dose of reality."

The attorney said, "Well, here's a list of options for you, but you will have to act swiftly on it because I believe there are quite a few more wheels rolling about right now."

Thomas asked, "What's the worst that could happen right now?"

"The worst would be to shut your business down."

"That doesn't even make sense," Thomas said. "If it shuts down the business, there's no revenue to generate."

The attorney explained, "This person is not looking to see what they can get from you from a monetary standpoint. They're trying to destroy you totally."

"I understand; thank you, gentleman, for making the time to come out. I will be in touch with you, now have a good night," said Thomas.

The two attorneys left and Thomas looked at Beverly and said, "Baby, you know that this means war has been waged?"

Beverly replied, "Yes, I'm afraid it has. What is it that you need me to do?"

"I need you to take the kids tomorrow and you all go and stay with your parents for a little while."

"What's a little while, Thomas?"

"Until I straighten out this madness."

"I want to stay around and fight this thing out with you. My place is by your side and if that means going down with you, then that's just what it means."

Thomas walked over to Beverly and grabbed her, bringing her closer to him, and it turned into an embrace. Thomas's face was cheek to cheek with Beverly's. He whispered, "Baby, I love you more than anything else in this world and you know it. I love my kids more than life itself. But I need for you to be with the kids; it's the only way I can operate the way that I need to and not have to worry about your safety when everything hits the fan, the way that I feel it will." A tear rolled down from the left eye of Thomas, as he kissed her on the cheek, and then a tear rolled down Thomas's right cheek.

Beverly asked, "Baby, is everything going to be alright?"

"Yes, it is," answered Thomas. "This time it's going to be right and even."

Beverly said, "You know, I don't even want to know what's going through your mind."

"Baby, the Marine Corps taught me how to win wars by being smarter than your enemies. Now, it's time to apply general principles."

The next day, Thomas was on the second floor looking at a spin class and Taria came running up to Thomas. "Mr. D, you better come down here fast." Thomas followed Taria, barely keeping up with the youngster. When they arrived on the ground floor level, they walked toward the front door and Beverly was having a heated discussion with deputy sheriffs.

Thomas walked up and said, "What's going on here?"

Beverly looked at Thomas and said, "These guys say that they have a court order to remove everything in this gym into those moving vans."

Thomas surveyed the scene and saw that there were four deputy sheriffs standing there. One of the deputies had a piece of paper in his hand holding it up. Thomas looked at the deputy and said, "Frank, is that you?"

The deputy smiled and said, "Yes, Thomas, it is me; how the hell are you doing?"

Thomas answered, "Well, Frank, I've seen better days, I can tell you that."

Frank said, "Thomas, can I talk to you in private for a moment?"

"Of course, let's go into my office." Thomas looked at Beverly and said, "Baby, I'll be right back. Can you please keep things together for a few?"

"Whatever you say, baby."

Thomas walked back to his office with Frank. They got into his office and Thomas said, "What's up, man?"

"Brother," said Frank, "I know that we served on the force together and I love you like a brother, but I have court orders to shut you down and remove everything you have in here. I have to do my job; I have no other choice. What I would be willing to do is allow you to take out of here whatever you want; I won't be looking, so I didn't see anything. Thomas, I don't know what the hell happened here, but whatever I can do for you, just let me know."

Thomas responded, "No, I can handle this one all by my lonesome. But, if you would, please let me gather my staff together so we can get all of the customers out, and then allow me to explain to the staff that we will be closing for a brief period, before the movers clear the place out."

Frank said, "Of course, take as much time as you need, Thomas; I'll have my men back off until you're ready for us."

"Thanks, bro'."

Thomas asked his staff to have the customers leave and then assembled a meeting. It was explained to the staff that the gym had to be closed due to some violations of safety codes by the city. The staff understood, and then Phil walked in.

Thomas said to Phil, "Just back my play, bro'."

"Cool."

They waited until all of the staff had left and Thomas called in Frank. He told Frank to begin and try to handle everything as fast as possible.

Thomas said to Phil, "Let me fill you in on what's going on."

After Thomas had filled Phil in on the happenings, Phil said, "Shit, this really pisses me off; I want to kick somebody's ass bad."

"Hold it down, bro'. We'll talk later, you understand?"

"Roger that," replied Phil.

It took every bit of five and a half hours to completely clear out the gym. Thomas looked around and said, "We'll be back, I promise you that."

Beverly could not help but let the tears flow. Phil walked over and embraced her and he allowed a stream to release.

Thomas looked around and said, "Let's get the hell up out of here."

As they walked out to the parking lot, Frank walked over to Thomas and said, "I have to put this notice on the window portion of the door and lock it with this chain and lock. Now, I took the liberty of making an extra key, so here you are," as he handed Thomas the extra key.

"You are truly a friend, Frank."

"Just don't let anyone know how close we are; remember, I'm a cop and my first duty is the job."

Thomas smiled and said, "Yeah, right." Thomas turned around and grabbed Beverly by the hand and said, "Baby, we have a lot of work to do and not a whole lot of time to do it in."

Beverly said, "Whatever that means, I do have your back."

Thomas looked at Phil and said, "Meet me at my place at 2000 hours."

Phil replied, "Ten-four."

Thomas asked Beverly to pack her things for a long-term stay at her parents' house; they only needed to get a few things for the kids because they had quite a bit of clothing at her parents' house already.

Thomas and Beverly got home and the kids were already there, running up to them to greet them in a happy fashion as always, but then again, they did not know what was going on at the time; however, they would soon find out. After Thomas and Beverly had finished with all of the greetings, Beverly said, "Okay, you young ones, we need to have a family meeting."

Tina (the younger girl) asked, "Aren't we going to eat first?"

Thomas answered, "No, baby girl, we need to have the family meeting first, then we'll get something to eat."

Beverly said, "Okay, everyone report to the family room." The whole family scampered to the family room and grabbed a seat and waited for the meeting to begin. Beverly looked at Thomas and said, "Honey, you start the meeting off."

Thomas said, "Very well. Okay kids, we have discussed before that when anything happens to us or with a family member then the whole family gets involved. We, our family, are one. I would like to start off by telling you that something went down with me and someone else, who was not in our family and I got involved with that person, which was a mistake. Your mom and I have had discussions about this and after sometime, we are on the same page. I'm not saying that it lets me off the hook, concerning getting involved in something that I should have not gotten involved in, but we all as humans make mistakes. I've made amends with your mom and now I'm making amends with you guys. I wish that I had the time to go into full details about the situation with you guys, but we just don't have the time. Now, I will say this, we are going to have to split up for a while."

Melvin shouted out, "What's a while, Dad? I don't want you to leave us!"

Elijah said, "Hey, Dad, you have been there for me, ever since I can re-member, and I would like to be there for you."

Beverly looked at Thomas and said, "Honey, can I butt in for just a second."

"Yes, of course, baby."

Beverly said, "You guys look, I want you to listen very carefully. Please understand this, your dad and I am not splitting up or anything close to that. What we are trying to tell you is that this whole thing has been blown out of proportion by a third party and something's that aren't so nice are going down. Your dad and I feel that we are not as safe here as we should be, so until your dad clears everything up, we have to hang out at your grandparents' house for a short spell. Now, I will be staying there, as well, and Dad will check up on us as often as he can."

Elizabeth asked, "How much time do we have to get ready? Because I get the notion that we should be in a hurry right now."

Beverly said, "You're right, baby girl; we need to pack now and leave. So, pack whatever you can in one suitcase and we have to go."

Elijah said, "I believe I understand what you're talking about and I just want to let you know that we have your back, Dad."

Thomas smiled and said, "I love all of you, but please trust me on this one; what I need for you to do is to stay safe. The only way that I know for sure that will happen is if you're not around me. I need to be able to operate without worrying about my family's safety. I promise as soon as this has blown over, we all will reunite and be a complete family again. Can I count on each and every one of you to do that?" he asked.

Everyone answered 'yes.'

Thomas felt a sense of relief at that point. Beverly told everyone to start packing and that they would reassemble in 30 minutes. Beverly headed toward her bedroom and Thomas followed. When they got to the bedroom, Beverly said, "You know I don't like this."

Thomas said, "Baby, I don't either, but for right now, this is how we have to do it and we don't have time to debate this."

"I know, but you better stay in touch and you had better not get yourself into any deeper trouble."

"You know that I will go one better than that; I will work it out so that all of our troubles and worries will disappear forever," assured Thomas.

"I don't know if I want to know what that means, but you go on ahead and do your thing."

Thomas looked Beverly in the eye and said, "Baby, if you've ever trusted me in the past, I need for you to reach down inside and trust me this time like you never have before. I'm telling you, I've got this one."

"Okay, Thomas, I'm going to trust you 100 percent; just let me know whatever it is you want me to do."

Thomas said, "I'm meeting with a couple of business associates at 2000 hours, so we need to step on it so I can get you guys out of here and get some grub, so I can get back."

"Let me go check on the kids; could you take my two suitcases down for me?"

Thomas went to grab the two suitcases and noticed that there were three more bags, as well, to go down. He just shook his head and picked up the suitcases first, and thought, *I'll just come back on a second and a third trip to retrieve the remaining bags.*

Everyone was downstairs standing by for further direction with bag in hand. Thomas shouted, "Elizabeth!"

She answered, "Yes, Dad."

Thomas said, "You're driving your car."

Elizabeth replied, "Yes, Dad."

Thomas said to Beverly, "Baby, I want you to take your vehicle, as well; I don't want any funny business going on and I want to keep people guessing."

"That's fine with me, but we're still going to need the space in your truck."

"Not a problem; I've already loaded you things."

"Okay," said Beverly, "well, let's get going."

Everyone began leaving and heading toward their perspective assigned vehicles as if it was rehearsed. Thomas and the family went out to a restaurant and dined together, and discussed communication plans, and when and when not to use landlines as opposed to cellular communication or hardwire. Everyone was of the same accord and fully understood the drill.

After dinner, they all drove over to Beverly's parents' home. Thomas felt safe enough there because her parents lived in a gated community—very remote and reserved. Security was present; however, if someone wanted to get in without being known, it would not be impossible, but very difficult to do so.

As they drove up to the turnaround area in the front of the house, Beverly's parents came out of the front door to meet them. Beverly's dad said, "You guys unload and I'll pull the cars into the back garage."

Thomas said, "I'll help you."

After everyone had gotten settled in and all the vehicles were put away, Thomas looked at his watch and discovered that it was 1935 already and said, "I really have to run."

Beverly's dad said, "Thomas, you be careful out there. I know that you are capable of taking care of yourself, but one slip up and it could be your last."

"Thanks for the heads up, Dad; I will be careful."

Thomas gave hugs and kisses to the young ones and Beverly said, "Honey, I'll walk you to the truck." When they got to the driver's side door, everyone else's view was obstructed. Beverly put her arms around Thomas and embraced him with a tight grip and said, "You had better come back to me."

"I'm coming back, baby. I have already thought this thing out and plans are drawn up." He opened the front door, reached into the console storage compartment, and pulled out a manila envelope. "Baby, take this; there are instructions on what you need to do. Now I want you to follow these directions to the letter. Everything you need is in here—plans, money, credit cards, birth certificates, passports—everything. Please, when you are alone, go over this, and then go over it again until you have it down solid. This is very important, do you understand?"

"Yes, I do understand, Thomas."

"Do not let anyone else see this envelope or know that you have it, please baby."

"Don't worry," said Beverly, as she tucked the envelope into her pants and covered it up with her sweater top.

Thomas said, "Now, I have to run, but I will call you in the morning."

"I'll be expecting to hear from you."

He kissed Beverly on the lips and she received a cold chill that resembled a last goodbye. However, she reserved revealing her true feelings to Thomas.

Thomas gave another wave to the family and jumped into his truck and took off. He had fifteen minutes to make it home before 2000 hours, so Thomas pretty much put the pedal to the metal and made the rubber hit the road.

When Thomas arrived at his house, he found Phil and the rest of the gang already there and waiting for him. Thomas pulled up, got out, and said, "You guys made it with one minute and eighteen seconds to spare."

Phil said, "The last thing we're going to be is late for you, Sarge."

Thomas laughed and said, "Let's go inside and rap for a spell."

They went into the den where Thomas pulled out a fifth of Jack Daniels Single Barrel and seven glasses. The men sat around where they could see each other and Thomas, as well. Phil picked up the bottle of Jack and said, "Here's to the good old days all over again," as he poured all seven glasses close to half full.

All the men lifted up their glasses and said, "Here, here, to the good old days all over again, oorah."

Thomas put his glass down and said, "What I'm about to share with you men will be sacred and requires an oath, the same as we took back in the thick of the jungles. We have to swear on our lives the code of silence and honor."

All of the men put their glasses down, stood up, and began to receive the code of honor. Then they sat down.

Thomas said, "First, I would like to fill you guys in on what this is all about. I will not give you a sob story about how I banged Suzie's rotten crotch and moved on. It's not about who got my sister pregnant and ran away or who shot my dad. This is about an honest person going through life, trying to make a decent living the best way that he knows how. All of a sudden, the bottom fell out; the big man decided that he wanted to put his foot on the little man and crush him, degrade him and his family, and figured the little man is powerless and can do nothing to stop him. Well, my friends, in the words of a great Japanese leader, 'they have awakened a gentle giant.'

"Now, I would like to reveal to you a plan, but before I do, I want to inform you all that you will be taking a risk, a risk that may not allow you to make it back safe...or at all." Thomas continued, "I love all of you like brother; hell, we are brothers. You Upchurch, Drew, Jackson, Toliver, Johnson, and Ortiz...each and every one of you have been through the thick of it and know what it is to go to hell and back. I'll give you the opportunity to say 'no, I would not like to take on this mission'." Thomas added, "To those who choose not to participate for whatever reason, I will understand and will not hold it personally against anyone. So what say thee, marines?"

Phil said, "You know, I'm in."

Ortiz said, "I'm in."

"You can count me in, as well," said Johnson.

Toliver said, "I'm in alright, but I know you, Sarge...."

Thomas said, "Well yes, Toliver, there is something in it for all of you. I actually was going to cover that next, once I learned who was in or out. But since everyone is in and we have our whole team, then we can proceed."

Thomas, in short, filled the guys in on what went down, or as close to the account as possible, then revealed the plan. Thomas said, "Everyone said that they were down with this, so there is no backing out now. We are going to hit a bank."

Phil said, "A bank? Man, what's up with that?"

"It's not just any bank," said Thomas, "it's going to be Western Stage Coach Bank."

"Why Western Stage Coach?" questioned Toliver.

"I'm glad that you asked. For starters, it's the bank that shut me down and put me out of the mix. Another reason that turns into opportunity is the fact that, on a certain day, the US Treasury will go through a transition and all of the monies that normally get put away with them and distributed to other institutions, will use this particular branch as a holding place."

Jackson asked, "But Sarge, once the money is in place there, then that place is going to be guarded like Fort Knox."

Thomas answered, "All of that has been taken into account."

"Then what the hell are we going to do," asked Jackson, "after the money is in place?"

"First, we're not going to wait until the monies are in place. That bank has an extremely large holding and storage facility. It has lock down capability of Level 5."

Ortiz said, "Level 5...we can blow up the building and still not get through a Level 5."

"Yes, that's right," agreed Thomas.

Phil looked at the rest of the group. Jackson looked back at Phil and asked, "Man, aren't you curious as to how we are going to even get through a Level 5 security area?"

Phil laughed and then said, "You guys must have forgotten how Thomas operates; I'm just waiting for him to fill us in on how we are going to do this thing, not if we can pull it off."

The men refocused on Thomas. "Now that I have everyone's ear...the plan is to hit them in the process of their delivery. What's going to happen is the bank will use armored carriers, a company called Stage Coach Armored Transport, SCAT for short. They are coming in six armored transport vehicles, scheduled for two at a time, ten minutes apart. That means as soon as two are unloaded, two more will pull up and begin unloading. That gives us 30 minutes to play with in the meantime."

Drew asked, "If we're waiting for all trucks to unload, how do we get the time to hit all six trucks?"

"This is where things are going to get interesting. They will still be in the process of transferring the bins from the trucks and into the vaults to the staging area. We will have men inside, removing the bricks of cash and loading them onto our retractable conveyer that will be ready to spring into action after the last truck has unloaded and taken off."

Phil said, "So, just in the event that a silent alarm is tripped, will we have the streets covered?"

"Yes, the streets will be completely covered. I'm bringing in additional help."

Ortiz shouted, out, "I'm not down with outsiders; they can't be trusted!"

"I agree," said Johnson, "plus, they will cut into our share of the take."

Thomas replied, "These outsiders are totally necessary; I assure you we cannot get by without them."

Phil said, "We will not question you, Sarge, so we are going to trust you 100 percent; just tell us exactly what we need to do."

"We're going to have another meeting the day after tomorrow, 2000 hours, and everyone involved will be present. One other thing, so I don't fail to mention it...I just saved the best for last. Each one of those bins will have $250 million in it, each truck will have a total of four bins; would one of you like to do the math?"

Drew stood up and said, "Thomas, you are the man," and sat back down.

Jackson asked, "Sarge, what are our chances realistically of pulling this one off and making it back home to our families?"

Thomas answered, "Honestly, brother, some of us may not make it home. My plan is to pull this off, this one time; the monies will be stored in a safe zone that no one knows except me and God. As I always have, I will be looking out for everyone's safety and welfare. If we operate as a unit and execute this plan to the 'T,' we have a damn good chance of making it out unscathed. Now, I'm hoping that we will not have to take the lives of those that are from our own American soil, but if it comes down to them or us, then we cannot for one instant hesitate to eliminate the threat factor, and I want that to be perfectly clear. Does everyone understand what I'm saying?"

All of the six men answered in unison, "Yes, sir."

Thomas said, "Now, the day after tomorrow when we meet, we will take sizes for vests and some other special items that we will use. Now, if no one has anything else..." As he looked around the room to see if any of the men were going to respond, Thomas continued, "Well, if nothing else...I'll see everyone day after tomorrow and I just want to make sure that it's clearly understood...this will not be discussed with anyone, including your wives."

All of the men nodded in agreement. Thomas walked everyone to the door and they all say their goodbyes. Phil hung back. When Thomas closed the front door, he walked back to the den. Phil had already poured himself and Thomas another drink and was holding up a glass in his hand for Thomas to take.

Thomas asked, "What's this?"

"Man, this thing is going to work and we are going to be rich as a son of a bitch."

Thomas smiled and said, "Yes, we are, but we're going to have to be smart, as well."

Phil asked, "Are we going to have to leave the states? Or the country?"

"No, because none of us are going to be a suspect."

"And, how in the hell not?" asked Phil.

"I wish I could tell you now, Phil, but trust me; you'll know why when the time comes."

Phil said, "Okay, cool. Oh, by the way, bro', I'm staying over tonight, so I'm going to have another drink."

Thomas replied, "Hey, man, you know it's not a problem."

"I'm going to get with Lisa tomorrow and let her know that I have a special project and I'll be going out of town for a couple of days, so if she says anything to you about it, we'll be on the same page."

"Okay," said Thomas, "but where are you telling her you're going?"

Phil thought for a moment and said, "Aspen, Colorado."

Thomas laughed and asked, "How in the heck did you come up with Aspen, Colorado? There are no black people there."

Phil said, "Well, I'm not going there to see any black people," and they both had to share a laugh. Thomas and Phil shared a few more laughs and a couple more drinks and then turned in for the night. The next day Phil got up, got cleaned up, and headed out to meet with Lisa.

The following day, Phil arrived at Thomas's house about 1730 hours. Thomas was talking on the phone to Beverly and the kids. Thomas let Phil into the house and they shook hands. Phil headed toward the den and said, "I'm going to pour me one, do you want one, too?"

Thomas said, "Yes, please, pour me a short one. I still need to jump into the shower and get ready."

"Cool," replied Phil.

Thomas finished up with his conversation with the family and got off the phone and went into the den where Phil was.

Phil said, "What's up, man?"

Thomas replied, "Holding it down, brother; what's going on with you?"

"You know, I'm just trying to get mine, like you got yours."

Thomas smiled and said, "Well, if you want mine, then you're in trouble." They both laughed.

"Here, man," said Phil, as he handed Thomas the glass of spirits that he poured for him.

Thomas said, "I'm going to down this and then I'm going to run upstairs and shower up. I hit it pretty hard in the gym."

"That's cool," Phil replied, "I'm just going to chill here and watch the San Antonio Spurs and Denver Nuggets game on your big screen," referring to Thomas's 72-inch plasma HD.

After Thomas got cleaned up and dressed, he came back to the den and asked Phil, "What's the score?"

"There's two and a half minutes left in the fourth period and San Antonio is ahead by 12 points."

Thomas said, "Now that's what I'm talking about."

It was 1930 hours and the doorbell rang. Thomas said, "Hey, bro', I'm expecting some guests, can you let them in?"

"Sure, bro', but who is it?"

"It should be Donald Morris with three other people," answered Thomas.

Phil said, "I'm on it." When he got to the door, sure enough, four people stood tall. Phil asked, "How may I help you?"

The gentleman, standing 6' tall, answered in a very stern voice, "Good evening, my name is Donald Morris, but please call me Don."

Phil extended his hand and said, "Pleased to meet you, Don," and they shook hands.

Don said, "These three gentlemen are my cohorts—Peter Taylor, Randy Favor, and Ralph Downs."

Phil shook each of their hands and invited them in. He said, "Follow me, Thomas is expecting you."

They all followed Phil into the den area, where Thomas was gathering up some papers, and placing them in order.

Phil said, "Hey, Sarge, your guests have arrived."

Thomas looked up and smiled and said, "Hey, Don, how are you doing, man?"

Don returned the smile and the two embraced. He then said, "I want you to meet my partners." Don introduced the three partners to Thomas and Thomas invited everyone to have a seat.

Thomas's den was very large; he would host parties and his den would accommodate his party guests with the help of the patio doors leading to the pool area out back.

Phil went out through the patio door and to the storage shed to get some folding chairs and bring them in. Phil asked Thomas, "Should I get any more chairs?"

"Yes, I believe that we'll need a few more."

Phil went back out to the shed and grabbed more chairs. Phil then went up to Thomas and said, "Man, who are these guys?"

Thomas answered, "You'll find out soon enough, brother," with a grin on his face.

At 1945 hours, the doorbell rang again. Phil said, "You want me to get it?"

"No, I got it," Thomas said, as he went to the door and opened it.

His guests this time were two of the drivers, Mitchell Payne and Lester Young. Mitchell shouted out, "Hey, Thomas, how in the hell have you been?"

Thomas walked toward Mitchell and said, "Man, I've been good, what about you?"

As they embraced, Mitchell said, "Man, I owe you so much; I owe you my life. When you called me, I told you whatever it was you needed me to do, then just say it and it shall be done."

Thomas said, "Great, man; come on in."

Mitchell said, "I want you to meet my buddy; you can trust him with your life."

"That's exactly what I need, people that I can trust."

Before Thomas could close the door, the rest of the boys from C Company were arriving, so Thomas just left the door ajar so they could let themselves in. The whole crew came in and started introducing themselves to one another. When everyone had finished with the introductions, Thomas said, "Can everyone please take a seat?"

After everyone was seated, Thomas said, "I would like to thank all of you guys for coming out tonight. I believe we all know why we're here, so I'll cut right to the chase. We are working on a payday. I have put together some material for you to review and lock into memory."

Thomas passed out a three-page detailed note for each individual to read. Thomas waited until everyone had a copy and said, "On the first page, you'll see the date for the job and everyone's name in place where they fit in and what their job entails. I need for all of you to lock this into memory. If you turn to the second page, you'll see the map and routes; you will follow these routes to the letter without detouring. If at any time you forget something and can't remember the route or street or time, then you get on the radio and ask for a update, but you will do this right away without delay. Remember, every man and woman will be counting on each other, and what each one does. Success depends on each one of us being on time and on the mark. If anything goes wrong, it could cost one of us, or a few of us our lives. If one of you fails to follow instructions because you failed to get the proper amount of rest or had a drink before the job or any type of mind altering substance, then you are going to be in a world of shit because we will have no, I repeat, no margin for error. If you don't die from any of our unfriendlies and cause one of your own to perish, then I will not threaten you with sudden death, I promise you that I will end your life as you know it in half a heartbeat. Does anyone have a problem with this?"

No one said anything; the attention was on Thomas, and if someone fired off a round, the attention would have still been on Thomas.

Thomas continued, "No one spoke up, so I'm going to take it that no one has any problems with this. Now, my next question is, does everyone understand what is expected of them? This will require a response of, 'Yes, sir.'"

Everyone shouted out at the same time, as if they had rehearsed it, "Yes, sir!"

"Very well then, now if you will turn to the last page. There you will see some numbers. These numbers represent what our payoff will be. It's broken down to what we will be taking in, what it will cost us in expense to operate, and then what each of us will have to take home in payoff. Does anyone have any questions concerning this?"

No one said anything.

Thomas said, "Very well, then. If everyone would review the paperwork and lock it into memory, I'll give you 30 minutes to study, and then I will be collecting the paperwork back from you." Thomas looked over at Don Morris and said, "Don, I need to see you and your crew."

Don said, "Right away," and called over to his crew and told them, "Follow me."

Thomas led them out the patio door and into the clubhouse in the backyard. Thomas told Don to come on in and have a seat. Thomas said, "So, Don, what do you think? You think you can pull this thing off?"

Don said, "I believe, I can." Don turned around and asked his crew, "Did you guys size everybody up and get an idea of what you could do with each individual?"

Pete answered, "Yes, we got a good chance to size everyone up."

"Yes," said Randy, "we pretty much know what we will do; this will work."

Thomas said, "Very well then, Don, I will contact you with more details. Now you have approximately eight days to get everything ready."

"That's just enough time," replied Don, "I'll be ready."

"Okay, I'll call you in five days. What I need for you to do is go around the side and use the side of the house to get to the front."

Don said, "Man, I don't understand, but whatever you say, you're the man."

Thomas said, "Make sure you go on the left side because the dogs are on the right side and they might not understand."

Don, with his eyes wide open and eyebrow lifted, said, "Thanks for that important information."

So, they took off.

Thomas went back into the house and was met by Phil, who asked, "Hey, bro', where are the other guys?"

Thomas said, "Man, keep your voice down and come with me." Phil followed Thomas into the living room. They stopped and Thomas turned around and shut the door. He looked at Phil and said, "Man, keep this completely under your hat. Those were my special project people; we need an edge and they are going to provide it for us."

Phil's said with a smile on his face, "Man, you are a genius, I tell you."

"Wait until we have pulled this off successfully before you give me that label."

"I now if you masterminded this," replied Phil, "then we can pull this off."

Thomas said, "The 30 minutes are up. We need to collect all of the paperwork that we passed out and make sure all of them are accounted for. I cannot afford to have this information out in circulation."

"It's done, bro'; I'll go and get them right away."

Thomas and Phil walked back into the den; Thomas cleared his throat and said in a loud and very distinctive voice, "The 30 minutes are up; please return the handouts back to Phil."

Phil walked around and collected all of the handouts. Thomas asked Phil, "Do we have all twelve copies?"

Phil said, "No, sir, I count eleven copies."

"Please recount."

Phil recounted and said, "I still come up with eleven copies."

Thomas said, "The last thing that I want to find out is that I cannot trust someone. I have one copy of the plans missing; so being the man that I am, I will allow the person that is attempting to steal from me amnesty for 30 seconds. After 30 seconds, I can only promise that you will learn that if you try and fuck me, the penalty will be more severe than you can imagine."

Johnson said, "Hey, Sarge, what happened to those other four guys? Did we collect the paperwork from them?"

Thomas said, "I personally collected their copies."

Phil looked over at Mitchell and then at Lester. He noticed that Lester was sweating. Phil said, "Mitchell, are you sure that you turned your copy in?"

Mitchell answered, "Yes, I'm positive."

Phil asked Company C; all of the boys in Company C stood up at the same time. Phil asked, "You boys turn everything in?"

All of them answered, "Sir, yes sir."

Phil said, "At ease," and they all sat down.

Thomas said, "Okay, 30 seconds are up. I now know that we have amongst us an unfriendly. I said in the beginning, I need people that I can trust. Jackson!" Thomas shouted.

Jackson returned to his feet. "Yes, sir."

Thomas said, "Come over here."

Jackson walked over to Thomas and stood in front of him. Thomas said, "With no loyalty there's no trust, and with no trust there's no bond, and with no bond there's no reasoning. If you can't reason with a man, what's left?"

"Death, sir," replied Jackson.

Thomas asked Jackson, "And how do we narrow things down?"

Jackson answered, "We look for the obvious."

Thomas reached under the desk and pulled out a pistol, Sig .40-caliber. He pushed the magazine release and let the magazine fall into his left hand. He inspected the magazine and saw that it was filled with rounds. He then slipped the magazine back into the magazine wall. He turned the pistol around and handed Jackson the weapon with the butt end first.

Jackson took the pistol from him and stood there.

Thomas asked, "Would you say that I handed you a loaded weapon?"

Jackson inspected the weapon and made sure it was loaded, and then answered Thomas. "Yes, sir; I would say that this weapon is loaded."

"Now, we have a traitor within, a turncoat, if you will, a Benedict Arnold…and now we'll have to go by the proper process of elimination."

Mitchell stood up and said, "Come on, Thomas; the last copy could have been thrown out, or misplaced, or anything like that."

Thomas looked at Mitchell and said, "I strongly suggest that you sit down and learn something." Thomas looked over at Lester and said, "Stand up."

Lester shouted out, "Hey, man, I didn't do anything, so don't get any bright ideas!"

Thomas said, "Jackson," and Jackson ran over and said, "What is it, Sarge?"

Thomas said, "Have this man strip down."

Jackson asked, "You mean make him strip down to his underwear?"

Thomas answered, "No, I mean make him strip all the way down."

Mitchell said, "This makes no sense at all. I have done nothing."

"Well, if you haven't done anything wrong," said Thomas, "then you have nothing to worry about, now do you?"

Mitchell said, "You're not going to find anything on me."

Thomas replied, "Now, it's time to stop talking and do as you're told."

Lester looked at Mitchell and said, "Well?"

Mitchell said, "Well what?"

"You brought me into this," Lester said, "now you have to help me."
Mitchell said, "Hey, buddy, you're on your own, just as I am."
This time Jackson said, "Shut up and strip down."
Lester began to strip down slowly.

"You have ten seconds to be completely naked," warned Jackson.

Lester took his shirt off, then his tee-shirt. He began to take off his pants and, as he unbuckled his belt, he hesitated.

Jackson noticed, once again, that Lester was sweating. Now it was running down the side of both his right and left temples.

Mitchell noticed Lester and his heart began racing. The thought of Lester trying to steal the plans from Thomas was going through his head. The thought also was that if Lester was stupid enough to attempt this, would Thomas believe that he was involved, as well.

As Lester began to release his pants, he looked at Jackson and said, "Hey, man, I'm sorry; I didn't think it was this serious."

Jackson told him to shut up and strip.

Lester again pleaded with Jackson, "Come on, man." Now Lester's eyes began to fill with water. As his pants hit the floor, the copies of the plans fell down from behind him. Lester began to plead for his life. "Please, I was just kidding; it's not worth killing me over."

Thomas said, "Shut up, now: I gave you a chance for amnesty, so it's too late. Now sit your ass down." Lester followed his orders.

Thomas said, "Looks like this concludes our meeting, Mitchell."

"Do we go as planned?" asked Mitchell.

Thomas answered, "Yes, we do. I'll supply another driver, and I'll be in contact with you. Now you can leave."

"Very well then," said Mitchell, "and you're sure we're cool?"

Thomas said, "Yes, we're cool."

Mitchell replied, "Okay, I'll wait for your call," then Mitchell headed toward the front door with Phil following behind. When they got to the door, Mitchell hesitated and Phil walked past him and opened the door. Mitchell asked, "Do you know what's going to happen to Lester?"

Phil looked at him and gave him the thousand-yard stare. The thousand-yard stare is a look that you develop when you've been in combat and have been in a position that you're looking death in the face, and come to the realization that you are going to kill or be killed, and whatever comes first, you accept it.

When Mitchell saw that Phil was giving him the stare, an ice-cold chill ran through his body, starting at his feet, moving upwards to his stomach, and stopping when it got to his brain. Mitchell had never experienced this feeling in his life, but there was no question that he would not ever see Lester again. Mitchell did not ask any more questions; he turned around and started walking toward his car. Mitchell had all kinds of thoughts running through his mind. *Why was Lester so stupid? Did he really think that Thomas would not figure out who took a copy of the plans? Well, with all of that said, I think that I'm lucky that I was not implicated; that's all I care about.* So, he jumped into his car and took off.

Phil closed the door and walked back to the den where everyone else was. Phil looked over at Thomas and said, "He's gone; are you sure Mitchell is okay? I mean is he cool?"

Thomas answered, "Man, I'll tell you, Mitchell knows that I'm all about business and the only thing that you have to do is stay on my good side and not cross me."

Phil said, "Man, I heard that."

Jackson asks Thomas, "Just let me know what we're going to do with this lowlife scum of the earth."

Thomas said, "Let's go downstairs to the basement."

The crew got up and went downstairs. Jackson led Lester in the same direction. Once there, Thomas instructed Jackson to bring Lester over to where he was.

Thomas said, "If your intentions were to steal from me, so that you could possibly use these plans for yourself or, perhaps, sell them to someone else or, maybe, just double cross me...I just want to let you know before you die that I do not take anything personal. I know that everything is business. Now, just to show you that even when you try to gaft me, I'm still a fair man, I offer you this. If your constitution and will to live are strong enough, then you will be allowed to walk up out of here a free man, debt paid in full. You just have to promise me that you will leave town and never return."

Lester shouted out in excitement, "Yes, sir; I swear on my mother's grave twice over, I'll leave and never come back if you let me go!"

"Not so fast there, quick draw. I did say it's up to you and how bad you want to live."

Lester said, "I want to live," as tears started to stream from his eyes, "I want to live."

Thomas replied, "Okay, we'll see." Thomas instructed Johnson and Ortiz to load up the bench, so they both went over to the bench press and began putting 45-pound plates on both ends of the bar bell.

They put four on both ends and Ortiz looked over at Thomas and asked, "Is this enough, boss, or do you want more?"

Thomas answered, "I want six wheels on each side."

"Hot damn," remarked Johnson, "this boy better want to live pretty bad," as they continued to load the two additional plates.

Thomas said, "Lester, take your shirt off, but leave you tee shirt on." Lester complied.

Jackson said, "Hey, Sarge; I'm not dumb or anything like that, but how much weight is that anyway?"

"It's not that much," Thomas replied. "It's not that much...it's only 585 pounds."

Phil said, "Good Lord, that a lot of weight!"

"Hey, bro'," said Toliver, "better you than me; now get on the bench, so we can see how bad you want to live."

Ortiz and Toliver grabbed Lester by his arms and led him to the bench.

Lester said, "Hey, man, that's too much weight; please give me a break?"

Thomas taunted, "You best shut up and save your strength for the Iron Challenge."

The rest of the boys shared a laugh. Lester tried to resist going to the bench, but Ortiz and Toliver's grip were too much for Lester to break free. They forced Lester down on the bench on his back. Lester began to plead for his life, once again.

Thomas looked at him and said, "Man, greed has taken more lives from man than any cancer or wars known. You gambled and lost; now you have a chance to live; remember I gave you a second chance, when you get a chance to reminisce in hell. Now lift."

Ortiz lifted one end the barbell and Toliver lifted the other end. Lester grabbed the bar and shouted out, "Please, I don't want to die!"

Thomas said, "Well, prove it!"

Toliver looked at Ortiz and said, "On three..."

Lester tried to brace himself as the bar was directly over the top of his chest.

Ortiz said, "Three, two, one...," and they both let go of the bar.

Lester gritted his teeth so hard he shattered three of them. The bar stayed up for two and a half seconds and Lester shouted out, "Ahhh!" as the bar came smashing down on the top of his breast plate. The sound of cracking bones echoed throughout the basement. Lester's hands fell to his sides helplessly and his head turned to the left.

Thomas said, "Lift the bar off of him."

Ortiz and Toliver did so and then re-racked the barbell. Toliver asked, "What should we do with the body?"

Thomas said, "Leave him there."

Jackson responded, "Leave him?"

"Yes," replied Thomas, "the man had an accident and we don't want to further injure him."

"Oh yeah, that's right," said Jackson.

Phil asked, "What now?"

Thomas said, "Now we finish our meeting."

"Do we have to stay down here with this dead fool?" asked Phil.

Thomas laughed and answered, "No, we can go back upstairs." They walked back up the stairs and reassembled in the den.

Thomas asked Ortiz, "Do you still have connections for arms?"

"Yes, sir."

"Okay," said Thomas, "then prepare to copy."

Ortiz took out a pen and pad and said, "I'm ready."

Thomas said, "Okay...I want one M-60 with the tripod, 2 m 0 magazines..."

Ortiz asked, "What model .60-cal. do you want?"

"I want the Dillon Precision mini gun."

Ortiz's eyes got big and looked over at Jackson. Jackson looked at Ortiz and nodded his head up and down in agreement. Ortiz wrote the request down, then looked up at Thomas and said, "Please continue, sir."

"We need four sets of 15 street spikes, and ten M-2 gas masks. We need twenty sets of Level III armor plates, two paint guns with red paintballs, six Level III ballistic shields...and make sure there are body bunkers. We need ten flash bangs, two remote signal scanners, and two remote cell phone blockers. We will need to get down to city hall and get the blueprints of the building plans. I want the exact square footage of that place. We need an operations plan drawn up with the number of cameras and the type of system, monitoring, and surveillance." Thomas said, "Drew."

Drew answered up, "Sir."

Thomas said, "When we have the dimensions for the target, I want you to locate a remote spot and set up a mock training center, so we can use it as a practice site."

Drew said, "Yes, sir; as soon as we gather their intel."

Thomas said, "Okay, Ortiz, you have one day to obtain this information."

"Yes, sir; that's all I need," Ortiz replied.

Thomas said, "Okay, I want Ortiz and Drew to team up; you're Team 2. Jackson and Toliver, you're Team 3. Johnson, you'll team up with me and Upchurch and your ID code is One Alpha. Gentlemen, remember, you will see other personnel that will work with you and we need to stay in communication by codes only. Does everyone understand their mission?"

The team responded, "Yes, sir," all in unison.

Thomas asked, "Are there any questions?" As Thomas scanned the room, looking at each team member, everyone nodded their head from side to side, indicating 'no.' Thomas said, "Well, that concludes this meeting. I want to hear from everyone with details of the operation by tomorrow at 1530 hours. Everyone is dismissed except for Phil and Sonnie."

The rest of the crew left the house and headed for their vehicles. Phil looked at Thomas and asked, "Man, what in the hell are we going to do with this dead body?"

Sonnie asked, "Do you want me to get rid of the body?"

"No, we are going to do this the right way. We were throwing up the weights and Lester was benching, I was on the lateral pull down across the room, and Phil was on the preacher curl bench. We both heard 'help' and then crunch. Sonnie had just come down the stairs from using the bathroom and saw us taking the barbells off of Lester. I examined Lester briefly and it was apparent that his neck was broken because he was extremely limp. I instructed Sonnie to go and call 911, which he did so we just waited for the response team to arrive."

Sonnie said, "That's exactly how I remember it, so I'm on the phone with emergency services." So Sonnie made the call and got an ETA. He hung up and went over to Thomas and said, "They will be here in approximately twelve minutes."

Thomas said, "Cool, I'll go upstairs and be on the lookout for them."

"Man, you want us to stay down here with this dead mother fucker even longer?" asked Phil.

Thomas laughed and said, "Man, you weren't afraid of him when he was alive, so why are you afraid of him now?"

Sonnie laughed and said, "Man, I'll stay down here with you," then Phil looked over and said, "Fuck you, man." They all laughed.

Thomas said, "Let's just keep this simple and it will play itself out."

"I got it," said Phil.

Sonnie said, "I got it."

Thomas went up the stairs and waited for the emergency response team to arrive. They arrived there after four minutes and Thomas let them in and led them down the stairs to the basement area where the gym was located.

The two paramedics immediately went to work on Lester's limp body. They transferred him from the bench to the floor and began taking his vitals. One of the paramedics said to the other, "We have no pulse and no breathing."

The other looked up at Thomas and said, "How long ago did this happen?"

Thomas replied, "Fifteen minutes or less, give or take a few seconds."

The first paramedic tilted Lester's limp head, in an attempt to begin rescue breathing. He stopped and looked over at his partner and said, "His neck is busted up pretty bad."

His partner said, "Well, just attempt to give him rescue breathing in that position."

The one began rescue breathing and the other began CPR. They worked for seven minutes and even tried switching up and rotating positions, but it was to no avail.

The first paramedic said, "Let's get him in the rig. Can you guys give us a hand getting him on the gurney and up the stairs?"

"Yes," said Thomas, "whatever you need, we want to help."

They got the body up the stairs and out of the house. When they got the gurney situated in the rig, one of the paramedics stayed in the rear compartment with the body and the other got out and said, "Whose home is this?"

Thomas answered, "It's my house."

The paramedic said, "I need you to write out a brief statement for me, it doesn't have to be to the letter or precise times or anything like that. It was an accident, so we will need something in writing to close this out."

"Sure, anything," Thomas replied, so he filled out the report and off went the rescue unit with the body of Lester Young.

Thomas and Phil went back inside and Sonnie was standing inside, and he said, "Man, that was smooth."

"Of course, just like I said it would," Thomas replied. "All we had to do was keep our cool about it. Okay, Sonnie, you have a lot of work to do, so you move on and get back with me tomorrow by 1530 hours."

Sonnie said, "Roger that, sir."

"Man," said Phil, "I'm going to sack out here tonight."

Thomas replied, "No problem, bro', we have an early start in the morning." Both Thomas and Phil turned in for the night.

Thomas was up bright and early the next morning and started working on the blueprint plans for the mock bank. Phil got up shortly after and first made a phone call to Lisa and then joined Thomas with the plans. As Thomas was making notes, Phil noticed that no names were being used when different positions were being assigned.

"Hey, Thomas, I know there is a reason why you're not putting any names to the positions, but are you going to let a brother in on the plan?"

Thomas answered, "I'll tell you like this, bro', the less everyone knows, the more the element of surprise will be effective."

"Man," said Phil, "I sure hope you know that I love you like a brother and I would give my life for you, too. I just hope this thing works because I'm putting all my trust in you."

Thomas smiled and said, "Hey, man, this thing is going to work; I just want to minimize the risk factors and, if we have to lose some to get some, I don't want it to be our own."

"I know that's right," replied Phil, "but can I ask this question on the for real side of things?"

Thomas said, "Of course, you can."

"I don't think it's a secret that you are very smart, I mean you leave me in you dust; but just so I can understand like I was a five year old, can we really win this thing and are you sure that our team will get out of this thing alive?"

"You know," Thomas replied, "I've never claimed to be the smartest person in the world, and I know that I'm not the dumbest, but this I will tell you. I have thought this out very carefully and this plan is actually a vision. If we carry out the plans of the vision to the letter, it will not only be successful, but we will be wealthy for the rest of our lives, our kids' lives, and their kids'. Now look at this blueprint. Can you take these pieces of wood and put together this mini mock building that represents the bank?"

Phil said, "Hell, yes; give me an hour and a half."

"You've got it and that will allow me to draw up the plans for everyone to follow."

They both worked diligently for two straight hours to complete their tasks.

Thomas said, "There it is."

"I'm done, as well," said Phil. "You want to check this out, Thomas?"

Thomas walked over and looked at the completed model. He looked at the model very carefully and inspected it inside and out. He looked over at Phil and said, "I'm impressed. You have gotten this scale model down to the 'T.' Now, I'll work on the numbers and schematics, so when we get the rest of the intel back from the team, we can put it all together and see what it looks like. Now, let's go and get something to eat, I'm starved."

Phil replied, "I'm past starved; I could eat a whole horse right about now."

"You can always eat a whole horse, man."

Phil had to laugh and agree at the same time.

The two of them went to the kitchen and rustled up some breakfast. They cooked some pancakes, turkey sausage, grits, hash browns, and eggs. They sat down and ate.

After breakfast, Phil said, "Man, I'm stuffed."

"Man, I'm as full as a Texas tick," and they both laughed. Thomas told Phil, "Come on downstairs; I want to show you some things."

They went down into the basement and Thomas said, "Over here," leading Phil to an area past the gym setup. Facing the wall, Thomas bent over and lifted up the mat covering the floor of the gym. He pulled it all the way back, then he took out a pocketknife and stuck it in between the tiles on the floor and removed one. He lifted a handle up that was flush with the floor and pulled it all the way up and back.

Phil was looking on in anxious anticipation to see what was next.

When Thomas got the trap door completely open, he began to descend down a flight of stairs. A light automatically came on and Phil followed Thomas without saying a word. When they got down the twenty-three steps, another light came on, which triggered more lights that completely illuminated the entire room.

Phil looked around the room and said, "Hot damn, you secured the whole armory."

Thomas said, "Close, do you remember the armory over in Lu Lu La, Pearl City?"

"Hell, yeah," replied Phil.

"Well, I just set everything up in here in the same format."

"But, how did you get everything transferred over?"

"Come on, this stuff did not come from over there. Do you think I turned everything over we found when we were with the LAPD?"

Phil said, "No shit, Sherlock; man, I was not even thinking. Back then, man, I wish I was as smart as you."

"Man, stop. I was just planning for the future, that's all, nothing more."

"Yeah, right," said Phil, "like that doesn't take any smarts."

"But anyway, just so that you know, we have all we need as far as ammo and firearms are concerned. I want to give you some heads up on some things."

Phil said, "Sure, shoot."

"Now, as far as the hit itself goes, I want only you and me in the bank."

Phil began to say something and had a puzzled look on his face.

Thomas stopped him and said, "Now, just hear me out first, please. There is a method to this madness. Now, to ensure everything goes by the numbers...the timing, exchange, and extraction has to be hands on by us. We need C Company on the ready because it's going to be an all points 311 response. That means we'll have the local PD rolling, as well as transit PD, Sheriff's Dept., CHP, and local fed agencies. Now, the team will be on point, so we'll have our backs watched. We'll have two snipers at both high rise level points, so we won't get pinned down. While we are transport and are in transition, we'll have to hold off any responders that are inside of the perimeter."

Phil said, "Aren't we going to have the outside perpetrators stopped up until we can break free with the escape route?"

"No," replied Thomas, "there is no such thing as stopped. We are going to slow them down, but we are going to be under heavy fire from pretty much all angles. What I want to do is choose our battlegrounds so that we have the advantage."

Phil said, "Okay, well how do you propose to do that?"

"Very simple," Thomas answered. "If we disable, let's say, at least six patrol vehicles, then it will buy us some time to bring in the big trucks to act as our cleanup crew, you understand?"

Phil thought for a moment and answered, "No, as a matter of fact, I don't get it."

Thomas said, "Don't worry, bro', you will. As we put each part of this plan together in segments, the puzzle will come together and it will be as clear as glass to you."

Phil asked, "Hey, man, what's next?"

"Well, it's 1430 now; we need to get to the simulated training area."

"Hey, I'm with you," said Phil.

So, they took off in Thomas's Yukon. Phil was sitting in the front passenger seat and looked over at Thomas and said, "Yo, bro', this is going to work, right?"

Thomas answered, "Hey, bro', beyond a shadow of a doubt this is going to work. As a matter of fact, now that we're on the subject, may I share something with you?"

"By all means, bro', please rap to me."

"I've had this idea for a long time now; I guess I was a young adult when I first thought about it. I would say to myself, if I was to attempt to pull off a bank job, I would do it right. I used to watch some of the movies with Bonnie and Clyde, Al Capone, Jessie James, and those guys, and I'd say 'these guys are stupid. They have no laid out plan, no contingency plans, no backup plan, and no master plan.'"

"This is big, man," said Phil.

Thomas continued, "There's going to be a hell of a lot of money in this. I mean we will literally be set up for the rest of our lives. The only question you have to ask yourself is, is this worth the risk? We are definitely going to suffer some casualties, that's a given, but we can minimize our losses, which means we are going to force the major loss to be our enemy's. Now our intentions will not be to collect dog tags, but to counter and strike hard and swift, by surprise and organization, and slip right out."

"Man, it sounds all good and all," responded Phil, "but, man, I still want to be around to enjoy it with my wife and make babies, I mean a bunch of them. I want at least four snotty-nosed, ashy-elbowed little Phils running around, Phil the II, III, IV, and V and then maybe a couple little pretty angel girls."

Thomas said, "Man, it's going to happen. When I roll out the plan, you'll feel more at ease, I assure you."

"Man, I feel better already. If you're cool with it, then I'm cool with it."

At this time, they drove up to an area that led up to a dirt road. As they took the dirt road, there was a closed fence with a sign that read, DUMP SITE. Thomas told Phil to get out, grab the bolt cutters, and cut the lock on the gate. As he cut the lock off, Phil opened the gate wide enough for Thomas's vehicle to drive through.

Thomas and Phil proceeded to drive into the dump site area, until they reached the end of the area where there was a pile of smashed up cars that were piled up three rows high. As they approached, Thomas slowed down to 3 mph in the truck. Phil looked at him and said, "Man, I sure hope you can drive through this pile of shit."

Thomas laughed and stopped the truck three feet in front of the pile. He said, "Let's get out."

The two of them got out of the truck and Phil looked over at Thomas, but said nothing. Phil was waiting for Thomas to make the next move.

Thomas walked over directly in front of the pile, stooped over, and lifted a large metal plate up, and then stomped his foot on the ground on a spot in the middle where he had lifted up the metal plate. He released the metal plate, stepped back, and allowed the plate to drop down. Thomas looks at Phil, smiled, and started counting, "Five, four, three, two, one…"

Phil looked at the piles of cars and noticed that they were moving backward, the whole pile at one time. Phil said, "What the hell is going on?"

"Just wait, look, listen, and learn."

The pile moved back five yards and the opening in the ground with stairs leading downward came into view.

Thomas said, "Hey, bro', follow me."

"Roger that, Sarge, but please don't get me killed," said Phil as they began their descent down the stairs, dim lights on both sides of the walls beginning to come on.

After they had gone down two and a half flights of stairs, Thomas told Phil, "Make sure you stay on this platform and stand completely erect."

Phil complied without question. After both of the men were standing on the platform, ten seconds later the platform began to descend downward. They went down one more story and the platform stopped.

Thomas said to Phil, "Follow me."

The area under the earth that was in a landfill served a dual purpose. Phil looked around and discovered that he was in an underground armory. The area looked like an underground city; it was the size of a large warehouse.

Thomas said to Phil, "Behold. This is my fallout shelter, as well as my armory; it is totally self-contained. I could live in here along with five other families for five years."

As Phil looked around in amazement, he looked back at Thomas and said, "Man, you never told me about this place, this is awesome! Did you design this yourself?"

Thomas replied, "Yes, I did. Took two years to build and the crew that built this, does not exist anymore. So, you are the only outsider that knows about this, do you understand?"

Phil said, "You're damn right I understand."

"Feast your eyes on this, Phil."

They walked over to a large wall on the left side of the area. Thomas uncovered a slate on the wall, pushed three buttons, and a tray came out of the wall with a key pad on it. Thomas placed his left thumb on the platform and another unit popped up. Thomas placed his head down on the unit and it read his eyes and scanned them. After ten seconds, the wall began to open up and, as Phil looked on in anxious anticipation, he couldn't help but get excited as to what would be next. When the walls had completed their opening, another room appeared.

As they walked into the room, the overhead florescent lamps began to automatically come on. There were three walls in the room and, in Plexiglas cases, were weapons of every type, as well as explosives and an array of protective gear from armor plates to protective vests.

As Phil looked in awe, he turned to Thomas and said, "Hey, man, now that I've seen what I'm seeing now, I know that this plan of yours is going to work. We have everything that we need to pull this off. I just hope that everyone will be on the ready. I mean our team has to be on point."

Thomas said, "Man, that's what we need to cover." He went over to the right wall, bent down, and picked up a large trunk. He opened the trunk and pulled out a large makeup kit.

Phil looked at Thomas and said, "Hey, man, I'm not going to dress up as a dead president or anything like that."

Thomas laughed and said, "Man, you don't have to be a dead president, but you have to put on head cover and glasses."

"Now, I can handle that," replied Phil.

Thomas said, "Grab this trunk, it's going with us."

Phil picked up the trunk and asked, "Is this all that we're taking?"

"No, Sherlock, this is only one of the things that we will be taking."

They walked over to the rear of the room and Thomas grabbed the handle of a large hand truck. Phil looked at it and said, "Man, this thing will still be hard to push."

"On the contrary, my dear Watson." Thomas responded. "This unit comes complete with remote controls."

"You think of everything!"

Thomas continued, "We need to grab two of these remote trucks, and just follow me."

"Thomas, how do you memorize what we're going to need?"

"It's quite elementary, my dear Dr. Watson. I have my note pad to assist my memory banks." They both shared a hearty laugh, and then Thomas said, "Phil, I need for you to listen very carefully and follow my direction to the letter."

Phil responded, "Ten-four, Sarge."

"I need for you to grab everything I tell you by the numbers; here we go: two M-40 grenade launchers, two .60-cals. w/tripod, four M-468 6.8 mm rifles w/28-round magazines, two .30-06 sniper rifles, two Dillon Precision mini guns, eight heavy-duty stretch spikes, ten Level III body armor vests with Kevlar linings, ten Kevlar helmets w/Level III ballistic, ten M-2 Phase III gas masks, stack of 10-gauge armor plates for the vehicles, four 30mm mini guns with tear gas launchers, four paint guns w/red paint (this would be used to blot out the surveillance cameras), ten ballistic shields w/full body bunkers, two signal jammers for cell phones and landline disruption, and last of all one remote disabler for helicopter and air support."

Phil looked at both carts and noticed that they are both stacked up perfectly and the carts were full to capacity. Thomas reviewed his note pad and said, "Man, this is everything. What we will do is get this stuff loaded into the truck, get back to my house, and get the team together."

Phil grabbed one of the remotes and headed back to the lift. They loaded the first cart onto the lift and brought the lift all the way to the ground level. They rolled the cart over to the vehicle and loaded the first cart. They repeated the process with the second cart and after the vehicle was loaded with both carts and all of the contents, Thomas told Phil, "Man, if you can stay topside, I'm just going to go down and make sure everything is secure down there."

He went down and re-secured the hidden wall and walked over to the key pad. Thomas pressed in a different code and the keypad displayed a different face. The face of the key pad was asking, 'To engage this command, please press the pass code.' Thomas punched in the pass code and the control asked, 'Are you sure that you want to set the self-destruct?' Thomas pressed, 'Yes please self-destruct,' and the pad then asked for a time frame. Thomas pressed in forty-eight hours.

Thomas looked around and said, "Well, this will be the last time I see you. You have truly served your purpose and have served me well, but now your tour of duty is ended. You're relieved of all duties." Thomas started walking back to the platform at a slow pace, as if he was reluctant to leave, knowing that this would be his last time seeing this very well developed and intelligently designed bunker and storage facility. As he went up, arriving topside, he forced himself not to look back.

His mind went back to when he was on assignment in another country and his fire team was involved in an extraction mission. His snipers had been placed and perched for three days in the same post. They had taken out forty-three unfriendlies and were waiting for orders from Thomas to move forward. The two snipers, Fernando Ortiz and Omar Toliver, were the best of the best, trained by Thomas personally. Ortiz radioed Phil and informed him that there was a whole city of women and children, and asked should they abort the mission.

Phil replied, "Standby, I'll have to confirm with headquarters." Phil radioed headquarters and informed them that the mission was compromised with women and children.

Headquarters responded, "It's your call, Sgt. Dugmal."

Phil called Ortiz and told them to abort. Ortiz responded, "Ten-four, Sarge, but what about the kids and women? They'll be left behind with those good-for-nothing, scum of the earth, shit bag unfriendlies."

Thomas said, "Men, we have to take a stand; if we go in now, everybody dies, and no one lives. If we abort, some of the children have a chance to live. So now it's time to walk away and just don't look back. The good Lord will take care of the rest."

It was extremely hard for the men of F Company (force recon marines) to leave innocent, defenseless little children and women behind, knowing that the women would be raped and killed and the children would be sold off or killed, as well.

All of the boys in Company F truly believed in Sgt. Dugmal and trusted his decision making, and all of them would give their lives for him and follow him to hell, waging war against Satan himself if Sgt. Dugmal was leading them. All of the marines of F Company knew that in order for a marine to die in combat, they had to have special permission from the commander in chief that lives in that special place in the sky and, if they were called for duty elsewhere, then it was by decision and special order to go and take care of business there, where it was needed. With great regret the boys of F Company began pulling out.

When they reached the designated safe zone, Ortiz walked over to Sgt. (Thomas) Dugmal and said, "Hey, Sarge, I know that what you did back there you had to do; we all understand and are all with you and behind you 100 percent."

Sgt. Dugmal looked around at all of the marines in F Company and said, "I hope that I made the right decision and God help me if I did not, but the bottom line is that all of us in this unit are going back and walking back and not being carried."

Thomas came back to reality, and began double-timing it back to the truck. He got in, put the key into the ignition and started the vehicle, and just sat there for a moment.

Phil looked at him and said, "Hey, bro', are you okay?"

"Yeah," responded Thomas, "I hope everybody is ready because it's going down."

Phil declared, "Man, I was born ready."

"Phil, I need you to call the boys in F Company. I need to get with them and go over the plans first. It will be the success of the first team that will allow for the whole mission to succeed."

"I know that's right," said Phil. "What do you need me to cover with them?"

Thomas replied, "I need for you to appoint each man his position. I want the same lineup that we had when we were in the shit."

"You got it, Sarge. That means Cpl. Ortiz and Toliver are snipers. I will have them recon the location and find the best perch. I will put Cpl. Johnson and Jackson with the 60mm. Do you want crazy Drew coming in with us?"

Thomas answered, "That's correct. I want Drew in before us. He will discharge the flash bangs to draw their attention and then dispense the NRT-2 agent."

Phil interrupted, "Hey, Sarge, you're putting everyone to sleep?"

"Yes," responded Thomas, "I believe that it is the best way to go; this means as soon as the vaults are open, we are expediting the cash and transferring it to our vehicles. We will only have a window of two minutes and thirty seconds to be in the bank, set this thing off, and be gone. We don't have time to babysit thirty or more civilians and make sure none of them uses their cell phones or other devices. We go in, put them to sleep, and do what we do."

"Hey, Sarge, and if things go to shit, what's the plan?"

Thomas looked at Phil and said, "Let's just say it's not my plan to takeout anyone in this mission, but if anyone gets in our way, this means that they are not friendlies, and we all know what happens to non-friendlies. To be honest with you, with the breaks that we got, we need to do what we need to do. The plan will be not to directly take out any law enforcement personal, but to disable their vehicles and means of attack. If their intention is to take us out, then we will have to eliminate the threat."

"Well, I knew that this was going to be deep, but now I'm thinking this is going to totally be a 10.2 rush," said Phil.

Thomas said, "We need to stay focused. The armor plates need to be placed in the door panels of the two Suburbans. These are the vehicles that we will be traveling in. I need the tires filled with nitro automatic refill, as well as the tripods mounted in both vehicles. Mount the .50-cal. there. As soon as the boys from F Company arrive, I need you to get on that right away. I want you to cover the drill, so that each man knows what his mission is, and what this is really all about. You must reiterate to them the importance of operating as one unit in order to make this work. The reason that we have our boys coming first is the simple fact that in the real world, we know that everyone is not going to make it back. Everyone that is involved in this mission is an asset. However, the outsiders are expendable assets and that's the way it is in the real world. I want my team as gunners because I know what they are capable of doing. Each man will be responsible for covering the next man, just like we trained and just like we performed it in the shit. This has to go by the numbers. We will cover our six, twelve, three, and nine. We will do exactly what we need to do to make it out of this. Our motivating factor will be the fact that our cut (as in F Company's) will be in the area of $13.5 million apiece. Outsiders' take will be considerably less, of course, due to the fact that we are the heaviest risk takers, and hell, we're trained for shit...bottom line."

Phil interrupted and said, "Hey, man, just what will be the take for the outsiders?"

"Each outsider has a specific mission and assignment, which determines their payday," explained Thomas. "This is what I consider a business and they are employees, which means they are on a payroll and being paid by their performance. It's all broken down by the job classifications, which they should have reviewed in the handouts that I provided for them in our meeting yesterday."

"What if they feel it won't be enough?" Phil asked.

Thomas paused for a moment and said, "Well, everyone had an opportunity to decline the offer and they all accepted it. The salaries were covered in the package. I'm thinking if four hundred thousand is not enough for just driving a vehicle to safety, then that's just too bad."

"Maybe I'm just getting a little paranoid about this, right," said Phil, "but you know how greedy people get when you throw money in their faces and there's a lot of money involved."

"I'm aware of this and I'm prepared, as well. I have no tolerance for greed and any disruptions on any level of the chain of command will result in heavy consequences and major repercussions, as well as casualties. I need for you to make this as clear as glass to all of the outsiders."

Phil smiled and said, "I can do that. That's what I do well."

As they arrived at Thomas's house, they went inside and down to the garage. Thomas opened up the garage door, ran outside, and began to pull the truck into the garage. Phil grabbed a hand cart and, as Thomas parked the vehicle inside of the garage, put the cart directly in back of the vehicle.

Thomas said, "Wait, man; let me close the garage door."

"Why did you not use the remote?" asked Phil.

Thomas said, "Pay close attention, my friend." Thomas went over to the wall and uncovered a panel in the wall that was not visible to the naked eye, and there was a key-code panel there. Thomas punched in the code, the garage door closed, and rods and rebar slid completely across the door and secured it.

"Man," said Phil, "you think of everything."

"I hope I've thought of everything. I need for you to make sure F Company will be here on schedule, so we can go over this one more time."

Now it was 1500 hours and F Company arrived together on time as one unit. Phil opened the door, greeted the men, and said, "Gentleman, let's go downstairs." Phil continued, "Let's sit in assignment order."

Drew sat first, then Jackson, Toliver, and Johnson, followed by Ortiz.

Thomas walked over to the men and said, "I will say this very briefly and that is it for me. Upchurch will cover everything else. I will get straight to the point. You all know what this mission entails and what the risk factors are. We are not going to paint a pretty picture for you or promise you a rose garden and a white picket fence. This is what it is. There is a very hefty payoff for each of us; enough to allow you to go away and live very comfortably for the rest of your natural born days. Just like when we were back in action, on assignment, and deep into the shit, the main focus will be that we look out for and take care of our own. My expectation is the same as back then. Is there any part of what I just said that any of you do not understand?"

All of the men answered at the same time, "No, sir."

Thomas said, "Okay then, I will allow Sgt. Upchurch to brief you on the details and remember F Company always completes its mission. Well then, men, as you were."

Phil said, "Okay, as usual, Ortiz and Toliver, you two are on point as snipers. I want you to take a look at where you're going to be on this map." Phil pointed out the hotel that was located on the north. "We have a room reserved at the Mission Deluxe Hotel on the seventeenth floor. This will allow you to cover our six where the bank is located. We also have a room reserved at the Holiday Inn on the seventeenth floor on the south end. This will allow for coverage for our three where the bank is located. Now, Ortiz, you are assigned to the Mission Deluxe and Toliver you have the Holiday Inn. If you two will walk over with me, I will introduce you to your new girly-type friends."

Phil led the two men to the garage and to the back of Thomas's truck. Phil opened up the back of the truck, opening the double side or 'suicide' doors.

Ortiz shouted out, "Mary, sweet mother of Jesus, I've made it to heaven!"

After looking into the back of the truck and seeing all of the weapons, Phil reached in and pulled out one of the Wakefield and Smith M-40 A3 sniper rifles. He handed it to Ortiz. Ortiz took the rifle in his hands and began to stroke it up and down, from the butt of the weapon to the tip of the flash suspense. He looked over at Phil and said, "Man, this is one beautiful weapon."

Phil responded, "Hey, bro', it's yours."

Ortiz thanked him and started walking back toward the door leading back into the house.

Toliver walked up to Phil and said, "I know that you have one of those for me, as well."

Phil smiled and said, "You're right, Marine; there is one with your name on it. Come and get it."

Toliver grabbed the rifle out of the truck almost before Phil could pull it out. Toliver said, "Man, I just got to get the feel of this beauty so that we can become one with one another."

Phil smiled and said, "I have always said that you snipers are some weird breed of people."

Toliver responded, "You just don't know. When God created snipers, he only made a few and he said to himself, 'These selected few are all that I need,' and then he made everyone else."

Phil said, "And you know that's right, man."

Toliver clutched his weapon tightly in his hands and started walking back inside the house. Before Toliver could get to the door, Phil shouted out, "Hey, man, send Drew, Jackson, and Johnson back out here!"

Toliver replied, "Roger that, Sarge."

Phil started taking some of the other weapons out of the vehicle and stacked them on the cart. He separated the vests into one stack and put the armor plates on the ground. The rest of the crew began to muster out into the garage area at this time.

Cpl. Johnson looked at the equipment that was sitting on the ground and said, "Man, what the hell, it looks like we're back in action again. What do we do next?"

Phil said, "I need for you, Jackson, and Drew to attach these armor plates that are on the floor here to the door wells of the two Suburbans that are in the rear garage. All of the equipment that you will need should already be back there. There's even a welding torch back there. I need this done and completed in two hours. Can you guys make this happen?"

Drew answered, "We'll have it done in under that time."

Johnson grabbed an empty handcart and began loading the plates on it. All three men loaded the cart and were off to the rear garage to complete their tasks.

Phil went back into the house and walked over to Thomas and told him, "We should have the vehicles knocked out in about an hour."

Thomas said, "Very well, the rest of the crew will be here at 1900 hours and I would like to have everything unloaded, separated, and ready for distribution at that point. Phil, make sure that they attach both of the tripods in the vehicles. We might need them."

In the meantime, the crew—Johnson, Drew, and Jackson—installed the armor plates into the door wells of both vehicles and they also installed plates inside the door wells of rear side-by-side doors of both vehicles. Jackson shouted, "This is done, boys, now let's get the extra inflated tires on these vehicles!"

They grabbed the rear garage entrance and began to lift both vehicles to begin the transition. It took them every bit of twenty minutes to complete this and begin to mount and bolt down the tripods. After this task was done they went back into the garage and grabbed the two .60-cal. guns with the ammo cans. They mounted the weapons on the tripod and tightened them down. Johnson opened the rear door and side passenger door and began testing the rotation of the .60-cal. Jackson jumped into the other vehicle and began the same process with the .60-cal. Both men were satisfied at this point that their weapons were well mounted and in operational condition.

After completion of loading the .60-cals. with ammo, they looked at each other and said at the same time, "Ready to rock 'n' roll."

They walked back into the house and went over to Phil and said, "What's next?"

"Let's get the rest of the equipment loaded into the vehicles," said Phil, "that way, when the rest of the crew arrives, all we'll have to do is go over the plan for the last time."

They went out into the garage and began to load the rest of the equipment and weapons onto the carts. After the carts were loaded up and Thomas's vehicle has been emptied out, the men began to load up the Suburbans. This took every bit of twenty minutes to complete and it was done.

The men went back into the house, approached Thomas, and said, "Sgt. Dugmal, we're ready to rock 'n' roll and we're all squared away."

"Very well then," replied Thomas. "We have time to eat some vittles. I've prepared a little something for us to eat."

Phil shouted out, "Man, that's right on time; I'm as hungry as a three dog fight!"

Drew replied, "Man, you're always hungry, anyway."

The whole crew got a laugh out of that.

"Okay, you guys," Thomas said, "let's chow down and get ready for Phase 2."

They all took a seat and began chowing down. Ortiz picked up a piece of chicken, took a bite, and said, with a drumstick in one hand and food still in his mouth, "This is kind of weird to me. This reminds me of the last supper. This reminds me of the fact that, after today, I will not be serving my own plate anymore. I'm going to have someone else serving me from now on with the money that I'm going to have."

Toliver said, "You know that's right. We will be in a position to hire our own private cooks and servants for once in our lives."

"Okay, then men, as you were," said Thomas. "Let's not lose focus on the goal first, and then we can share pipe dreams. Until this mission has been completed, I want each and every swinging dick to maintain focus and stay on the ready."

All of the guys at the table recovered and resumed eating their meal.

Now 1845 hours rolled around and the doorbell rang. Thomas says to the crew, "Everyone standby." He went to the door and peeked out the peep-hole. He could see that it was the makeup crew. Thomas opened the door and was greeted by Donald Morris.

Donald greeted Thomas with a handshake and a, "Good evening, Mr. Dugmal; we are a little early, but we wanted to make sure that we had the time to go over the particulars."

Thomas said, "Not a problem, come on in."

Donald was followed by Pete Taylor and Randy Favor.

Thomas asked Donald, "What happened to your fourth member?"

Donald looked at Thomas and explained, "Well, let's just say that I had some trust issues with Mr. Downs, and now we don't have to worry about him. Can we keep it as that?"

Thomas replied, "That's fine by me."

Donald proceeded down the hall and went directly downstairs to join the rest of the crew.

Thomas went to the back of the house where the master bedroom was located, went into his room, and secured his door. He went over to the large dresser and bent down and opened the fourth drawer. He pulled out a box, picked it up, and walked over to the bed. He put the box on top of the bed and then sat down. He looked down at the box and then opened it. He pulled out the contents of the box and it was wrapped up in plastic bubble wrap. After unwrapping the bubble wrap, he pulled out a cellular phone marked Cell-One. Thomas picked it up and said, "Thank God for pay-as-you-go phones." Thomas punched in some numbers and waited for it to ring. He heard the phone on the other end ring and allowed it to ring six times. On the sixth ring, he hung up. He placed the cell phone on the bed beside him and then lay back on the bed.

Six minutes passed by and the cell phone began to ring. Thomas allowed the phone to ring five times and on the sixth ring, he picked up the phone and pressed the answer button. He paused for a moment and then said, "Baby, is that you?"

Beverly answered, "Yes, sweetheart, it is me; are you okay?"

"Yes, I'm fine," Thomas replied, "you're calling on the Cell-One phone, correct?"

Beverly answered, "Yes, just like you asked me to do."

"Very well, how are the kids?"

Beverly told him they were all fine, they were just worried about him. "What do you want me to tell them?"

"Baby, just tell them that I am on a special assignment and I'm not allowed outside communications. Can you just tell them that for me? Tell them that I will rejoin them as soon as the mission has completed."

Beverly paused for a moment and said, "Thomas, I can tell them that, but you had better be careful and make sure that you come back to me. The kids need you and I need you. I can't do this by myself."

Thomas said, "Baby, I promise that I will be back and that everything will work out fine."

"Okay then, I do feel reassured."

"Okay, baby, I have to go now," said Thomas. "I will contact you three days from now. Get rid of that first phone and stand by with the next phone for contact. Please kiss the kids for me and tell them that I love them."

"You just make sure that you are in a position to tell them yourself," said Beverly.

"You can bet on that. I'm signing off; I love you." Then Thomas pressed end.

Beverly paused for a couple of seconds and said, "I love you," and pressed end.

Thomas got up off the bed and left the room. He walked over to the living room and stood in front of the fireplace. He turned on the gas-operated fireplace and waited until there was a full flame and took the cell phone and tossed it in. He waited until the phone had completely disintegrated.

The doorbell rang once again. Thomas walked to the front of the house and looked through the peep hole. He could see the remainder of the crew—Mitchell Payne, along with his crewman Mike Simms. Mitchell greeted Thomas with a handshake and an embrace.

Thomas said, "Man, I forgot to tell you, I will need for you to get six additional drivers to stage some vehicles in different locations around the city."

"That's not a problem," said Mitchell. "I can get any fools to do this without any questions. What's the payoff for them?"

Thomas replied, "Well, they do not have to know what we're doing, so all they have to do is have the vehicles at their perspective locations at the assigned times."

"Man, give me 30 minutes and it's done," said Mitchell.

"You need to make sure that these people are reliable and realize that, if they are late by as little as 30 seconds or screw this up in any way, shape, or form and it is not done precisely by the numbers, then it will...and make it clear...I did say it will cost them their lives."

Mitchell replied, "Man, trust me, I got this. I have the people who can handle this, plus, they don't get paid unless the job is completed."

"I'm okay with that," Thomas said. "Now, let's go to my study. I want to show you the scale map and go over time and plan of execution."

Thomas was very careful not to mix the different crews up as he had learned that too much information was too much for some people to handle; plus, this kept all of the parties involved focused on their individual tasks and limited the desire to get greedy or plan a double cross.

Thomas and Mitchell went to the study and Thomas pulled down the window shade so it became rather dark, and they were relying on the room light from the lamps and overhead light. Thomas cleared his large desk, opened a drawer, and inserting his index finger into the open drawer, the top of the table lit up and LED lights began to appear and form the shape of the city.

In the middle of the city, a structure took the shape and form of a bank, a large bank. There were streets on this large luminous map, as well as street lights, stop signs, and other buildings and structures.

Mitchell looked at Thomas and said, "Man, this is so good, it scares me. Are you sure that you're not working for the other side and, if you're not, why the hell not?"

Thomas paused for a moment and answered, "Mitchell, I used to work for the other side. I've done some things that I am not proud of... Some things that this government asked me to do for them, and I went along with it, without question or hesitation. I've gone on assignment where, in my mind, I did question my orders, but I carried them out nonetheless. As I look back, I know that I can't take back or reverse all of the lives that I've taken in combat and while on assignment. Deep in my mind, I know that one entire family was not the cause of drugs coming here to the United States of America, or even covering up an aircraft going down in Asia during a summit meeting. I, along with my team, carried out these orders right, wrong, or indifferent. I realize that the majority of wars that have been started here in the United States of America have been for greed, selfishness, and the establishment of dominance of power. We have been used, abused, misled, and forgotten.

"What I'm going to do is no different than what's always been done. There's only one difference. The fox that taught the sheep has turned from a fox and is now the hunter—the smart and intelligent one, and they will have to figure this one out. The best part of all of this is they will never figure this one out.

"So, to answer your question, Mitchell, this is all about the little man doing what he has to do in order to make the big man realize that no one is going to just sit back and take abuse from anyone anymore. Forces are going to strike back."

Mitchell bowed his head and looked at the floor. He then looked back up at Thomas and said, "Man, they should not have pissed you off. I've always heard of payback, but this is the granddaddy of all paybacks, this is the *Tora! Tora! Tora!* of paybacks. I could even say that this is the big payback."

Thomas smiled and said, "Let's refocus." Thomas began to point out what streets were going to be affected. He instructed Mitchell that it was vitally important that at 0901 hours, the motion be set off, so everything had to be in place on time.

"Now, the main arteries into the city downtown areas are Main St., Post St., Broadway St., and State St. This is where I will need the vehicles placed and blocking these streets."

Mitchell interrupted and asked, "You're telling me the bank is located dead slap in the center of the city and you plan escaping with that amount of cash?"

"Trust me," Thomas replied. "There is a method to all of this madness, I assure you."

Mitchell smiled and said, "Sorry, man. Please proceed on."

"Thank you very much," Thomas replied. "Now, when we strike at 0901 hours, we will be moving at warp speed and everything will go by the numbers. Once the bank alarms are set off, we will have twelve minutes before all local law enforcement is dispatched and rolling hot. The stations that are furthest away will be the last point of response and will not move in. They will set up perimeters, blocking off the throughways within a quarter of a mile radius using their judgment on time and distance of travel. Now, after they're set up, that's when your people plug up streets with vehicles that I've provided for you. All you will have to do is make sure that your people put out the spike strips, just in case a few of the police feel the need for speed and watched too many episodes of *Barnaby Jones*, deciding to use the sidewalks, patrol bikes, or motor bikes. Either way, we're covered. Just make sure that as soon as your team has completed their assignments, they get the hell out of there without being identified."

Mitchell assured Thomas, "Don't worry about my people, Thomas; I have loyal people that trust me just as you do, and they know that to let me down is just as good as suicide."

"That's good enough for me," said Thomas. "I need for you to study this map. Memorize it...lock it into memory. I'm instructing you not to discuss this with anyone, except for your team. Let's go downstairs and join the rest of the crew. We will cover time frames and locations where we will meet up after we have completed our missions. I will say this only once, Mitchell, there will be no room for failure or non-execution of this mission, and there will be no turning back from this point on. I have invested too much time, energy, and effort at this point and I will not turn back. I hope that I have made myself perfectly clear."

Mitchell responded, "Thomas, I am with you all the way, even if it's to the end." They turned to each other and embraced. They grabbed each other in what seemed to be a confirmation that there was a chance that this would be the last time for this opportunity and this moment.

Thomas reached his finger into the desk drawer, once again, and pressed a button. This time, as the LED light faded out, they began to bleed together as if they were melting.

Mitchell asked, "Are the lights melting?"

"Yes, they are," replied Thomas. "This table will be nothing more than a slit in approximately forty-five seconds. Let's head downstairs and join the rest of the crew, shall we?"

Thomas went downstairs to the basement area and Phil had just finished up briefing the crew about the precise time for operation and responsibilities. Thomas said, "Okay, I want everyone to fall in with Donald Morris and his makeup artists and do not give them a hard time. This man is a professional in his own right and has worked with several movie stars and stage performers, so you will give him your complete cooperation."

Donald stood up and walked over to the area of the garage where the sinks were set up and chairs with foot lifts attached. He said, "I need three people at a time to come over and have a seat in one of these chairs."

Jackson, Toliver, and Ortiz were the first ones to walk over and take a seat. Ortiz said, "I do not want to look like Donald Duck or Elmer Fudd."

Jackson said, "No, don't do that, it might be an improvement." They all shared a laugh.

Donald and his crew began to work on the men. After the first crew had completed their makeup, Donald called over the next crew.

Jackson looked over at Ortiz and said, "Man, you don't look that bad with blush on."

Ortiz responded, "Man, I would not talk if I were you. I sure hope that none of my friends see me like this."

Donald and his crew continued making up everyone until his work was completed.

Johnson asked, "Donald, how long will this make up last? Will we wake up in the morning and it will be off of us?"

Donald smiled and said, "Don't worry, this is scheduled to last for 36 hours and then you won't even have to wash it off. It will come off on its own, and then you will realize why they call me an artist. I must admit, damn, I'm good. After looking at all of you, you guys are my creations. This is simply put, beautiful work."

Thomas looked around and agreed with Donald. "You're right, Mr. Morris, you are good…the best. Now, your work is done and I'm going to have to ask you to leave, Mr. Morris."

Donald said, "Not a problem." He gathered his belongings and looked around at the crew and commented, "Damn, I'm good. Okay, boys, let's boogie."

Thomas said, "I will walk you to the door," and then he, Donald, and Donald's crew walked back up the stairs and headed for the front door.

When they arrived at the front door, Donald said to his people, "You guys wait for me in the car; I'll be right there."

Peter said, "That's cool; let's go you guys, I have the keys anyway."

After they cleared the doorway and walked down the driveway, Thomas shut the door and told Donald, "Hey, man, I'll be right back; wait here, I have something for you."

Thomas took off down the hall and into his den area. He walked up to the fireplace and bent down, reached under the hood cover of the fireplace, and pulled a metal box down and out. The box looked like a silver cash box. He walked over to the coffee table and picked up a brown shopping bag. He looked over at Donald and motioned for him to come over and join him.

Donald walked over and said, "Why do I get the feeling that this is going to be a farewell, not a so long?"

Thomas looked at him and said, "You have been a great friend. I have gotten you involved in this as far it needs to go. We will not see each other again and I do wish you the best. Please take this box. It contains $300 thousand. I know that it's not a lot, but as a token on my appreciation to you, I offer this."

Donald said, "You don't have to give me anything; you are my friend, Thomas."

Thomas looked at Donald and said, "Yes, that is true, you are my friend, but you know that your crew needs to be paid for their work and after today, you don't know me anymore. It will be better this way and you can live with a clear conscience."

Donald replied, "Thomas, I don't know and I don't want to know what you're going to do, but you have my blessing and support, no matter what happens."

"That's good to know."

The two men embraced for the last time. Thomas grabbed the brown paper shopping bag and inserted the silver box into the bag and handed it to Donald. Donald extended his hand in a motion to shake Thomas's hand. Thomas extends his hand and they shook hands one last time. They turned and began heading toward the front door. Thomas opened the door and Donald proceeded to walk out. He paused for a moment.

Thomas said, "Donald, please don't turn around. The easiest thing to do is to just continue walking forward, trust me."

Donald complied with Thomas's instructions. Donald was halfway down the driveway and said loud enough for Thomas to hear him, "You have always been a good friend to me; I will always remember you, Thomas."

Thomas did not respond and allowed him to continue walking toward his vehicle. In Donald's mind and in his heart, he knew that Thomas was a good man, as well as a good friend. Donald knew that Thomas was all about business and very strong-minded and strong-willed. By being this way, he understood that Thomas had a very tough outer shell because he had to, but inside Thomas had a good heart that was endearing enough for people to hang on. Donald smiled as he felt an inner peace come over him, as if an angel confirmed to him that everything would be alright and not to worry.

Donald got into the car on the right passenger side and kept his head straight, looking forward. Pete was sitting in the driver's seat and Randy was sitting directly behind him in the rear. No one was saying anything. Donald kept his head straight forward and, in a whisper, said, "Pete, our job is complete here. Please drive us home."

Randy asked, "Hey, Don, are you alright?"

Donald answered, "Yes, you know, I believe that I am alright now."

Pete started up the vehicle and they drove off.

Thomas went back into the house and down the stairs. All of the crew was sitting around in their chairs, no one saying anything. Thomas walked over in front of all the men and said, "Phil should have briefed all of you by now, so there is not much that I need to say. I would like to, however, say this… Tomorrow morning, we will make a hell of a lot of money. As we all know, this will not be easy and the stakes are extremely high, as well as the risks. As always, I expect excellence and execution. I would like to avoid casualties, but the possibilities are imminent. Our plan is 'execute and extract.' There can be nothing and no one in our way. At one time, we all took an oath to defend the Constitution of the United States of America, whether foreign or domestic. May God help us all. Men, I need all of you to go and get some sleep. We have an early morning. This basement, as you can see, has been supplied with cots for your sleeping pleasure. Just grab one and pick a spot here in the basement. If you have a need to nourish yourselves, the refrigerator is stocked with food and drink, and the bar is open until 2330 hours, so gentleman, help yourselves."

Thomas looked at Phil and told him, "Man, I need to see you upstairs."

The crew began to choose a cot and the space that they would occupy for the night. Phil went over to the bar and grabbed a bottle of Jack Daniels Single Barrel and headed up the stairs.

In the meantime, the team began to raid the fridge and take advantage of the food that was provided for them. Toliver grabbed a plate and piled some spaghetti and baked chicken on it, and put it into the microwave oven. While he is waiting for the timer to expire, he went over to the bar and selected his beverage. He grabbed a bottle of Miller High Life from the mini bar refrigerator. He turned around and asked, "Does anyone else want a Miller's?"

Jackson shouted out, "Hell, yeah. It's Miller time!"

Mike Simms responded, "Me, too; I'll take one of those bad boys."

Johnson shouted out, "I'll have one, as well!"

By the time the microwave timer went off, Toliver shouted, "Your services have been suspended; my meal is ready. The rest of you ladies will have to serve yourselves!" They all shared a hearty laugh.

Phil went to the refrigerator and grabbed two Miller High Life from the kitchen upstairs and joined Thomas in the study. Thomas was already sitting behind his desk and reviewing some notes.

Phil walked in and said, "Hey, man, I brought the shit."

Thomas smiled and said, "Man, come and have a sit down."

Phil placed the bottle of Single Barrel on top of the desk. He opened up the bottle of Miller's and handed it to Thomas. He then opened his and lifted the bottle, looked at Thomas, and said, "Hey, man, this is to success."

Thomas reached into the lower bottom drawer and took out two small drinking glasses and set them on top of the table. He grabbed the bottle of Single Barrel, poured some into Phil's glass, and then poured himself some.

Thomas lifted his glass and said, "This is to the big payback."

Phil lifted his glass and said, "Hear, hear."

They both downed their glasses at the same time. Thomas set his glass down and grabbed his bottle of Miller's and took a sip of it.

Phil looked at Thomas and asked, "Hey, man, I know that this is going to work, but just tell me one more time how much cash are we really thinking about in this deal."

"Phil, if I told you, you would not be able to sleep tonight or even concentrate on the job in the morning, so let's just say that your cut out of this alone will be over $300 million."

Phil paused for a few seconds and said, "Man, I need to have another drink." So, he poured another round of Single Barrel. He downed it and said, "I'm just going to grab another couple of Miller's," and Thomas added, "Make sure you grab me a couple more, as well, I know that we will drink up plenty tonight."

Phil ran to the refrigerator and grabbed four more beers and went back into the study and joined Thomas. Phil picked up the bottle of Single Barrel and poured two more shots for himself and Thomas. Phil said, "Is all of our paperwork in order and plans set in place?"

Thomas said, "Everything is in place and ready to go and, if we perform everything to the letter, Phil, this thing will work. We are going to lose some people on both sides, but because we are trained and rehearsed as well as we are, law enforcement will not be ready for us. We have the latest technology and firearms. We will have them in every manner of offense and defense. I'm telling you, Phil, everything that they will not be expecting will be thrown in front of them. That's what will keep them off balance. Law enforcement works from a response reaction. From air elements to communications we will constantly bombard them with, by the time they think they have this figured out, it will be over."

Phil paused for a moment and said, "You know I'm down with you and I'm ready for this."

Thomas replied, "I trust you, Phil, because I know that I can, and I cannot do this without you. This job is going to take everything that we have to pull this off, but it's going to happen."

Phil poured another round in the shot glasses for himself and Thomas. He looked at Thomas and said, "This one is to us."

Thomas agreed, "To us."

They both turned up their glasses and Thomas finished off his bottle of Miller's. He looked at his watch and glanced at the clock on the wall. He said, "Man, its 2330 hours; I think I'm going to turn in now. Our day starts in five hours. I'm up at 0430 hours."

Phil said, "Man, wake me up, I want to go over the entire inventory in the vehicles one last time."

"You got it, bro'. I'll see you in the morning."

"You can bet on that," replied Phil.

They both left the study and Thomas went down the hallway leading to his master bedroom, where he went to retire for the night. Phil went the opposite way, leading to Thomas's son Elijah's room. It was a fairly large room and very comfortable for Phil to rest in.

Meanwhile, Beverly was sitting up watching television with her mom, Cassandra. Beverly looked as though she had a lot on her mind, as Cassandra looked over at her and noticed a blank look on her face. Cassandra picked up the remote and turned down the sound of the television. She asked, "Okay, Beverly, please tell me what's on your mind."

Beverly replied, "Not much, Mom. I'm just thinking about Thomas and I hope that he is going to be alright."

Beverly's sister Ericka walked into the den where the two ladies were and said, "You guys are still up? I'm going to make some popcorn and hot chocolate, does anyone want any?" Cassandra and Beverly responded they would love both of those. Ericka said, "Okay, I'll be right back."

After five minutes passed by, Beverly's dad, Jedadiah, walked into the den, looked around, and asked, "Why in the hell is everyone still up? If there was going to be a party, you could at least have invited me."

Cassandra laughed and said, "Jed, shut up and come over here...sit by me. Beverly was just going to share some thoughts and concerns that she has about what's going on with her family and Thomas."

Jedadiah replied, "Okay, now that's what I'm talking about; we as a family do not sit down and rap about things as often as we should anymore." Jedadiah walked over and sat down on the couch on the right side of Cassandra.

Ericka walked in with two large bowls of popcorn and said, "Hey, I thought that I heard more voices, so I brought extra popcorn. I have to go back for the hot chocolate." As she sat the two large bowls of popcorn down on the coffee table, she turned and started back toward the kitchen when Beverly's brother Kamal walked into the entrance of the den.

He asked, "Is this a family meeting?"

Jedadiah shouted out, "Shut the hell up and come over here and join us! Beverly is just about to fill us in on what's going on with your brother-in-law."

Kamal smiled and asked, "Is it another large business investment and all of us are going to be rich?"

"Not quite," replied Beverly, "just have a seat and listen, little brother."

Kamal said, "Just because you're four years older than me doesn't mean you can order me around like you used to do when we were kids." They all laughed.

Ericka said, "I will be right back."

After everyone had settled down in the den and had started enjoying the popcorn and hot chocolate, Beverly said, "Now that I have everyone's undivided attention, I just wanted everyone to know just for the record, that there is nothing going on between Thomas and I that you guys should be alarmed about. I just wanted to tell you that something went down a while back and it caused some ripples in our lives. We had to shut down the business."

Jedadiah interrupted and asked, "You mean you lost the real estate business and gym?"

"No, not exactly; please, Dad, just listen carefully. I still have the real estate company and that's where, Mom, you and Ericka come in. I have paperwork here that you two need to review and sign off on. I'm turning over power of attorney to you, Mom and Erica. I'm appointing you CEO of the People's Choice Real Estate Co. Now, I will remain as president, but I will assign you two as operators of the company. Now, can you two do this for us?"

Cassandra said, "Baby, I'll do whatever I need to do to help you guys out."

Ericka responded, "Sis, I love you, and there's nothing that I would not do for this family and that includes Thomas, as well. You know that I love him just like I would a blood brother. He has been good to you and my nieces and nephews, as well."

Beverly looked to her dad and said, "Dad, this is where you come in."

Jedadiah answered, "Baby girl, you know that I put fifteen years of my life into serving the United States Marine Corps; I did five tours in Nam. Thomas served in the Corps, as well, so that makes us more than father and son-in law, it makes us brothers. Just knowing Thomas the way that I do, I know that he is going to take care of business and I have a feeling that what you are telling me is that someone or some people have fucked with the wrong person and pissed him off, and now have awakened a sleeping giant. Whatever the situation is, I'm in, and you can count on me to help in any way I can."

Beverly smiled and said, "Dad, that is very reassuring. You don't have to swing back into action or anything like that, but what I'm going to need from you is to get ready to go on a trip with us...you and Kamal. Listen carefully. We have already booked reservations for airline tickets and hotels. You two need to pack some bags—only enough clothes for one week and make sure that all of the clothes are summer attire. We are going to Buenos Aires. I have all of your passports and other documents for travel and we leave at 7:00 tomorrow morning."

Kamal stood up and said, "No problem; I thought that you were going to say that we were leaving tonight. Well, can I bring Maria with us? She would love to travel to that side of the world?"

Beverly said, "As much as I would like for Maria to join us, I'm afraid that we can't. I do not want to raise any suspicion or get any outsiders involved, at this point. Now, I know that she is your fiancée, but she is not family, yet, and you know what Dad taught us about only being able to trust family all the way to the grave."

"Okay," said Kamal, "but I'll have to call her and explain to her what's going on."

Beverly replied, "Kamal, just tell her that we have to make an emergency trip for business investment reasons and convince her that you will fill her in as soon as you return. Now it has to be exactly like that, do you understand?"

"It's not going to be the easiest thing to explain and convince Maria, but still 'n' all, I will do it."

"Thank you, Kamal. Now, what I'm going to tell you guys has to stay only with us, and please understand that Thomas is still a good man that has his back up against the wall and that's a very dangerous position for the people that backed him into it to be in.

"They shut down his business and froze all of his assets, investments, lines of credit, and brought in the IRS to liquidate all tangible assets and further assets. In other words, they screwed him royally and did not even have the common courtesy to use any K-Y jelly or the opportunity for a reach around. So, Thomas is taking things into his own hands. It's going down tomorrow morning and that's why we will be on our way out of the country, while this is going on.

"Now I'm not going to inform any of you guys as to any specifics of what's going down, so if it were to ever come up and someone asked you what you know about this, you can honestly say, 'I don't know anything about what happened or what the hell you are talking about.'"

All of the family members took a look around the room and at each other, and no one said anything. The whole room was filled with complete silence.

After 30 seconds, Jedadiah took a deep breath and stated, "With all that said, baby girl, I'm sure in and I just want you to know that I do trust you and your decision to stick by your man."

Beverly stood up and said, "Come on, Ericka, let's review the paperwork, so that you and Mom can sign off."

Kamal stood up and said, "Dad, we need to go and get packed."

Jedadiah agreed, "Let's do it."

Cassandra asked Beverly, "Are the kids packed and ready to rock 'n' roll?"

"Mom, they came here ready to rock 'n' roll."

After everyone met in the center of the room, they embraced each other and reassured each other. Beverly and Cassandra shared a tear together. As she was hugging Beverly, Cassandra whispered in her ear ever so softly, "Baby, I really do hope you are doing the right thing. I mean in your heart of hearts."

Beverly responded back softly, "Mom, I love you very much and I do believe that I am doing the right thing."

They all picked up after themselves and departed the room. Beverly, Cassandra, and Ericka went to the study and they all sat down. Beverly reached down and picked up a briefcase. She carried it to an awaiting table and sat down in a chair behind the desk. Cassandra and Ericka joined her, as they began going over and signing off on paperwork.

The next morning Beverly was awakened by the alarm clock. She turned off the alarm and saw that the time was 4:30 A.M.

They had a 7:00 A.M. flight and had to be at the airport by 5:30. As Beverly came out of the bathroom already showered and dressed, Cassandra met her in the hallway and said, "Good morning, baby; the kids are up and I'm cooking breakfast so come to the kitchen and eat because you know that the food on those airplanes is nasty as can be."

Beverly laughed and responded, "Yes, Mom, you are absolutely right about that."

Cassandra went to the kitchen and finished the breakfast. As she was setting the table, Beverly walked in and asked, "Can I help with anything?"

Cassandra answered with a bright smile, "Yes, can you please help me put the food on the table?"

Cassandra had prepared a complete spread for the family to enjoy. She cooked pancakes, grits, turkey bacon, turkey sausage, country fried potatoes, and sautéed tomatoes, onions, and avocados. She had scrambled eggs and now put milk and orange juice on the table.

Ericka walked into the kitchen with her nieces and nephews, looked on the kitchen table, and asked, "Is this Christmas morning?"

Cassandra smiled and said, "Don't be silly, young lady; you know that when we have all of the family here at the same time, then I go all out. That's just my way of saying I love all of you and I appreciate all of you being here and around me."

Melvin said, "I don't have to ask why. I just need to know, where do I sit so I can chow down?"

Cassandra began giving seating instructions as the table was set up for nine people with nine place settings. Jedadiah and Kamal walked in and Kamal said, "I want to sit next to my little nephew Elijah."

They all sat down at their respective places at the table and began to partake of a festive meal. Jedadiah looked across the table and observed that everyone was about finished with their meals and said, "After everyone is through, I need for anyone that is under the age of twenty-one to double-time up the stairs, brush you fangs, wash your mugs, and standby with all of your travel gear and prepared for inventory and inspection."

Melvin looked at his grandfather and said, "Tata, did you and Dad serve together at the same time or something?"

Jedadiah smiled and answered, "Son, yours is not to question why, yours is only to do or die."

Melvin responded, "With that said, I'm gone."

They all began to get up from the table. Cassandra reminded everyone, "Make sure you clean up your area of the table, and scrape and stack your plates on the sink. I love you all, but I flunked out of maid service school." They all shared a laugh as they got up from the table and followed Cassandra's instructions.

Cassandra looked at Ericka and said, "Can you please assist me in stacking these dishes in the washer, after I've rinsed them?"

Ericka replied, "With pleasure, Mom," and Beverly said, "I'll help, as well."

Melvin said, "Can I talk to you for a quick minute, Mom?"

"It will have to be quick; we're pressed for time here."

Cassandra said, "You go and talk to the boy, Beverly; we can handle this."

"Okay, Melvin; let's walk and talk."

Beverly and Melvin were walking down the hallway and Beverly asked, "Are you ready to go; everything on schedule?"

Melvin answered, "Yes, Mom, but I still need to talk to you about something."

"Okay," said Beverly, "you have the floor."

"Mom, I don't quite know how to say this, so I'm going to say it the best way I can. How it comes out, is how it comes out."

Beverly replied, "Well, you have my attention."

"Mom, I know that I'm the youngest son, but I love Dad, we do everything together; I just need to know why he does not want my help. I need to be with him because I can help him, just like he has always helped me. I remember when Jonnie Solis was picking on me and I told the teacher about it, and he called me a punk and not to rat on my classmates. Dad told me to pretend that I was afraid to fight him, play up to him like he was my friend. Dad said, invite him to go and have ice cream with you after school, and confront him then while he's not in his comfort zone and on a platform. I did what Dad told me and Jonnie fell for it. When we got away from the school, but before we got to the ice cream parlor, Jonnie looked at me and said, 'Hey, punk, you're going to pay for my ice cream and I'm going to eat yours, too.' I looked at him and said, 'That's fine with me, but I have a better idea. I'll fight you for the ice cream, and if you whip me, I go along with you and pay for yours, but if I whip you, then you're paying for my ice cream, plus everyday when I see you in school, you're going to come up to me and ask me if you can carry my books and give my your lunch money.' Jonnie said, 'You must be crazy. I'm going to kick your butt up and down this street.' I put my hands up in the defensive stance that Dad taught me and Jonnie took a swing at me. I blocked his punch and countered, and I hit him in his nose with the palm of my left hand and Jonnie fell back on the ground. When he got up, I stood over him and he was holding his hands over his nose. I noticed blood coming out in between his fingers. Jonnie said, 'I think you broke my nose.' I said, 'This is not over, Jonnie.' Jonnie said, 'My nose is broken, I can't fight anymore.' I walked directly in front of Jonnie and said, 'Let me see it.' Jonnie removed his hands and I punched him in the mouth. He fell back down to the ground. I stood over him and he looked up at me and said, 'You just broke out one of my front teeth,' then he stood up. I said, 'Let me see.' He removed his hand from his mouth and I punched him again, this time in the eye. Jonnie fell to the ground again and rolled over on his stomach. He yelled out, 'Okay, okay you win; you kicked my ass, man.' I told him to turn over on to his back. Jonnie said in tears, 'I don't want to get hit again. I told him, 'Just turn over and you won't get hit again.' Jonnie turned over onto his back. I looked down at him as he was looking up at me. I then remembered what Dad told me, if a man is on his back and does not get up; then he is down. I started to walk away and Jonnie shouted out, 'Are you just going to let me sit here like this?' I said, 'You have permission to get up now.' I continued to walk away and Jonnie started staggering down the street, bleeding from the nose, mouth, and a cut that was above the right eye. Jonnie said, 'I just need to know.' I stopped, turned around, and asked, 'Know what, man?' Jonnie said, 'Why did you keep hitting me after you broke my nose with the first punch?' I told him, 'I kept hitting you because you kept getting back up. If you had stayed down on the ground, you would have not been a threat to me; but by you getting back up, I attacked until the threat was eliminated.' Jonnie just looked at me with this dumbfounded look and did not know what to say.

"When I returned back to school, for about two weeks straight, I didn't understand why people kept coming up to me and asking me questions about what to do if this happened or that, or if someone messed with them, what should they do? It was then that I learned that Dad taught me not to just beat people down when they deserved it, but to beat their ego and pride down, as well. To this day, I think that is not just a respect level that I have at school, but it's more the fear factor. So, these kids are not sure of what to expect from me, so they don't even try me. I just want to be there for Dad when he needs me."

Beverly said, "That was a very good lesson about life you learned; a little severe, but good. Your dad does need you this time, in a different way. He is not here right now, so he wants you to help take care of the family, along with Elijah. He is trusting in you, too, to take care of the rest of us. Now, can he count on you?"

Melvin looked at her and replied, "Mom, you're in good hands and Dad will be proud of me." Beverly smiled and said, "I believe that. Now let's get ready so that we can get out of here and not miss the flight that we have to make." So, they caught up with the rest of the group and went over their last minute procedures.

Beverly said, "Mom, we're going to take Dad's truck; that way, we will not have the need to wait on anyone to pick us up from the airport when we return from our trip."

Jedadiah said, "Fine with me; I'll start loading up." He looked at Kamal and his two grandsons and said, "Okay, men, let's start loading up the cargo." Jedadiah led the pack to the garage where the vehicles were parked inside and all they had to do is enter the garage through the side kitchen area.

They loaded all of the suitcases in the rear of the Escalade SUV. Beverly and the rest of the family hopped into their respective places. Cassandra walked over to the front passenger window, where Beverly was sitting. Beverly closed her door and rolled down the window.

Cassandra looked at Beverly and said, "Everything will work out, I'm sure of it."

Beverly said, "Mom, don't worry; it will be fine. Now, just follow my instructions to the letter and you'll be good. I will call you when we get there and my contact numbers have and will not change. Call Dad on his cell phone, just as you always have. Remember, we have to treat this situation as if it's business as usual. No sudden changes."

Cassandra said, "I have it now; get going before I get emotional."

Cassandra walked over to the driver's side and Jedadiah was standing in front of the door. He extended his arms out to reach for Cassandra, who practically fell into his awaiting arms. Jedadiah kissed her on her lips and again on her forehead. He reassured her by telling her, "Baby, you know that I'm not going to let anything happen to our daughter and our grandbabies."

Cassandra said with a tear running down both of her cheeks, "I know, honey, I said I would not get emotional and look at me now. You guys get out of here before you're late." Cassandra opened the garage door for them and they drove off down the street.

Thomas was lying on his back with his eyes closed and resting, not really asleep. He took a deep breath and opened his eyes. He glanced over at the alarm clock and saw that it was 0345 hours. He thought *what the heck, I may as well get up; I've gotten all the rest that I need. I will get more rest when I die.* So, he got up and hit the shower. After showering, he put on his clothes and began to re-do his makeup. As he was glaring into the mirror, he laughed out loud, *I better follow complete instructions that Donald Morris gave me.* I don't want him getting upset that we messed up his artwork. Thomas continued preparing for the day. There was a knock on the bedroom door and Thomas shouted out, "Who is it?"

Phil answered, "It's me, Sarge; are you up and at it?"

Thomas answered, "Man, I never went to sleep."

Phil opened the door and said, "Well, I'm ready to rock; I'm going to go downstairs and check on the boys."

Thomas said, "Ten-four, I'm going to make us a light breakfast, with coffee and some tea."

Thomas went into the kitchen and pulled out a tray of fresh fruit, bagels, and cream cheese. He got the coffee pot going and the kettle on the stove. Thomas was sitting down eating and Phil walked into the kitchen and joined him. Phil pulled up a chair right next to Thomas.

Phil grabbed two bagels and filled his plate up with fruit. Thomas watched him as he piled the fruit up. Thomas said, "Man, how can you eat so much in one sitting?"

Phil laughed and said, "Man, this machine does not run on meals which only weigh three ounces. It takes fuel for me to run." They both burst out in laughter.

After ten minutes had gone by, the rest of the crew began to muster in the kitchen area. Jackson, being the first one, looked around and said, "I sure hope that you guys saved enough for me; I'm as hungry as a horse with two stomachs."

Thomas smiled and said, "At ease, marine; there is enough food here to feed the whole third marine fleet."

Jackson grabbed a plate and began to dig in. Ortiz come into the kitchen and grabbed a plate, heading straight for the food.

Phil said, "Hey, man, aren't you going to say good morning, or screw you guys, or something?"

Ortiz said, "Not until after I've eaten something; I don't talk to no one until I've had chow." They all laughed at Ortiz and said, "Gangway and let the animal eat some chow." Ortiz just looked around, not saying anything to anyone and began to eat as though this was going to be his last meal.

Mitchell Payne, one of the driving crew, walked in to see what was going on and looked very perplexed.

Jackson asked Mitchell, "Hey, man, are you okay?"

Mitchell replied, "Is there anything I should know about you guys?"

Phil answered after he stopped laughing, "Man, you're safe alright. Just don't get in the way of a hungry marine and his food."

Mitchell said, "That's good to know; I mean this is why I want you all to listen. I want every one of you to enjoy your meals. I just want you to know that every meal is a blessing and the good Lord may see fit that it's you last. So, I want you to thank Him for this meal and if He calls for you to serve duty in another time and space, I want you to serve proudly wherever God reassigns you."

Phil stood up, "Oorah; hear, hear for you civilians." Everyone got to their feet and cheered back.

Thomas looked around and said, "Men, let's get prepared to do this."

They all disbursed from the kitchen area. Thomas went into his room and broke out his notebook. He reviewed it one more time. He grabbed his gear, put on his vest, and then put on his combat jacket. He scanned the room and walked out. He walked to the den and over to the fireplace. He turned on the automatic fireplace and the fire came on. He waited 30 seconds to ensure the pit of the fire had reached 500 degrees and then he placed the notebook directly into the eye of the fire. He watched the book burn into ashes, then turned off the fire. He reached down in back of himself and picked up a bottle of hydrochloric acid. He carefully poured it onto the ashes that remained on the floor of the fireplace. It took six seconds and what used to be ashes disintegrated into nothing; it vanished as if there was nothing ever there.

Thomas left the den and headed for the garage. When he got to the garage, he took a look around and checked out the whole crew. He made sure that every one of them had complete disguises on and that they looked the part. Thomas inspected each individual until he was absolutely satisfied. When he felt that he was satisfied, he said, "We're ready to do this; let's set this shit off." All of the men began to get fired up and started high-fiving each other and knuckling one another and shaking hands.

Thomas looked at Phil and said, "Man, where is my case?"

Phil replied, "Right here, Sarge."

Thomas took the nylon case, opened it, and began to inspect it. He made sure that he had two signal jammers and one remote disabler. After he was satisfied that he had his primary equipment, he instructed Phil to conduct a last inventory of everything that was needed for this operation.

Phil completed his inventory and reported to Thomas. "Inventory is 100 percent complete, Sarge."

Thomas said, "Very well, we take these two vehicles and let's do what we do."

Mitchell got behind the wheel of the first vehicle and strapped in. As soon as he started the vehicle up, the garage door began to open. The garage door was in sync with the vehicle's code and ignition.

Mike Simms got behind the wheel of the second vehicle and started up the engine. He strapped in and readied himself for the drive. He took a deep breath and closed his eyes, and whispered a brief prayer. "Lord, I know that I have not always been right in your sight and I don't talk to you as often as I should, but I'm asking you this one time to be with me as I feel that I'm doing the right thing. If I'm not and you see fit to take me, then I come with a clear conscience."

Ortiz and Toliver walked over to each other. Ortiz told Toliver, "Turn around and I will square you away." Toliver turned around and Ortiz began to ensure that Toliver's backpack was secured tightly onto his back and his side compartments on his motorcycle were secured tightly. Ortiz told Toliver, "Your M-40, scope, and intra-vision are secured. Just don't forget that your ammo is in the side compartments, along with your handguns."

Toliver replied, "Roger that."

Toliver instructed Ortiz to turn around and began the inspection on him. After Toliver's inspection has been completed, he informed Ortiz, "You're squared away."

Ortiz replied, "Roger that. Let's do this."

They both hopped on their individual Harley-Davidson 1500 Night Rods.

Thomas and Phil got into the first vehicle with Mitchell Payne. Thomas looked at Mitchell and said, "Okay, let's roll; what the hell are you waiting for, a personal invitation?"

Mitchell replied, "No, sir," and took off.

Mike Simms followed in the second vehicle and Ortiz and Toliver followed on their bikes.

After the bikes cleared the garage driveway, the road sensors indicated that all vehicles had cleared and the garage door closed and secured itself. The crew was off, and on course to fulfill their mission

As they drove down the street, Thomas looked at Phil and said, "Man, we have to do this by the numbers. If we do this by the numbers, it will work; I know it will. We have to keep in mind, that we are taking them by surprise. However, being that this will be the largest transference of cash and currency ever, they are operating on a low key status and they will be on high alert. When this goes down, keep in mind, it's going down. When we get into the banks, we will hit Phase 1 very quickly and clear them out and be ready for Phase 2; because of the size of the cash bins, the armored car guards will not be able to see what's going on in front of them.

"Now, they will have two spotters that will go in first, but they will only signal the other guards if something is wrong. This is where we have the advantage. These guards are untrained and not prepared for this type of action, but remember what I taught you guys…never underestimate your opponents."

Phil responded, "Yes, sir."

Thomas reminded the men one more time, "Once we're inside, there will be no communicating with names; we will use our codes. We do everything by the numbers.

Thomas picked up his radio and made sure that his ear piece was plugged in. He turned on the radio unit. He stuck his earpiece in his left ear and called out to Phil, "Red Hawk to Red Dog, radio check."

Phil responded back and said, "This is Red Dog, I hear your 10-2, now copy?"

Thomas responded, "Ten-four, Red Dog."

Thomas went on all call at this time as the vehicles were reaching the city limits, "Red Hawk to all units, roll call."

Ortiz responded, "Red Eye 1 to Red Hawk, 10-2."

Toliver came through, "Red Eye 2 to Red Hawk, 10-2."

Drew responded, "Snake 1 to Red Hawk, I read you, 10-4."

Jackson called out, "Snake 2 to Red Hawk. I read you, 10-4."

Johnson called out, "Rooster to Red Hawk. I read you, 10-4."

Thomas called out, "All units are present and are accounted for. I'm going off the air and clear."

Ortiz and Toliver were riding side-by-side on their own at this time. The whole group was approximately three minutes outside of the city limits. Toliver looked over at Ortiz and nodded his head in a gesture of reassurance. Ortiz responded back, with thumbs up. As they reached the city limits, the two SUV vehicles continued traveling on to the expressway, and Ortiz and Toliver broke off from the motorcade and took the street route.

Jackson, who was traveling in vehicle 1, began to perform a systems check on his weapon. He checked the action bolt and the slide handle action lever, then swung the .60-cal. from left to right and up and down. He then checked that the tripod was bolted down to the floorboard. He inserted the magazine into the magazine port and locked and loaded the weapon and drove the safety lever to safe. He then took the metal box that he had filled with rounds already packed into the magazines and ready for action. It was apparent that he was prepared for a heavy gun battle, if the opportunity presented itself. In all, Jackson had five cases with two thousand rounds of ammunition.

Meanwhile in vehicle 2, Johnson was conducting the same systems function that Jackson performed, but Jackson seemed to be a little more enthusiastic about getting the opportunity to use the services of his deadly, but efficient new toy. Johnson had visions of sending his rounds downrange and just knowing that the rounds that he was using were armor piercing and could go completely through a car from both sides including the engine. Johnson felt completely empowered and he had to constantly remind himself that they were still on American soil and engaging on American soil would only be a last resort and destruction of property would be first and life second. Yet still, his adrenaline was at the ninth power.

As the vehicles continued down the expressway, Mitchell turned to Thomas who was sitting in the passenger seat and said, "Sir, this is our exit."

Thomas said, "I'm aware, Payne; proceed as planned."

When the exit came up, Mitchell engaged his turn signal and proceeded turning off of the expressway and looking up at the sign reading STATE ST. He turned off and exited the expressway and was driving down State St.

They drove down five blocks and Thomas looked over and noticed two large dump trucks loaded with dirt. He smiled as he noticed that the trucks signs on the side of them read, NO JOB IS TOO DIRTY. These were the trucks that were working for him. Thomas looked at his watch and noticed that the time was now 0845 hours. Thomas smiled and thought to himself, *It's really coming together.*

Meanwhile, Ortiz and Toliver were traveling down the street together on their bikes and they came to a fork in the road. Both of them came to a stop. Ortiz looked over at Toliver and said, "Hey, man, Post St. is to the left here; that's where I'm going."

Toliver nodded his head in agreement and said, "And I'm going right toward Main St."

Ortiz said, "Let's do this, man."

Toliver agreed and said, "Hey bro', do or die recon company to the end."

They both took off, speeding away and showing off the power and speed of the Harley Night Rods.

Toliver rode until he arrived on Main St. It took him seven minutes to arrive at his location. He reached in excess of 65 mph and this excited him so much that when he stopped, he had goose bumps from joy. He pulled up to the Holiday Inn and into the parking structure, and then into the inside parking garage. He parked his bike in the motorcycle parking spaces and went into the hotel.

Two minutes after Toliver arrived at the Holiday Inn, Ortiz arrived at the Mission Deluxe Hotel. He pulled into the parking structure and into the parking garage. He hopped off of his bike then adjusted his backpack and headed off to the hotel.

Both Ortiz and Toliver already had keys to their hotel rooms because Thomas had already checked in.

Ortiz made it up to the seventeenth floor from the elevator and reached into his pants pocket, pulled out his room key and read it. The room number was 1722. He walked down the hallway and tried to be as quiet as possible, in an effort not to bring any unnecessary attention to him. On the way to his room, he did not see a single soul. He thought to himself, *Good, all of the chickens are still sleeping. Now the eagle can go and nest.* Ortiz hurried to his room and began to unpack his backpack. He went over to the window that faced the north and looking out, he discovered that he could see the bank that was located on State St. He began to unpack and set up—first the tripod, and then he broke out his baby, the M-40 A-3 sniper rifle. He assembled the rifle and then attached the scope. He walked over to the window, lifted it, and opened it to a quarter and a half. Ortiz carefully attached the rifle to the tripod and measured his distance from the open window to three and a half feet back.

He put on his knee pads, knelt down on one knee, and began to sight in on his scope and set his distance, elevation, and windage. He took out his distance meter and set his asmouth. After he stabilized his asmouth, he placed his can of ammo directly in front of him, slightly to the right. This was to ensure that he would only have to reach half an arm's length to obtain more ammo to load. After Ortiz was all set for action, he got on his radio and called to To-liver, "Red Eye 1 to Red Eye 2, come back."

Toliver responded, "Red Eye 2 to Red Eye 1, go."

Ortiz asked, "Are you perched in your nest?"

Toliver responded, "Affirmative. I'm perched, locked, cocked, and ready to rock; how are you?"

Ortiz responded, "The same; it's show time, out."

Toliver responded, "Out."

Toliver had set up shop almost simultaneously with Ortiz and in the same order of operation. It was blatantly obvious that these two marines trained together, thought alike, and reacted alike. This was the reason they were alive to this day, and these men were extremely good at what they do.

Meanwhile, Thomas looked at his watch and noticed that it was now 0903. They were half a block down from the bank. Thomas instructed Mitchell to drive down and park the vehicle at the location they had desig-nated. Mitchell pulled up directly across the street from the bank and there was a utility truck parked alongside the sidewalk.

As the first SUV pulled up alongside of the utility vehicle, Thomas rolled down his passenger window. He looked over at the driver behind the wheel of the utility vehicle and nodded his head. The driver of the utility vehicle nodded his head in return and then started up his vehicle and pulled off. Mitchell pulled into the newly occupied space.

The second vehicle, driven by Simms, pulled up directly behind vehicle 1. As both vehicles turned their engines off, a truck pulled up in front of the bank; the engine was left running and, from the back of the vehicle, two men jumped out wielding 12-gauge shotguns. Thomas looked at the printing on the side of the truck and saw that the writing said Stage Coach Armored Transport. Thomas went on his radio and said, "This is it, we move."

Thomas exited the vehicle from the passenger side. He was holding a large briefcase. Drew got out of the vehicle and joined Thomas as he started walking across the street.

Upchurch looked at his watch and counted off thirty seconds and then got out of the second vehicle. He too was carrying a large briefcase. He proceeded across the street as Thomas had just entered the bank. The guards had completed uploading the first two bins. There were two guards pushing each bin. The four guards began pushing the bins into the bank; the two guards with shotguns followed and were the last two to enter the bank.

Dugmal walked over to the area for new accounts and special needs. Thomas saw a desk and some chairs, but no one was sitting behind the desk. He took a seat and placed his briefcase on the floor beside him. Drew walked all the way over to the other side of the bank where there was an ATM machine located. As he was walking over, a man wearing a suit met him and asked if he could assist him with anything in particular. Drew replied, "Yes, as a matter of fact, you can. I need to conduct a systems check on the ATM machine. I'm with Wells, Inc. and we do random checks on different machines; here's my card." Drew handed the man his business card.

The man reviewed his card and then said, "No problem, the ATM is located right over here," pointing to the ATM machine a few feet ahead and on the right-hand side. Drew thanked the man and said, "This will only take about fifteen minutes, and I'll have the ATM back up and running. I just need to read some data and I'm gone."

The man asked, "Do you need anything from me?"

Drew said, "No thanks, just inform anyone that needs to use this machine for the first fifteen minutes they will have to go to the outside ATM."

The man said, "Not a problem."

Drew walked ahead and smiled, "Man, is he stupid," he said about the man who joyfully assisted him without knowing what was about to go down.

The first two bins had entered the bank and the men were taking them to the vault area. The bank was very large in square footage. It had 17 thousand square feet and had the storage capacity that no other in the area had.

The bank's vice president assisted in opening up the vault door and was just babbling in conversation with one of the armored car carriers. At this time, Upchurch walked into the bank. He entered and walked over to the merchant's teller area. One of the tellers looked over at him and said, "It will be just a few minutes before I can help you, we're kind of short staffed this morning, and we have a large shipment coming in."

Upchurch smiled at her and said, "I understand, take your time; I'm not in a hurry or anything."

175

The teller smiled and said, "Very well then, if you don't mind, you can have a seat and I'll make sure that I'm the one that takes care of you."

Upchurch smiled at her and said, "I'd really like that."

The merchant area was an area that was isolated from the outside business area so that the merchants could conduct business in private, away from the general population. Upchurch sat down and began to take items out of his bag.

Dugmal looked at his watch and now it was 0914 hours. He looked toward the front door and noticed that the second armored transport truck was pulling up. As he was looking, the guards were heading out of the rear vault area. The vice president remained in the vault with the first two bins.

The four guards began heading toward the front door with the two shotgun carrying guards bringing up the rear. Two of the guards opened up the double doors, allowing the next incoming bins to have an easy entry. The guards greeted each other and then proceeded to push the bins toward the vault area.

Dugmal stood up and radioed Upchurch. "Red Hawk to Red Dog, secure the front door."

Upchurch jumped over the small door that separated the merchant's area. He put a long pipe against the front door that was made of titanium. When the bar was secured, Dugmal jumped back over the door and into the merchant area.

Dugmal radioed to all units and just said, "All units, move."

Drew placed the same bar on the exit door on the opposite end, ensuring that no one came into the bank or left it. He then reached into his bag and removed two handguns that dispensed paintballs. Upchurch reached into his bag and pulled out three flash bangs, as well. Dugmal radioed Phase 2 and pulled all three pins of the flash bangs. He threw one behind the tellers' desk and then another on the opposite end of the tellers' desk. Upchurch released the pins on his flash bangs and threw two of them in the vault area. The last one was in the middle of the bank where Dugmal had thrown his final flash bang in the same area.

Five seconds later, all of the flash bangs went off at the same time.

There was a loud explosion followed by a very bright flash; the light from the flash was so bright it was blinding. Although the blinking was only temporary, most people are so startled by the noise from the explosion, they believed they are blinded for life.

Everyone in the bank began screaming; that's when Dugmal and Upchurch were already in motion to dispense the canisters of Ef2A nerve and sleeping gas. Upchurch and Dugmal dispensed two canisters apiece and as the gas began to fill up the air in the entire bank, Dugmal, Upchurch, and Drew donned their protective M-2 Phase 3 masks.

Drew had already reconned the bank and assessed that the bank had 27 cameras. Cameras 8, 10, 12, 13, and 16 were linked live to the distress center. Drew quickly donned his mask and went over to cameras 8, 10, 12, and 13 and blasted them with the paintball gun so that the cameras were non-functional.

The people that were in the bank were coughing and crawling around aimlessly, trying to find some relief or a way out, but it was to no avail. After three minutes had elapsed, all of the bank employees, armored couriers, and bank customers were out like babies.

Dugmal went to the vault and was followed by Upchurch and Drew. Dugmal pushed out one of the bins from the vault. Drew began pushing the second bin, as Upchurch was following the first two men...the only difference was pushing two bins...one in front of the other and the bins were moving fluidly.

When they got to the front door, Dugmal instructed Mitchell and Simms to drive the vehicles across the street to the front of the bank.

Upchurch ran to the front door and removed the bar that he had placed on the door to secure it. By the time both vehicles flipped a U-turn and parked in front of the bank, Dugmal was walking out of the front door with the first bin. The two armored trucks were parked directly in front at curbside. Both vehicles 1 and 2 parked as close to the armored cars as they could.

Dugmal pushed the first bin out to the sidewalk, off of the curb, and into the streets. Mitchell pushed the rear cargo door release and both cargo doors opened. A lift came down. Dugmal pushed the bin onto the lift; Mitchell lifted the first bin and it attached to the rail tracks and was locked in place in the truck. Drew was right in back of Dugmal with the second bin. Upchurch pushed both bins off of the curb and the second bin heel got stuck on the curb. Dugmal was just about to load the second bin and noticed that Upchurch was struggling and directed Drew to run over and assist Upchurch. Drew ran over and grabbed the second bin. Dugmal loaded the second bin onto the truck and made sure that the lift retracted properly.

He looked at what was going on at the bank. It was still quiet in the bank, but people began to slow down walking down the street and beginning to take notice at what they were doing. Dugmal walked over to the second vehicle. He was questioned by a passerby who questioned as to if they worked for the bank. Dugmal responded, "Yes, we do, now keep on moving; we're on a timeline."

The man on the street responded, "You guys don't look like bank employees to me; I'm going to check this out." The Good Samaritan walked into the bank.

Dugmal looked over at the crew in vehicle 2 and said, "Let's double-time it; this slack jam sissy dog just went into the bank and I believe that he is going to cause trouble."

The Good Samaritan came running out of the bank coughing and screaming, "Help, there's something wrong; these guys are doing something wrong."

Dugmal ran over to the Good Samaritan, grabbed him, and dragged him over to vehicle 1. He put the guy on the ground, strapped his hands and feet together, and stuck the man's tie in his mouth to shut him up. By this time, a young lady that was standing by looking at the action build up took out her cell phone and started dialing. Dugmal glanced over and saw the young lady looking their way and on the phone. He got on the radio and said, "All units we have been made; we have 30 seconds to disappear from here."

Dugmal got into the passenger seat of vehicle 1 and pulled out his remote signal jammer. He pushed the disrupt button and looked over at the young lady, and saw that she was shaking her phone and checking it in an effort to try to find out why it was not working anymore.

By now, Upchurch and Drew had just completed loading the fourth and final bin in the back of the truck. As the bin was locking into the tracks, the men began to hear sirens. Upchurch radioed Dugmal and asked, "Red Hawk, do you hear what I hear?"

Dugmal responded, "Affirmative; they are very close…about two blocks away, let's move."

Both trucks started their engines and started driving off. When they got to the first block, a patrol car pulled in front of the truck. Mitchell asks Dugmal, "What should I do?"

Dugmal answered, "Go through him."

Mitchell did not hesitate one bit. He pushed the accelerator and drove through the police cruiser. Vehicle 2 followed directly behind him. The police cruiser was completely disabled. As Dugmal sped off down the street, the second vehicle being driven by Simms followed tight behind him.

Dugmal radioed Upchurch and instructed him to make sure that Simms followed him in vehicle 2 and do not, at all costs, let him lose us. We have got to stay together as one unit.

Upchurch responded, "You got it."

Thomas directed Mitchell to make a left onto Florence Ave., which was the next turn. They arrived at Florence Ave., which was quite sudden because Mitchell was going at a speed of 60 mph. When they turned left onto Florence Ave., Simms turned, as well. Both vehicles proceeded to drive down Florence.

The patrol vehicle that began the pursuit called into headquarters and reported two vehicles traveling at a high rate of speed heading west on State St. As the report to dispatch went through, one unit that was on Florence Ave. responded, "Did I hear two SUV vehicles?"

Dispatch responded, "That's a 10-4, Mobile 362."

Unit 362 replied, "I have a visual on two black SUVs traveling at high speeds heading west on Florence Ave. and I'm in pursuit."

Dispatch radioed, "Calling all units in the vicinity of Florence, State, Main, Post, and Broadway to respond and back up unit 362. These suspects are believed to be armed and dangerous and connected with a bank robbery at Western Stage Coach Bank on State St. at 0920 hours."

At this time, Thomas was listening to his law enforcement scanner and picked up everything that was being tracked. Thomas instructed Mitchell to proceed down Florence Ave. until he gave the order to change directions.

At that time Upchurch called Dugmal on the radio and said, "Red Dog to Red Hawk, come back."

Dugmal responded, "Red Hawk, go."

Upchurch said, "This cruiser is right on our ass and two other units have just joined them, what do you want to do?"

"Hold steady our course and I will advise," replied Dugmal.

Thomas looked back to take a look at what was going on with the responding police officers. Being that Thomas had served in the sheriff's department in the past, he realized that now he had to think like a cop would think if he was in this situation and pursuing a suspect. As Thomas contemplated what would be the next move, Jackson said, "Hey, Sarge, guess what? We have a road block up ahead of us about half a click."

Thomas looked ahead and said, "Okay, I thought that we could avoid this, but it looks like we can't."

Mitchell asked, "Avoid what? What are you going to do?"

Thomas said, "I need for you to shut up and only do what I tell you to do from this point forward. I can get us out of this and I can also keep you alive, as well; so do only what I tell you when I tell you. Is that clear?"

Mitchell answered, "Crystal clear, sir."

Thomas got on his radio and called out to Phil. "Red Dog, when we reach that Radio Shack just up the street on the left, we will be approximately forty feet from the road block ahead. I need you to instruct Simms to pull up and get side-by-side with us, right now."

Simms sped up and pulled side-by-side with vehicle 1. Thomas said, "Now, once we get to the Radio Shoppe, stop the vehicle, pull in front of us facing the barricade with the right side of your vehicle and we will face the opposite."

Upchurch looked at Simms and said, "Did you get that, man?"

Simms answered, "I got it; I got it!"

When the vehicles reached Radio Shack, both vehicles stopped, the police vehicles that were in hot pursuit slammed on their brakes and stopped back 3-5 feet. The police that were in back and in front of them watched in amazement and in curiosity, as vehicle 1 pulled around 2 and, before you knew what was going on, vehicle 2—Upchurch's vehicle—was facing the blockade and Thomas's vehicle 1 was facing sideways looking on to the pursuing police vehicles.

All of the police units got out of their vehicles, opened the car doors, and knelt down in an effort to use the car doors as shields for cover. One of the trailing police officers ran to the trunk of his vehicle, opened it, and directed two other officers to come over. As they joined the one officer behind his trunk, he starts handing them shotguns—riot shotguns and one SMG automatic rifle. After the police officers collected their weapons of choice, they began to take position behind their vehicles.

Meanwhile at the other end, the police officers at the blockade point were walking in position and one of the lieutenants began to speak on his megaphone. "This is the United Cities Police Department. You are all under arrest. We need for all of you to come out with your hands held high where we can see them. We have you completely surrounded. If you don't comply, we will start firing upon your vehicle. You have ten seconds to comply."

Thomas talked on the radio and said, "Just hold at ease, men."

Thomas turned on the loudspeaker that had been attached under the hood of the truck. He keyed up the loudspeaker and said, "Attention; I need for all of your units that are blocking our paths and the patrol units at the opposite side of the street to listen carefully. I need for all of your units to back up and away from this area immediately. I know that the majority of you guys have families back at home and you want to make it home to see them again, but if you don't back the fuck up and clear out of here, this will be your final day of being alive. I know that your salaries do not dictate risking or losing your lives like this. Most of you guys will never understand what's really going on here right now. I will give you 30 seconds to clear out for those of you that would like to live. I will only say this once and then what will happen next, I will not be responsible for."

The police lieutenant looked at one of the sergeants and said, "Do you believe this guy? He must be out of his fucking mind. Does he think that we're Boy Scouts or some shit like that?"

The sergeant responded, "Hey, Lieutenant, something is not right about this situation. You said yourself the way these guys stayed together while traveling at high speeds and the way both vehicles stopped on a dime at the same time…either these guys are a well organized unit or they are some kind of law enforcement or military. Maybe we are in over our heads or something, and they are giving us an opportunity to clear the way."

The lieutenant said, "Get yourself together, man. You're a sworn police officer, sworn to uphold the law, at all cost."

The sergeant said, "You're right…to uphold the law…not commit suicide. We know nothing about these guys, what they are capable of, or what they have with them."

The lieutenant said, "Okay, I suggest you get back to your positions, and anyone that takes off from this will be fired. I will fire your asses myself."

At the other end of the street, two of the uniformed officers looked at each other. One of the officers said, "Man, I have a son that's two and a half years old and my daughter is seven months old. I want to make it home to see them."

The other officer kneeling with him said, "You know, you're right. These guys are no joke; something about these guys tells me in my gut they are nobody to play around with."

The first officer said, "Let's get out of here."

They both re-holstered their side arms and eased back to the last patrol car. The second officer said, "This is our cruiser and it's not blocked." They both jumped in and drove in the opposite direction.

Dugmal said, "You guys have ten seconds left; this is your last warning."

The lieutenant got on the radio and said, "Dispatch, have you dispatched the SWAT unit yet, and what's their ETA?"

Dispatch responded, "That's affirmative, Lt. Barnes; their ETA is twelve minutes."

Lt. Barnes replied, "Dispatch, you tell the SWAT unit to get here in five minutes; we may have an uncontrollable situation here in twelve minutes."

Dispatch responded, "I will relay your info, Lieutenant."

Lt. Barnes looked back at police Sgt. Knowles and said, "Make sure every officer is in position and ready to move on these fuckers. I want every officer to unload on these two vehicles and not stop until I give the command to cease fire. Do you understand, Sgt. Knowles?"

"Yes, sir, but I'm going to tell you now that we have lost some units."

Lt. Barnes asked, "What in the hell do you mean we have already lost units? I have not heard any shots fired, yet."

Knowles responded, "I know, sir; but, we did have some units that pulled away already."

"I thought I said for all units to stand fast," said Lt. Barnes. "I want the names of all of the officers that pulled out without authorization."

"Well, Lt., I'll do that if we live through this. If you look at your watch, it should show that we are plum out of time."

Lt. Barnes glanced at his watch and said, "Damn it; where's the SWAT unit?"

Dugmal keyed up the megaphone once again and said, "I was really hoping that all of you police officers would have pulled out by now. To all of you with families I'm sorry for this, but I'm not sorry for those that are willing to engage and die unnecessarily."

Lt. Barnes got on his megaphone and said, "Hey, wait just a minute. You guys don't have to die like this; this is your choice."

Dugmal responded, "I have nothing else to say at this point; you all have made your choices."

Lt. Barnes shouted out on the megaphone, "All units open fire!"

Officers at the east end began firing at the two vehicles using their handguns, 12-gauge shotguns, and SMG semi-automatic weapons. Right after that, the police officers that were on the west end joined in on the barrage of gunfire.

They continued to rain down on the two vehicles with everything that they had for three and a half minutes.

Lt. Barnes looked at the two vehicles and noticed that with all the rounds of ammunition being fired, the two vehicles appeared to be completely intact.

Sgt. Knowles looked at Barnes and said, "I don't know if you noticed yet, sir, but both of these vehicles appear to be reinforced with armor plates. Hell, we're not even scratching the inner portion of their vehicles."

Lt. Barnes shouted, "Continue firing; we'll hit something sooner or later!"

Barnes said, "Lieutenant, we're wasting rounds. They have not even returned fire as of yet."

Barnes said, "That's right you dipshit; that could mean that they were just bluffing the entire time. Maybe they weren't ready for us."

"Or maybe," said Knowles, "they are waiting to see if we run out of ammo before the cavalry comes. So all that we have to do is keep up the fire power until that special unit arrives, and more units arrive to back us up, if needed."

Barnes said, "We can last until then."

Four minutes passed by and Knowles said, "Lieutenant, we need to see if these guys are willing to give up, yet."

Barnes said, "You're right; let's see if these guys want to give up as of now."

Lt. Barnes gave the order, "Cease fire; cease fire!"

All of the police units ceased fire while the smoke from the gun powder filled the air and it looked like a war zone. After a few seconds, the smoke began to clear and all of the officers that were looking on began to notice and talk amongst one another. They said, "Look at that; there are no windows broken out or tires blown out at all." The officers began to get very uneasy.

Barnes shouted, "You people that are in the vehicles; are you ready to come out, yet? Have you pieces of shit had enough, yet?"

Dugmal looked over at Jackson and said, "It's time to go to work."

Jackson responded, "I'm ready to rock 'n' roll, Sarge."

Dugmal got on the radio and told Johnson, "It's time to go to work."

Johnson replied, "This is Rooster, Red Hawk, and I'm ready to scratch this itch."

Dugmal said, "Gunners to your marks."

Both Jackson in vehicle 1 and Johnson in vehicle 2 locked and loaded the .60-cal. and braced to fire.

Dugmal said, "All units, engage."

At this point, Mitchell placed his right index finger on the door release and the side door began to open from the hydraulic system.

At the same time, Simms engaged the release in vehicle 2. The doors began to open in both vehicles at the same time.

Meanwhile, all of the officers that were looking on began to say, "Hey, the doors are opening!"

Barnes said, "You know, I think these bastards are going to surrender."

By this time, three other units showed up and joined the west end where Lt. Barnes gave a brief update to the officers that just joined them. Barnes said, "These pieces of shit robbed the Western Stage Coach Bank this morning and now we have them cornered here. There are two vehicles, both Chevy Suburbans. They seem to have armor plates protecting both vehicles, as well as reinforced glass that seems to be shatterproof. The tires must have some type of filler because they won't go down. Now, I believe that they are going to give up because the doors are beginning to open."

Cpl. Wayans, the police officer who just joined them, looked at Lt. Barnes and asked, "There are hundreds of spent casings around here, was there a fire fight?"

"I gave the order to open fire on these pieces of shit," replied Barnes. "I gave them ten seconds to give up and get their asses out of the vehicles and their time expired. I think that they got the message now."

Cpl. Wayans looked at Barnes and asked, "Man, how long have you been on the force?"

Barnes answered, "What the fuck kind of question is that? I know what the fuck I'm doing. I've been on the force for nine years and I always win."

Wayans looked at him and said, "No disrespect to you, Lieutenant," and said, "you dummy. I have only been here for two minutes and I can see that these guys are not getting ready to give up. You mean you can't see that? These guys are ready for an all-out war and I guarantee they are more ready than we are. As a matter of fact, I'm pulling my guys back far behind your perimeter!"

Barnes said, "I'm giving you a direct order, Corporal, to stand fast or I will have you up on charges!"

Wayans smiled and said, "Do whatever you want, but I'm pulling my men back."

Before Barnes could say another word, one of the officers that were looking on shouted out, "The doors are open, I can see…" and then he said nothing.

Barnes shouted, "See what? What the fuck do you see?" Just as Barnes finished his question, there was no time to receive an answer before it all started going down.

As the doors completed the open cycle in both SUVs, Jackson and Johnson began firing the .60-cal. machine guns. Jackson rotated from left to right and Johnson from right to left. As the rounds began to go down range, they found their targets in the parked police vehicles. The first vehicle struck was on the east end. The officers sat helplessly behind their vehicles as they hoped the car would prevent the rounds from striking them. One of the officers that was sitting up against the rear end of the cruiser, looked ahead toward the front end; as he looked on, rounds traveled down from the front to the middle of the driver's door and back passenger door. He noticed that the rounds were going completely through the car...in one end, and out of the other. The first thing that was going through the officer's mind was, *OH, NO! I'm going to die today.*

In a frantic motion, the officer fell down, dropping on the ground, and as he opened his eyes, he could see that holes were appearing in a straight line heading toward him, but above this head. He held his breath and the rounds went past him, almost as if they were going in slow motion. As he waited to see if this really was his time to go, he noticed that the rounds and firing did not stop, but they were past him. He lifted up his head and looked down to see if he could see blood on him and where. He scanned his left arm and saw nothing; scanned his right arm and saw nothing. He scanned down his body and when he looked down at the ground to his left, he saw and felt something wet and warm. He gasped and took a deep breath. He said, "Lord, if you just let me live through this, I will leave the force like Jenny wants me to." He gathered himself and patted his left thigh; he couldn't feel any pain or injury. He then looked and felt the right side and, again, if he felt or saw anything, that would confirm he had been hit. He looked down at his crotch and began to giggle. *OH, NO! I pissed my pants. That's all. I never thought that I would be happy that I pissed in my pants!*

As Jackson continued his rotation and firing of 3.3-second rounds, it did not take long before the rounds found their next target. There were four officers behind the next vehicle. They had their bodies pressed against the vehicle in an effort to allow the vehicle to stop the rounds from finding them. The first officer at the front of the vehicle let out a loud yell as he fell quickly to the ground. The officer kneeling next to him noticed that blood from his fallen comrade had sprayed all over the front of his uniform. It was not long after, the officer seeing blood splatter on him, felt a round go through him. As he fell forward, the round struck him in his right arm, going through his chest from one side to the other, and exiting through the left arm. He, too, fell on the ground. The next two officers fell to the ground without even knowing what hit them.

As Jackson rotated the .60-cal. back to the right, the police officers that were behind the vehicles on the right saw what was going on. One of the officers said, "Do you guys see that? The bullets are going right through our vehicles; let's get the hell out of here!"

The officers on the right side began to scramble away from the cover of their patrol cars and tried to run away. As Jackson sprayed rounds into the patrol vehicles; it looked like the police vehicles were toys being shredded by hot welder's rods. As the officers ran away one by one, they would fall to the ground after being cut in half by the force of the .60-cal. rounds. Some of the officers had the wherewithal to dive on the ground and lay prone while the rounds would pass over their heads. Other officers that were not as fortunate fell victim of one of the worst rounds that a human can get hit with, and stood no chance of surviving after being hit by them.

On the other end, Johnson had begun sending rounds eastward and finding targets as easy as he wanted.

Lt. Barnes yelled to the other men...as soon as they reloaded, to commence firing on them.

Sgt. Knowles said, "You dumb shit, you can't see the forest for the trees, they're using armor piercing rounds on us; we don't stand a chance against them! We're lucky if we live through this!"

Barnes said, "Shut the fuck up and return fire!"

Sgt. Knowles thought to himself, *I'm going home tonight to my wife and six kids. The asshole can die today like he wants to.* Knowles grabbed his pistol and lay prone on the ground.

Barnes stood up and placed his pistol between the unit and the open front door of the patrol car and started firing anyway. As Johnson continued rotating the .60-cal. to the right, Barnes emptied one magazine, dropped it out, reached into his magazine holder, grabbed a full load, and inserted it into the magazine well; he brought the cartridge and slide handle home, and continued firing his pistol in the direction of vehicle 1.

As Johnson continued barraging rounds into the patrol vehicles and randomly finishing police officers, bodies were falling by the numbers on the police side. As Johnson got within three feet of Barnes, one of Barnes' rounds found its way into the right arm of Johnson. He did not even flinch and continued firing the .60-cal.; two rounds found their way into the left chest and middle breast plate of Barnes.

Barnes continued firing. He was dying, but did not believe this, yet. Barnes emptied another magazine. He repeated the process once again and reloaded. He fired off five more rounds when he noticed that blood was coming out of his mouth and nose. He stopped firing and looked down at Knowles on the ground and said, "Well, what do you want to do, dummy, live forever?" He fell to the ground next to Knowles and spit with his dying breath, "Fuck them!" He closed his eyes and went to sleep.

When Johnson and Jackson had completed two cycles of rotating with the .60-cal., Dugmal said, "Cease fire, gunners!" They both stopped firing. They began to reload the .60-cal. ammo as Thomas stepped out of the vehicle wearing a Dillon press mini gun; at the same time, Upchurch stepped out with a mini gun just the same as Dugmal.

Dugmal looked around and saw that some of the vehicles that were parked back behind the first six vehicles were sitting intact. Dugmal radioed Upchurch and said, "Let's finish this."

Upchurch said, "Let's do it."

Dugmal started walking ahead and began firing the mini gun. The windows in the police vehicles began to explode out and parts began to fill the air and sprinkle down like dust particles. The police officers began to run away from the vehicles and try to escape the rounds that were overwhelming them.

Upchurch began firing rounds on the opposite end. As police officers scrambled, Upchurch sent rounds into the remaining vehicles. The police officers desperately tried to avoid being in harm's way, but some were not so lucky and got hit as they were running away. Police officers were falling down while others saw them going down bleeding, but were not able to do anything to assist them in an effort to save their own lives.

Sgt. Knowles was still lying prone on the ground as bullets flew above him. He was just watching as fellow officers ran and fell in front of him and to the side of him, and could only hope that the barrage stopped as suddenly as it started.

Cpl. Wayans crawled over and stopped next to Knowles and said, "Yeah, bro', it looks like we're in a hell of a mess!"

Knowles responded, "Yeah, you're right; we are in a hell of a mess."

Wayans asked, "Where is Barnes?"

Knowles paused for a second and said, "He's over there, next to that cruiser."

Wayans looked over at the police cruiser vehicles near them. He noticed that Lt. Barnes was lying prone, but there was no movement whatsoever coming from the body that was on the ground. Knowles looked at Wayans and said, "Yes, Barnes will not be giving any orders to anyone else." Wayans dropped his head down and whispered, "Well, Barnes was a hard ass, but this is not the way that I thought he would go out. I knew that he was coming hard, but I would like to have believed that he would have been more careful than this." Wayans looked over at Barnes' lifeless body and shook his head and said, "You know what, Knowles, we have to get the hell out of this alive."

Knowles said, "Yes, we do, and the way we do it is by playing it smart; we are not out manned, but we are definitely out gunned by a long shot."

Wayans asked, "What shall we do at this point?"

Knowles said, "Well, they told us to back off; and that is just what we're going to do for the time being. But, this is what I want you to do in the meantime. I want you to ease back there behind the fourth cruiser over there; it's already been destroyed, so they have no reason to revisit that one. Use your radio and call our dispatch and inform them that we are not dealing with an advance bunch here; these guys are totally organized and armed to the teeth. I don't know who they are, but we have reason to fear them and to proceed with caution."

Wayans said, "Ten-four, I got you; I will also let them know to inform SWAT when they arrive to come in code six and we need to flash them, as well."

Knowles said, "And let them know that I need eyes in the sky, as well. Get the chopper as soon as possible and keep the news choppers the hell away."

Wayans eased back slowly until he found some cover behind a disabled vehicle. He began to call in for help from dispatch. After all the information had been relayed, dispatch asked, "Who are these guys anyway? And how many of them are there?"

Wayans answered, "We have counted eight of them, but there may be more. We have no idea who they are, but if you pull the information from the plate on their vehicles, run them; maybe we can get some type of idea what or who we are dealing with."

The dispatch operator responded, "We're on it as we speak. You guys just try to stay alive. I'm dispatching the highway patrol and sheriff's departments, as well. Don't worry, help is on the way!"

Wayans said, "Okay, 10-4, I'm signing out." Wayans signed off of the radio and looked around from the rear end of the vehicle in an effort to see if the coast was clear. He could see from a distance that Dugmal was still walking around and dispersing rounds from his weapon. Wayans looked down at his pistol in its side holster and grasped the 12-gauge riot shotgun in his hands. He thought to himself *this will do nothing against their weapons.* He just braced his back up against the rear end of the vehicle and smiled to himself. I'm just a sittin' turkey here for a while and wait it out.

Several police officers have split and run for their lives in whatever direction would render them safety. As Dugmal continued walking and dispersing rounds, he tried to be sure to target the vehicles and not actual people. Upchurch was following the same philosophy. When there was no more threat by law enforcement and no return fire up on them, Dugmal re-joined Upchurch and instructed him to back off. Jackson and Johnson remained in the vehicles and provided cover for Dugmal and Upchurch.

Dugmal began to back up in the direction of the vehicles; Upchurch began to do the same. Dugmal called out on the radio to Jackson and Johnson and said, "Red Hawk to Snake 2 and Rooster, maintain cover for our six o'-clock and twelve o'clock."

Rooster responded, "Ten-four, Red Hawk;" Snake 2 responded back, "Ten-four, Red Hawk."

All of the police officers remained on the ground as Dugmal and Upchurch grew closer to vehicle 1 and 2. As Dugmal reached a vehicle, he opened the front passenger door and as he was getting in, Drew took his hand piece off and said, "Hey, Red Hawk, we have SWAT arriving here and will be on point in 30 seconds. We also have some eyes in the sky."

Dugmal asked, "Which department do we have airborne?"

Drew answered, "We actually have three arriving. We have United Cities, Highway Patrol, and Sheriff's Department. Oh, yes, and just to let you know, all of the departments that are airborne are sending patrol units, as well, and ground unit SWAT departments."

Dugmal said, "Very well, then. Let us now prepare for Phase 3."

Drew responded, "I did not know that we would have to take it to Phase 3, but I guess that it's not such a bad thing; we're all still alive."

Dugmal smiled and said, "Just follow directions and you all will stay alive." Dugmal instructed the crew to shut the doors in the vehicles.

Upchurch called Dugmal on the radio and asked, "What's the next move, Red Hawk?"

Dugmal responded, "We sit tight and wait until the rest of the responding units arrive, and then we do what we do, and we are going to head back over to our rendezvous point."

Upchurch responded, "Ten-four, Red Hawk; we will follow your lead and we will be right with you."

As the two vehicles just waited to see what was going to be the next move by the police department, the emergency sirens could be heard coming down the street and were getting very loud as they drew closer. It wasn't long before the sirens stopped and you could then see three mobile units from SWAT in vans. They stopped at the east end of the barricade. Then three more units showed up on the west end. The units began to deploy officers out of the back of each unit as they came to a stop. They began to run and take cover behind some of the disabled units, some of which were even still smoldering from bullets that sprayed them and cracked glass and paint; and some vehicles had actually burned up.

The units began to pull out a small barricade and set up mini guns on tripods.

Upchurch called Dugmal on the radio and asked, "Are we going to wait until they get set up before we strike?"

Dugmal responded, "We can't move, yet, until the air units arrive. It makes no sense to scram now because they can track us. Just stay down until their air units arrive and then we move."

Upchurch responded, "Ten-four, Red Hawk; I sure hope you know what you're doing."

As the SWAT unit alone set up and positioned themselves, the SWAT team leader made his way very carefully to where Sgt. Knowles was squatted down and embracing cover from behind one of the squad cars.

SWAT team leader from United Cities Sheriff's Department Lt. O'Malley put his back up against the squad car alongside of Sgt. Knowles and introduced himself, "Sergeant, I'm Lt. O'Malley, Swat Unit, and we're here to clean up this shit. What's the situation?"

Knowles took a breath and said, "Are you ready for this?"

O'Malley looked at him and said, "Are you asking me if I'm ready for this? My men and I are highly trained. We go through special training and tactics in preparation for this kind of action consistently, and we can't wait to close this out and go home to our wives, girlfriends, and family…and have steak and potatoes for dinner."

Knowles smiled and said, "I wish that it was going to be that easy, but I assure you that it's not."

O'Malley looked at Knowles. Knowles said, "Just look around you; take a good look and then let me know when you're ready to shut up and listen to what we're up against."

O'Malley gasped and said, "I'm all ears."

Knowles said, "These guys are heavily armed and we don't even have a count on how many of them there are; every time we've attempted to return fire, they take us out. These guys are extremely organized and every one of them hits their target when they shoot; I mean they have not missed a target, yet."

O'Malley asked, "Who's in charge, someone has to assess this situation?"

Knowles said, "Look over there. He was pointing to the direction of Lt. Barnes' body lying on the ground behind their unit and in front of another disabled unit. Barnes would not listen to me when I suggested that we wait and see what they wanted first."

O'Malley asked, "Well, what did they want?"

Knowles responded, "They instructed as to pull out and allow them to escape. They told us if we wanted to live, we should comply with their demands."

O'Malley asked, "That's all they wanted?"

"That was enough for me," replied Knowles. "You know, it wasn't what they demanded; it was how they demanded it."

"How was it demanded?"

Knowles said, "They sounded very confident; it was like they knew something that we did not know about them. It was almost like they knew that their weapons outmatched ours and their training was far superior to ours. If I had to take a wild guess, I would say that these guys are former military, like Navy Seals or United Stated Marine Corps."

O'Malley looked at Knowles and said, "That sounds totally unbelievable. By looking at all of these bodies of our fallen, I know something is not right. I'm going to radio in and have dispatch look up all of the members of recently released military and the ones that were Special Forces and other Special Units, and the one's that may possibly have psychological disorders. We can at least start there. I will also check for recently released prisoners; we might have a situation where some of the charters have joined together from different crime wave sets and are trying to pull off something big, thinking they are going to outsmart law enforcement."

"That's a good start," Knowles replied, "but my gut tells me something else."

O'Malley asked, "What does your gut tell you?"

"When they gave all of the officers the opportunity to pull out..."

O'Malley interrupted him, "What do you mean gave them the opportunity to pull out? That's an option that we would give, if it was an option."

Knowles continued, "Well, what they said is, their intention was not to hurt any law enforcement officers, but to leave the area and get away."

"You know that just makes no sense at all," said O'Malley. "What the hell were they talking about? It sounds like a bluff."

Knowles said, "Funny, that's what Lt. Barnes thought just before he gave the open fire command."

O'Malley asked, "You mean you guys fired first?"

"We fired everything we had at their vehicles and we had no penetration at all; not even the tires. It was as though they were expecting a heavy firefight, were prepared for it, and just toying with us; that is what's scaring me. We have no idea of what we're up against and, yet, they still have the audacity to show honor."

O'Malley asked, "What do you mean show honor?"

Knowles says, "After we opened fire on them, we had to expend at least 50 thousand rounds. They waited, and watched us scramble around looking for more armor; and then when we were collecting more armor, while it was being distributed, they came out blasting, and I don't mean small arms and small fire. They came out with the big dogs."

O'Malley asked, "What do you mean big dogs? Shotguns, AK-47s?"

Knowles gasped, took a deep breath, and said, "I don't think that you heard what I was saying. I said big dogs, .60-cal. armor-piercing rounds. They were shredding our vehicles like you would Wisconsin cheese. But, they showed sportsmanship in doing so. They targeted only the vehicles, at first."

O'Malley asked, with excitement, "What do you mean, at first?"

"They only shot the officers that were returning fire; that's how Lt. Barnes bit it. I told him to stay down under cover, but he had to play commando."

O'Malley looked at Knowles and said, "You talk like you admire these criminals, and I hope that's not the case here; you are a sworn police officer, and that means you take risks, and if it means dying for the cause, then that's what it means. I expect you to get your shit together and pull your head out of your ass and get into this war, Sergeant."

Knowles smiled and said, "I have no problem doing my job. I've done it for twelve years. I made sergeant in the first three years after I joined the force. I have decorations and citations. My record is exemplary. I have a Bachelor's of Arts degree in Criminal Justice. I say from my professional experience that until we find out who these guys are, and what we're up against, I say we bypass time and we just might stay alive."

O'Malley replied, "Well, I'm going to wait for intel from dispatch and I should have a negotiator here."

"That's good; at least we will have someone talking to these guys. And maybe they can talk some sense into them," said Knowles.

Dugmal was looking out of the window and listening to the police scanner. He heard Lt. O'Malley call into dispatch and ask, "Where is my negotiator?"

The negotiator came on the air and said, "This is Epstein; I'm looking for Lt. O'Malley."

O'Malley said, "This is O'Malley, come over to the patrol unit that is seven cars up toward the front of the barricade to the right."

Negotiator Epstein made his way to where O'Malley was located. O'Malley introduced himself to Epstein and the two met. O'Malley briefed Epstein on what was going on and said, "This situation is different than what I'm used to dealing with. We have no hostages and they're not asking for any ransom."

O'Malley responded, "Yes, that's true, but they robbed a bank and are sitting on a few million dollars. We don't know for sure if there are not any hostages with them. So, until we find out for sure, then your job is to negotiate, so negotiate."

Epstein said, "Okay, here we go."

Before Epstein could key in on the megaphone, Cpl. Wayans shouted out, "Here comes the news media!"

O'Malley looked toward the streets ahead of the barricade and saw three news media vehicles pulling up. They got out and started setting up their equipment. O'Malley radioed to Wayans, "The news media stays back as far as possible."

Wayans took off and ran into a situation with the news crews.

Dugmal was listening in on the scanner and radioed to Upchurch, "Hey, all units, stand down at this time until I give instruction."

Simms looked around at Upchurch and said, "Hey, man, we are sitting ducks just waiting here like this; we are going to be like sheep waiting for the slaughter."

Upchurch said, "Man, shut up, and hold it together. Dugmal knows what the fuck he's doing. You don't know shit. We have been in the shit before and have come out of it. All you have to do is hold it together and we will make it out of this."

Johnson started to laugh. Simms said, "Man, I don't know what's so funny. I've never been in a situation like this and I've seen some bad situations, and the outcome has always been unfavorable for the bad guys."

Johnson said, "Well, for one we are not the bad guys here and two, you don't know Dugmal." Johnson looked at Upchurch and asked, "Hey, man, do you remember Kuwait in 1983?"

Dugmal laughed and answered, "Of course I do; now, that was the shit."

Simms asked, "What happened in 1983?"

Johnson said, "We were on Operation Head Storm; it was a rescue and extraction mission. We thought it was going to be an overnighter. Intel informed us that we were spending it with a couple of hundred insurgents."

"Hey," said Upchurch, "I mean that was truly the shit."

Simms asked, "What's the shit? You keep saying that."

Johnson said, "We started out with only our team; we were scouts. We placed our snipers ahead to render cover. Ortiz reported to us that what we thought was a couple of hundred armed, turned out to be a couple of thousand insurgents and they were armed to the 'T.' Ortiz reported his findings to Dugmal and Dugmal responded, 'Now, it looks like the odds are just about even, that's about twenty-seven to one; this is going to be a good day and if our time comes and the good Lord calls us up to that big green place in the sky to guard the gate of heaven, it will be a pleasure to have served with you few fine marines. But in the meantime, let's invite these lowlife maggots to hell.'"

Simms said, "Well, what happened then?"

Johnson laughed, looked at Simms, and said, "There were two thousand of them and seven of us to start with. We engaged with them at 2120 hours on Thursday. Sgt. Dugmal had Ortiz in an abandoned building on the right-hand side of town and Toliver in a hotel that was still occupied by hotel guests. Many of those pricks ran into the town, as Ortiz and Toliver would pick them off one-by-one. They had M-46 sniper rifles and they averaged one shot every 3 seconds," Johnson said, "and you know what the best thing about it was?

All of the shots were headshots and they went down right away, dropping just like flies."

"What about the rest of the insurgents," asked Simms, "what happened to them?"

Johnson said, "Dugmal had us set blasts every half a click, and two perimeter spreads. These assholes were blowing up left and right; there were arms, legs, lips, and asses flying all over the place."

Simms inquired, "There still were a lot more of these guys left, what happened then?"

Upchurch smiled and said, "Hey, as they ran for cover all disorganized and 'discombobulated,' we would fire and watch them fall down. When their numbers diminished down to under a hundred, Dugmal ordered us to grab the scumbags' dead bodies, put their clothes on, and go out into the streets as though we were them. Those fools thought that we were them and did not even pay any attention to us, as we wiped them out. We recovered the hostages and called it a day."

Simms said, "Hot damn, you guys are fucking heroes; I mean you've shown what made all of the headlines in every newspaper in the country."

"Okay, not so fast, cowboy," said Johnson.

Simms asked, "What, what is it?"

Upchurch replied, "We were on Special Ops. What we did is what we do. We don't get recognized, no flags flying or parade. It's what we do for a living and we do it well. That's why I say that we have been in the shit before and came out of it under the direction and leadership of Sgt. Dugmal."

Simms paused and said, "You know, just hearing that, I feel more confident about this situation; I'm not worried anymore. What will happen, will happen, and I'm ready."

Upchurch said, "That's good to hear, man, because we have to be ready to respond without hesitation as soon as Dugmal gives the order."

"I'm ready," said Simms.

As Dugmal looked, he saw that more units were showing up as re-enforcements and were attempting to get set up and organized.

Now, Epstein began to speak on the megaphone. He said, "Attention to you people that are in the subs; my name is Detective Negotiator Epstein, may I please speak to whoever is in charge."

Dugmal got on his loudspeaker and said, "This is Red Hawk Leader and that's all you need to know about me. Keep in mind, that I don't want to be your friend and we will not make plans to meet later at the barn and hold hands to the wee hours of the morning. I say this only to you, and I will say this only once and then this conversation will be terminated; remember we have the upper hand here and we have nothing to lose. This is a job and the job is on us to stay alive and take the lives of others, and I would like to inform you that business for us is good."

Epstein paused for a moment, he looked at Knowles, and said, "I, I don't have a comeback. I usually have an answer or response quicker than the other person, but these guys are different. They are definitely military. Let me try this. We need to know what you want, that's all.'"

Dugmal said, "We want you to hear what we really want. You are in our way and we need to pull out. You can't stop us, even if you wanted, and we would not enjoy spilling any more American blood, if we can help it. You guys need to really think about this carefully. The money that we already have in our possession is 'Federally Insured.' It can and will be replaced. Your lives can't be replaced. Now the way I see it, it should only take five seconds to think about this and say to yourselves, 'No, it's not worth it,' and pull out and be able to go home to your families. This is non-negotiable and time is not on your side."

Lt. O'Malley said, "He's bluffing; we will have the intel on these assholes soon, we just need to stall them. Hell, we have more manpower and more guns than them. They cannot have the upper hand on us."

"That's the same way Lt. Barnes was thinking, about 13 minutes before he died," said Knowles.

Meeks said, "Maybe we should think twice about it before we rush in like this. I don't believe that they're bluffing because the results are all around us, lying on the ground."

Epstein said, "It's not my call anymore."

O'Malley got on the radio and said, "I want my eyes up in the sky with sharp shooters; I want to take these fuckers out. We blast; we use explosives and whatever it takes."

Five seconds lapsed and there was total silence on both sides. As Dugmal sat in waiting for the next move by law enforcement, he was as cool as a snowball in the freezer. As he glanced at the blockade and saw different officers from the different SWAT units scamper for better positions and better cover, he looked up and, in the distance, he could see one chopper heading toward the area. He could not hear it, but he could see it coming.

He radioed to Upchurch, "Red Hawk to Red Dog, I have a vision on a bird approaching."

Upchurch responded, as he looked in the direction of the west, "I can't see anything. What direction are they coming from?"

Dugmal replied, "They're coming from the northeast at my two."

Upchurch turned and looked into the direction of the northeast from his position. He responded back, "I have vision on him. It looks like just one of them."

"That's affirmative; he seems to be solo," replied Dugmal.

Upchurch asked, "Should we bring him down?"

"Negative," said Dugmal, "we hold steady."

As the chopper approached, Dugmal picked up his binoculars. He zeroed in on them and could see that the chopper was from the FBI and there were two snipers on the ready with rifles. They were dressed in black and khaki uniforms with baseball caps and sky masks. Dugmal radioed his crew again. "All units, stand down; no one fires a single shot unless I give the command." All of the crew complied with Dugmal's orders.

Upchurch turned around and looked in back of the vehicle, facing the opposite direction. He saw another chopper rapidly approaching from the west side. He called to Dugmal, "Hey, Red Hawk, I spotted another bird flying swift from the west."

Dugmal looked over to the west and saw the second bird heading in the direction of the two vehicles that were occupied by his crew. He smiled and said in a low voice, "These Americans. They are trying to flank us, and then have an all out attack from the air and ground."

Upchurch grabbed his binoculars from the floor and looked through them at the approaching bird. He called Red Hawk and said, "Red Dog to Red Hawk, I'm picking up a 60mm cannon mounted on that bird. We can't take very many blasts from a 60mm cannon." As he looked closer at the chopper, he noticed that on the side mount of the chopper were 112 launchers, as well. He informed Dugmal on what he saw.

Dugmal said, "Calm down. Trust me; they will never get the opportunity to launch them off. I'm waiting until they get within range to fire."

Simms turned to Upchurch and asked, "How does he know what range they have to be before they fire?"

Upchurch answered, "Trust me, he knows that the range of fire for maximum penetration is 330 meters. Anything closer will risk the concussion of the blast affecting them."

"I just hope that he is accurate," Simms said, "and not off by a millimeter." Upchurch laughed and said, "You'll see, man."

Dugmal picked up a handheld remote unit, looked out at Drew, and then asked, "Are you at the ready?"

"Ten-four, Sarge," replied Drew, "ten more meters to go." He was holding a perimeter meter gauge. Drew continued, "We are at 360, now 350, now 340…"

Dugmal flipped the switch to 'On,' and the unit lit up. It flickered three times. The LED light flashed red three times and then turned to solid green. A smile came to Upchurch's face. In his mind he was thinking, *these bastards really don't even have a clue that we are prepared to counter what they attempt to throw at us.*

Drew continued his countdown, "335…."

Dugmal placed his thumb on the press down button.

Drew counted out, "330 meters…"

Dugmal pressed the button that read 'disable.'

As he was pressing the disable button down, the gunner on the chopper began to fire the 112 cannon. The first shot rode right over the top of vehicle 7, where Dugmal and his crew were. The shot continued down range and hit the street just in front of five of the disabled squad vehicles. The round went into the ground and traveled three and a half feet into the earth. The impact propelled rocks and sandy particles from the asphalt and tar into the air and in the direction of some of the officers that were using the cover of the police vehicles. The officers were beginning to dive toward the ground in an effort not to get hit by falling and flying debris.

The cannon released another round and, this time, the round found its target and hit the top rear of the vehicle that Dugmal and his crew were in. Drew braced himself against the side of the vehicle and clutched the 40cm pistol. Mitchell dropped down in his seat behind the steering wheel and began to recite his last rites and Hail Marys. Dugmal just continued to sit in his seat and not move. It was almost as though he had made up in his mind that, either the disable was going to work before they were hit, or they all were going to die… And, either one was fine with him.

Dugmal had stared death in the face several times and dared death to take another step toward him; and during the stare off, death backed down. Dugmal did not possess any fear of any living man, woman, or animal. Fear was taken away from him long ago when he was forced to take lives, save lives, and cause cities to fear him in fear of destruction, as the charge was ready to make contact with the bolt hammer in the 112 cannon.

The engine in the chopper shut down. The pilot reviewed his instrument panel; he saw that all of his gauges had gone to zero. He had no reading from the tachometer readout of his computer.

One of the gunners yelled out to the pilot, "What the hell is going on, my cannon won't fire? And, why don't I hear the motor running anymore?"

The co-pilot yelled out, "We're in trouble. We're going down."

The gunner asked, "What do you mean we're going down, are we out?"

The pilot responded, "I have no power at all; I can't even slow this son of a bitch down until we get level."

The co-pilot looked at the pilot and said, "Man, what do we do?"

The pilot replied, "There's nothing we can do."

The chopper began to fall toward the earth at a very rapid speed. The nose of the chopper was diving; and as the vessel dropped, it picked up speed in its descent. The pilot continued to attempt to pull the throttle back, but there was no response. The co-pilot started pushing the engine on and lift bottoms, but there was no response. The gunner continued to embrace his cannon, thinking to himself that once they got close enough to the earth, maybe he could jump out and be injured, but still alive.

As the chopper came closer and closer to the earth, the gunner's thoughts of jumping were dispelled. He believed that the chopper was moving way to fast to jump. It would be a worthless effort. Then reality set in. He gave in to the fact that he was going to die, along with his comrades. He began to wonder to himself if his wife would be okay by herself. The kids we're in high school and they had time in their lives to recover and rebound from something like this.

The chopper finally made contact with the ground below and burst into flames. There was a very loud explosion followed by a large fire ball. The chopper was totally engulfed in flames; they were riding with a full tank of fuel and carrying four cases of ammunition. Debris from the wreckage sent parts of one of the propellers flying and became impaled in the side of one of the police vehicles.

The officers on the ground began to run back and take cover at a farther distance. A large fireball from the explosion was followed by black smoke bellowing 70 feet into the air. The flames and smoke could be seen for miles in every direction.

The second chopper began its descent toward the earth ten seconds after the first chopper began to go down. The pilot looked out of the front of the windshield and saw the chopper hit the ground. He said in a monotone, "Oh, shit."

The co-pilot was making every attempt to restore the functions of the instruments. The pilot looked at him and said, "It's no use; this was planned. These fucking guys were waiting for us to come here like this. They set us up like wolves would do to a kill."

The co-pilot cried out, "But I don't want to die!"

The sniper in the rear undid his harness and threw his rifle out of the open side hatch, as the second sniper asked, "What the hell are you doing?"

The first sniper looked at him and said, "Hey, man, I'm not going to die on their terms. I'd rather die on my own terms; that's how I roll!"

The second sniper said, "Hey, man, that's stupid; don't jump out."

The first sniper looked at him and gave him a half smile and said, "See you in hell." He stood in the open doorway as the chopper fell rapidly toward the earth. He took in a deep breath and then leaped out of the aircraft.

The co-pilot watched as the chopper descended at a faster rate of speed than the airborne sniper. The second sniper continued to look at him until he could not see him any longer. Tears begin to stream down the face of the second sniper as he closed his eyes and allowed his body to hang lifeless in the support harness of the aircraft that kept him from falling out of the chopper. The co-pilot released a loud yell, followed by uncontrollable gases from his panic-stricken body. As the aircraft came closer to the ground the pilot and co-pilot grabbed a tighter grip on the control stick and control panel. Suddenly the aircraft made contact with the ground. The chopper was not as fortunate as the first one that only hit the ground.

This time, the second aircraft hit directly in front of the mobile anti-intrusion buster that the FBI had planned to ram the suspected vehicle with in an effort to disarm them. The agents in the anti-intrusion vehicle (which was built in the form of a tank) took the concussion of the blast from inside of the unit. A large fireball engulfed the whole unit, melting the steel and metal on the vehicle, causing the release latches to melt together. The agents could not open the release harness to escape and, as they struggled to get out, it was apparent that it would be impossible to escape. They were trapped inside and the heat from the fire and fuel of the aircraft continued to intensify.

The two agents began to get hotter and hotter. After one minute and fifteen seconds of intense burning, the agents were being overcome by smoke and with the heat of the fire, their brains began to boil more with their blood, and after ten more seconds, they passed out.

The officers that were standing and kneeling close to the anti-intrusion vehicle took off down the street to take cover farther away from the fire and out of harm's way.

Simms looked at Johnson and shouted, "Hot damn, that shit was intense! I've never seen any shit that comes close to this!"

Johnson looked at Simms and said, "Just wait, man; this ain't over, not by a long shot."

"What is next, man?" asked Simms. "What are we going to do?"

Upchurch looked over at Simms and said, "Stand by there, Sherlock."

Dugmal radioed Upchurch and said, "Red Hawk to Red Dog; what's your damage report?"

Red Dog responded, "We took no direct hits and are fully functional; how are you?" Dugmal replied, "We took one rap with very little damage and we are fully functional."

Upchurch asked, "What's our next move, Red Hawk?"

Dugmal responded, "We wait and see. I'm expecting emergency vehicles to arrive and assist with the downed birds and when that happens, I will inform them that they can assist and recover their wounded and we will pull out."

Upchurch replied, "Ten-four, Red Hawk; that seems like a plan to me."

Dugmal was waiting and listening in on the police scanner and he heard radio traffic about the responding emergency units—arrival times and where their safe zones were going to be.

Epstein crawled over to O'Malley and said, "Sir, I have never seen anything like this before. These guys are organized and they are good. They are more prepared than us and the way I see it at this point, we can no longer think with our penises. It's not about being macho or having bigger balls. We are losing and we are losing big. Look how many lives have been lost so far. We need to find out what the hell they want and rethink this."

O'Malley paused for a second and responded, "The way I see it is you're half right and half wrong. Yes, we are getting our asses kicked, but there is no way in hell that I'm going to back down or even just let them walk the hell out of here. Now we have seen what they are capable of doing, but they have not seen what we can do. Now, I say that we do listen to what they want and then ask them to at least gather up our wounded and dead and get help for them. Now, that will buy us some time to set up a counterattack, and then we move on them and take these fuckers out."

Epstein smiled and said, "You guys in blue just kill me; I guess you're not keeping up with current events. You talk about countering them. The last move was on us…they countered us, you dumb shit! I'll tell you what I will negotiate…a truck to recover the dead and wounded, and then I'll get the hell out of here; in the meantime, my work will be done at that point, and I'll watch the rest of this contest of who has the biggest balls at home, sipping some Irish whiskey and watching the developments on the news."

O'Malley said, "Go ahead and run off; just buy me a little time and I will do the rest. I'm going to win this battle, and kick some ass and take some names in the process. Now, if you don't want any of this action, then that's on you. But, I'm taking these pieces of shit down and calling it a day."

"Very well, then, have it your way." Epstein called out to Dugmal on the loudspeaker and said, "Leader of the group Red Hawk, do you read me?"

Dugmal answered, "Yes, I read you. Go ahead with your traffic."

Epstein said in an almost a fearful tone, "I…or we have a couple of requests that I would appreciate if you could grant us."

Dugmal responded in an almost a taunting manner. "Det. Epstein, it doesn't seem like you guys are picking up the dynamics of this situation. Before you even ask me, yes, you can bring in your team of emergency units to recover you dead and wounded. It was never my intent for this to go this far. Your request is granted."

Epstein responded, "For some reason, it's clear that you do value honor, but what I can't understand is why you are willing to allow so much blood to be spilled on America's soil for such a non-American act."

"I lost my sentiments years ago, and please do not mention anything about American acts. We have spilled a lot of blood in the past for selfish reasons and personal gain. Just check your history books and some novels about races that have been eliminated for senseless reasons, but did not make the history books.

"But you know what? I'm not here on a political platform, right now. I will allow you to collect your dead and wounded, but it will be on the conditions that while you are doing the collecting, we are allowed to pull out."

O'Malley soon grabbed the megaphone from Det. Epstein and yelled, out of control, "This is Lt. O'Malley; now you listen, you disgusting piece of goat shit, you're not in a position to negotiate or call any shots! You have killed in cold blood several of my men and destroyed police and FBI property! Now the way I see it, you have only one option—you allow us to collect our wounded, the dead are dead; I don't give two shits about that, because you fuckers are going to pay anyway! There's no way in hell that I will allow you idiots to just waltz off into the sunset like this is your favorite Western movie or some shit like that! Now, you have ten seconds to comply!"

Dugmal began to speak on the megaphone, but paused and thought for a minute. Drew looked at him and asked, "What is it, Sarge? What is wrong? What are you thinking about?"

"Well," responded Dugmal, "I just have to think before I speak. What they are trying to do is get us worked up so that we will be unable to think because we're upset. It is a law enforcement game that we all used to play to get the other guys off guard, and it usually worked."

Johnson said, "That's right, but they don't know that Sarge invented that game." They all had a laugh.

Dugmal said out loud, "As you wish, men, at ease." He pressed the key on the mic and said, "It seems that Lt. O'Malley has no regard for his men's lives, but is trying to make a name for himself in the media. What I propose in the name of what's left of humanity, I do not want to rush into taking any more lives if it can be helped on account of some non-thinking egotistical idiot; so, having said that, I will only speak to Det. Epstein.

"Now, what I have proposed to you, Det. Epstein, is what I will honor. In case there are some doubts in the group, just reflect back to about forty-five minutes ago; you guys thought that you had the upper hand, and you saw that you didn't. The evidence is lying all around you. No one else has to die. It's up to you. I'll start counting from ten and I'm already on nine."

O'Malley looked at Epstein and said, "We are not going to give in to the assholes, no way, no how!"

Epstein commented, "Just in case you didn't notice, he asked only to speak to me."

O'Malley replied, "Okay. So maybe he has a heart now for you, or he likes your voice or something. I can't get into who likes who, I have a job to do; I'm pissed off and I will not allow another man to go down on my watch if I can help it, or if there is any breath left in my body." O'Malley continued, "If they don't come out and surrender, I will give the order to attack and let them have everything we've got."

Epstein said, "Okay, now I'm officially putting you on notice that I'm calling the shots from now on. You are out of control; you have demonstrated that you are thinking from emotions and not from your brain. You're acting just how they want you to respond in this situation. You'll keep coming at them with full force and they'll continue to counter and kill all of your men and, in the process, feel justified is in doing so because, at that point, they will be defending themselves because you are the aggressors. Don't you see?"

"The only thing that I see," replied O'Malley, "are fallen comrades and wounded brothers and sisters that took an oath to defend justice and honor in the American way. You have rank on me and it's your call, but remember, I'm not for this."

Epstein pressed the key on the mic and asked for Red Hawk to come back in. Dugmal responded, "Go for Red Hawk."

Epstein said, "Okay, comrades, you got it; you allow us to bring in the emergency crews and pick up the people that are down, and you guys can pull out. Now, this will only happen after we have pulled all of our people out and have gotten them back to safety; that's the deal. That's the best that I can do for you, you have my word."

"That's a bargain and a gamble," Dugmal replied, "but I have no choice. It is interesting working with you, Epstein; I guess when the shit hits the fan again, you won't be around. You have done your job so, so long to you."

Epstein responded, "So long to you back."

O'Malley asked, "What was that all about?"

"You still don't get it, man! This guy or these guys are former law enforcement, I guarantee it. They know our every move and can anticipate our counter. No one outside of being on the inside could be that good."

O'Malley said, "You have a point."

O'Malley called to Meeks, "Get over here. Fall back and get on the horn to dispatch and find out what officers left the report about go statewide, and check for those who have been released going back ten years from today. I want info from rank and file officers to who left as chief. I don't care if they retired, quit, or were fired; I want the whole list and we only have a 30-minute window. Make sure that Operations understands this."

"I'm on it," said Meeks. He called back, and began his requests with dispatch.

Upchurch radioed Dugmal, "So, we allow these guys to collect their trash?"

Dugmal replied, "That's affirmative. They are attempting to contemplate their move against us, while they're regrouping and waiting for more backup and heavier equipment to arrive."

Upchurch asked, "Are we just going to wait for them to build up their attack forces?"

Dugmal answered, "Hell no, as soon as the wounded and dead have been collected, we move. When we move, we will go right through the heart of their exiting emergency team. We will use this opportunity as an escape route and then the cavalry will not be in position to recover."

"Well, that plan works for me," said Upchurch.

Dugmal said, "After we clear this area, I will introduce my next plan that we will use to put some distance between us. I really don't want to continue to eliminate these opposing forces. This is no fun and it's not fair. I need for you guys to be on the ready when I give the order to move. If they attempt to initiate the engine disabler, I do have a signal blocker, but I only have ten seconds to operate within."

"I got it," said Upchurch, "just let me know, I'm ready."

As Dugmal and Upchurch sat and waited, they looked on as the emergency units arrived; men got out, and began to run over with stretchers to whoever was laid out.

As they assessed the emergency situation, the chief of fire department advised O'Malley, "Some of the people will not make it back to the local hospitals; we'll have to set up triage locations. Some of these officers have been bleeding for some time now, and are going to need blood ASAP, and we will need to stop a lot of the wounded from bleeding before we can transport them out of here."

O'Malley said, "I don't know if they will allow us to do that."

Captain Ferguson of the United Cities Fire Department said, "You don't have a choice, my friend."

O'Malley countered, "Chief, you don't understand. If we set up triage here, we will allow these bad guys to just drive out of here because we will not be able to attack them while you guys are working on our people."

Ferguson replied, "Well, that just means that you hold off on your attack if you want our people to live; and I know that I don't want any of my people in the line of fire while they are saving your people's lives in the battle zone. Now, think about that, O'Malley."

"Damn it, you win! We hold off our attack. You save as many of my people as you can, do you understand me?" asked O'Malley.

Ferguson said, "I hear you alright; now just stay out of my way and allow us to do our jobs!"

O'Malley put his head down, looking at the ground as though he was a little kid upset that his favorite toy was just broken.

The emergency team began to move in and pick up wounded police officers. Chief Ferguson arranged ladder units to set up seventy feet back and line the units up from front end to back end, as s shield just in case any bullets started flying around, his people and the triage center would be safe.

Dugmal looked on as the emergency units set up, while EMTs and ambulances moved through rubbish, still burning vehicles, and what was left of the helicopters.

Dugmal said to Upchurch, "Listen carefully, in ten minutes, start the engine of your vehicle and stand by. I have 1145 hours."

Upchurch confirmed, "I have 1145 hours, too."

While the emergency crew were rushing to assemble triage teams and pulling people out of some of the rubble and wreckage, O'Malley called over Meeks.

Meeks ran up to O'Malley and said, "Yes, sir."

"Run to the mobile unit and grab the vehicle disabler," said O'Malley.

Meeks replied, "Yes, sir," and ran off to the SWAT mobile unit. He grabbed the portable disabler and ran back to Lt. O'Malley. Meeks handed it to him and asked, "If we're going to allow them to clear out, then why are you going to disable their vehicles?"

O'Malley said, "I'm going to wait until they get one block away and then I'm going to take the fight to them. We will be clear of this area and that will give us the opportunity to surprise them and take them down."

Meeks asked, "Are you sure about this, because I'm not sure. What if something goes wrong and they attack us and then go for our wounded and innocent rescue team who are only trying to do their jobs and get our people out of here?"

"We have to do something, damn it!" said O'Malley. "I can't just sit back and wait for the next move of these assholes!"

As more rescue units arrived, Dugmal was looking on and worrying and waiting for the right moment to make his move. As the last emergency unit pulled up, they were busy gathering up wounded police officers and deciphering which would be taken to triage and which ones would go into the expired pile. The officers that had not been wounded were standing by and waiting for the word from O'Malley to attack and open fire.

Dugmal looked over at Jackson and said, "It looks like as good a time as any to head to the mark."

Jackson replied, "Sounds good to me, let's go."

Dugmal radioed Upchurch and said, "We move now!"

"Ten-four, Red Hawk," responded Upchurch. "We're right behind you."

Dugmal tapped Mitchell on his shoulder and said, "Let's roll."

Mitchell took a gulp as though he was swallowing some whiskey and said, "Okay." Mitchell put the truck in gear and began to pull out slowly. As the truck rolled forward, Simms put his vehicle in gear. He waited for Mitchell to pull ahead.

Dugmal said, "Start heading west."

Mitchell complied and started heading west. He maintained the speed of 15 mph. As he pulled out thirty feet ahead, Simms began to turn the truck around. When he completed repositioning the vehicle, he picked up his speed and caught up with Mitchell's vehicle. Then he slowed down in order to stay directly in back of Mitchell.

Dugmal said, "Jackson, stay on the ready with that .60-cal."

Jackson responded, "Sarge, I stay on the ready."

Dugmal went on the radio and said, "I need for all of you guys to stay on the ready. I don't know if they are planning something, as far as an attack is concerned, but we need to stay on point and be ready to counter them."

All of the men replied back to Dugmal in agreement.

O'Malley was looking on with the remote in his hand, just waiting for the chance to push the disabling button on the unit. He could not wait and he was itching just like someone would if they had a bad case of dandruff. He looked over at Meeks and Wayans and signaled for them to follow him. The two ran over to O'Malley and he took off in the direction of the two trucks driven by Mitchell and Simms. O'Malley and the two officers trailing him, headed around and behind parked vehicles, which they used to cover themselves.

As Mitchell approached two squad cars, he saw that they were parked face-to-face against each other. He asked Dugmal, "Should I go around them?"

Dugmal answered, "No, go through them. Our grill is reinforced with solid steel connected to the frame of the truck. We can take the impact."

Mitchell said, "Let's do this!"

Dugmal looked over at him and instructed, "Don't gun it; just push them with the weight of our truck."

As they approached the front vehicle, O'Malley and the other officers were rounding and taking positions in preparation to launch an attack. As Mitchell drove directly in front of the two squad cars, he gave it a little more gas, and brought his speed up to 35 mph. He crashed through the two vehicles and the two squad cars separated like Tonka toys. Simms stayed right behind them. After Mitchell cleared the vehicles, Simms followed fifteen feet behind.

O'Malley stood up and pressed the disable button on the remote box.

Simms stepped on the gas in an effort to keep up with Mitchell. As the two vehicles pulled out from the blockade, they got 45 yards down the street and Simms' vehicle just died. He stepped on the gas, but the accelerator did not respond. The vehicle began to slow down and Simms watched as Mitchell's distance began to increase.

O'Malley radioed to all units to move in on the disabled vehicle.

Dugmal heard the call go through on the police scanner as he looked around and saw that Simms' vehicle was not moving. He radioed Simms and asked if they were down. Simms did not answer. Dugmal called for Upchurch and he did not respond. Dugmal looked around and saw police officers running down the streets with their weapons drawn and heading toward Simms' disabled vehicle. He picked up his remote disabler and pressed the button.

Simms continued to turn the key in the ignition in an effort to start the vehicle. Upchurch tried to call Dugmal on the radio, but he was getting no response.

Johnson said, "Hey, man, I think that they blocked our signal. We have no communication!"

Simms said, "What do we do? Do we get out and make a run for it?"

Upchurch replied, "Hell, no, we wait to see what Dugmal is going to do. He's not going to just leave us out here."

Jackson looked at Dugmal and asked, "What do you want to do, Sarge? Do we go back or what?"

Dugmal answered, "No, they will have to continue to try and get the vehicle started."

"Look," said Drew, "those assholes are getting close to where they are!"

Dugmal said, "I can see that. Upchurch will have to make Simms continue trying to start the vehicle."

As the SWAT team approached within 25 yards of the vehicle, Upchurch shouted at Simms, "Start this piece of shit up and get us the fuck away from here, now!"

Simms turned the key one more time, the engine kicked over, and started up. All of the crew inside breathed sighs of relief. Upchurch said, "Go man go, go, go!"

O'Malley saw the vehicle start up and started to take off once again. He shouted out, "No fucking way; no way! I disabled that fucking vehicle; no way should it start back up!"

As Simms drove away and put more distance between him and the police officers, he smiled. Dugmal saw them advancing toward them and said, "Now that's just what I'm talking about!"

O'Malley shouted out, "Stop, everyone! Let's go back and get our vehicles. We are not going to let these assholes get away! We are going to chase them down and eliminate them!"

O'Malley stopped, turned around, and began running back in the direction of the squad cars. All of the other SWAT team members turned and followed him.

Meeks looked at Wayans as they were running back and asked, "I think O'Malley has lost it, what do you think?"

Wayans said, "I think that you're right. Let's just see how this turns out."

O'Malley ran up to the first patrol car he saw, got in, and started it up. He opened his window and shouted, "I want three officers to come with me; get in my vehicle!"

Three officers ran over and got into the vehicle with O'Malley. The rest of the officers ran over to different vehicles and jumped in, and then waited for O'Malley's next move. There were seventeen vehicles total and there were two to three officers in each vehicle.

When O'Malley saw that he had properly rounded up a posse, he radioed to all units, "Let's move out, and pursue these fuckers!" One-by-one and two-by-two, the vehicles began to speed off in the direction that Dugmal and his team was headed in.

Upchurch looked around and saw all of the units in the distance in pursuit and closing in. He radioed Dugmal and said, "Man, they are coming after us hard and heavy."

Dugmal replied, "I knew this was coming. Okay, follow me. We are going to take a stand and I'm going to pick the place for it."

Drew asked, "Dugmal, what do you mean you're going to pick the place?"

Dugmal looked at the team and said, "When I was coming up as a boy, back at home, there were a couple of kids—they were brothers, in fact—and they would go around bullying people. They were bigger than the rest of the kids. Most of the kids on the block were afraid of them. I was telling my dad about them one night at dinner and my dad said to me, 'Son, if they come in your face and it's two against one, it's okay to back down if you're not properly prepared; choose your battles wisely. Then when you see them again and you are prepared for them, invite them onto your turf and under your conditions. This will give you the advantage over them.' I follow what my daddy told me to this day and to the letter. We have to get to the designated battleground and this fight is ours to win. We do everything by the numbers, we come out of this on top. Now let's move out; our destination is mid-town and get the setup."

Dugmal radioed Upchurch and told him, "Red Hawk to Red Dog, come back."

Upchurch responded," Red Dog, go."

"Let's get first to Post St. and set up shop," replied Dugmal. "We need to follow Drill 1, Phase 1."

Upchurch responded, "Ten-four, Red Hawk. When we get to Post St., we will park at three o'clock and you guys park at six o'clock."

"Ten-four, right by the numbers," answered Dugmal.

Both vehicles began to accelerate and reached a top speed of 70 mph. The streets had been cleared of traffic when the ordeal first began, so both of the vehicles driven by Dugmal's team readily had clear streets, except for parked vehicles on the street sides.

O'Malley saw that Dugmal's team had pushed the pedal to the metal, and picked up the mic and radioed to the crew, "Step on it! I want everyone on their asses, so close that they will think that we're pimples popping out all over!"

O'Malley's crew followed his lead and stepped on the accelerator, picking up their speed. At this point, O'Malley's crew hit speeds of 110 mph.

Wayans looked over at Meeks and said, "Man, you were right. O'Malley has lost it. We are in pursuit at high speeds and we're on city streets."

"Hey, man," replied Meeks, "this fool has turned this thing into a personal vendetta!"

Wayans replied, "No shit, Sherlock. These guys have a bad feeling about the man. Check this out. We had them pinned down back there and they broke out 60-cals. These guys are no amateurs; they know what the fuck they're doing and they're doing better than us."

"When do we back off, 'cause I want to go home to my family? I ain't scared of no man," said Meeks, "but these guys are far from your average guys and, yes, I'm scared of them."

"Well, let's pull back to the end of the pack," said Wayans, "and see what develops from that vantage point."

"I'm with you, brother."

They began to decrease their speed and eased to the rear of the pack. O'-Malley saw Meeks' and Wayans' vehicles, looking at them in his rearview mirror. O'Malley picked up the radio and called out to them and asked if they were okay.

Meeks looked over at Wayans and said, "Man, you answer that sick fuck!"

Wayans responded on the radio to O'Malley, "We're fine; we're falling back to the anterior position just in case they try something stupid."

O'Malley thought for a moment and said, "Good point. Just make sure you keep an eye on these assholes and make sure they don't surprise us with anything."

Meeks and Wayans looked at each other and gave each other a smirk.

Dugmal and Upchurch got to the intersection of Post St. and Main, and both vehicles braked, as Dugmal turned to three o'clock and Upchurch turned to six o'clock and both vehicles stopped.

Toliver jumped out of the vehicle and ran toward Main St. He was carrying a backpack and had his rifle in a carrying case draped over his left shoulder. He ran all the way down Main St. until he arrived at 1714 Main St. in front of the Holiday Inn. He ran through the lobby, went to the elevator, and pushed the button. The elevator was waiting on the ground level, so the door opened and there were four people in the elevator who were laughing and talking about the bride's gown that one of them had just won. Toliver ran in and started pushing them out of the elevator and said, "What's wrong with you folks. Get the fuck out now."

The people looked at him and seemed to have lost the joy they once had and were willing to follow the orders of Toliver without questions or comment. Toliver pushed the seventh floor button, went up to the seventh floor, and got out. He ran to room 1722 and waited, removing his rifle from his shoulder and taking off his backpack. He unzipped the carrying case, took out the tripod, and attached the rifle to it. He opened his backpack and pulled out a scope. He carefully attached his scope to the back of the rifle and then pulled out a case and set it down by the window. He opened the case, reached in, and pulled out bullets. He loaded them into the rifle and pulled the bolt, inserting a round. He positioned the scope, focusing in on the street where Dugmal's vehicle was parked.

Upchurch pulled his vehicle over headed to six o'clock and stopped. Ortiz jumped out of the vehicle, running toward Post St. Ortiz had his rifle draped over his left shoulder and was carrying a backpack. As Ortiz ran to the entrance of 1714 Post St., he turned and ran into the Mission Deluxe Hotel. As he ran in, he saw two United Cities' police officers in the restaurant section of the hotel, facing the entrance. All three of the men looked at each other at the same time. Ortiz froze in his tracks. The two cops stopped drinking their coffees and quickly glanced at each other and then made eye contact with Ortiz.

Ortiz unstrapped his rifle and allowed it to drop to the floor. The two cops watched in amazement as though they were staring into the headlamps of a car approaching at night. Ortiz dropped to one knee and reached to the small of his back and pulled out a Sig .40-cal. He went back on one knee and extended the other leg out in front.

When the two cops realized that they were encountering one of the participants of the robbery crew, it hit them that their discovery was a little too late. They turned and began to run in the opposite direction. Ortiz took aim and then unloaded. He fired off six rounds. He hit one of the cops in both legs and put one round in the leg of the other cop.

They simultaneously fell to the ground and began to plead for their lives. Ortiz laughed and said, "Relax, gentlemen, if I wanted to kill you, you would have been dead already. Now give me your weapons and radios and just lay down there and bleed for a while."

One of the officers asked, "So, you are not going to kill us?"

"If you don't shut up," replied Ortiz, "I might change my mind."

The other officer turned to his partner and said, "Can you just shut up before *I* kill you."

Ortiz ran over to the entrance and pressed the button. He looked around and noticed that there were twelve people in the lobby and café area. He looked at them as the bell sounded on the elevator. He said, "Anybody that doesn't want to die today, should keep their mouths shut and say they didn't see or hear anything."

The elevator door opened, he went in, and pushed the button for the seventh floor. He got off the elevator and ran to room 1722, unloaded his backpack and brought out his rifle. He quickly set up the tripod and attached the scope. He began to set his sights on Upchurch's vehicle.

Dugmal got on the radio and said, "We have unfriendliness approaching; I need everyone on the ready."

Toliver radioed in, "Perch One's ready."

Ortiz radioed in, "Perch Two's ready."

O'Malley was listening on his radio and heard "We have shots reported fired on Post St. at the Hotel Mission Deluxe."

O'Malley responded, "Dispatch, I need to know who is involved in that and what the disposition of the situation is."

Dispatch replied, "Please stand by for update."

O'Malley shouted, "To hell with standing by, give me the status on the fucking situation right now!"

"All units, be advised that this is a Code 3," stated Dispatch, "we have two officers reported down and disabled. The subjects are believed to be our guys in the bank robbery."

O'Malley radioed, "All units step up, and let's get to this location."

Dugmal radioed, "Dump unit 1, dozer unit 1, are you ready?" Dugmal was referring to dump truck driver one and driver two.

Javier responded, "Dump 1 is on the ready."

Korette responded, "Dump 2 is on the ready."

Benivais responded, "Dozer is on the ready."

O'Malley radioed to his patrol crew, "I need units 6, 7, 8, and 9 to circle around east on Mission. I need units 10, 11, 12, 13, and 14 to circle east on Post St. I need units 15, 16, 17, and 18 to circle south on Post and units 19, 20, 21, and 22 to circle south on Main St. Do it now!"

As police units got through, nine arrived at Mission St. They began to form a barricade with the patrol vehicles end-to-end. Dugmal radioed, "Dump one, move into position."

Javier put the large dump truck into gear and began to pick up speed as he approached the patrol vehicles from Post St. The patrol units were not looking for the dump trucks at that time because they thought they were part of a construction crew that was parked on the side of the road, so this plan of action was taking them by surprise. By the time the officers saw the dump truck coming, it was too late. They could only retreat and attempt to run away in an effort not to get plowed over by the rapidly moving heavy vehicle. As Javier plowed the first patrol vehicle, the impact forced it into the second vehicle.

The officers were running frantically out of the way, diving onto the ground, and rolling out of the way as fast as they could. Javier continued plowing the patrol vehicle and shouting, "Hey, man, you want some of this? Hey, come get some, you *pincha putos!*" It was obvious that Javier was enjoying himself. As he came to the last patrol vehicle, he ran atop of the vehicle smashing the hood and completely disabling it. He backed up and ran directly into the middle of the vehicle's side, smashing the vehicle and moving it against the curb. Javier was laughing out loud and shouting, "Come and get some!"

O'Malley was looking at the incident taking place and could not believe what was going on. He got on the radio and stated, "All units, open fire on that fucking truck; take that truck the fuck out!"

After some of the officers had recovered from rolling and running out of the way, they drew their firearms and pointed at the windows and windshield of the dump truck and began firing at Javier. There were so many bullets blazing at the same time that Javier had no time and no room to find cover. Bullets struck Javier in his arms and body, the truck began to slow down, and Javier noticed that he was losing strength. He looked to his left and shouted out, "Fuck you, guys!" A single bullet struck him in his face as several more bullets riddled his body. The truck came to a complete stop and Javier was looking out of the windshield. There were six officers standing directly in front of the stopped truck. Javier laughed as he coughed up blood and it ran down both sides of his mouth and chin. Javier said, "Is that all you pussies got?" The six officers dropped their magazines and replaced them with a full magazine and began to fire at will into the dump truck, striking Javier until he just slumped over and was lifeless.

While the officers were still focused on the events surrounding Javier, Korette began her part of the attack with her dump truck. She picked up speed and was able to collect 60 mph in her approach from Broadway St. She started plowing the patrol vehicles that were positioned on the south end. Patrol units 19 through 22 were taken by surprise and Korette had approached patrol units 19 and 20 so rapidly that they did not have a chance to escape the vehicle; she plowed into the side of the first vehicle, knocking the vehicle in the air and landing it on the second vehicle, killing the officers instantly. She backed the truck up and started building her speed back up. The officers in the remaining vehicles had time to escape their vehicles and fled for their lives. Korette plowed two more patrol vehicles and had to back up to regroup and go after the rest. As she backed the dump truck up, she stopped back seventy-five feet and said to herself *I'm going to cut these sons of bitches right in half!*

As she was putting the truck into gear, one of the officers ran in back of the truck and climbed into the dump deposit. Korette was so fixed on getting the vehicle into gear that she did not see the officer. She finally got the massive truck into gear and began her journey once again. As she picked up speed, one of the officers that was in the patrol vehicle and had fled happened to break his ankle in his escape attempt. Korette saw him crawling in an effort to get to the other side of the street where his fellow officers were. The officers that were standing on the curbside were cheering him on in an effort to encourage him to hurry to the curb where he would be safe. Korette saw this as an opportunity to taunt her prey before the kill. As the truck approached the crawling officer, the officers on the sidelines became more frantic in their efforts to get him safely to the side. There was a look of total terror on the face of the officer as he watched the rapidly approaching vehicle. As Korette continued to stay fixed on her prey, the other police officer was making his way up and over the dump bed onto the roof of the cab.

Korette continued to accelerate and the officers on the sidelines became more frantically intimidated as the officer looked at the distance between the truck and himself. He just stopped and realized that he was not going to make it. He turned on his stomach and whispered , "Hail Mary full of grace..." and right before he could finish, Korette came pushing strong and shouted, "Payback is a mother fucker, ain't it?" and ran him over. The back tire of the dump truck ran over the officer's head and brain fragments shot everywhere. One of the officers standing on the sidelines caught some skull fragment and brain matter in her face. She began to yell and cry. She fell to the ground and curled up. Several of the other officers turned their heads and broke down and cried.

Korette laughed and said, "You bastards, you haven't seen nothing, yet." As Korette drove 45 feet down the street, she slowed the truck so she could turn around; at this time, the police officer on top of the truck took advantage of the truck slowing down and climbed onto the roof of the truck. As Korette turned the truck around and was correcting the vehicle in the direction she wanted to go, she looked down the street, smiled, and said, "Eenie, meenie, miney, moe."

She stopped moving forward and the officer on the roof crawled over to the driver side. He carefully pulled out his handgun and looked over the side that the driver was on and noticed that the window was down. He eased his hand down the window side and pointed the barrel in the direction of the driver. At this point, Korette did not see the officer because she was so fixed on her next kill. She focused on the officers that were standing on the curb as she figured they were distant and confused and would be an easy kill. As she positioned the vehicle to head in the direction of the pack, the police officer squeezed off six rounds in the direction of the driver's seat. The officer returned his handgun to the holster and gripped both hands onto the roof of the truck in an attempt to embrace for impact.

Korette never knew what hit her. The first round struck her in the neck and arm. The truck came to a dead stop after striking the back end of a patrol vehicle. The officer that took Korette out jumped down off the roof of the truck and onto the ground. He began celebrating and jumping up and down. The officers on the curbside began to applaud and cheer for him. He started running toward his fellow officers.

Toliver was watching everything from his seventh floor window and whispered over the radio, "I have that pussy ass prick lined up in my sights. I'm going to take the shot."

Dugmal responded, "Man, negative. Do not take the shot due to the fact that you will then give your position away and then we lose."

Toliver responded to Dugmal, "Ten-four."

Dugmal radioed, "Dozer, start your roll."

Benivais responded, "I'm on it."

O'Malley shouted out over the radio, "Hey you fucks, you pieces of shit, we're going to take all of you out, one by one or all at once, just watch!" O'Malley radioed, "East units move in on the two parked vehicles. Patrol vehicles 9, 10, 11, and 12, start moving toward Dugmal's and Upchurch's vehicles."

Upchurch saw the vehicles advancing toward them and said, "Hey, Red Hawk, do you see this...should we respond?"

"No," said Dugmal, "we sit and stay the course." He radioed Benivais and said, "Your timing has to be right on the mark."

Benivais replied, "Yes, sir, that's my name."

Moving as the patrol units approached the two parked vehicles, the officers in patrol unit 9 smiled and said, "Yes, now it's time for some payback."

O'Malley was looking on and laughing, and said to his fellow officers, "Now, we're going to show them what we're all about. These fuckers are going to realize that they have messed with the wrong Irish party!"

Benivais was barreling down Stoke St. and O'Malley had no idea he was on his way. Benivais said, "If my calculations are correct, I will cut them off 23 feet before they get to our guys."

O'Malley shouted, "This is it; you pricks you're going to pay dearly!" O'Malley radioed his units, "When you guys get in front of the two vehicles, I want you to get out and blow these pricks away. I don't want to see any of the fuckers alive; kill them all!" All of the patrol units responded, "Ten-four."

When the patrol vehicles approached within twenty-five feet of Dugmal and Upchurch, one of the officers said, "Well, they don't know it, yet, but this is when the lights go out for them," and they all enjoyed a brief laugh.

Just as their patrol vehicle hit the 25-ft. mark, the bulldozer pulled in front of them and caught them off guard and by surprise; so much so, that the vehicles did not have enough time to stop. Two of the patrol vehicles plowed directly into the scoop of the bulldozer. Benivais lifted the scoop of the dozer, while lifting the two patrol vehicles up into the air. The other patrol vehicle eventually stopped and began to look up at the lifted patrol vehicles in utter amazement.

O'Malley got on the radio and shouted, "All units, open fire on these pricks!" All of the officers began to open fire on the bulldozers and on Dugmal's and Upchurch's vehicles.

Dugmal radioed the sharpshooters to stand down until ordered. Dugmal radioed the rest of the crew to stand down until given the order to engage.

O'Malley had focused his attention on the bulldozer and his two patrol vehicles stuck in suspended animation. As he observed the officers firing at the dozer and at the other two bandit vehicles, he realized that the bulldozer was completely bullet retardant. He began to believe that he was being sucked into something.

One of his officers looked over at him and said, "Hey, Lieutenant, what's wrong? Why do you have that look on your face?"

O'Malley said, "I believe I sense a rat."

The officer asked, "What do you mean? What's happening?"

O'Malley answered very excited, "I don't know exactly, but something just doesn't feel right! Do I have my SWAT unit in place?"

One of the officers answered, "Yes, they are here."

O'Malley said, "Order them to move in and take out the vehicles."

Twelve members of SWAT emerged a parked van and formed a wedge formation advancing toward Dugmal's and Upchurch's vehicles. They advanced within 35 feet and then stopped. The front three members of the

SWAT team dropped their ballistic bunker shield and lowered themselves to a prone position on the ground, while pointing 30 mm mini guns at the two vehicles. Two of the middle team members were standing up, pointing two more mini guns at the two vehicles.

Upchurch was looking at what was going on and said, "Well, are we going to engage on these guys?"

"No, not yet," replied Dugmal. "I'll let you know when it's time, but stand by and be on the ready."

Upchurch said, "Okay, man; we won't be able to withstand too many hits from those mini guns."

Dugmal says, "I am well aware of that, just trust me; I know what I'm doing here."

The SWAT team began to fire on the two vehicles. The heavy shells began to knock out the headlamps and chip away at the top of the vehicles. They launched grenades under the under carriages. The impact lifted the vehicles, but the solid steel lining was holding, for the time being.

Mitchell asked Dugmal, "What are we waiting for? I know that you have a plan. Come on, sir; share it with us!"

Dugmal smiled and said, "Just wait, you're going to love this."

The SWAT continued to barrage the two vehicles with rounds and blast off grenades in between. The two vehicles were well prepared for the attack, but were taking on heavy fire. The barrage continued for over eleven minutes, however, it seemed like three hours to Thomas's crew.

O'Malley shouted to the rest of his team, "Continue to pour it on these fuckers, they'll break!"

One of the SWAT team members turned to a team comrade and said, "We have just about expended all of our ammo."

The team leader said, "We are going to cease fire and then assess the situation with these guys."

The message was relayed to Lt. O'Malley, who shouted, "Hell, NO; we ain't going to cease fire or slow down until I know these assholes are down!"

The SWAT leader said, "Hey, if we continue, we are going to be out of ammo and will have not confirmed that these guys are down, yet. They could be playing possum. Now we know that these guys are not amateurs and they are hurt, but still dangerous, very dangerous just like a wounded bear."

"I'll take my team and advance," O'Malley said, "and you just provide cover for us."

SWAT Team Leader Sgt. Meeks said, "Man, I'm telling you still, we need to assess this situation; I just have a bad feeling about these guys. They are too organized. They definitely have combat experience and know combat tactics. I'm just saying, let's wait this out."

O'Malley said, "Wait, hell; let's rock 'n' roll!"

At this point, as Thomas was sitting in his vehicle, a smile came to his face. He looked over at Drew and said, "I need for everyone to stand ready. It's time. They are regrouping and confused, and not sure as to what they really want to do. This is exactly what I was waiting on." Thomas got on the radio and said, "Benivais, start moving out."

Benivais responded, "Ten-four." He started the engine in the bulldozer and revved up the motor, black smoke pouring up in the air as the entire police department looked in amazement. Benivais still had two patrol vehicles in the scoop shovel. He shoved the release lever forward and the two vehicles went falling down and smashing to the ground. Benivais revved up the engine once again and continued to stay in the same spot.

O'Malley looked over and said, "What the hell is he doing?"

Meeks whispered to one of his team members, "Get ready for a train ride."

The young team member responded back to Meeks and asked, "What do you mean; what do you think is about to happen?"

Meeks looked at him and said, "Son, this is what you signed up for. Now, you're actually going to have to work for your money and fight for your life. I'm going to level with you, son; you're about to see some shit that you've only seen in the movies. This is what I truly feel and I feel that all of us will not go home tonight, and that's a fact."

The young team member just looked at Meeks for a couple of seconds and thought to himself, *I have to make it home; my wife would never be able to bring up three kids by herself.*

Thomas called Benivais on the radio and ordered him to start moving out. As Benivais began to move the extremely large vehicle forward, O'Malley looked around and ordered Meeks to cover the bulldozer.

Meeks responded, "We can't damage that thing. It's solid steel all over. Hell, even the tires are solid rubber all the way through."

O'Malley asked, "Can you blast that damn thing?"

"We can give it a try," said Meeks. He called over Gibson, who was the explosives expert.

Gibson ran over to Meeks and said, "Yes, sir."

"Do you think that you can blow that thing?" asked Meeks.

"Well, yes," Gibson replied, "I can blow that thing, but as the thing is, I would have to use something so powerful that it would take him out and us, as well... as well as this city block. We would have matter flying in every direction and the impact would be devastating."

Meeks thought for a few seconds, and then he said, "Just stand by on that one. We might need to take a different approach."

"Ten-four," said Gibson. "Just let me know what you want to do."

Dugmal got on the radio, "All units, fall out of the vehicles and form battle group formation."

Upchurch said, "Well, it's about damn time; that's what I'm talking about!"

Dugmal and his team exited the vehicle and formed a group. Thomas was at point with Mitchell at three o'clock, Drew at nine o'clock, and Jackson anchorin' the .50-cal.

Upchurch exited his vehicle along with the rest of his crew, and once everyone was clear, they quickly teamed up with Dugmal's team. Now, Johnson took the nine o'clock position with the .50-cal. and Jackson took the three o'clock position with gun in hand.

O'Malley was observing the two teams as they left their vehicles and teamed up as a group, and O'Malley was struck by shear surprise and admiration at the same time. The way the two teams came together, grouped up, and formed a tight group tractor formation was like watching an extremely poised dance at the same time.

O'Malley was so star struck that he forgot to give any direction or instruction to his team. O'Malley finally came to and realized that he was preparing to engage in an all out battle that would probably end with very bad results on both ends.

Thomas shouted, "Move out!"

The group began to move east on State St. Each member began their steps with their left foot and as soon as their left foot hit the ground, the right foot was following, and the group moved as one in perfect harmony. There were no gaps in between the men and they moved methodically down the street.

O'Malley looked around at the group, moving as if they were just one. He looked at his team and said, "Stand by." He took a step forward and shouted out to Thomas and his team, "Halt, stop, drop your weapons, and surrender, or we will be forced to open fire on you! I will not repeat this! You have ten seconds to comply!"

Thomas shouted, "Are you sure that you want to set this off? Because, if you want to, it's fine with us! We are prepared to die! As a matter of fact, this is a good day for dying and the blood spill will help the grass to grow! So, ask yourself and have your men ask themselves the same question, what are you prepared to do?"

O'Malley shouted, "I'm not asking you, you pieces of shit, we'll do this!" O'Malley began firing with his handgun into the direction of Thomas's team.

Thomas gave the order to don the shields, referring to the ballistic body bunker shields. Simms, Mitchell, and Drew covered the entire group with a 30-degree angle in circumference with the complete knowledge that the bullets could strike any of them.

Meeks yelled to O'Malley, "Hey, man, let's back off and regroup!"

O'Malley responded, "Hell no! Let's advance!"

"No," yelled Meeks, "I'm pulling my team back until we can get some support!"

"You dumb shit," O'Malley shouted, "this is all the support that we are going to get! These punks took out over half of five departments! Now we have them outrun and pinned in here, so let's finish this!"

Meeks asked, "What are you not understanding? They are not even returning fire, yet, does that not concern you at all?"

"Hell no," answered O'Malley, "and we will continue to advance." O'Malley shouted out, "Red team cover south, blue team north, green cover east, and yellow will cover the west! Now we will have them closed in!"

"No, man, what the fuck are you doing?" Meeks shouted, "We will be drawn into a cross fire with our own team!" Meeks ordered his team to stay back and cover O'Malley's team along with the local units.

As O'Malley's team got into position, O'Malley said, "Let's bring them down!"

Thomas gave the command for the team to halt; as the team stopped dead in their tracks, at the same time Thomas gave the order of, "Force ready!"

Jackson and Johnson responded, "On the ready."

Thomas shouted, "Red light!"

At that command, Simms, Mitchell, and Drew turned the shields to a 45-degree angle and dropped down to one knee at the same time, in perfect harmony with each other. At the same time that they were dropping and turning the shields, Jackson and Johnson stood erect and reached that position at the same time, and began firing the .50-cal. in a sweeping motion exactly 45 degrees. The two firing together at a 45-degree angle were able to clear a 160-degree angle, thus, wiping out the entire team led by O'Malley.

O'Malley's team began to fall like raindrops during a heavy rainstorm. O'Malley was watching as his eyes became as large as the balls on a pool table. O'Malley and his team were fully engaged and at a point of no return. There was a look on O'Malley's face that showed defeat. O'Malley continued to look around as each of his team members dropped like flies. Finally, a bullet struck O'Malley in the right shoulder. He let out a loud cry and shouted, "You pieces of shit; is that all you have?"

He changed gun hands and transferred his sidearm from his right hand to his left. He fired a shot off and looked around. He adjusted his right arm where he had been hit by the round and that was when he realized the .50-cal. round had torn his shoulder almost completely off. He was losing a lot of blood and becoming weak. He fired four more shots off and then fell to his knees. He looked over toward the north side of the street where Meeks was attempting to hide behind cover because the bullets from the 50-cals. were going completely through the patrol vehicles and some of the barriers that were set up.

As O'Malley refocused his attention on the shooters, another round from the .50-cal. found its mark on O'Malley once again; this time, striking him in his lower stomach. O'Malley dropped his sidearm at this point. He looked up toward the sky; he saw that the sky was blue and not a cloud in sight. Everything became quiet at this point and seemed to be going in slow motion. O'Malley tried to speak, but no words came out of his mouth, only blood. O'Malley began to bat his eyes, almost uncontrollably; he fell completely forward onto the ground with his face first and he was lifeless.

Meeks looked on with a feeling of disgust and sympathy. O'Malley was the last team member to go down, so there were no remaining special unit members from O'Malley's team.

Thomas looked around and saw that none of the remaining officers from the different departments were engaging, at this point. Thomas started to recover. Johnson and Jackson returned to their position within the inner group and the shields came back up. Thomas gave the command, "Forward help!" The team began to move forward, once again, in uniformity. Thomas said, "Let's keep on moving and stick to the plan."

As Thomas continued to move his team forward, two more police departments gained the position themselves next to Meeks and they greeted one another.

Meeks said, "Guys, I'd bring you up to speed, but it would take up too much of your time. I'll put it to you this way; we have some guys here that are some major bad asses. They have to be either former law enforcement or military or both. They are literally kicking our asses."

The new officers asked for recent actions that have been attempted.

Meeks said, "We have to be extremely careful with this because they have disabled our eyes in the sky (the chopper) and even jammed our communications."

Roberts, the newly arrived officer said, "Who's in charge here?"

Meeks replied, "He's the one on the ground over there with his shoulder and mid-section taken out."

Roberts said, "Damn, man, these guys are no joke."

"That's an understatement," declared Meeks.

While all the shooting was going on, Benivais had driven the bulldozer over to where the vehicles were parked, had gotten out, and transferred all the bags with the money from both vehicles into the bulldozer and driven off down to Broadway St.

Roberts gave his guys the order to open fire on Thomas as they continued to advance down the street.

Thomas gave the order to Drew, "The shields again," and the shields went up. Thomas said, "Let's get these bastards!"

Upchurch and Simms reached into the cargo pockets of their Pluck sweats and each pulled out two canisters of tear gas. They pulled the pins out and tossed the canisters in the direction of the police officers that were standing across the street and two where the officers were hiding, using their patrol vehicle for cover.

Three minutes later, you could hear people coughing and hacking almost uncontrollably. Meeks' voice could be heard shouting, "Get your gas masks, everybody!"

Thomas looked around at Upchurch and said, "Now, we set this off. Let's put out a small screen."

Upchurch smiled and said, "It's about damn time," as he pulled out two canisters of white phosphorus smoke screen. He turned to Simms and asked, "Are you ready?"

Simms responded, "I was born ready."

Upchurch and Simms tossed the canisters directly into the arena of all the police officers. After two and a half minutes, there was a cloud of smoke over the area becoming so dense that it was very difficult to continue to see anything in front of you.

Thomas looked around at Upchurch and said, "Let's move out." They began to move out.

Meeks shouted, "All officers, every man and every woman, side-by-side, we will form a wall!"

Barnes asked, "Are you sure? Then, we will be directly in their line of fire."

"Hey, we cannot afford to allow them to escape," said Meeks. He gave the order to begin firing.

One of the officers standing at the police wall looked over at his buddy to his left and said, "Man, I can't see a damn thing, I just hope that we don't hit any innocent bystanders or anything like that."

His buddy replied, "Man, you're right; plus, we cannot see those guys coming at us, either."

Meeks shouted, "Barnes, take your squad and move around to the left flank!"

Barnes replied, "Ten-four. Okay, men, all of you follow me."

Meeks then said, "Knowles, take your team and come in on the right flank."

Knowles responded, "Ten-four," and said to his team, "Okay, ladies, you heard what the man said, let's go, double-time it."

Johnson said, "Dugmal, sir, they are spreading out. I can't see everything, but they are going for what looks to be a right flank."

"Just keep your eyes and ears open," Thomas said.

Meeks called out to his team, "Is everyone in place?"

Each team responded, "Ten-four, we are in place."

He said, "Let's move forward and begin firing."

Meeks and all of his team began to fire in the general direction of Thomas's team. Thomas's team heard bullets whiz by their heads and shoulders. Sometimes bullets would hit the ground next to them.

Upchurch said, "The smoke cover is starting to thin out and we are not at our rendezvous point."

"I'm aware of that," said Thomas. "It looks like we are going to have to take a stance and fight this one out again."

The team was trying to reach the end of the block on State St., at Post St. They were at least two hundred and thirty feet away from it. There was a heavy breeze that blew through and the smoke cover was becoming thinner and thinner. The team advanced forty more feet and Drew said, in a very excited tone, "We are visible and I see them, as well; they are all around us, sir!" Thomas looked around as there was little, if any, more cloud cover smoke.

Meeks gave the order to open fire. The police units opened fire at Thomas's team. The SWAT teams were on the right and left flank of Thomas's team, firing on them. Drew was not able to redirect his angle of cover with his shield as he lost his grip on the handle due to the vibration from all of the bullets striking it. As he tried to recover, he was struck in the shoulder by a bullet. He dropped one side of the shield and was hit again in the chest by a bullet that was followed by another bullet, finding its way to Drew's neck. His chest was protected by his vest, but the shot to the neck was devastating. As Drew lowered the shield, he fell to both knees. The shield fell forward and uncovered Simms. Simms received two bullets in his right arm. He directed his aim with his right arm toward the direction of officers on its right flank. He fired off three rounds and struck three officers in the top of their necks. The officers fell immediately. The remainder of the officers stepped over the bodies of the fallen and continued to fire at Simms and Drew.

At this point, Thomas and team continued to press forward. Upchurch looked over and cried out for Dugmal, "Simms and Drew are down."

Thomas said, "Wait a moment!" Thomas looked around and saw that they were taking heavy fire and, if they went back, they might not make it.

Upchurch asked, "What do you want to do, because we need to act fast!"

Drew was attempting to keep pressure on his neck in an effort to control the bleeding. Simms took two more shots to his right and left legs. He went down to the ground and crawled over to Drew. He continued firing off rounds at the police officers that were advancing toward them. He started shooting from left to right. The magazine emptied and he dropped it out, went into his belt, and pulled out another full clip; he inserted it and continued to fire five more rounds. He looked down at Drew and asked, "Hey, man, how are you doing?"

Drew replied, "Man, I've been better; this blood won't stop, I think I'm done. You go ahead. I think I'm just going to stay here for a little longer and just rest."

"You're a crazy mother fucker," said Simms. "I'm not going to let you be the only one to get some rest. I'll rest here for a while with you."

Drew smiled at Simms and said, "And, you call me the crazy one."

Simms shouted to Thomas, "Hey, don't come back for us, you guys go ahead! We will provide cover fire for you!"

Thomas looked at Upchurch and said, "We don't leave our own behind."

Upchurch then said, "Hey, man, if we go back, you know what that means; and if that's what you want to do, then I'm down for you, all the way. And so is the rest of the crew. We would go to hell and fight Satan himself with you; all you have to do is say so."

Thomas looked at Upchurch and said, "Man, I'm responsible for all of you guys."

Jackson said, "Hey, Johnny," respectful of Thomas's rank when they served together. "Those two are guarding the gates, this is now their post, and we need to complete our mission."

"That's affirmative," said Upchurch.

Thomas looked back at Drew and Simms and shouted, "This is your final assignment men. Your orders are to secure this post and do not allow any unfriendlies to cross."

"Copy that, gooney!" Simms shouted.

Drew grabbed Simms' hand and said, "Hey, man, I want to die fighting; give me a weapon."

Simms smiled and said, "That's what I'm talking about." Simms reached into the inside of his jacket and pulls out a .40-cal. He inserted a fully loaded magazine, and released the slide handle as the hammer locked back into place. He put the pistol into Drew's hand and said, "Let's dance."

Drew pulled out a .45 pistol in his left hand and 40cm in his right. As the team of police officers advanced toward Drew and Simms, Simms yelled out, "Sons of bitches!" They began to fire at the advancing units as the units returned fire back, finding their targets with no problem. Drew slumped over onto the side of Simms and Simms continued to fire away with both weapons blasting, while receiving shots to his body at the same time. Simms continued to fire until he had no bullets left in his two pistols. The advancing officers continued to fire away at the two downed men.

Simms lowered his arms. At this point, he could no longer feel any more pain and everything seemed to be moving in slow motion. He batted his eyes a couple of times and seemed to develop a smile of peace on his face As the life rapidly left his body, his mind drifted back to when he was a little boy of twelve years and he was playing outside in a field with his older brother and two friends. They were butterfly hunting with nets and carrying large Mason jars to put the butterflies in once they caught them. It was a very warm day with just a slight breeze. The boys sat down in the field to rest and began to compare with each other who had the most butterflies and Simms said to his older brother, "I have the only double-wing swallow tail. His older brother said, "You're right, you do. I am so proud of you, little brother." Simms felt on top of the world at that point to have had his older brother so pleased with him.

Simms then opened his eyes and looked around, then his eyes shut for the last time, and he slumped over onto the limp body of Drew.

Meeks and his team advanced directly in front of Drew's and Simms' limp bodies. Meeks gave the order to cease fire. The police units just stood in a complete circle around Simms and Drew. One of the officers said, "Now this is good."

Meeks looked over at the officer that made the comment and said, "You secure that kind of shit talk. These people served in the military at one time. I don't know what the hell happened for this kind of shit to go down, but it must be bad." Meeks took his semi-automatic rifle and slung it over his shoulder and said, "Peoples and Scott, cover these bodies and then join us. We're going after the rest of these sons of bitches so we can end this." Meeks and his crew turned and started jogging in the direction of the other police units that were in foot pursuit of Thomas and his crew and were nearly to closing in on them.

Thomas and Upchurch were moving down the street until Thomas said, "Okay, let's slow down." There was still gunfire exchange going on between Thomas's crew and the police units. They came to a point and Thomas looked around and said, "Stop." There was noise of gunfire all around them and Jackson was bringing up the rear, dispensing rounds from his .50-cal. rifle and he did not hear the 'stop' order. Thomas then raised his arm in the air and extends his arm with his fist clinched. Jackson and the rest of his crew saw this and stopped immediately. They all took a knee. Jackson put the ballistic shield in place. Johnson put his shield in place as bullets bounced off and ricocheted away.

Upchurch looked over at Thomas and asked, "Hey, are we making a standpoint?"

Thomas replied, "This is checkpoint. We need to get to that general store over there on the right side of the street."

Upchurch looked around and saw police units in front of the general store and, basically, in all directions. He looked over at Thomas. He took eight shots at the police crew standing behind a parked city bus. The windows broke out and one of the front tires of the bus flattened, and then Upchurch said to Thomas, "Hey, man, if we only need to get over there to that store, then this is going to be easier than I thought." Jackson and Johnson began to laugh out loud, almost mimicking hysteria.

Barnes heard the men laughing and shook his head.

One of his officers asked, "What are these guys laughing at, are they crazy or what?"

Barnes said, "Yeah, they are crazy like a fox. When you see people in a situation like this where your lives are in danger and they're still laughing, it's scary. This could mean more than one thing: 1) They're not afraid to die, 2) they're not afraid to kill, and 3) they know something at this point that we don't know."

Another officer asked, "What might that be?"

Barnes said, "I believe we're going to find out very soon what that is."

Where Thomas had the crew held up at the checkpoint, it allowed Meeks and what crew he had remaining to catch up with Barnes' crew. Meeks crawled over to Barnes and said, "What's next, man?"

Barnes replied, "I'm not sure, but they stopped for a reason; it could mean that they're wounded and trying to recover, or that they're expecting something or someone to care. Whatever the case may be, then I want to be ready."

Thomas looked around at his crew and said, "This is it. We're hurt. I'm about to set this off." Thomas radioed to Toliver and Ortiz, "Red Hawk to Nest."

Ortiz responded, "Nest 1, on the ready."

Toliver responded, "Nest 2, on the ready."

"All nest units...on my go."

Meeks looked around and said to Barnes, "Something just doesn't smell right here. Is he talking on a radio?"

"Yes," replied Barnes, "it looks like he is."

Meeks said, "Do you see anyone else around here that he may be talking to?"

Barnes said, "No, but have your people look out for possible backup for these guys."

"Let's spread out and take these guys out," said Meeks.

"Ten-four," Barnes said. "I'm taking my units and come in on his left flank."

Meeks replied, "Good. We will close in on his right and just have the support unit move in on the front side."

As all of the police units began to move closer to Thomas and his crew, they continued to exchange fire from both sides. When the police units got within forty yards of Thomas and his crew, Thomas radioed to Toliver and Ortiz, "Take them out!"

Toliver sighted in from his perch point on the seventh floor. He locked his sights on one of the police officers firing off an SMG 1 fully automatic. He squeezed off a round and the officer with the SMG rifle dropped to the ground from a single shot to the head.

Ortiz locked sight on another officer, squeezed off another round, and dropped that officer with a single shot to the head. He smiled and whispered, "One shot, one kill."

Toliver and Ortiz continued to drop the police units one by one, each with a single shot. They alternated their shots as though it had been orchestrated and they were competing against each other. Their shots become frequent and simultaneous.

Meeks was advancing on Thomas's position and there was an officer right beside him firing. All of a sudden, the officer at his right dropped to the ground. Meeks looked down at him and asked, "Are you okay?" There was no response from the downed officer. Meeks dropped to his knees, bent over the fallen officer, and saw blood coming from his forehead. He lifted the head of the dead officer and looked at the back, and saw that there was a larger exit hole. He said to himself, "I knew it; we have a sniper." He stood up, got on his radio, and called for Barnes.

Barnes responded, "Go, Meeks, I'm a little busy right now."

Meeks said, "I know where the backup for these guys are now…"

Barnes interrupted, "It would help if you look…" and as Meeks was about to finish his sentence, a bullet went down through the back of his head and out of his mouth. One officer that was standing beside him actually heard the skull cracking and bone crushing from the single bullet. Meeks fell to the ground dead. The officer that was standing next to Meeks looked down and saw blood pooling in the street around Meeks' head. The police officer dropped her handgun and yelled. There were several fellow police officers that heard her scream and they looked over at Meeks on the ground. The police officer ran in the opposite direction.

Barnes radioed and said, "Meeks, you broke up. What were you saying?" He got no answer. Barnes radioed, "Any unit in the area of Meeks go over and make sure he's okay."

One of the units responded, "Sir, I'm near Meeks and he's down."

Barnes asked, "What do you mean down, is he okay?"

The officer replied, "No, no, he's not okay, he's dead."

Barnes shouted, "Damn it to hell!" He looked over where both units were engaged in a firefight with Thomas and his crew. Barnes saw officers dropping like flies. He said to himself, *what the fuck, these guys could not be this good. Who the fuck is helping them?* He looked up at the hotel and saw a particular open window. As he observed, he could not see a barrel of any sort that would lead him to believe they had a sniper. He looked across the street and scanned the hotel that was opposite on First Ave. As he scanned up, he noticed an open window. He focused in and then looked across the street at the first hotel's open window. He thought for a moment and then looked back at the second window and whispered, "Son of a bitch, those open windows are on the same floor." He watched carefully and could see a faint flash every 3 seconds. He said to himself, *these guys are more than good, they're trained; I think we're fucked!* As he turned and looked at the first hotel's open window, Ortiz had his sight fixed on Barnes. Barnes batted his eyes twice and Ortiz squeezed off his shooter. He hit his target somewhere between the eyes. Barnes dropped with no movement. Another officer that was standing next to him looked down and saw Barnes' body just lying there. It did not take long for the blood from the head shot to pool around the dead man's head. The officer looked without saying a single word. He turned around and shouted, "Take cover, take cover!" The other police units heard the officer yelling to take cover and saw him running. All of the surrounding units began to turn and run for any cover that they could find.

Thomas said to his crew, "Just by the book, we start moving toward the general store." As they started to make their way toward the store still with the shield up protecting them as they move along, there were more police units behind a patrol vehicle firing only at Thomas and his crew. As one of the officers got ready to pull the trigger on his handgun, he noticed a pain in the middle of his chest. He looked down and saw a small hole in his vest. He thought to himself, *no, this couldn't be a bullet hole. I have a vest on and a trauma plate.* He took his left hand and placed it on his chest between his vest and inner clothing. He pulled his hand out and saw what he actually did not want to see. Blood was on his hand. He said to himself, *Damn it, I just bought this under armor.* He fell to the ground dead.

Ortiz and Toliver were taking turns dropping them one by one. The police began to retreat back for cover at a further distance.

Thomas radioed Ortiz and Toliver and asked, "How are we on ammo, Nest One and Nest Two?"

Toliver responded, "I'm good," and Ortiz responded, "I'm good."

Thomas said, "Continue operation Blanket Cover. We have two-thirds of a crew left."

Both Toliver and Ortiz responded, "Ten-four, sir."

More and more of the police units began to run for cover from as far a distance as they could possibly get.

Ortiz radioed Toliver and said, "Hey, man, watch this."

Toliver focused in on where Ortiz was sighted. Ortiz fired off a shot. His aim was a policeman who was hiding behind a parked vehicle in the rear between the trunk and passenger door. The bullet went into the rear portion of the patrol vehicle's outside, through the inside of the vehicle, and out through the opposite side. The bullet finds the hiding officer in the right side of the neck and out of the left side. The shot killed him instantly. The other two officers saw him drop to the ground and there was blood spurting out from a severed carotid artery. It blew going two feet in the air.

The police officer looked for ten seconds and then took off running. As they were running off, one of the officers asked his partner, "Do you think that we will get in trouble for running off like this?"

The other officer responded, "Man, if I survive this ordeal and they put me in front of a panel , then I would cheerfully say I don't really give a fuck about what you think of me at this point, but I can tell you pricks this, I'm still alive."

Thomas and his crew made it to the general store and went in. He made sure all of his crew was in and closed the door behind him. He peeked out of the door window and noticed that no one was pursuing them. They were too busy attempting to find cover for protection. As the police departments were in total disarray and scrambling around in total confusion, the focus on Thomas and his crew was lost. Thomas radioed to Ortiz and Toliver, "Nest 1 and 2 disengage and fly away."

Ortiz and Toliver responded, "Ten-four," and ceased fire and began to break down their weapons and put them away in the green case and backpack.

The men quickly got their gear packed away and began to get their brass picked up until there was no spent brass on the floor at all, as though it was never there.

Ortiz looked at his watch and radioed Toliver, "Red Eye One to Red Eye Two, are you ready?"

Toliver responded, "Red Eye Two, ready."

"Ten-minute drill," replied Ortiz.

Toliver said, "Copy."

They both left their respective rooms and took the elevator down all the way to the basement level. Toliver walked over to the parking section where he took out a key, and walked over to some parked motorcycles. He took his rifle off his arm, walked over to a nearby dumpster, and placed it in. He covered the rifle up with garbage and went back near the bike. He got onto a Suzuki Hayabusa, blue with flames on the gas tank. He started it up and took off out of the parking garage. He exited through the rear of the building. Ortiz had duplicated Toliver's actions while he was continuously looking at his watch. When he exited the parking garage, it was from the rear, as well. Toliver made two left turns and was on Main St. Ortiz made two right turns and was on Main and Madison. Ortiz rode up on the left side of Toliver and they both did a high-five. They took off down the street at a high rate of speed and no one even suspected them.

Meanwhile, Thomas and his crew were going to the back of the store and into a locked backroom. They went in and shut the doors behind them and locked them. They walked over to an elevator and went inside. The elevator went down one story; they got out, and started making their way through what was a very elaborate tunnel with lights. They walked twenty-five yards in the basement of the hotel. They began to change clothes.

Upchurch started laughing, "Man, you are a sweet mother fucker. You thought this shit out and pulled it off. I think you should be in Hollywood."

Upchurch said, "Man, you know he's right; that shit was ingenious."

Thomas smiled and said, "You guys hurry and get changed. It's not over until we are out of the country."

"Hey, I'm just saying man," Upchurch added, "this was well thought out; we went by the numbers."

Thomas said, "Okay, maybe one day you can write a story about me."

"One day he can write, hell," said Upchurch. "You write it yourself." Thomas just smiled.

Meanwhile, Benivais had pulled the bulldozer over a manhole cover and was transferring all of the bags of money from the engine of the carrier, and dropping them down into the open manhole. He was dropping bag after bag after bag. He did not have to rush because no one was paying any attention to him because of all the commotion going on with the shootout. He finally finished his transfer. He dismounted into the manhole and closed the cover.

When he got to the underground, he loaded all of the bags in a mobile tram with five compartments being pulled by the engine tram. He drove underground 750 yards until he arrived outside of the city limits and was at the PG&E conductor yard. He came to a lift where he loaded the bags and started ascending. He surfaced on the inside of the building where a mobile full-service utility van was parked and waiting. He loaded the bags into the vehicle and left the building. He left the yard and drove off.

Back at the scene, the FBI had arrived and began doing their investigation. They started with the bank. They retrieved the surveillance tapes and began to interview witnesses.

Soon after the arrival of the FBI, the ATF arrived; they began to investigate the areas where they had the shootouts. The ATF lead investigator found the bulldozer and called over to Sgt. Cantolli of the United Cities Police Department.

Cantolli asked agent Peters, "What can I help you with?" Cantolli walked over, shaking his head.

Agent Peters said, "We should have been contacted a lot sooner, like before it got out of hand."

"You know you guys think that you can just come in, step on our toes, and take over after the fact," replied Cantolli. "Look at all of the officers, what I list. This shit is no joke. No, you're going to jeopardize the integrity of the crime scene and just screw everything up."

Agent Peters responded, "First, I'll say I'm sorry for your loss of life, but this is what you signed up for. Second, I would like to say this is not your crime scene, it's mine."

FBI Lead Agent John Starks walked over to the two men arguing and said, "At ease, men. I need you, Cantolli, to have what's left of your force lock this city down completely; no one in and no one out. I mean busses, planes, and even trains. Nothing goes in and nothing goes out. I want perimeters set for major highways, expressways, and junctions for 25 miles. Is any part of this confusing to anyone? Good, let's get started." John Starks continued, "You guys brief your crews, give them instructions, and then come and see me. We need to get going on this right away because I don't know how much of a jump they have on us. You guys have plenty of time so come and see me in, let's say three minutes. I hope that's enough time for you." Cantolli and Peters just looked at each other and ran off to get their people briefed.

Investigator Starks was sitting in the local café, drinking some coffee with some paperwork and reviewing pictures. Peters and Cantolli joined him and sat down. Starks broke out some photos that were retrieved from the bank and local vendors in the area. Peters looked at all twenty-five photos and commented, "How typical."

Cantolli said, "What do you mean typical?"

"Well," said Peters, "just look; all of these guys are white males between the ages of twenty-five and forty."

"It's typical because they fit the profile of usual suspects in organized crime scenes such as this," Starks said.

Cantolli asked, "What the hell are you guys saying, that blacks and other minorities cannot think up a crime like this and carry it out?"

"Well, to be honest with you, no," Starks answered. "I especially do not believe that blacks would be able to sit down and plan something like this out and organize anything like this and be able to put it together; now, if we're talking about Russians, or Germans, and maybe Columbian-types, but that's about it."

Cantolli said, "This is about as much horse shit as I have ever heard. Anyone of any race is capable of carrying out a crime like this with proper training."

"And," asked Peters, "where would somebody from the ghetto get that type of training?"

Cantolli questioned, "Who says that they have to be from the ghetto?"

With a smile on his face, Starks asked, "Where else would they be from?"

Peters and Starks shared a laugh together.

Cantolli said, "I still say that the idea it had to be white only is a crock of shit."

Starks distributed the photos and said, "Take these to your people and make sure that they all have and get familiar with what they look like, talk like, smell like, walk like, their height, weight, and build. Now let's get on it."

Thomas and his crew finished changing, went out to the basement area, and walked up to two waiting vehicles parked side-by-side. The first vehicle was a Chevy Equinox—Mitchell got in the driver seat, Thomas in the front, and Jackson in the back. Mitchell looked over at Thomas and noticed that he had on a thick sweater and overcoat. He asked Thomas, "You're not cold, are you?"

Thomas replied, "I sweated a lot and I'm cooling off; I'll be just fine when we get out of here."

Jackson laughed and said, "You know that's right."

Johnson walked over to the next vehicle and opened the door. This vehicle was a Chrysler 300. Upchurch got into the front passenger seat. Upchurch looked over at Johnson and said, "It looks like it's just the two of us here, big guy."

Johnson smiled and said, "Let's just get the hell out of here."

Both vehicles pulled out of the garage driveway and drove off.

FBI Field Agent Starks was walking back with Peters and Cantolli after their briefing. Cantolli turned to Starks and asked, "Are you sure that there were only a dozen of them? These guys did a hell of a lot of damage."

Starks replied, "From all of the preliminary reports and surveillance footage, we came up with twelve. However, they could have had more help along the way and they were just undercover."

Peters added, "Or, unless they were former law enforcement or worse, recently released, or war veterans."

Cantolli looked at the two and said, "Heaven forbid if they were former marines. These guys did a lot of damage to this town and what, my friends, is the MO of a Marine Corps Unit?"

Peters said, "Bullshit, man, they were just a group of under privileged prep kids trying to get attention. Let me take a look at these pictures, anyway. You notice each individual in these photographs are fit and in good condition. There are no fat bodies here. You can clearly see that they do exercise, a couple of them look like bodybuilders."

Starks said, "And, let me remind you, that all of them look to be close to the same height, as well. Okay, enough of this; let's go out and get these bastards."

The three men walked in different directions. They all went to brief their perspective departments on what information was released, photographs, and descriptions of the subjects. All of the various departments began scrambling around to make sure everyone had all of the necessary information on the subjects. There were checkpoints on every major intersection and on ramps to freeways, highways, expressways, and junctions. Vehicles were being stopped and some members of the public were becoming outraged. The members of the public were asking why was it them that fit this profile. The various departments were telling the general public that they would be obstructing justice if they did not cooperate. The entire city was in disarray and a state of confusion.

Thomas and his crew drove up to the entrance of Interstate 110 and they were stopped at the checkpoint. The sun had gone down, but it was not completely dark, yet. Upchurch was in the tail vehicle, right behind Thomas. Two officers walked over to the driver's door of Thomas's vehicle. Two different officers walked over to the passenger's window, stood there, and looked at Thomas.

The officer asked Mitchell to roll down his window. Mitchell complied. The officer proceeded to ask Mitchell, "Have you seen anyone that might look suspicious to you or anyone acting strange?"

Mitchell replied, "No, I can't say that I have seen anything strange."

The officer said, "Okay, proceed; be careful while driving. If you do see anything strange, don't attempt to take care of the situation yourselves; these guys that we're trying to locate are very dangerous."

"Thanks for the advice," said Mitchell. "I will keep my eyes open."

The officer on the driver's side looked over at the two in front of the passenger's window and shouted, "They are clear." The two officers stepped back from the vehicle. Mitchell drove off.

Johnson approached the checkpoint; the same officers asked them to stop the vehicle, so Johnson stopped the vehicle. The officer asked Johnson to roll down the window, and Johnson complied. After the window was down, Johnson put his hands on the steering wheel. When asked, "What are you doing, sir?" Johnson said, "Man, I just don't want a mistake to happen." The officer started laughing out loud. Johnson asked, "What's so funny, may I ask?" The officer looked at him still laughing and said, "Sir, you can go."

Johnson drove off.

Upchurch breathed a sigh of relief and said, "Man, I thought that I was going to have to take those guys out. Now that was too easy."

They drive down the highway headed to their rendezvous point.

Benivais arrived at the checkpoint just before the 110 entrance. He put the hazard lights on as he approached. The checkpoint officer said, "Good evening."

Benivais responded, "Good evening."

"Do you have an emergency that you're responding to?" asked the officer.

Benivais answered, "Yes. Someone reported a downed power line in Palmdale."

The officer looked at Benivais carefully and said, "Okay, man, you can go."

Benivais took off down the highway.

As Thomas and his crew got closer to the meeting place, Thomas grabbed his right side and gripped it with his left arm. He groaned and grimaced with his face.

Jackson asked, "Are you okay, man?"

"Yes, I'm okay now," answered Thomas. "I just twisted my body wrong and tweaked my rib cage, but I'm okay; I'll be just fine."

They pulled into the fenced-in area and Thomas got out of the vehicle and unlocked the gate. He got back into the vehicle and off they went down the road to the spot.

Upchurch followed directly behind them. Benivais pulled up. They all went inside the safe house.

Benivais asked Thomas, "Are we going to let the money just sit there?"

Thomas said, "No, man. The money comes in, as well. Don't worry; I have that taken care of."

They went inside and Upchurch high-fived everyone. Upchurch said, "Yeah, man, we did this shit, didn't we?"

"Okay," Thomas said, "let's come to order here. Everybody take a seat and let's come to order." They all sat down and Thomas continued, "I would first like to say congratulations to all of you that made it out of this. All of you are rich people now. I felt that if you can pull off something this big, then you deserve to have the money. You guys are going to give up everything that you did before because things as you knew them before are no longer…from cars to bars and toys. Your new life will be in a different country. You will hang low for thirty days. Then you will begin your journey to a different part of the world. If you look to the rear of the room, you see the gentlemen bringing in all of the bags. I just felt that now, you don't have to carry your own bags anymore, you can afford for someone else to do it for you." The men on the team began to clap.

Thomas allowed them to have their moment of joy. He then said, "I would like to take this time out now to bow our heads and give thanks and, in a moment of silence, to remember our fallen."

They bowed their heads down. One minute passed and Thomas said, "Thank you, all of you guys. I'm honored and privileged to have served with you. I wish you guys all the success in the world and the happiness and joy that comes with it. It is important that you guys continue to follow the plan to the letter… and you guys cannot be touched. I wish that I could see you guys in your success, however, that was just not in the cards."

Upchurch stood up and said, "Hold the horse, gunny, you and I are going to the same place as planned; so what the fuck are you talking about?"

"Gunny," Jackson said, "you're not making any sense."

Thomas said, "At ease, men. Plans do not always go as they should. Now, what I'm telling you guys is that I have different orders than you guys." Thomas grasped his side and paused.

"Hey, gunny, are you hit?" asked Jackson.

Thomas smiled and sat down in a chair. All of his crew ran over to him and encircled him. Upchurch grabbed Thomas's hand and said, "We can get you to a hospital or have a doctor come out here for you."

"Hell no," Thomas replied. "Listen, I've got different orders than you guys; I'm willing and ready to accept this."

Johnson said, "Let me at least look at you, gunny."

"Johnson," replied Thomas, "I've been hit low and on the outside of the abs. The blood that I'm losing is dark; what do you say now?"

"Gunny, you took one in the liver."

Thomas said, "That's right; but man, the bottom line is that we pulled this shit off and got away with it. You guys will never be suspected of any crime because they're looking for twelve or more white men and guess what, last time I checked...all of you guys...you are dark people. Some very dark and some less; but bottom line is none of you are even remotely close to being white." They all laughed.

Upchurch said, "Man, I've got to ask you, how did you come up with the white men idea?"

"It was easy. White men do this all the time and it is expected of them," Thomas answered. "They simply call it 'white collar crime.' They're going to have to rename this one if they ever figure it out, which they won't. To make this plan, I thought like an upper class white male and pulled this off."

The entire room laughed.

Jackson said, "Gunny, you can't leave us."

"I'm not leaving you, I just have different orders," replied Thomas.

"Man, I'll make sure your family gets your share and all of the information," said Upchurch.

"I need for you guys to grab your things soon and continue to follow the plan, and I will meet up with you guys in the afterlife."

Upchurch was holding Thomas in his arms. There were tears flowing down Upchurch's face.

Thomas said, "Man, secure the tear shit, this don't even hurt anymore; but I'm tired, so I think that I'm going to rest for a while. See you later..." Thomas closed his eyes for the last time.

Upchurch held Thomas tight in his arms and said, "I don't give a fuck what you said, I'm just going to hold you for a little while here."

Upchurch reflected back to when he and Thomas were young men serving in the USMC. He went back to when they were in a bar in Korea. The two were sitting at a table having a drink. Two young ladies came up to them and introduced themselves. Phil said, "I'm Phil, but you can call me Devil Dog."

The young ladies laughed and one of them asked Phil, "Why do they call you Devil Dog?"

"Well, it's a long and interesting story and I cannot discuss it while the sun is shining." They all shared a laugh.

The young ladies asked Thomas, "What's your name? And, what's your story?"

Thomas said, "My name is just Thomas and there is no story behind it, only in front." They all shared another laugh. Before you knew it, the young ladies had joined them having drinks and laughing it up, having fun.

Three guys walked in and walked over to the table and said, "Are you boys in the Marine Corps?" The three men were white.

Phil answered, "That's a two part question, and you did not follow the three rule chain of command."

Thomas laughed and said, "Oh shit, you guys have done it now."

One of the men said, "Are you guys supposed to be funny or something? This isn't the Heckle and Jeckle Show, or Amos and Andy."

Phil looked over at Thomas, stood up, and said, "I got this, bro'. Rule 1, if you cannot kick a person's ass, don't call him a boy. Rule 2, you never have to ask if a person is in the Marines. The Marines are in the person, so that's it."

One of the men that approached them said, "You boys can't even count. That's only two rules."

Thomas stood up and said, "Man, I got this." Thomas turned to face the person standing in the middle. Thomas said, "Rule 3, if I stand up it's already too late for you guys." Thomas kicked the man standing in front of him in his balls, and when he slumped forward, Thomas uppercut him in the face, striking him in the nose. The man fell back and landed on the floor on his back, bleeding and out cold.

Thomas looked at the second guy standing to his left and said to him, "You can't leave, I want to play."

The guy stepped back as Thomas approached him and caught the front of his shirt. He said, "The next time you feel the urge to call somebody a boy, don't." Thomas punched him in the throat with his fist. The guy clutched his throat with both hands in total agony. He went to the floor on both knees. Thomas walked in front of him and asked, "Does it hurt? Well, let me show you a little something that I've learned to help you take your mind off the pain." Thomas kneeled down and punched the guy in his left lower rib. The punch was so loud that you heard the rib crack. The guy fell down to his left side.

Thomas walked over the third guy and said, "I'm surprised that you stuck around."

The guy said, "Hey, I'm stupid; I'm in the Navy, so that should tell you something about me."

Thomas replied, "I'll tell you what. I need a storyteller, so I appoint you. I want you to make sure that you tell it right to your friends and neighbors here and back at home in the world. Inform all of your slack- jawed faggot friends that you do not attempt to fuck with the power of the Marines, you got that?"

The guy was standing there with the look on his face like he had just seen a ghost.

Phil looked over and burst out laughing and shouted out, "Hey, this fucker just pissed his pants!"

Every one that was in the bar looked down at the guy standing there in total embarrassment and everyone began laughing.

Thomas said, "Hey, man pick up your two girlfriends and get the fuck out of here!"

The lone standing troublemaker responded to Thomas, "Yes, sir." He assisted his two buddies up from the floor and they all stumbled out of the door while everyone in the bar laughed and applauded Thomas.

Thomas walked back over to the table where they had been sitting with the two young ladies. Phil looked at the ladies and then back at Thomas and said, "I know I know; we have to go."

Thomas replied, "Hell no. I was going to say, I've worked up a mean thirst, so order up some more drinks." They laugh once again.

Phil looked at Thomas and said, "You have got to be the craziest son of a bitch that my sorry ass has had the distinct pleasure to meet."

Upchurch came back to reality and said, "Okay then; I guess we move forward."

Upchurch gave the order to all of the men working on bagging the stolen monies and dividing it up and packing it up, "All this is done within one hour."

Upchurch looked around and made sure that the building was spotless. Jackson went over to Upchurch and asked, "What do we do about Dugmal?"

Upchurch answered, as if he was upset with the questions from Jackson. He responded, "I've got him; I'm taking him home. Now, you guys just get the hell out of here. We will never see each other again."

Jackson and the rest of the crew figured enough had been said already and goodbyes were not in order, but everyone understood nevertheless. The crew left the building without looking back. No one said anything to each other on the way out. They just loaded their vehicles and drove off.

Phil grabbed Thomas's body and carefully placed it in his vehicle as though Thomas was just sleeping from a drunken time out with the boys. He arrived at Thomas's home and went down to his basement and placed him in a box that Thomas had prepared, as though he knew that this was going to happen before it all began. Phil closed the lid and secured the latches. Light came on surrounding the box and you could hear power come on. Phil looked and saw a thermostat. The gauge was set at 27 degrees. Phil looked at the box and said with tears falling from his eyes, "Later, bro'."

Phil left the house and got into his vehicle and drove off. He picked up his cell phone and dialed a number. The phone rang six times before someone picked up.

Beverly answered and said, "Is this the way it has to go down?"

Phil paused for ten seconds and said, "I'm sorry. All of the information and packages are at the house and a recording for you to see and listen to from Thomas. I'll never see you guys again, so I won't say goodbye, but I will say so long."

They each hung up from the other.

Beverly called the family together and said, "I have an announcement to make; Thomas did not make it. His assignment has ended and I'm not going to go into details about it; this is the way that Thomas wanted it."

The entire family huddled together and wept uncontrollably.

End of Assignment

CPSIA information can be obtained at www.ICGtesting.com
Printed in the USA
LVOW04s1514240815

451304LV00002B/253/P

9 781480 910836